CONTROL ME

THE COMPLETE BOX SET

CJ THOMAS

CONTROL ME

City by the Bay series
Alpha Billionaire Romance
Complete Box Set

CJ Thomas
& Jordan Lace

All rights reserved.

Copyright © 2017 CJ Thomas

No part of this book may be reproduced or transmitted in any form or by any means, electronic or mechanical, including photocopying, recording, or by any information storage and retrieval system, without permission in writing from the author and/or publisher. No part of this publication may be sold or hired, without written permission from the author.

This is a work of fiction. Names, characters, places and incidents are a product of the writer's imagination and/or have been used fictitiously in such a fashion it is not meant to serve the reader as actual fact and should not be considered as actual fact. Any resemblance to actual events, or persons, living or dead, locales or organizations is entirely coincidental.

The author acknowledges the trademarked status and trademark owners of various products referenced in this work of fiction, which have been used without permission. The publication / use of these trademarks is not authorized, associated with, or sponsored by the trademark owners.

cj@cjthomasbooks.com

ABOUT THE AUTHOR

CJ lives in the Green Mountains of Vermont. You can find CJ skiing, hiking, and spending time with family when not typing away on the latest hottest read.

Connect with CJ:

cj@cjthomasbooks.com

FREE NOVEL

Join my newsletter and read my never before published novel, Boss Me, FREE!

CONTROL ME, SERIES DESCRIPTION

Virginities were the commodity, and I sold them for money to the highest bidder.

I'd invited him to hold that honor so that he could be her first. Except billionaire Odin Thayer wanted to sink his teeth into me, even when I wasn't on the menu.

Then he offered a deal of a lifetime I couldn't refuse. A way to scale my business and take the auctions to the ever exclusive clientele of Black Velvet.

And when my past collided with the present, I was determined to break the shackles of fear that kept me in full control of the dark secret I harbored.

Control was not a game for me. It was a way of life. There was only one way I'd move on from my damaged self, and it was to have him control me.

1

Get caught up with the series and read my Take Me box set before beginning this story. Control Me is the fifth story in my City by the Bay series that begins with Ruin Me, followed by Promise Me, Save Me, then Take Me. Each are standalone stories and Control Me can be fully enjoyed without having to read them first. This story will have you in bed and snuggling under the covers with the one you love. Enjoy!

Ashley

"You're beautiful, darling." I touched Audrey's hair, setting one auburn curl in place and touching her shoulder gently.

She was nervous; all the girls were at this point before the auction, no matter how well they'd handled the decision to lose their virginity in exchange for ridiculous sums of money. The amount they garnered mattered less to me than the empowerment this choice gave them.

"Are the guys here?" Her voice shook and I turned her so she faced the antique mirror in the hallway outside the restrooms of Trent's bar where I held the majority of my auctions. I wanted her to see herself and remind her why she'd come to me to take this route to sell her virginity.

Despite the rumors and occasional bad press, I didn't go looking for these girls, didn't coerce them into this; my clients came to me via word of mouth and I turned away nine out of every ten. I'd learned the hard way that drama wasn't worth the price those girls brought, and finding the perfect combination of confidence and beauty ensured that the money a girl earned in one of my auctions served to change her life, not send her down a path of destruction and entitlement that quick money can often bring. It took me far too many disasters to figure that out, but I'd adjusted and accelerated, which was how I did life.

"The gentlemen are here. I hand-picked four that will ensure tonight is one to remember."

Her gaze met mine. "I'm nervous, Ms. M."

I smiled and stepped beside her, threading my arm through hers. Audrey and I were physical opposites: her henna-red hair curved against her low back while my golden tresses were neatly contained in a low pony. She was athletic and out-doorsy with a physique to match; her long lean limbs showcased in the black dress clasped over one shoulder, leaving the other bare. Her curves were graceful and lithe. If she'd let herself, she had a body made for pleasure.

I did too, but I'd played it down tonight, wearing a silver wrap dress and a pair of black Louboutins. "I understand. Losing your virginity is always a nerve-wracking moment. You've just chosen to have the ultimate control over how it happens. Somewhere tonight, a college girl just like you is drunk and losing hers to a random guy at a frat party. She'll have nothing to remember, no money, and a hell of a hangover. You're still more than welcome to walk away now and do that next week, but this way you'll have all your student loans paid off. Remember why you're doing this. The men out there know why they're doing this, they know why you're here, and there's absolutely no shame in that. This is a win-win for everyone."

She nodded and straightened, her slender shoulders tipping back. A slow breath released from her tight chest and she shook out her hands, making the diamond and silver bracelets on her wrist tinkle and chime. "This will make it so much easier to take the right job instead of one that I have to take to pay these loans."

I smiled. "Exactly."

She gave me another nod, this time looking like the professional who'd walked into my office a few months ago. As an architectural student at the University she'd fallen under the trap so many of her colleagues had: walking off the graduation stage to a lack of high-paying job offers. After a year of working multiple part-time and intern positions, she was feeling defeated, and as the loan payments came due, now that she was out of school, the impossibility of her situation had seemed dire.

Thankfully, she'd run across one of my previous clients who'd spoken highly of how my auctions worked and what she stood to gain. Her age was a fantastic factor. There weren't a lot of women who made it all the way through college with their virginity, but Audrey had maintained a steadfast focus to graduate top of her class, further embedding the myth that she'd step straight into a six-figure position at a top architecture firm. Honestly, if the universities knew what was good for them, they'd let me give a consulting session to every girl on the first day she set foot on campus. Not only would they end up with less partying and more magna cum laudes, but student debt would be at an all-time low. Alas.

I turned her toward the room where the men awaited her, millionaires and billionaires I'd vetted and selected to fit her personality and sexual appetite—whether she knew it or not. I had a knack for reading people's desires and giving them what they didn't know they wanted. Money was what brought them through my door, but money wasn't what I gave them. My girls left with dignity, self-awareness, and expectations of what a man could do for her. After a night with my clients, they rarely settled for drunken college boys who didn't give her everything she desired.

I gave them control not only over their bank accounts, but over their orgasms, too. All of which brought me down this path; I'd had control of neither when my virginity had been ripped from me in college.

"Remember, highest bidder isn't necessarily who I'll send you out with tonight. At every chance, let me know which way you're leaning or if you have any concerns about any of the men. While I've done my very best to vet them, competition has been known to turn men into monsters. Sometimes the smell of virgin blood is too much for them to handle," I teased.

She laughed and it was then that I knew she'd be okay. If the thought of losing her virginity still terrified her, we'd stay back here until it didn't. It mattered to me that she was okay about this at every stage. I was not sending a lamb out for slaughter. This was her choice, had been since the moment she'd walked in, but that didn't mean she couldn't change her mind at any point in the evening. It didn't happen often, but it did happen. A girl doesn't make legal age with her virginity by being loose and fast and open to anything. The very idea of a virginity auction toyed at their sensibilities, creating the potential for a war inside them. I'd had to talk more than a few off the ledge of bailing when the pressure became too much. Mostly, they worried about disappointing the men who were about to pay exorbitant amounts for the opportunity to spend the evening with them. Usually it didn't take too many reminders that their alternative was to lose their virginity to a guy who might or might not know what he was doing and who might or might not even bother buying her dinner, let alone the level of romance and elegance that came from being a treasured gem of one of my auctions.

There were strict rules as to how the men behaved once they left here with the evening's woman. They had to take her to a nice dinner at an upscale restaurant and have her back to the location of her choice by noon the following day. Whatever arrangements they made past the 24 hours she was under my tutelage and care was their business. I made them sign contracts agreeing to all those details. If they balked at any of them, they were out, and they knew it. Being hand selected as a bidder was as much an honor as being chosen as one of my women. My name flew in all the right circles and men clamored over the chance. Yes, it took a strange set to pay for an evening with a virgin, but we all had our own guilty pleasures, now didn't we?

We paused just outside the reach of the doorway's sight line, placing her at an angle that allowed her to see the men mingling on the other side of the door, but they couldn't see through the soft lighting to see her. I let her drink her fill. "Take your time. Let me know when you'd like me to make the final decision."

She nodded and inhaled, her fingers trembling only slightly against her hips. I left her to go check on the men; they'd been on their own for nearly twenty minutes now, and their strong personalities wouldn't hold for much longer. They always complained that it took too long to meet the girls, but I did this for a reason, as with everything. The longer they bumped up against men as strong as they were, the higher the bids.

While money might not be the most important consideration, it was still a consideration. I wanted Audrey going home with as much money as we could garner with these men, and the more competitive they became, the higher the bids.

Odin Thayer, Wilder Easton, Ryder Viera, Asher Mayer-Roe, between them, thirteen companies, five countries, and over three billion in assets. These were worldly men, men who would appreciate Audrey's mind as much as her body.

This was a tighter set than I usually invited. Six was a particularly suitable number and made it easy to give the girls a variety of men to choose from. Audrey didn't need variety. Too many choices would overwhelm her.

I'd stopped taking notes during consultations years ago, learning to trust my intuition and hearing what the women never said. Audrey needed a strong hand, quick mind, and huge personality to match her style. These men's names had popped into my mind within the first few minutes of meeting her and I hadn't found any reason to change my original list.

They'd been all too happy to oblige.

Three had been past customers, all enjoying the rush of getting to be a woman's first and setting the bar for her future lovers. Odin was the only newcomer to the set. We'd had several interactions prior to tonight, and his pedigree was impeccable. He was a man of his word and a serious ladies' man who treated women with respect and, apparently, had a voracious appetite for sex. He'd fit right in with the other three.

I glanced at him now, standing with one arm casually draped over the lip of the bar, the silver hair at his temples glinting in the soft lighting. He was a handsome man with a natural tan and square jaw. A self-made billionaire, he had a drive that made men envious and a smile that made women simper. He commanded a room, unless he didn't want to, then he could blend in and disappear among the narcissists that ruled our world.

Tonight, he was impeccably dressed in a dark gray suit, red tie, and matching red pocket square—though if I asked, he'd probably withdraw a handkerchief, his ancestral roots showing. Odin was the kind of man who exuded charm and grace and old-world sophistication. I'd had no trouble researching his backstory; the papers were littered with articles about his triumphs and failures, as with all the men in the room.

Wilder walked over, his lean figure moving smoothly across the space. He'd made his fortune in adventure, first with sponsorships of his high-adrenaline mountain climbing treks, then with a line of clothing and accessories. He'd quickly become the face of the industry. He and Audrey shared a passion for the outdoors and he was clearly in shape to wield incredible stamina. While she might not benefit from all that he had to offer tonight, I had a feeling there might be a future for the two of them long past this evening.

It wasn't rare for the auction pairing to make a match. I was good enough at giving them both what they wanted that they often lingered with each other far beyond the limited slice of time that the men's wallets purchased. That was one of the reasons I required both dinner and a hotel; I wanted the girls to feel safe on neutral territory as opposed to going to his place, and I wanted them to be able to get to know each other. So often on dates, the noise of *will we* or *won't we* becomes so loud that no one can hear what the other is saying. That was one luxury I could give them tonight; sex was a sure thing, so they could bask in each other without having to worry about reading signs or sending the wrong signal. In return, they often found that they really liked each other.

Wilder was definitely my personal favorite. He kept his blond hair cropped close to his head and sported a longer-than-normal beard tonight, which did nothing to detract from his looks. Creases crinkled at the corners of his eyes, skin prematurely wrinkled from days on a mountainside. His overall look was rough and rugged and insanely attractive. He took my hand and kissed the backs of my knuckles. "A pleasure."

I cocked a hip and gave him a smile. "I'm pleased you came. Perhaps tonight you'll be my high bidder."

He smiled. "Maybe."

Wilder had been to several auctions, but hadn't liked the woman enough to stay in the fight. He'd often opted out after the first round. Occasionally I used him to up the bids, but for the most part, I left him to be a spectator. Sometimes I wondered if that was what drew him to these; the adrenaline and rawness of bidding on a woman's virginity. Much as I tried to keep it classy, at the end of the day, there was something to be said for calling a spade a spade.

Wilder excused himself and I moved toward the final two men, lost in quiet conversation. I'd expected some heated debates, so the softness of their conversation surprised me, so much so that I almost detoured around them to let them finish. Ryder spotted me, winked, and extended a hand toward Asher. "Thanks for the info. Appreciate it and I'll let you know." They split from each other, Ryder coming toward me and Asher heading toward the bar where Trent, the bar's owner and my long-time business partner, was holding court and pouring drinks.

Ryder inclined his head, but didn't shake my hand. If I remembered correctly, he had some weird germ issues; funny for a guy who was into buying strangers, but I wasn't one to judge. I'd always liked him and he'd won both the heart and panties of the girl from the first auction he'd attended. They'd dated for nearly a year and, last I'd heard, had an amicable breakup. I'd always liked Ryder. He'd come from money but hadn't ridden anyone's coattails, quickly taking his father's fortune and doubling it with what had seemed risky investments at the time but had proven to be sound timing and strategy.

He looked nothing like was expected of an IT genius and billionaire, preferring flannel shirts and worn jeans and boots to the high-profile suits. Tonight was no exception. He'd rolled the cuffs of his sleeves, exposing forearms that looked like they'd chopped a cord of wood before coming tonight. He was a burly man, but exuded a gentleness that women flocked to and men admired. His silence was his strength and, as with the other three men, he'd been a perfect fit for tonight.

2

Odin

Her movements stirred the very air around me, making me aware of Ms. M's entrance the moment she stepped into the room. I could feel her. How anyone could miss her was beyond me. The woman was power and sex all wrapped up in a seductive package. I sipped my drink and turned ever so slightly to watch her stride toward Wilder.

My fingers tightened on my glass as his lips brushed her skin. I was insanely territorial of her, even now, wanting her for myself. Truly, she was the reason I came to her event tonight as I had little taste in inexperienced women. I would climb a mountain to see her, and I despised the cold climates; the elusive Ms. M simply had that much of an effect on me.

Tonight, my awareness of her occurred at a nearly-subconscious level. If I were to turn away, I would know her movements.

If she was aware of mine, she made no notice of it, enraptured as it was with Wilder. He was a fine enough man, I was certain, but I wanted her to myself.

Even now.

Our paths had crossed at art gallery openings, restaurants, and a few of San Francisco's VIP underground lounges. My reaction to her was the same each time; my blood raced, my chest expanded, and I wanted to drag her from the room and back to my bed for days on end.

Yet there was something alluring about her that went beyond who I believed she was in the bedroom. There was a worldliness that lived in her every graceful movement.

And there were secrets hidden there, too.

I knew about secrets.

I took another sip and she dispensed with Wilder. As she walked away he glanced back over his shoulder to watch her walk. Not that I blamed him, but the motion ignited a fury in me that I was resistant to tamp. Let him look my way and see the fire burning beneath my lids, I silently challenged.

She engaged with Ryder and I had no more time for Wilder and his looks. Ryder, at least, didn't touch her and I was glad. But the way she looked at him…

The woman was a natural, the way she interacted with her clientele. My team could learn a thing or two.

"Odin." Asher drew up beside me and ordered a Hennessy, neat. I nodded in greeting and took another sip of my own scotch.

Mr. Fenner—a man I'd had no dealings with before this evening—poured a glass and slid it across the bar, then turned to me. "Odin? You want another?"

I downed my glass and mimicked his movements, sending the glass across the polished wood. It stopped beneath the neck of the bottle and Trent raised an eyebrow before pouring me a glass of the Hennessy.

"I'll drink Asher's pick."

The glass came back and Trent left us. I wasn't sure what he thought of Ms. M or her auctions but he seemed liked a nonjudgmental fellow and I liked that. *Live and let live.* Unless you're touching my money, my woman, or my scotch. A man's gotta have rules.

Asher lifted his glass in salute. "May the best man—"

"For God's sake, Asher, this isn't that kind of contest," I admonished him and his crassness, immediately reassessing my original impression and taking a dislike to him.

"I know. Christ, Odin, lighten the fuck up, ya old coot."

My impression of him darkened and I bid him good evening and stepped away. My life was full of assholes, I didn't need to spend tonight in his company when there were two lovely ladies in need of my attention.

I moved slowly toward Ryder and Ms. M, hoping they'll finish their conversation organically before I had to interrupt. I didn't want to appear rude in front of her, but I also wasn't going to stand by patiently in the wings. She well knew my attitude and asked me here anyway. I was intrigued by that, and this entire process.

She'd explained the rules and they seemed simple enough. They came down to *don't be a dick.*

On some days, and in some situations, that was a difficult one for me, but for Ms. M, I would be on my best behavior tonight.

Ryder sensed me and wrapped up his story, excusing himself as I approached. She turned to me and the room ceased to exist. There was only her, and she was a goddess come to life.

She was sheathed this evening in a silver wrap dress that clung to her curves, leaving barely enough for me to imagine once I had her out of it. She was sex come alive and I wanted her.

The growl rose in my throat before I could trap it and her eyes dilated in response. I grinned and held out my open palm for her. "I'm honored to be here this evening. Thank you for inviting me."

"Thank you for being worthy of the invitation." She didn't miss a beat and took a step closer. I could smell her perfume and wanted to scent her, bury my face in the nape of her neck and infuse my lungs with her unique fragrance. A gold necklace lay at the base of her throat and I watched the pulse beating beneath her skin.

I wanted to taste her there. And everywhere. All evening.

Her golden hair shimmered nearly bronze in this lighting and she'd pulled it back neatly at her nape, exposing just enough of the back of her neck that I could find a spot I wanted to taste there, too. With my teeth.

"You look divine this evening." My voice was a low growl and I did nothing to pull back my desire for her.

"As does Audrey." She glanced over her shoulder. "Look, here she is now."

3

Ashley

Oh, yes. I smiled to myself as I turned away from Odin. He'd do nicely.

I'd already decided that I wanted him to have Audrey. With her approval, of course. But I could sway that decision easily. Odin would be a superb lover; strong, but careful and considerate on her first time.

Heat bloomed at my cheeks and I quickly shook off the unusual response to my client. They were always handsome and wealthy, but Odin was raw and smooth, like steel.

Too bad I never allowed myself to have one-night stands with my clients. He might have been fun.

Audrey strode into the room, shoulders back, looking each man in the eye, a small smile playing at her lips. Ah, that was my girl. She'd come into my office defeated and feeling like she had no choice, but now she was a woman about to earn a sizable sum in exchange for a lovely evening of fun and flirting. I'd given her no rules. She could pick whomever she wanted and I'd do my best to run up the bids so the evening turned out how she wanted.

Rarely did I have to go against who'd been the high bidder, but I did it sometimes, especially if she wanted another—and I agreed with her reasoning. If I didn't, I'd do my best to persuade her. The girls often bailed out on their perfect match because he scared her, but I knew all too well that fear was the exact thing they needed to open them to the rest of their lives.

I receded from the mingling and left Audrey to meet the men, watching her interactions and noting her body language. And theirs.

Trent wrapped his fingers around my elbow and drew me behind the bar. "How's it going?" he whispered, his eyes on our guests.

"Still early. I have my favorite. What do you think?"

He smiled and crossed his arms over his chest. "I think your favorite is a lucky man."

I sniffed. "That's not always true."

He cast a sideways glance without moving his head. "Mm hmm."

"Stop it." Trent had known me long before I'd become Ms. M. Our last year had been fraught with all the things that had created the reason for both my new name and persona. I'd created my empire one hard-working week after another, and the girl I'd been had fallen under the weight. And I'd never looked back.

Until the last few months when I'd had no choice.

And through it all, Trent and his sister, Vi, had been there for me. They were the only family I had.

But that didn't mean that he could treat me like that girl in this venue. Here, I was Ms. M, businesswoman extraordinaire and a woman who'd been where every one of these girls had been—with my virginity very much intact.

Now, thanks to a horrid set of events, I could prevent these girls from being where I'd been on the next day—having lost my virginity to an awful human being who'd taken it from me when he'd raped me. I'd never be thankful for what he'd done, but I was grateful for the lessons that had come of it; I was resilient, independent, and in control. Now and for always. No man would ever change my strength.

"Oh shit." Trent tensed beside me and I snapped back to the situation at hand. Asher's hand had drifted down the small of Audrey's back and she was doing her best to remain polite and shift to the left and out of his reach.

I didn't prohibit touching while they mingled, but only—ever —if she wanted it. And I could tell Audrey had no interest in Asher's advances. He'd come on too strong, too hard, and she needed an out.

I hurried over. Behind me, Trent said he was right here if I needed him.

I didn't and wouldn't, but it was a nice gesture and I appreciated it.

I came up behind Asher and put a strong hand on his shoulder, pulling his hand away from Audrey's waist. She drew a huge breath and moved closer to Odin. He gave me a look that said he understood my concern and drew Audrey to his side, hands perfectly placed on her forearm.

"Well, now that you've all had a chance to meet Audrey, what do you think of this evening's belle?" I gave Asher's arm a tight squeeze and gave him a look that would serve as his only warning tonight, and he knew it. We'd been in this situation before, but he'd been intoxicated and had blamed the heat and his lack of meals. Tonight, I'd not put up with an excuse from him. If he miss-stepped even slightly, I'd send him packing and he'd be blacklisted for all time.

The men made their perfect compliments and kept it up until she relaxed. Odin took a step to the left to give her more room to move and I gave him a grateful glance. He winked at me and my belly responded. Surely due to the events with Asher and my concern for Audrey. A small hint of regret rose beside the heat in my belly and I snuffed them both quickly. Asher was here and there was nothing I could do about it now. He would either mind my rules or leave.

"If you're all ready, we'll move to the one-on-one time." I stared at Audrey. "Unless you'd like to take a small break to catch your breath?"

She nodded and I moved quickly into action, capturing her hands and drawing her away from Odin. "Would you ladies prefer an escort?"

I placed a hand on his forearm. "No. Thank you." He held my gaze and the heat in my belly doubled. He was kinder than I'd realized and my respect for him increased a few notches. I quickly drew Audrey past the bar and into the back room.

Trent paused at the door, his question directed at Audrey. "You okay?"

She nodded and twisted her fingers. I covered them with mine. "Trent will escort anyone out if you're uncomfortable." She glanced from me to Trent and back to me. She swallowed, took a breath, and shook her head. "I'm okay. I can do this."

Trent stepped into the room. "You sure? I don't have a problem with any of these guys."

I took a half-step away, wanting to give her space to breathe and take a minute to collect herself. It wasn't unusual to have to draw the girls away for a moment to regroup. This was a big deal and I wanted to make sure that she hadn't lost all her confidence from when she'd come out the first time to meet the men. We'd stay back here as long as she needed. I trusted that Odin would handle any altercations that arose while we were away. I had a feeling he would put up with less crap than I would.

She flattened her hands down her stomach and took a shaky breath. "Sorry, I'm just nervous."

I took her hand. "No apologies. Not for anything. We go at your pace."

"Sorry—" She swallowed again and Trent grabbed a glass and

pitcher off the corner of his desk and poured it for her. She took it and carefully drank half the glass, then handed it back to him.

He wrapped his fingers over hers and held her hand for a minute. "Whatever you need, whenever." He released her and held her gaze. "I'm serious."

"Thank you." Her body relaxed and she turned to me. "I'm fine. I just wasn't ready for all that so soon."

"Which is fine. They get to respect your boundaries. They're not paying to rule you or do anything you're not comfortable with. I picked these men because they're gentlemen, not because they're rich. Just as I'm particular about the women, I'm ten times more scrupulous with the men. I have to know that I can trust them after they leave here, and I don't pick just anyone." To me, that sounded like a justification for what had already gone wrong...which was minimal in comparison to some of the touching that happened during some of the alone time, but the girls were okay with it and some of them had even initiated it. All fine by me, but Asher had clearly overstepped.

"Let's do this." She brushed past us and down the hall before Trent and I recovered and followed behind her. Odin met her at the door, concern etched on his handsome face. With her permission, he escorted her back to the crowd and stood behind her like a large guard.

I put a hand on his arm in thanks. His soft gaze expressed concern for both of us and I tried to reassure him. I wanted him to be her final date to hopefully solidify her decision to pick him. I knew he had the funds to come up with the high bid no matter where it fell. And he seemed like he wanted to please both of us.

"Ryder, will you take her first?" From what I'd been able to tell, they'd hit it off well and her body language certainly spoke to how much he appealed to her.

"I'd be honored." He stepped into her and offered his hand which she placed both of hers in.

"Gentlemen," I looked to the remaining candidates, "I need a drink."

4

Ashley

With two men to my left and Odin to my right, we walked to the bar, leaving Ryder and Audrey to make a connection. I hoped that he could draw her out and leave her with the confidence she'd need to get through the rest of the night. I'd let Asher go after she had time with Wilder and before she talked to Odin.

Trent had drinks ready for us, a whisky sour for me and the men's drinks from earlier in the evening. They waited for me to take a sip and then tasted their own. I met each gaze. "This goes without saying, but I'm going to say it anyway: You move on her terms." I held Asher's gaze. "I'm not kidding and it pisses me off that I have to tell you this at all."

"Not all of us." Wilder gave Asher a look. "Most of us can mind our manners."

"I grabbed her ass. You all are acting like I fucked her on the table."

Odin stepped into the center of the circle and consumed the space before Asher. "I'll remove you myself."

They glared at each other and I didn't bother diffusing the situation. Odin could certainly handle himself and I wanted Asher in his place. Dammit, I should have listened to my gut and only had the three front runners. I'd liked Asher the first time and I'd made exceptions for him since.

Even if we made it through tonight without anything else happening, I wasn't sure that I'd have him back. This was too stressful and I didn't need any more of that in my life at the moment.

Conversation switched to lighter topics and they had me laughing and at ease. They were good men and I was solidified in my choice by the time Ryder brought Audrey back to our group.

I drew her away and checked in. "I'm going to send you with Wilder, then I'll check in again. I'd like to save Odin for last."

She glanced at him over my shoulder. "He seems nice."

Not quite the reaction I'd wanted for the devastatingly handsome man, but I knew he could charm her during their time alone and he could quiet anything that Asher incited in her. "How was Ryder?"

She smiled and ducked her head. "Yeah," she whispered. "I like him."

A blush crept up her cheeks. She'd make one of these men very happy as her rosebud blossomed open tonight. Much as I wanted Odin for her, I'd be willing to let Ryder be the high bidder. Other than Asher, any of the men were perfect for her.

Now I needed to start driving up the bids. They'd been ready to start competing for her since the moment she'd walked out and I'd pushed off the discussion about money until the one-on-ones started. "Go with Wilder, have fun." I hugged her and sent her on to the next private session.

Asher and Ryder were in conversation, with Odin overseeing Audrey's walk toward Wilder. His eyes swung toward me and warmth flooded my body. I was relieved he was here and glad to have him as a heavy. He set his glass on the bar and walked to me.

"Do you need another drink?" His dark voice melted into me, touching off that warm spot in my stomach.

No, I most certainly didn't need any more intoxication.

"Water, anything?" There was a hint of seduction in his question and I didn't dare answer him until after I took a moment. There was something incredibly appealing about him.

I shook my head and took a small step away from him. "I'm fine. Thank you for everything tonight."

His warm gaze slid down my body, coming to rest at the hollow of my throat before moving back up. "My pleasure." He made it sound like there wasn't anything he'd have rather done than come to my and Audrey's defense. I liked him a lot and he'd definitely be appearing at more of these.

But I needed to get us back to the reason he'd come.

"What's your bid for Audrey?"

His eyes flickered and he smiled. "How much do you want from me?" Again, the tone of his voice didn't quite match the words, like there was a teasing secret behind the question.

But I was all business when we were talking about money and could easily resist his charm. Besides, I needed him spending it on Audrey. "Will you start the bid at a quarter million?"

"Gladly." He didn't miss a beat, lifting my fingers to his lips.

I left him and pulled both Asher and Ryder aside, increasing the bid fifty thousand more from each of them. If I worked them, I could easily have her to half a million without much effort. I'd set my goal at 600K and that was well in excess of what she'd wanted. Being able to send her on her own with that much money and debt free would be a spectacular start for her.

I left them, checked on Trent, powdered my nose, and came back as Wilder returned Audrey to the circle. She met me at the door and admitted how much she'd enjoyed her time with him, too.

"This is going to be a really tough choice." I warred with the idea of telling her how much I had in bids already. Sometimes I told the girls, but rarely. The money was usually far more than what they were used to and it had soiled the events in the beginning when I'd told them the amount. For now, I let her know that the men had all given me their starting bids and that I'd keep checking in on them.

"Okay, great. Please don't tell me any of that part. I just want it to show up in my account when this whole thing is over."

I smiled and squeezed her hands. "We can definitely talk about all that later. For now, are you good to go hang out with Asher? I'll set the men close-by in case you need any of them?"

She shook her head. "No. I've got this. Both Wilder and Ryder flirted pretty hard with me." She blushed. "And there was some touching."

I laughed softly. "There's going to be more of that tonight."

"I know. It's just so strange to be getting it from so many guys all at once. So many rich and attractive guys. It's easy to get a bunch of douchebags to hit on you at a party. This is different."

"Your life is going to be different after this." I looked at her earnestly. "If you want."

She exhaled and stared at the wall behind my head. "I do want that. This last year has been tough on me and I'm ready to at least eliminate one stress from my life."

I patted her hand and steered her toward the men. "More money comes with its own stresses, just remember that."

I handed her over and gave Asher another stern glance, which he dodged. Before I could ask, Trent and Wilder pulled up chairs at nearby tables, far enough that they couldn't overhear the conversation, but close enough that they could step in if needed.

5

Odin

The woman could have asked anything of me. Two hundred and fifty thousand dollars was a small price to see her delight at my agreement to her request.

Asher's refusal to play by her rules bothered me. The man was an arrogant ass and one to take rules too lightly. He wanted Audrey, he'd made that incredibly clear with his comments every time Ms. M drew her away from us. I would pay to be the highest bidder just to keep him from having his way with her tonight.

Not that I was eager to deflower the lovely Audrey, but I would treat her well and show her a thing or two that she could take to her future lovers.

The woman I wanted to take home was the lovely and amazing Ms. M. Her handling of Asher was superb, and though she hadn't needed any of us, I'd been happy to assist.

"God dammit, Asher!" A slap reverberated through the room and a flurry of bodies in motion had me racing to Audrey's side.

Ms. M beat us all to the incident, grabbing Asher by his lapels and hauling him out of the booth where he'd been sitting with a now-flustered Audrey. "You're out of second chances."

He didn't say anything, nor did he look chagrined. Clearly, whatever moves he'd put on Audrey had been uncalled for and I hoped that Ms. M would stick to her word to escort him out.

Mr. Fenner stepped in and took over, man-handling Asher with rough movements and heading him toward the door. Ms. M followed while Wilder and Ryder checked on Audrey. I stood in the middle of the floor feeling helpless. I should have helped Mr. Fenner escort the offender out. As it was, I couldn't help now or I'd look foolish.

So I waited.

Ms. M came back in the room, Mr. Fenner escorting her as they talked in low whispers. I wondered at the protocol for such events. Would they have to press charges? Was it up to Audrey? Had they had issues of that nature in the past?

This entire production was so peculiar, and yet I admired the intention behind what Ms. M had created. For a girl like Audrey, this was money that had the ability to kick-start a serious career or business endeavor. I, for one, would have killed for a cash influx like that back when I'd been getting started.

Now that Asher was out of the picture, I wouldn't need to protect Audrey and could see about the possibility of pursuing Ms. M. But for now, I wanted to make sure that Audrey was both all right and that she felt safe enough to continue with the evening.

6

Ashley

My hands were shaking. Trent and I hadn't had to do kick out a bidder before, and now the air was charged with the negativity of Asher's actions. I needed to tip the scales. And quickly.

I clapped my hands. "All right, gentlemen. Clear out for a minute, give the girl some room." Wilder and Ryder stood and walked over to where Odin held court in the middle of the floor. I swept into the booth beside Audrey and covered her trembling hands with mine. "You want to call tonight off?"

She shook her head. "No. If I do, I'll never get the courage to go through with this again. I can't pay those loans. I have no other choice."

I tugged her hands and made her look at me. "You always have a choice, okay?"

She nodded, a single tear slipping down her cheek. "Do I have to do the rest of the dates?"

"There's only Odin left. He's your high bidder right now. I wouldn't make you chat with him, but I feel like he's a good fit. I'd like you to spend some time with him." I brushed a lock of hair behind her ear. "If you feel up to it."

She sniffed.

"Want to tell me what happened?"

"No."

I waited, weighing my decisions about how to proceed best. "That's fine. It doesn't matter. He's gone."

"Can you just make a call and tell one of the guys who won?"

I shook my head. "No. It doesn't really work like that. I mean, it can. We have the option to change the rules at any point, but I really think you should at least spend some time with Odin. Let him smooth over what just happened. He might seem intimidating, but he's very kind. While the two of you are chatting, I think I can get another hundred-grand out of the other men."

She nodded but didn't make any move to get out of the booth.

"If not Odin, who's your favorite?"

"I'm not sure I'm the best judge anymore. I usually go for guys like Asher and end up right where we just were. The rest are all nice. You pick."

I sighed. Never mind that I'd already done that, but I wanted her to have a voice in this. I didn't need her chickening out as they left the restaurant later. I wanted her turned on and willing. If Ryder or Wilder was the guy to get her through this, then I'd gladly get them to the highest bid.

"You and Ryder seemed to hit it off; is he who you want to win?"

She chewed the lipstick at the corner of her lip. "You said you hand-picked these men. Did that include Asher?"

I laid my hands over hers. "Yes. And I'm sorry that he couldn't behave himself. I knew you'd be attracted to him and I thought he could keep his word and not be an asshole. If you want to call this whole thing off, I'm fine with that. Just say the word."

She shook her head without hesitation. "I meant what I said

earlier; if we don't finish this tonight, I'll regret it. I'll meet with Odin. Ryder is my first pick for now."

I nodded and patted her hand. "You're going to be fine."

She smiled. "I know."

I eased from the booth, worried at how poorly I'd put all the players together in this one. Audrey swung like a pendulum between a strong woman and a meek, virginal girl. The latter would not serve her in this room, nor out in the bigger world.

I'd had the smallest inkling during our first meeting that she'd been bluffing and high on desperation, but she'd held herself together and yes, perhaps some of my own drama that had been playing out at the time had swayed my normally-unshakable intuition. Now I had to make the best of it, and that was sending Odin in; he would make a suitable evening for her and would wash away any of her insecurities.

If I'd managed to judge him right.

He stood a dozen feet away, his gaze never wavering from me, like he'd been keeping an eye on Audrey and me the entire time we'd talked. There was a solidness to him that I admired, like nothing rocked his world. I'd been that way for a lot of years and I'd get back there again—was almost there now—I just needed a few more really great months, and the past would forever be behind me.

I approached and he opened his arm, inviting me closer. I stepped into the space beside him to ask my request. My hand lifted to his chest and I couldn't help the small inhale that slipped past my lips. Tonight had wrung my emotions and nerves to their breaking point and Odin felt like a safe harbor in this moment. I tipped my face up to him and his nostrils flared. "Audrey wants her time with you. I'd like you to be the high bidder tonight."

His gaze wandered over my face like a man perusing a fine piece of art he wanted to collect. For another moment I regretted asking him here tonight and making him a client. "I'd like other things."

I swallowed and smiled at him. "Oh?" I couldn't help myself. I wanted to know.

"You. I'd like to be taking you home this evening." His gaze dropped to my cleavage and he growled low in his throat. "Very much, Ms. M. Very much."

For the first time since I washed my hands of my former identity, I wanted someone from this life to call me by my name. I wanted him to call me Ashley.

I really was a mess. Maybe I needed to take some time off. There were so many auctions coming up I couldn't do it soon, but perhaps an afternoon at the spa would be enough to hold me over. The last thing I needed was for my past to mingle with my present and screw up my future.

His hand found the small of my back and he pulled me close. "But I will do as you request and I will take the girl." Again, the heat of his desire was unmistakable in his eyes. "As long as you know that I much prefer a woman with the right kinds of experience."

I laughed softly. "I definitely have the wrong kind of experience."

He leaned close and kissed my cheek. "Not to me."

He stepped away and I blinked, gathering my equilibrium. Without a backward glance he made his way to Audrey, giving her his full attention. I turned to find Wilder and Ryder watching, easy smiles on their faces. Wilder winked and I shook off Odin's effect on me. Now that the men had met Audrey and they were all feeling protective of her, it would be easy to raise the bids.

If I was lucky, we'd all salvage what was left of the night and leave each other on a good note. Wilder and Ryder had both proven themselves tonight as long-term clients; they'd both be coming to future auctions and I had the perfect girl in store for Wilder. Ryder might still be going home with Audrey, but I had a feeling Odin was going to win her over.

There wasn't a woman in the world who could say no to a man like him.

7

Ashley

Odin finished with Audrey and I touched Ryder's arm. Both of the men had added another fifty grand to their bids, and if Odin had done what I'd expected and won her over, it would take merely a request from me to have him up his bid. I wouldn't come back to them for more, wanting to leave Odin as the highest bidder. Audrey would walk away with more than enough to pay off her debt and create a nest egg, leaving her able to pick the cherry of a job she wanted instead of one she had to take for the money.

The couple paused a few feet away and Odin lifted Audrey's hand to his lips, placing a gentle kiss on the back. She simpered for him and a sweet blush rose to her cheeks. He dropped her hand and turned her toward me, winking over her head, and I gave him a nod of thanks.

"Gentlemen," I took Audrey's arm and tucked it in mine, "we'll discuss the bids and Audrey's choice. Please make yourselves comfortable." Trent set new drinks on the bar and I grabbed mine and Audrey's. She took hers greedily and I walked her quickly to the back room.

Settled, I let her take a drink and a breath. "How was it?"

She smiled. "He's kind."

I bit back my laugh. Odin was anything but. Beneath that exterior hummed a wicked man who would turn her inside-out before the night was over. He would be gentle and giving and exactly what she needed, but kindness was not the word she'd use to describe him tomorrow morning.

"Is he your choice?"

She looked up at me with big eyes. "What do you think? Should he be?" Her nerves shook her body and left her trembling slightly. I leaned over and tipped the bottom of her glass, raising it toward her mouth. I didn't want her drunk, but she still needed to take the edge off before they left tonight.

She took another drink and licked her lips while I pondered the choices. Odin was still the best one. The other men would work suitably, but Odin would give her growth and confidence that she needed in this space. It was fascinating to me how she could be so capable in one area and so skittish in another.

"I could be. He'll treat you exceptionally and leave you with a memorable experience. But I don't want to make this decision for you, either." I told her the current bids for each of the men. "Odin will meet or exceed any of those, if you want to choose him."

She nodded. "Yes. I trust your input."

"As you should, dear."

She smiled. "Thank you for this, for putting all this together. I really did have a nice time."

I held out a hand for her. "Good. That was my hope." She put her hand in mine and stood. We finalized her contract and I promised the funds would be deposited by the end of business tomorrow. "Go ahead and grab your things; I'll let the men know, and if you'll give me ten minutes, Odin will be the only one in the main room."

She nodded and finished her drink.

"Fix your lipstick." I left her to touch up her hair and makeup, and I'd send Trent in with another drink for her; something a little lighter like a gin and tonic.

I let the men know the results. Ryder and Wilder were gracious and I allowed Wilder to be a last-minute addition to the next one, thinking Brittny would be the perfect girl for him. Ryder was out of town for the next three and I promised that we'd get in touch. I walked them to the door, Trent locked it behind them, and I turned, ready to chat with Odin.

I was not, however, ready for the unmistakable heat in his gaze. It smoldered with desire. I smiled and walked to him, ready to put that desire to work. He leaned casually against the bar, one arm propped against the fine grain of the wood, drink in hand. "Congratulations."

He nodded. "To your girl, as well. I'd say she made fine business this evening."

"Thanks to you."

He lifted the glass to his lips, his eyes never wavering from mine. "I'd do anything you ask of me, Ms. M. The girl will have an entertaining evening."

I smiled. "I'm sure."

Audrey came out and he turned that smoldering look to her, making her steps falter. I reached up and touched his elbow. "Go easy on her."

He laughed. "She'll have no complaints."

Audrey stood beside him and he curled an arm gently around her waist. No, I didn't imagine she would.

Trent stood at the main door, hand on the deadbolt, ready to usher them out into the evening. Odin would take her to dinner, then on to the hotel for a night of exploration and coming into her own. I kissed her on the cheek and whispered, "Call me tomorrow."

Trent held the door and watched Odin escort her down the

sidewalk to where his town car waited. I watched through the window, then let out a sigh of relief as he closed the door. "Another one in the books."

"I wasn't sure. It got a little touch and go for a bit." I took a seat on one of the barstools and swiveled as he walked behind the bar to make us both a drink.

He brought them around and handed me mine, then we toasted. "To virginity," he said.

I shook my head. "To empowered choice."

He took a drink and looked at me. "Tonight wasn't so much about Audrey's choice, it was about yours."

"Not true." We'd gone rounds about this before tonight. Trent cared deeply for anyone and everyone who ever crossed his path. It was one of the reasons I liked doing the events at his place; the girls and their well-being mattered to him. He never gave the evenings over to anyone on his staff. He closed the bar entirely for the duration—they'd open again in a few hours after he got it set for a night of patrons. "Odin was the right choice and she agreed. I wouldn't have forced him on her."

"He wanted you."

I waved Trent's comment away and sipped my martini. "He said as much."

"No, I mean *wanted* you."

"Yes, Trent. I know the meaning of the word. I wasn't on the menu tonight."

He shook his head, smiling. "Not for a one-night-stand. The man wants to *keep* you."

I laughed and ran my finger down the length of the glass, then touched it to my lips. "I think you're mistaken."

"What do you know about him?"

"He's a gentleman, wealthy, obviously gorgeous and experienced. What's your concern?" Trent rarely voiced displeasure in anything about the auctions. I didn't vet the men through him or with him. Some of them I should have, but it was hard to know who Trent knew and who flitted in and out of his circles because of the bar. As possessive and protective as he was about the women in his life, it was difficult to take his judgments at face value. Once a girl set foot in his bar, he felt obligated to care for her.

Audrey was no different.

Trent shrugged, finished his drink, and stood, ready to get the bar prepped for the night. "None. I just think you should take a longer look at him. You vetted him for your girl, but what about taking a look at what he could do for you?"

"Do for me? Trent, darling, I'm only ever going to let him do one thing for me, and I guarantee the man can fuck like no other."

He pressed a kiss to my forehead and laughed. "You know, one of these days you're going to meet a man who won't let you take over. I think Odin's got your number."

I stared at my drink, mulling over Trent's statements. Odin had been remarkably attentive on the occasions I'd seen him and he'd always been the ultimate gentleman. Tonight was the first night he'd overtly told me of his desire, but there'd been no mistaking it during our earlier meetings. He was unabashed in the way he spoke to me, giving away every bit of how much he wanted me. He flirted hard and with intention. But I'd seen only a man who I could add to the roster. Perhaps one I could have shared a fun evening with.

There were so few of those lately.

I'd fallen so deeply into the pit of my past with my demons coming back to haunt me in ways I never could have planned for. Sex with Odin could have drawn me out of that, but I'd pushed him away.

Now I had to wonder if Trent had seen what I had subconsciously. If that was why I hadn't responded to Odin's come-ons as I did with my other one-time flings; because I sensed that he'd want more from me.

I didn't do relationships. Men couldn't be trusted and I'd never given them a chance to prove me wrong. I was perfectly happy building my empire and fucking men whenever I needed one. I certainly didn't need one right now, and Odin would be around for a while if I wanted to engage him later.

I did like him as a benefactor for the auctions, however. Tonight he'd been easy to manage and more than happy to spend money to secure Audrey.

And besides, I could live vicariously through her tomorrow when she called.

8

Odin

The hostess seated us in the back corner of the restaurant, away from the sprinkling of couples placed elsewhere in the dining area, as I'd requested. Audrey looked lovely, and maybe on another evening I could have enjoyed her beauty. She was youthful and her red hair glimmered in the dim lighting. She smiled and I held her chair.

"Thank you."

I bent down and kissed the side of her neck, just below her ear. She purred, warming up nicely. "My pleasure."

I'd expected her to take most of dinner to warm up to the prospect of letting me bed her, but Ms. M had plied her with just the right amount of alcohol to calm the nerves that had plagued her for most of the evening. I was glad Audrey and I had been the last to chat, as that conversation was fresh on her mind. And her skin.

She was an intelligent girl, open to ideas and well-versed in some of her own. I was grateful for both. While I'd have done this with any girl that Ms. M would have asked me to escort, doing it with someone I could effortlessly converse with was a bonus and would make for a more enjoyable evening.

The waiter brought wine and poured us each a glass. Audrey sipped hers and I watched her, dousing my hunger for sex so as not to scare her. "Which firms have you applied to?" She'd told me when we'd chatted earlier of her desire to become an architect, having recently finished school. I applauded her for not taking the first job she'd been offered.

She set her glass down and leaned forward, arms delicately perched on the table. "Most of them. There are still a few I haven't heard from."

"And your preference?"

She sighed. "Long and Teller. That's where I'd really like to work. Their projects are on such a grand scale and they're using cutting edge designs and materials."

"Marcus Long? His firm?"

Her eyes lit up. "Yes! Do you know him?"

I laughed and sat back in my chair, relaxing and swirling the wine in the bottom of the glass. "Marcus was the first architect I hired. He designed the reno on my first building."

"Really? Oh, I'd love to see it. It's probably gorgeous. Which one?"

We discussed the building at length and I drew her in with a conversation about the colors and fabrics and the way Marcus had opened up the loft with lighting and demoing half the walls.

Maybe Ms. M had been right in this choice. Audrey and I had more in common than I'd first realized. She was a smart girl, and when she stepped into her business persona there was a glow about her that made her all the more sexy.

I reached across the table and took her hand in mine. "You're a brilliant woman. Marcus would be lucky to have you on the team."

She ducked her head and smiled, a little of her confidence waning. Not that I wanted to compare her with the illustrious Ms.

M, but that woman never shrank from a compliment. She owned them and usually came over the top with another one of her own.

I loved a strong woman, but not bossy-strong, confident that she had a right-to-own-the-world strong. Audrey might get there. One day, with the right set of circumstances. Maybe tonight would set her on the way.

Once again, I admired Ms. M's business prowess. Tonight hadn't been only about making sure that Audrey succeeded monetarily, but as a woman.

"Thank you. I hope to get the chance to prove you right."

I smiled. Maybe next week I could put a call in to Marcus. I didn't want to tell Audrey that, unsure if she'd be the kind of girl who'd appreciate a helping hand or would rather do it all on her own. I wanted her to be the latter, so I left the comment unsaid for now.

Dinner came and we fell into an easy conversation. I'd visited most of the cities she wanted to and I plied her with details that surpassed what she'd read about in her classes. "Where would you go first?"

She sighed and set her fork beside her plate. "There are so many to choose from. Paris, of course, or Milan, but then there's Sicily and Rome. Berlin would be amazing."

I laughed softly and touched her hand, drawing it into mine. I caressed her fingers, letting mine wind slowly over her skin. "You'd love them." I touched my lips to her palm. "The cities would love you."

She giggled, the wine working its way through her system. "I'm not sure about that."

"It's true." I reached forward and tugged her chair closer, bringing her knees between mine. My hand lifted to her nape and I stared into her soft eyes. She was delicate and willing. I kissed her softly, brushing my lips against hers. She set her hand on my thigh and squeezed, inviting me farther. My tongue swept across the bow of her lower lip and she sighed into my mouth. I'd have to take my time, but she'd open for me like a rose beneath a summer sun.

Beneath the pressure, her lips parted and I slid into her, pulling her close and tipping her head to the side, deepening the kiss. Her other hand found its way to my thigh and she slid them higher along the soft fabric of my pants, lifting the hair on my thigh. I would have no problem getting hard for her.

She was a quick learner. Her tongue slid along mine, twisting its way through my mouth, tasting, seeking, wanting more. One hand slid higher and I let her take the exploration as far as she wanted. If she was this brazen in the public air of a restaurant, then she would be open to my requests tonight. I wanted her as fearless as she'd come, willingly opening herself to the pleasure I could give her.

I suckled her bottom lip, drawing it into my mouth and scraping it lightly with my teeth. She moaned and her hand slid against my growing erection. I waited for her to pull back but she leaned forward, running her hand along the length.

I deepened the kiss, pushing my tongue deep into her mouth. She didn't resist, matching the swirl of me with her own.

Her gentle stroke against my cock made it harden more and I lifted my head, cradling her face between my hands.

But hers wasn't the face I wanted to see flushed with desire. "I'm sorry."

She blinked her eyes open. "Don't be." A slow smile curled her lips. "I liked it."

"As did I." I sighed. "But I'm afraid I can't go through with this."

She laughed. "I think we can leave. We don't have to finish dinner. We just have to start here."

I stood, peeled four hundred-dollar bills from my wallet, and tucked them beneath my plate. I curled a hand beneath her elbow and urged her to stand. "I'm afraid I won't be very good company."

She cocked her hip and pressed into me. "I don't know about that."

I patted her hand and moved to put space between us. "I'll call you a cab."

Her face fell and she rolled through waves of emotion. I felt remorse at ending the evening this way, especially after we'd hit it off so well.

I was not the man she needed; I would take her virginity tonight and she'd want more from me. While I wasn't adverse to dating women, I was too consumed by another. I couldn't go through with the evening's planned events.

Not with Audrey, anyway.

9

Ashley

I slipped my shoes off at the door and dropped my phone and keys in the bowl on the table beside the door of my penthouse. Beyond the dark windows, San Francisco sparkled like diamonds.

I stretched my neck and tugged the elastic from my hair, letting my curls fall over my shoulders. Tonight had been another success but there was still a heaviness surrounding my days. I sighed and padded silently to the kitchen, ready for a cup of tea and a quiet night on the couch before bed.

If anyone knew who I was behind closed doors, they'd laugh. For all that I loved the action and socialization of the big city life, I treasured my solitude most.

This was one of the huge reasons I'd never date anyone seriously. Beyond all the other things that went with getting in a relationship, I didn't share my time. I loved sex and had a voracious sexual appetite, but then I wanted them to go home.

And never call me.

More than a few men had tried to start something long-term

with me and I just wouldn't have it. Some of them had gotten downright ugly about it the more I'd said no, which reminded me of why I'd become Ms. M in the first place. While Odin might be a good time, the fact that he might be interested in more was enough to keep me from pursuing anything there.

I wondered if Audrey was having a good time. I checked my watch. They'd only been on the date for a few hours and I hoped Odin was going to take his time and ease her into this. They'd probably be through with dinner in the next hour, then to the hotel.

I tucked my feet under me and pulled my skirt down to cover my knees, tugging a cashmere throw off the back of the couch and spreading it across my lap. Guiding the voice-controlled remote that controlled the entire sound system, I asked for some slow jazz and adjusted the volume verbally, sinking into a nice evening as my surroundings soothed away the day's rough edges.

My phone rang and I reached forward, tapping the Bluetooth button on the remote that connected it to the home system. "Hello?"

"Ms. M? It's Audrey."

I leapt from the couch and ran to the bowl with my phone in it but didn't pick it up just yet. "Are you okay? What's going on? How's the date?" I strained to hear any anxiety in her voice.

"He cancelled on me."

I stuttered to a stop. "What?" Fumbling, I reached for my phone and disconnected the Bluetooth. "Audrey, tell me what happened."

"He just cancelled. Can he do that? Do I have to give back the money? Is there something wrong with him? If there something wrong with *me*? I can't give back the money, not when I'm this close to being out of this situation. Will you call him and make him fuck me?"

"Hold on. Just hold on." I ran a hand through my hair. "Tell me what happened. Where were you when he cancelled? What did he say exactly?"

"We were at the restaurant. We had a great time. I thought. He kissed me and then said he was sorry." She sniffed. "Does this mean I'm a bad kisser? Is he worried that I'll be bad in bed? Is that what this is about, how I'm a virgin and don't know anything? I know some things. I do."

Her voice was nearing hysteria. Being on the brink of losing hundreds of thousands of dollars will do that to a person. I totally understood.

What I didn't understand was what the hell had happened.

"That's it? He just said he was sorry? What happened after that?"

"He called me a cab. I tried to ask questions and reason with him but he wasn't talking to me. He looked sad. This is because of me, isn't it?"

"No. It's definitely not because of you." Anger burned in my stomach. What the hell had happened? He'd been ready to take her, and Odin didn't seem like the kind of guy who suffered from performance anxiety. Especially not with someone inexperienced like Audrey. I was pissed. "Where are you now?"

"I'm in the cab. It's pulling up to my building."

"All right. I'll get this taken care of. Don't worry about anything. And no, you don't have to give back the money. I'll fix this."

I hung up and clenched my teeth. "What in the *fuck,* Odin?" I scrolled through my phone and dialed his number. He picked up on the first ring.

"Ma chérie."

"Do not try to sweet talk me. You had better have a damn fine fucking reason that Audrey went home alone. Meet me in one hour."

"My place or yours?" His voice flowed like brandy and he wasn't the least bit upset at my tone, goddamn him.

I wasn't about to meet him at either, and Trent's would be crawling with barflies by now. I pressed the tips of my fingers to my temple and thought about where we could meet.

Vi wouldn't be at the gallery where I'd first met Odin; she'd had an opening two days ago and I knew her next one wasn't scheduled for at least a week. I had the code and there was a bar next door so I could get a drink after dealing with all this bullshit. We could speak at the gallery in relative peace.

And I could yell at him and give him a piece of my mind without causing a scene.

I gave him the address and fumed. "One hour."

"Until then, ma chérie."

I hung up on him, not trusting my voice and not wanting to completely alienate him. This was an unfamiliar situation and he and Audrey were both my clients. I couldn't defend her without pissing him off, and vice versa. I had to find a solution that benefited both of them, and I really needed to make sure that he kept his end of the bargain.

Trent and I both got paid off the auctions. The girls gave up ten percent, Trent getting a share of that. So keeping Odin—and all the bidders—happy was a huge part of my livelihood, my whole paycheck, really. And I wanted him to come to other auctions.

But that didn't mean I was about to let him off the hook for what he'd done to Audrey tonight. Bad enough that she'd had to call me and let me know like this, but so much worse that he'd shunned her on a night that was supposed to be a new beginning for her. I didn't understand how I'd misread him.

I stomped back through the house, changed out of my skirt and into a worn pair of boyfriend jeans and a white tee. Tonight, he'd see the fierce side of Ms. M and I wasn't about to be hindered by a hemline or a pair of heels. I grabbed a pair of slingbacks and stormed out the door.

So much for my quiet nice night at home. He was going to get an earful about that, too.

I slammed the car door and gripped the Bentley's steering wheel. This was not happening. Not when I needed at least one thing in my life to perform as expected.

I roared out of the parking garage, furious and ready to take out my anger on him, which was not good. I needed to figure out a strategy to find out what had gone wrong and how to fix it. Audrey needed to be taken tonight, or tomorrow, but he was not about to get out of his contract. Whether he deflowered her or not, she'd at least get to keep the ten thousand dollar retainer that was required for a bidder to attend. I'd put that in place after the first one had turned into a bunch of assholes who'd come for a show.

Every lesson I'd learned had come with an incredibly high education. I was tired of learning. I really wanted things to go back to how they'd been for the last couple years; auctions, fucking, drinking, gallery openings. I'd had the perfect life until that fucker, Carter, had popped back up on charges. He'd ruined my life all those years ago, and it pissed me off that he was coloring things now. I thought I'd been ready to put all of it behind me, and truthfully, most days I was. But then there was something that smacked me upside the head and wouldn't let go, forcing me to relive all those awful moments.

And now this.

I slapped the top of the steering wheel and took the exit. I wanted to be past this, past the hurt and the upheaval. For all that challenges were supposed to make us grow, I was ready to do a little stagnating for the rest of the year.

10

Odin

I hadn't expected her to call so soon. Or to sound even more beautiful when she was angry.

I made it to the bar early on purpose, wanting to watch her walk in. It wasn't lost on me that she'd chosen the one beside the gallery where I first met her. I sipped my Hennessy and had a gin and tonic waiting for her—the drink she'd had the night I first met her.

While I'd believed that I could go through with fucking Audrey, there was no heat in it. She was a good girl and not the one I wanted. I'd only gone to the auction for Ms. M, wanting to please her and work my way closer to her. She was amazing and powerful and intoxicating.

I wanted her.

My cock hardened at the thought of taking her in the back room here, but I also wanted to take my leisure with her. Wanted to stretch my body over hers and make her squirm with wanting and watch her orgasm around me. I wanted to taste her and feel her and bury myself in her wetness.

She walked in and cum dripped from the tip of my cock, ready for her. She'd changed into a casual outfit, probably so she could kick my ass. Fury rolled off her, turning her into a brazen stunner. Her hair flew out behind her, and when she saw me she scowled, clearly furious at having to come down here and give me a talking-to. If I was lucky, maybe she'd turn me over her knee and punish me properly. God damn the woman was fine.

She marched up to me and crossed her arms.

I took a sip and winked.

"What in the fuck, Odin?"

Oh, I did love the way she said both my name and fuck. I wanted to hear them both again. While she was naked.

"I like the way you say *fuck*." Fury burned from her gaze and I lifted her glass. "Have a drink."

She ignored the drink and shook her head. "Explain."

"Have a drink."

We stared at each other, each ready to make the other bend. I wanted to please her; I wanted to be pleased by her. God damn she was gorgeous.

"Come with me." She turned and stalked away, then tossed her hair over her shoulder. "Bring my damn drink."

I grinned and stood, obeying her commands and following her as she pushed through a small door that connected another room with the bar. I hadn't seen it when I'd come in, but now we stood in the empty, darkened gallery. I wanted to toss both glasses to the floor and scoop her in my arms, then have my way with her.

"Stay here. I'll turn on the lights." Her angry footsteps carried her away and the perimeter of the room illuminated with audible clicks as she flipped on some of the lights. She left the front of the gallery dark, giving us a private space toward the back to talk.

I watched her walk with a hungry gleam and did nothing to hide it. She could ask me why I'd left Audrey and I'd tell her in no uncertain terms what I wanted. The girl could keep the money; hell I'd double it for an evening with Ms. M.

She took the drink from me, careful not to touch my fingers, then set it on a table beside her and crossed her arms again. She didn't repeat the question, confident that I'd know what she'd come for and what she wanted.

I did, but I needed her to know what I'd come for as well.

I took a sip and watched her jaw clench. "When was the last time you were this mad?"

"You mean, when is the last time someone backed out of a contract on me?"

I shook my head and gave her a smile. "No. I meant only the question I asked. You look unbelievable, so alive, so aware."

"Cut the shit, Odin."

I set my glass beside hers and walked toward the wall where two chairs stood as castoffs from the last gallery opening. I curled my fingers around the backs and carried them to her, offering her the first. She glared at me, then shook her head. I shrugged and sat, then picked up my glass again. "Suit yourself."

She paced a short track in front of me, still mute, still waiting.

"I couldn't do it."

She paused, then resumed her pacing, still waiting.

"The girl was beautiful, charming, funny." I took a sip, making her wait a bit longer. "But she wasn't you."

That made her feet stop. She whirled and looked at me. "What?"

I set my glass down, glanced at my fingernails, flicked a bit of lint from my thigh. "You heard me."

"We had a contract."

"You can keep the money."

She slapped her arms against her sides. "That's not what this is about, Odin."

"Isn't it?" I smiled. She was so easy and pliable when she was this heated. I needed to make her angry more often. God I wanted to fuck her right now.

"No, dammit. It's about Audrey, about how she felt completely rejected and down on herself that she couldn't even pay a man to have sex with her."

"That's not true."

"Yes it is! I just talked to her not more than an hour ago."

"And did you get her to calm down and understand that it had nothing to do with her?"

"Yes, but that's not the point."

I took another sip. "You seem to be missing a lot of them tonight. Perhaps you need a drink."

She tapped her toe against the floor. I wanted her so badly my cock strained against my pants.

"Audrey will be fine. She's a smart girl. The worst thing that could have happened to her would have been for me to take her home and fuck her while I was thinking about you."

She blinked and looked at me. Her jaw ticked. She didn't say a word.

But her chest rose quicker, her pulse pounded at her throat, and her toe stopped tapping against the ground. I'd affected her. Good, because the woman had intrigued me since the day I'd met her, standing here, in this very space.

I stood. "Do you remember the day we met? I do." I stepped closer, setting my drink down and sliding my hands into my pockets. I walked behind her, making a slow circuit around her while she fumed. "You were over there." I nodded toward the far wall, beneath two spotlights that she'd dimmed, leaving shadows caressing the corners of the walls and displays. "You'd chosen a green dress that tied at the base of your neck. I wanted to kiss you there." I leaned close, letting the last word caress her skin, right where the dress had buckled.

I wasn't lying one bit. She'd been mesmerizing that night, clad in an emerald vision that stood out from all the little black dresses that had been in the room. I'd had eyes for no one but her that night. She'd been drawn to me and we'd chatted carelessly all night. I'd flirted, I'd charmed her, I'd said all the things I'd thought would earn her bed that night. But she'd rebuffed me and promised that she'd be in touch. When she'd called a week later with an invitation to the auction, I hadn't cared why or what it meant, only that I'd get to see her again.

I should have known that no other woman would have been able to tempt me or turn my head. Not until I had the elusive Ms. M. Even now, dressed in jeans and a worn, comfortable t-shirt, she looked elegant and sexy.

My cock throbbed in my pants and I wanted to press against her ass as I walked behind her. "I wanted to kiss you everywhere." She shivered. "I wanted to taste your skin, your lips, *your* pussy."

I paused in front of her and she wet her lips. Yes, that was what I'd wanted, a reaction that was undeniably charged with the sexual tension that hummed between us.

"Then why agree to the auction? Why not ask me into your bed."

I threw my head back and laughed. "You are amazing." I stepped close and touched her chin, tipping her face up. "And I want you."

11

Ashley

I stepped away. He had me unnerved and forgetting why I'd come. We had things to discuss, Audrey's money to negotiate, and terms to configure. I didn't need him using his sex appeal to get out of the contract. I hadn't had time to call Wilder or Ryder, but I was sure one of them would fix what Odin had broken.

I hadn't expected the answer he'd given about coming to the auction. It was ridiculous that he'd refused to have sex with Audrey because his desire for me was so great. We could have had sex next week. Never mind that I never had sex once a man was a bidder in one of my auctions, but we could have worked something out.

Now I didn't know what to do with him. He couldn't be a bidder again and I couldn't sleep with him. He'd fucked up everything!

And there was still the matter of the money.

"According to the contract, by refusing to uphold your end of the bargain, you forfeit all rights to your monies. You'll still be required to wire them to me in the morning."

"Fine." His fingers slid around my neck, the barest whisper of a touch. I fought the full-body tremble that coursed through me, singing along my nerves.

The man exuded sex and confidence, and his desire for me had been visible since I'd walked into the bar. And now he was telling me that he couldn't sleep with a twenty-one-year-old virgin because he'd rather have me.

I bit my lip and looked at him. His silver hair glimmered in the lights, the barest hint of stubble emerging on his cheeks. I wanted to touch his face, run my fingers along his lips, taste him.

I swallowed and forced my hands into fists to keep them from running the length of his abs. He was in fine shape—for a twenty-year-old, let alone a man of his age. He was seasoned and beautiful and cocky and suave. Under any other circumstances, I'd let him take me to the floor and fuck me right here.

But he'd gone back on his word. Something that was sacred to me. When people didn't keep their word, it hurt me deeper than most. I hated not being able to count on people.

His other hand found its way to my waist and he pulled me tight against him. "I did not mean to let you down. The money is Audrey's. Plus another fifty grand for the trouble. Plus the cost of her next evening out with Ryder or Wilder or whomever you pick for her." His breath caressed my face and he lowered his lips toward mine. "Plus whatever payment you wish to extract from me."

Damn him.

I pressed my lips into his, biting his lower lip and making him growl. He squeezed my neck, tilted my head, and plundered my mouth. His teeth ground against mine and he possessed my mouth. I bit him and he pulled away.

We traded the upper hand and he laughed in my mouth. The man was sexy as hell and demanding and, based on the length pressing into my thigh, huge as hell, too. He'd made his amends and I wasn't sure what else to ask of him. He had a point that letting him deflower Audrey while he was obviously so hot for me might not have been the best way for her to lose her virginity, and I could more than make it up to her, plus what he'd promised to add to her pot. I'd deal with all that later.

My hands unclenched and I lifted them, sliding them around his waist. As I'd thought, he had a rock-hard midsection to go with his hard cock. I was wet instantly, and now I had a choice to make: either rescind every personal rule I'd made since becoming Ms. M, or send him home, hard and wanting me, to which there would be ramifications of that as well.

He'd promised Audrey compensation far beyond what he'd put in the contract, but those things were verbal only. I had a feeling if I rebuffed him now, he'd take them with him.

Not that I wanted to have sex in exchange for getting Audrey more money, but I wanted to make sure that, inside, I was making the right choice.

For me.

There was no mistaking that I'd been attracted to him since our first meeting. Tonight was no different. He was splendid in his suit and that tie. I wanted to stroke it, wanted him to take it off and tie me up with it. I wanted to give myself over to him and not have any of my past bullshit in the way. I wanted to be able to roll back the clock to the first night when we'd met and make this our future instead of putting him with Audrey; instead of forcing him into a position where he let me down.

He was a magnetic man and I'd been drawn to him all night, pushing it off on what I wanted for Audrey. But I'd been attracted to him since the moment I'd walked into this gallery and spotted him.

I could let him go again, and miss out on what promised to be a memorable night. Or I could grab this one, salvage what was left of the mess he'd made for us, and let him have what he'd wanted since he'd walked into Trent's tonight.

I wasn't surprised that he'd remembered everything about it, from the place to what I'd been wearing that night. We'd been magnetic and attracted to each other, I'd just thought him better suited as a bidder than one of my lovers.

Now I was crossing lines that I'd put in place for my own sanity.

But Carter had forced me across them all months ago when he'd fucked up my life again.

Odin pushed a thigh between mine and backed me against the wall. I sucked his tongue into my mouth and he pressed his cock into me.

God damn I'd made the wrong call about him and we should have been doing this the night we'd met.

But I didn't want him fucking me here, either. We needed to go back to my place.

He grabbed my ass and lifted my legs, wrapping them around his hips. Maybe we could stay here just a little longer.

I moaned and pressed into him. Jesus! The man knew his way around a woman. Audrey was missing out. But then, she wasn't experienced enough to really enjoy this.

I was, though. I was so going to enjoy this man's experience and expertise.

He suckled my lips, my tongue, my ears. I tilted my head and let him have more of my skin. He swirled his tongue against my throat, then nipped me gently with his teeth. I had a feeling that he might be willing to get rough with me. And I wanted to see how far I could push him. We couldn't do that here. Not to the extent that I wanted to enjoy him.

Never mind what Trent said about Odin wanting more of me than just a one-night stand—and walking out on Audrey to put a lot of weight behind that theory. I was going to get all I could out of him tonight. There would be no second time for us, or third, or relationship. I had one-night stands. Period.

I'd never dated, never wanted to. Men weren't trustworthy.

Even the one between my legs had let me down when he didn't keep his end of the bargain. Well, he'd be taken to task tonight, for certain.

He lowered my legs and ground against my clit, making me moan. I squeezed his shoulders, ran my fingers down his arms, clutched his back. The man was amazing and I wanted more. He ran his hands over my breasts, squeezing them gently, and then his thumbs hooked beneath my shirt the same time he lowered his face, moving slowly south as my shirt came up. A soft breeze ruffled against my skin, then his lips grazed my belly. I inhaled swiftly and threaded my fingers through his hair. His beard raked lines across my bellybutton and he dragged his cheeks purposefully from one side to the other, making my skin leap and jump beneath his touch. I grabbed his hair and pulled his face away. "Quit."

He laughed and bit my stomach. "I'll do what I want."

I smacked the back of his head. "You'll do what I tell you."

He pulled his face away, a wide grin exposing his white teeth. "You think you'll be in charge tonight, Ms. M?"

"Only if you want to bed me."

He laughed. "You are unbelievably sexy. I do want to bed you. I do want to allow you to direct my actions." He rubbed his beard against my stomach while he held me tight. "And I will do my best to follow your orders."

"I think you're not very good at following my orders." The truth of that stung and sobered us both. He stood and cradled my face between his hands. His look was earnest.

"All I can do is apologize for my grievances against you. Would you rather I be doing this to Audrey right now? Hard with wanting to bury myself in her pussy?" He tightened his grip and brushed my lips, featherlight. "Kissing her. Making her wet?"

I wasn't about to whimper, or make a plea that this was where I'd rather he be, but I also wasn't willing to examine what I truly wanted out of the evening's events. Fact was, he was here, I was here, he was hard, and I was wet. Nothing else mattered. We'd part ways in the morning and I'd figure out what to do with him going forward.

For now, I was going to take him to my place and let him have his way with me.

I hooked my fingers in the waistband of his pants and yanked him close. "Prove to me that you're a man of your word before you waste my night."

One corner of his mouth lifted in a mischievous grin. "Your wish, ma chérie."

"Eat me."

He laughed and dropped to his knees, snapping the button on my jeans and flicking the zipper down before I had a chance to catch my breath. The jeans puddled to my knees and his face sank into my flesh. The first flick of his warm tongue against my skin stole what was left of the air in my lungs. His fingers slid up my thigh, teasing my opening, wet with wanting him. One hand grabbed my ass, his fingers moving everywhere. I tried to spread my legs to give him more access, but my ankles were shackled by the loose fabric of my jeans.

"Bend your knees."

"You're not giving the orders." I grabbed his hair, needing something to hold onto.

He shifted his weight, pushed his shoulders closer and forced my knees to break. I slid down the wall but only as far as his hands. He held my weight, never pausing in the strokes of his tongue. My clit swelled and he tasted me there, switching between sending his tongue between my thighs and circling my clit.

I moaned, and the rest of my weight fell onto him. He held me; held me up, held me close, held me on the brink of a dizzying orgasm.

The seduction of our location swirled around us. Art hung from the ceiling, stood in reliefs on pedestals, and made shadows that reached for us.

I reached for him. I gripped for a handhold on the wall. I fell into him and let him catch me.

Hoping against all hope that he would keep his word in this and not let me down twice in one night.

12

Ashley

My orgasm crashed over me like waves against a cliffside. I did not come easy, but like a ship coming apart on the shoals. This man would be my undoing if I let him. And I would not.

He kissed my thighs softly in contradiction to the ravaging he'd placed on my womanhood. I needed more of him, needed all of him tonight.

And I did not need.

"Take me home." My words trembled on my breath and he rose, guiding my jeans up and buttoning them gently back in place. "Yes, ma chérie." He gave me his elbow, we locked the gallery together, and strode to our cars. "May I escort you?"

My fingers rested gently on the insides of his arm, testing the warmth and strength of his bicep. If we went to my place, I could easily Uber back here in the morning.

I smiled up at him. "Please."

He held the door for me, his fingers grazing against the small of my back, the curve of my shoulder. I sank into the seat, muscles depleted, yet energized.

This man was remarkable. I had a feeling tonight was going to be a night to remember.

I'd had no shortage of amazing lovers, but Odin held a strength about him that was old-world sophistication and honor. All pieces that would make him so much fun to control tonight.

His door opened and he slid in, pushed the ignition, and sped us away. "I'm afraid I don't know your address."

I gave him directions and we stole glances of each other while I pretended not to be interested. His hand found my knee, sliding higher until, if I'd have had my standard skirt on, he'd have traversed beneath the hem.

A low growl sounded in his throat and we pulled into the parking garage. He shifted the car into park and rested his hands on the wheel, staring straight ahead at the concrete wall inches from his car's bumper. "I don't think I've ever wished for my driver more than I did on that drive."

His erection stood out starkly against the fabric of his pants—the same ones he'd worn to the auction.

"Oh, would that have made a difference?" I feigned ignorance, knowing exactly what would have transpired in the back of his town car.

He growled and turned toward me, his hands wrapping around my back and pulling me into him. He stopped when our noses nearly touched. The desire burning in his eyes was unmistakable. "Only that I would already be inside you."

I laughed softly. "You think so, do you?" I admired his confidence. It was my favorite trait among my lovers. The confident ones knew their way around a woman and also weren't so weak as to not be able to take instruction. I had a feeling Odin wouldn't need much in the way of how to please a woman.

His lips grazed my throat and he growled again. "I know so. Now get us inside before I take you right here on the front seat."

"I'm not opposed to that," I teased him, knowing that I wasn't interested in a quick fuck by the glow of the dashboard lights. I wanted him all night and possibly into the early hours of the morning. We were losing time by sitting here arguing about who was going to be in charge.

He pulled away, touched my cheek, and got out of the car, coming around to my side. I stepped out, letting my body graze against his before walking toward the private elevator that would take us to the penthouse. The doors opened as he walked up and I stepped inside, not fully prepared for how he'd consume the space once the doors closed us in.

His fingers played at my hip and I admired his restraint. Mine was quickly fraying at the edges and I wasn't entirely sure we'd make it past the foyer before I let him take me. The soft ping of our arrival plucked at my already-frayed nerves and he held out a hand to escort me inside. I settled my hand in his and drew him past the doors, closing silently behind us. The jazz I'd put on earlier still serenaded the empty rooms, sounding more contrived than I would have wanted for bringing someone home.

Odin trailed behind me, his fingers lazily stroking mine. I wanted them on my skin. Soon.

"Care for a drink?" I glanced over my shoulder to ask and his gaze drew upward from where he'd been appreciating my ass.

He smirked and shook his head, then returned his gaze to my ass. "I think we can skip the refreshments."

"I thought you were going to do what I asked."

He laughed and pulled me back against him, his fingers sliding down my stomach and dipping beneath the waistband of my jeans. "I will do everything you ask that pertains to having your naked body on mine, beneath mine, or beside mine."

Waves of desire and pleasure washed over me. I wanted this man badly. He was intoxicating. But I also wanted to draw these moments out as long as I could.

I lifted one arm and threaded it through his hair, feeling the thickness against my palms and fingers. His fingers slid lower, over my wet clit, circling, knowing exactly the right amount of pressure and location.

Oh, yes, this man would be a superb lover.

I swallowed and tried to catch my breath. "I didn't give you permission to touch me."

"I don't remember asking." His lips pressed into my neck, and my knees trembled. My skin lit on fire everywhere his lips touched and I pushed back into him. "Ah-ah," he admonished me, lifting his lips for a second. "I also don't remember giving you permission to rub against my cock."

I laughed. "I don't need permission."

He bit me, holding my skin lightly between his teeth. I ground my ass against his hard erection, left then right. He pinned my hips into his, pumping his once and driving his hard cock against my ass. He felt so good and his fingers hadn't stopped their motion even during our teasing. The man was going to make me come before we even got started. It had been a long time since I'd been so easily played.

"Do you want me to fuck you here, against the wall, or would you prefer a softer landing?" He'd released my skin and moved on, kissing and nibbling the delicate spots of my throat and ears. His voice was a murmur against my ear. I wanted him to fuck me everywhere, but I wanted to start in the bedroom.

A moan slipped past my lips and I yanked on his hair as my orgasm built. He stroked me hard, then soft, then barely a whisper against my swollen clit. His fingers slid easily across my body, slick with my own wanting. He stroked another circle, then eased his hand from my pants. I moaned louder and clenched my thighs together.

I'd been on the brink of orgasm.

By the look on his face, he'd known it.

"Lead the way."

13

Odin

She was everything I'd imagined and more. The woman never shrank from any of my advances, doing her best to control me.

I grinned and stepped away from her, wanting to spend time devouring her body, exploring every inch and teasing her to orgasm after orgasm.

The woman was wild and untamable and I wanted to bury myself in her wildness. Doing her bidding would be the most difficult task I'd had in a long time, but I also hardened at the thought of her telling me how to pleasure her. She would be my undoing tonight, and I would gladly go under.

Her penthouse was not what I'd expected. I'd assumed she lived well, but this was decadence on a scale near grand as I lived. She was poised, elegant, and had clearly done well for herself. There was no question that she did not live off money she'd acquired from a man, that just was not her style.

Soft music played from hidden speakers and I smiled. This was the same system as mine and I was not about to fuck her to a string quartet. On the way to the bedroom, I tugged my phone from my pocket, swiped open the app, and started my playlist.

She barely lost a step, glancing over her shoulder with a rueful smile and shaking her head. "I should have known."

I winked and followed her up the glass stairs, across the open balcony, and into her boudoir—there was simply no other name for it. Furs draped the giant four-poster that commanded the center of the room, silks hung from the floor-to-ceiling windows that crafted the far corner of the room, and brocade chairs and couches made up small settees throughout the room.

This was a bedroom of a fine woman, the one holding my hand and leading me toward my certain doom. I wanted her far more than what was prudent, given the way she'd rebuffed me. The woman wanted a one-night stand, and while I would have agreed on most occasions, on this I wanted more from her. She was just too intriguing and everything about her hinted at rich confectionary with layers upon layers of decadence. I wanted to taste them all.

And I would not ask permission.

She turned in the center of the room and tucked her fists against her hips. I adored her spirit and would do nothing to break it. I'd already disappointed her by reneging on the deal with Audrey, but I would not have had that any other way. And, in truth, going through with the evening with Audrey would have damaged all of us more than canceling. She'd come around to see my way before the night was over.

But first, I wanted to taste her, wanted to taste all of her.

I stopped just short of where she stood and let the smile tug my lips upward. She was as fun as she was fiery. "May I have the pleasure of fucking you?"

She smiled and held up a finger, asking me to wait. I shook my head in revelry; this woman was the first to tell me to wait. Most of them were naked and beneath me within seconds, wary of the possibility that I might change my mind if they gave me too much time to think about it.

Not her though; she possessed a confidence nearly as large as my own. She knew—as did I—that I wasn't going anywhere. Not until I had my way with her, or rather, whatever way she let me have.

A large chest stood at the foot of the bed, half-covered in the furs that spilled from the bed. She pushed them aside and lifted the lid on the antique piece. I stepped closer, craning my neck for a better look at this hidden compartment that might give me some insight into the elusive Ms. M. She withdrew bits of satin and lace, making my cock harder.

She lowered the lid and turned, the pieces hidden behind her back. "Are you ready to do my bidding?" Her hip jutted to the right and she had a hard time keeping the smile from her lips. I wanted to kiss that smile away, make her moan my name and beg for release.

I bowed slightly. "To the best of my ability."

She laughed. "That's not really an answer."

I straightened and looked at her without hiding a bit of the intensity. "No. It's not."

Her back straightened as she took my challenge head-on. Bringing her hands forward, she held out a black blindfold. "Put this on."

I shook my head. "No way am I going to miss out on seeing your beauty."

Her face fell slightly. "This is important to me."

I tipped my head to the side, startled at the vulnerability in her voice. "Truly?" I tugged it from her fingers. "If that is true, then I will wear it." I cocked an eyebrow. "Until I cannot take it any longer."

"You'll wear it until I tell you to take it off." With one swift movement, she lifted her shirt and tossed it aside.

I blinked. Her creamy skin glowed in the room's soft light and my mouth watered. She was every bit as stunning as I'd imagined. I wanted her.

"Put it on."

I shook my head and took a step closer. "Not yet." I dipped my head and tasted the line of her collarbone, the hand with the blindfold coming up to caress her bare breast. She'd had no bra on and I'd been able to see the outline of her nipples beneath the soft fabric of the tee, but my imagination had been unable to conjure what stood before me.

The woman was perfection, even in jeans and bare feet. I wanted her. Wanted her badly.

14

Ashley

The twist of satin brushed against my nipple, making it harden into a tight bud. His fingers played lazily against my skin, and his mouth was hot on my neck. I could easily fall into him.

My hand found his shoulder and, though I'd meant to squeeze and push him away, I found my fingers tightening and pulling him closer. Odin was so very confident and yet charming. He slid behind my defenses before I knew he was at the gate. His other hand slid around my waist and pulled me close, dragging my bare chest against the stiffness of his shirt.

Lips climbed higher, playing at my neck, my ear, before taking my lips in a plundering kiss that was not meant to be ignored. Odin possessed, he claimed, he left his mark. If I wanted there to be anything left of me on the other side of tonight, I needed to get control. Fast.

With a shaking breath, I took a step back and pointed at the blindfold. "Now."

He grinned and held it out to me. "Put it on me."

It was a compromise, but one I was willing to make.

Without touching him, I withdraw the silk from his fingers and walked behind him, lifting up on my tiptoes to reach high enough to wrap the fabric across his eyes. He inhaled as my bare breasts pressed into his back. The heat of him raged through me, making my pussy clench and my thighs slick with wanting. I balanced and found a way to not fall into him. His hands reached behind and cupped my ass, both balancing and unbalancing me. I tied the silk quickly and stepped away.

He growled as his hands fell to his sides. "Command me, ma chérie." His voice echoed like a low rumble through the room and straight into my bones.

I took a couple deep breaths and gathered myself before starting this game with him. I wanted to tame the desire that threatened to rage out of control. In all things, especially sex, I was in command and in control. I knew always how the night was going to progress and when he was going to leave. I didn't always know how many orgasms I was going to experience, but I did know how long we were going to toy with each other's bodies.

Odin, however, was a wild card.

I had a feeling he would exploit every inch I gave him. In a very good way, but that would leave me without control.

I dragged a finger down his spine, along the waistband of his pants, and to his front as I circled him. Beneath my hand, his muscles jumped and flexed. "Can you see me?"

"I can smell you. I have no need for sight. Blinding me only robs me of the vision that is you."

Whoa. This guy was good.

I was going to have to stay on my game if I was going to come out of this with any sense of myself when the night was through. I'd had a few guys who'd been experts at the games of sensuality and I'd come close to wanting another night with them, but I'd never experienced the sincerity of someone like Odin. His words were meaningful and not meant to get me to change my stance on anything. He liked that I was in control, I could tell. Most men struggled with it, willing to play the game for a little while and pretend I was in control while secretly waiting until I'd had enough fun and then they'd put themselves firmly back on top.

Which was when I sent them home.

Control was not a game for me. It was a way of life. If I kept every bit of my life carefully constructed, bad things stayed at a minimum and were always manageable. Even in sex. Sex led to men thinking that they owned a piece of me and that they were entitled to more. The few who'd let me stay in control still wanted more; those men turned into serious cling-ons. The night would show what Odin revealed about his true nature.

I flicked the first button of his shirt open. Breath hissed through his teeth and his hands found my hips, digging into the softness on the sides of my flat stomach. I wanted to knock them away until I told him he could touch me, but the press of his fingertips sent shivers through me.

He brushed his thumbs lazily over my skin and I undid another button, trying to focus on my own task while his hands played at my skin. I bit my lip and slid the rest of the buttons free. His t-shirt clung to the muscles of his torso, revealing every dip and definition. I swallowed.

"I hear your breathing, ma chérie." His voice sent a shiver through my body, settling in the wetness he'd already laid claim to. "I hear it hitch when you look at me. I want to see your chest rise and fall, want to watch your eyes dilate in delight." He leaned closer. "As I think you want of me, as well."

"Stop trying to persuade me."

"Never." He laughed. "You think you know what's best for you, but you're depriving both of us of feasting."

I pushed the dress-shirt off his shoulders, tugging it free of the waistband and letting it float to the floor. My hands explored his body, feeling the heat and hardness of him. "I'm feasting just fine, thank you."

His hands went to the hem of his shirt and he yanked it off, managing not to dislodge the blindfold. I inhaled swiftly and he grinned, tossing the shirt over his shoulder. "I hear you," he whispered. "Tell me what you see."

I smiled and traced the line of his shoulder. "Power. Seduction. Charm."

He licked his lips. "Yes. What else?" His hands found my hips again and pulled me half a step closer. Heat radiated off him, drawing his cologne into my nostrils. I inhaled and shivered. "Ma chérie…" It was a plea and a curse. His fingers slid higher on my back and I let my eyes drift closed. He felt so good and I wanted to make this last.

I lifted both palms to his chest, rolling them slowly over his nipples, feeling the crests press against my skin. I bit my lower lip, wanting to taste him but not yet ready to take us there. Things would escalate quickly and I wanted to touch him for a while longer. I ran my hands down his arms, cupping the muscles, feeling them flex and bunch beneath my exploration. My fingers slid between the muscles, fanning lightly across the tendons as they moved with his hands at my hips. He was a gorgeous man, molded and pristine. He took care of himself and I liked it.

I moved behind him, hands at his waist. The span of his back was glorious and strong. I gave in and tasted him, touching my tongue to his spine, licking the indentation between his shoulder blades.

It was his turn to inhale sharply. I bit the muscles as they bunched and played. He growled and reached behind us to cup my ass again, grabbing hard and pulling me into him. I fell forward this time, letting my arms come around his waist and slide between the indentations of his abs. Our breath hardened, coming fast with desire. I reached up, cupping his pecs and playing his nipples again.

He clenched his teeth and the muscle in his jaw bunched and hardened. I loved the play of his body. My hands coasted down, stopping for a moment above his belt. He held his breath; mine flowed across his skin.

His hands held tight to my ass, his stomach clenched, waiting, anticipating my next move. I withdrew my hands and quickly slipped out of my own pants, kicking them to the side. Naked, I moved in front of him.

"I hear you," he whispered. His hands reached for me, found my bare ass, and pulled me against his hard erection. "Undress me."

"You're not in charge." My voice was soft, teasing.

"I don't have to be. Undress me."

My fingers slid his belt from its harness, then undid the button of his pants, only taking time to linger on the zipper. I leaned forward and brushed my breasts against his chest until he inhaled and licked his lips. "I want you, Ms. M. Want you beneath me in the worst ways."

I sucked his nipple. "Is that so?" My fingers hadn't moved from their spot on his zipper.

He growled and bent over, scooping me up and carrying me over to the bed. I didn't resist, amazed at his deftness at moving through the space with the blindfold still on. He lowered me to the bed, pushed his pants off and slid between my legs.

I arched up into him, feeling him with my entire body.

His hands slid beneath me, spreading wide across my back as he nudged my thighs wider with his. I didn't want to tell him to stop, didn't want to voice a single thing.

The silk still hid his eyes and I wanted what he'd talked about, wanted to see him when he drove into me for the first time.

I reached up, trailing my fingertips along his jaw. He turned and mouthed my fingers, drawing them against his teeth. My eyes fell closed and I drew a deep breath, focusing on the tingling sensation spiraling down my arms. Without opening my eyes, I pushed the blindfold up and off of him.

He chuckled softly. "Look at me, ma chérie."

I did, and saw the desire mirrored in his eyes. He drew his gaze down my body, trailing his fingers behind as he held himself up on one hand. I watched him move, so intently as if he were memorizing each line and curve of my body.

His hand grazed my hip, slid down my thigh and the back of my calf, drawing it up and around his waist. I slid the other behind his knee, locking me nearly against him, save the tension-filled inches between his cock and my slicked opening. His hand slid back up my body and brushed the hair from my face, sliding back to cradle my head. I tipped my face up into his and he lowered his cheek to mine, his lips at my ear. "You are delicious and I intend to taste every single inch of you."

He pushed his hips forward, sliding the head of his cock into me. I gasped and tightened my legs, pulling him deeper.

"Ma chérie…" He held my gaze and our bodies moved in tandem. He drove deep into me, held there, and pushed deeper. Then withdrew, making me empty with wanting him to fill me again.

He did.

Over and over, pressing into my body with a relentless tender pursuit that had me wanting and needing him and yet resisting the hold he had on me. I was supposed to be in charge tonight but there was something comforting about him that made me think I might—for the first time ever—be able to let myself go with him.

The weight of that thought hit me and I pushed up, rolling him over and straddling him.

His hands found my waist and his movements didn't change, pushing deep into me and holding me tight so my clit ground against the hardness of his hips. My orgasm expanded, spiraling outward until it touched every corner of the room. Odin moved beneath me, his hands roaming my body, lifting me and returning me back, sending our bodies in a wild movement that couldn't be contained.

"Come for me, ma chérie. Come for me."

I settled my hands on his chest and rotated my hips, swiveling them left and right, moving with him and against him, pulling our bodies apart before they crashed together again. I wanted the pressure to build higher, more, faster. I wasn't ready to let it go yet, but I wanted to start it all over from the beginning and let him take me to this place again.

My hips slowed, stilled, and I watched him intently. His eyes smiled as wide as his lips and he lifted my hand to his mouth, drawing my fingers inside, grazing them against his teeth. "You take no orders, do you, ma chérie?"

I traced the line of hair that split his abs, stroking his skin up and down, feeling the heat of him outside as well as inside my body. "Nor do you."

He laughed, and the movement made our bodies vibrate together. "You tempt me to take them."

I smiled and drew my hands up to his chest, letting the muscles fill my palms. He flexed them, making them pop against my skin. I liked his playfulness as much as I liked his strength.

15

Odin

She was going to be my undoing.

With little persuasion, I'd admit she already was. I did the blindfolding, not the other way around, but I'd wanted to experience this with her, wanted to see how she'd handle my blindness.

Her body vibrated so loudly that I could see her beyond the tight blackness of the silk, hear every movement of her skin, feel every quiver of her lips as she played them against my body.

The image of her played in my mind, stark against the blackness of the blindfold. Yet, when she'd removed it, I'd been delighted at how incorrectly I'd cast her.

She was a stunning woman, all curves and ivory skin. Her dark hair stood out in stark contrast as it played across the bed beneath her, curving around her like a living thing. I wanted to touch her for hours, play her body with every part of my own—and I would.

But first I'd had to bury myself in her and find my own relief. She felt amazing, wrapped around me, and it had taken all my willpower to keep from exploding inside her with my first thrust. She was elegant and sensual and so fucking beautiful.

When she'd rolled us over and loomed above me, I'd been struck again by her beauty. The soft glow of the city radiated through the room, scattering diamonds across her skin. Her hair tumbled over her shoulder, loose and wild like she was. I stroked her body, lifting her and lowering her, wanting to hold her tight but knowing she'd never allow it. The woman was hard and soft and every dichotomy between. She was wild and sweet, a stunning mix of all that a woman should be.

I slid my hands to her thighs, giving her the floor and letting her move over me. She swiveled her hips and moved to a beat of her own. I pulsed inside her, taking her farther again and wanting her to come while she rode me. Then again beneath me. And again while I tasted her.

For all that Ms. M wanted to give me orders, a secret part of her wanted to let go and give in, finding someone trustworthy enough to allow that to happen. I'd broken her trust earlier tonight and she would not give that over to me yet.

But I would earn it back.

One orgasm at a time.

It crashed over her and shook her body, leaving her trembling and collapsing into my chest. I held her and waited for the aftershocks to subside. Her hair hung damp at her temples and I pushed it back, in awe of how she'd given herself over to the experience. Everything she did, it seemed, she did with her full attention and devotion. I'd seen that earlier at the auction, and most certainly here in her bedroom. The woman was a powerhouse.

I wanted her for more than tonight.

She was amazing and there was so much to her that I wanted to discover. I wanted to peel each layer back slowly so as not to startle her, wanted to see what secrets lay beneath this complex woman.

With a smile, she lifted up, tossed her hair over her shoulder, and ran her hands across my chest. I was still hard and buried inside her. She'd had a single orgasm and I had so many more to take her through.

I slid my hands up her body, curling them around her waist and rolling her onto her back. She lifted her legs, curling them around me, but I lifted up on my knees and tipped her to the side, putting both of her knees over my right knee.

And I began to move.

She watched me, a quiet smile playing at her lips, her lids drooping closed a little with each thrust. My hands caressed her thigh, her ass, her legs. I encircled her ankle, tugging it tight against my lower leg, holding her in position as I thrust deeply into her. She was powerless to move with me from this angle, and it didn't please her to be so out of control.

I wouldn't hold her here long if it panicked her. She'd revealed the tiniest slip earlier when she'd told me that the control and the blindfold was important to her. Many of her rules and boundaries were important to her, I understood that.

I wanted to know why and who'd caused her this pain.

And I wanted to be the one to soothe it all away.

To get there, I had to play by her rules.

She whimpered and pushed against me, struggling to move with me and hindered by the angle. I cupped her ass and shifted her, flipping her over onto her stomach. My cock slid out of her warm pussy, making both of us moan in agony. She squirmed beneath me and I held her gently, moving over her and pressing my chest against her back. "I want to take you like this. Will you let me?"

She stilled, her breath quick and hot. "Yes. Take me, Odin." Her voice trembled with the same want and need that coursed through my body. We were overheated with desire for each other and I would not get enough of her tonight.

"Your command, ma chérie." I buried myself inside her, making her buck forward and grab for the sheets. Her ass moved backward with each thrust, driving hard against me as we moved together. My fingers bit into her flesh, holding her tight as my own orgasm threatened to break me. "I cannot hold much longer, ma chérie. Come for me."

She twisted, making eye contact with me and biting down on her lip. "Take me hard, Odin."

"Yes." I tightened my hold and drove into her with a fierceness that belied how tenderly I wanted to hold her. She consumed all of me and, together, we broke through as our orgasms claimed us, crashing over us and filling the room with a noise that overtook all the sound we made together.

16

Ashley

He lay curled at my back, his semi-hard cock nestled in the cleft of my ass, his big arm wrapped around me, his lips at my neck. "I want you again."

He stirred and ran his hands over the length of my side, over my hip and back. "Your command."

I laughed. "I think you did a pretty awful job of listening to them tonight."

He rose up on an elbow and kissed the path his hand had taken. "I ravaged you, as requested."

Another chuckle passed over my lips, swollen both from his kisses and my own need to pull them between my teeth while he'd fucked me.

The man had ravaged me, that was for certain. My entire body tingled and I felt like I was still on the brink of an orgasm. He'd taken me to places few lovers had been able to, touching parts of me that had nothing to do with my body. There was a tenderness to his movements that made me want to trust him, and that bothered me. I'd shoved my concerns away during our first round and let him take me as he'd wanted, doing my best to maintain control as we'd moved together.

He'd proven that he was skilled at the art of sex and I wanted more from him. We'd gotten our frantic sex out of the way, hot and needy with desire for each other. Now I wanted to let him move over me and inside me, taking me to another level that I had a feeling he was very capable of. Tonight was going to be one for the memory bank and I was going to miss the way our bodies moved together.

While I'd had ample lovers—a few phenomenal ones in the bunch—there were a couple who just synced with me, moving seamlessly between thrusts and positions as if we were one being, capable of taking each other higher together than we could separately. Odin was a suitable match tonight, diligently giving of himself, making sure that my pleasure came before his own, and moving inside me with an intensity that revealed a depth to him.

I smiled while he trailed kisses against my skin, carrying out his promise to taste all of me. I rolled over, landing beneath him as he loomed over me, pleased to let him explore my body with his mouth. Sensations radiated out from every one, rippling one after another, overlapping each other and sending shivers across my skin. He licked and bit me, sending bigger ripples to overtake the little ones. I smiled and played my fingers through his hair, threading the tips from the crown down his neck, pleasuring the feel of his face against my skin as much as he clearly enjoyed the opposite. "You taste of expensive things."

I laughed. "Oh? Like what?"

He bit me. "You mock me."

"Mmm." He touched the inside of my thigh and made me quiver.

"You taste of wine and diamonds and luxury."

I laughed again as his stubble tickled the inside of my foot. "I've never been told that."

He lifted up on his knees, glorious in his naked pride. "Truth?"

I nodded. "Yes. That's the most original compliment I've ever had."

He puffed up and drew my leg over his shoulder, then turned and started kissing on the other foot, nibbling at my toes and making me squirm again. "Then I will tell you more of them." He bit my heel, making me squeal and twist away.

His hands drew me back, dragging my skin against his. His hands played at the corners of my body my elbows, my knees, the edge of my heel. I wanted him to find every one of them and exploit them until I couldn't take it anymore. He took me to the brink of what I thought I could handle and held me there, forcing me to trust him.

I didn't do trust and it was a strange new feeling.

But he never pushed too far, never made me feel uncomfortable. I'd had lovers like that, ones who thought all I needed was a strong hand to get over my issues. Those men had been escorted straight from my bed and to the door. I didn't bother getting dressed when I'd shown them out. I knew what I needed and most definitely did *not* need a strong hand. I had my own two hands that were plenty strong.

What I needed from a man was not his power, but his obedience.

Odin had struggled with it tonight and I'd been very aware of it. He'd wanted to please me, to obey my commands, but he's also wanted to exude his strength. Yet, he'd relented, allowing me to make the decisions tonight, much as he'd wanted to be the one calling the shots.

"You are champagne." He kissed my ankle, lifting my leg and licking his way up my calf. "My favorite cognac." He nibbled my knee. "My Breitling."

I laughed. "Great. I taste like a watch."

He bit the inside of my thigh, hard enough to make it sting. "Luxury, ma chérie. You taste of elegance and the most expensive beauty."

I purred, enjoying the feel of his lips as they traveled up my inner thigh. He lowered himself and brushed his chin across the points of my hips. His breath pooled in my bellybutton and flowed over my sides. His tongue caressed my skin and I fell into him as he tasted me, devouring me with a completeness that he'd brought to the sex. He tasted me to my next orgasm, kissing me so thoroughly that I could barely breathe.

My hands fisted into the sheet and I arched up into him, planting my thighs tightly against his cheeks. He did not let me go easy with one, but he stayed between my legs, licking and lapping me onto my next one, taking me higher this time and keeping me there until my lungs compressed into nothing. I gasped for breath, unable to draw enough air.

He kissed his way up my stomach, taking his time and in no hurry to move to the next thing. He did that with each part of tonight; luxuriating in whatever we were doing without any pressure to move on. He was a man of the moment and it was so apparent in everything he did, every touch he left on me.

He rose above me, hands beside my head. I trembled beneath him, my body not fully recovered from the back-to-back-to-back orgasms. He kissed the side of my jaw, my neck, and brushed his lips against mine. "I could taste you all night."

"Mmm." I curled into him, dragging my toes up his legs. "Me too."

I rolled us over, pushing up so I straddled him again. "But first, it's my turn."

He grinned and propped his hands behind his head. "Yes, ma chérie."

17

Odin

I didn't want tonight to turn to dawn. She was exhilarating and took every challenge I gave her head-on. Tonight had exceeded my expectations of her and I wanted more.

So much more.

She was a fascinating woman and I hadn't been exaggerating when I'd told her that she tasted of the most elegant things I'd experienced.

Her hair tangled across my chest and I watched her move down my body, licking and tasting me as I had her. The first touch of her tongue against my cock made me growl and moan and fist a handful of her hair. She pinned my hands to the bed, not pausing in her torment of my body. Her tongue swirled and slid across my cock and my eyes shuttered closed, much as I wanted to watch her taste me.

Her hands worked in concert with her mouth, sucking me and stroking me into another dimension where we'd already traveled. I wanted her fiercely and she was a willing participant, giving as much as she took. My hips thrusted off the bed, in time with her movements. Her hands were everywhere; on my cock, my hips, my thighs, my balls. She stroked me with an expertise that unnerved me. She was incredible.

I wanted so much of her. So much more. I didn't want to come in her mouth, I wanted to be inside her again.

I tugged her upward, drawing her against me and rolling us over, placing myself between her thighs. "I wasn't finished."

Her mouth drew in a tight pout and I kissed her gently, wanting to please her and knowing she wanted to please me as well. "I need to be inside you. Will you let me?"

She pouted again. "I wasn't finished."

I lingered in my kiss this time, playing at her lips, teasing them open, tasting her mouth and drawing her tongue into mine. I knew she'd had a strategic plan for this evening and I wanted to push her boundaries, even if just a bit. I rose above her, settling our bellies against one another, waiting. She rubbed her cheek against mine and shifted beneath me, spreading her thighs and curling into me.

"If you truly want to finish me, I'll take you at your command."

She wiggled her hips against mine, rubbing her thighs against me. "You'd better prove to me that you're what I need."

I chuckled. She'd made me laugh several times tonight and I liked it. "I'm definitely what you need, woman."

She pressed her chest into mine. "We'll see."

I nibbled on her neck, making her squeal. "You'll be saying that a lot where I am concerned."

She pulled away and looked at me. "You think?"

I rose above her and winked, nudging my hard cock toward her warm pussy. "We'll see."

She arched into me and I dove into her, wanting to be enveloped by her. She wrapped her legs around my waist and I thrusted into her, meeting her movements and driving us both to ecstasy. She grabbed my shoulders and arched into me, whispering my name and curling around me.

Bodies slick with sweat, we crashed into each other as the orgasm claimed us again.

I slept with an awareness of her all night, our bodies entangled together. She slept fitfully, waking with a start and barely coming full awake, only to find me and curl against my body. I cradled her against me, tucking her into the safety of my arms until she drifted off to sleep again.

I slept little, preferring to watch her slumber beside me. Beyond the windows, the city slept, waking a few hours before dawn. With any other woman, I'd have dressed and gone home, leaving her with the promise that I'd call—which I sometimes kept.

This one, though... I brushed a lock of hair from her face and she stirred in her sleep, tucking closer to me and sighing heavily.

This one made me do strange things, things I'd never considered with the other women in my life. Rarely did I date long-term; my life typically had time for an occasional lover, or a woman to take on my arm to an event. But something about Ms. M made me want for more, for longer days, for a larger collection of hours. She was extraordinary, and not just in bed, though that had been an experience I'd not soon forget. She would have me thinking of her for days to come. Along with wondering about her name. She'd not given it to me tonight and that had surprised me.

Dawn broke in a startling display, waking me from a short nap I'd fallen into while I'd watched her. This time, it was she who looked on as I woke. "Good morning." I reached for her and she let me wrap an arm around her and pull her close. "Surprised to see you."

I kissed her forehead and nudged myself between her thighs. "And miss this?"

She stroked my arm and back, her touch soft in the early morning light. "Don't get any ideas that we're doing this again."

I rubbed against her, stroking the outsides of her gently, but not entering yet, not going beyond where she was willing to let me go this morning. "Do you mean to leave me in this state?" I rubbed my cock against her inner thigh, shifting slightly higher until she arched into me.

"No." She shifted, drawing her thighs tight around me. "I just mean once you leave here. I'm a one-time kind of girl."

I rubbed my cheek against hers. "That is not how it seemed last night."

She purred and lifted her hips, cradling the head of my cock barely inside her. I longed to be able to drive deeper and make her moan.

"Oh, I'm all about multiple orgasms; I'm just not sure about multiple days." She smiled and kissed me softly, holding my face between her palms. "It's not my style."

I pushed into her. "We'll see."

18

Ashley

He threaded his tie beneath his open collar while I watched, clad only in my silk robe.

I'd shunned his request for breakfast, feeling the hidden request that we become something beyond what we'd been last night. I had no interest in that, much as Odin attracted me with his suave features and actions. The man had been talented and obedient last night—much as he could be with his own need to be in charge. I'd enjoyed him, and waking up to him hadn't been horrible.

He stepped to me, sliding his hands around my waist and pulling me close. His lips hovered above mine.

I smiled, not leaning into him. If he thought I'd push forward and close the distance, he had a lot to learn about me. Things that I'd never reveal, not now that we were finished with our connection to each other. "Have you considered Black Velvet for your auctions?"

I fought the tension springing to life in my belly. *Had I?* Only every week since it had opened. Black Velvet was the premier place for luxury, and dark enough for debauchery the way the upper class liked it. Black Velvet was the desire of my soul. I wondered at why he'd picked that location to ask me about. "I have. It's beautiful and would be a perfect backdrop."

His lips shifted to graze my jaw. I sighed and leaned into the pressure of him. He was beautiful and sincere and pleased me well enough last night. A small part of me was bummed we were through.

"Let me know if you'd like me to make an introduction to Sampson. He and I go back for years. Black Velvet is in the first building I ever purchased, so that one is special to me. I think you'd fit in well there."

I kissed his cheek and stepped out of his arms. Too much longer there and I'd ask him to stay. "I'll let you know. I have a few coming up that would be perfect there."

He lifted my hand to his mouth, brushed his lips across my knuckles, and stared at me for a long moment. "I hope to hear from you soon, Ms. M. You have my number."

He walked out and I watched the doors close.

If I knew what was good for me, I'd immediately dismiss the idea of Black Velvet. I'd tried on my own to get in there for years to no avail and it needed to stay that way. Using Odin to get in would only encourage him, and lord knew the man needed no encouragement.

He'd tossed Black Velvet out to entice me, and it had worked.

I walked into the kitchen and made coffee, thinking I should have done that earlier and offered Odin a cup before he left. My gaze drifted over the marble island that stood sentry in the kitchen, picturing him laying me down on it, spreading my legs and devouring my pussy.

I bit my lip and let my head tilt back, my fingers sliding beneath my robe and touching my swollen clit, already damp at just the thought of Odin's tongue. He'd used it well last night, tasting parts of my body with an eagerness. I tasted my lips, running my tongue over my teeth, missing what he'd done to me last night. One finger slid inside, mimicking the feel of his.

I'd had plenty of great lovers, and Odin was no exception; what attracted me to him was the way he moved out of bed, with a surety and confidence that he knew I was going to call him. If not to have him inside me again, then about Black Velvet.

We'd see about that.

19

Ashley

I hung up with Vann Wolford and smoothed the hem of my skirt, brushing my fingers across my thigh. Vann was the last bidder for tonight's auction, a finance manager who'd made millions during the housing bubble. Now he dabbled as an angel investor for small businesses and continued to increase his net worth. He was gorgeous, smart, funny and a possible match for Brittny, tonight's virgin.

If Wilder didn't snatch her up.

I hadn't been sure about him at first, reading some bad press on him that had come out with a purchase-gone-bad a couple years back. When the deal didn't finish like he'd expected, Vann took out his frustration on the owner of the company he'd been working with, leaving a huge marketing disaster that he'd been unable to erase. That was one of the things about the internet, once news showed up there, it was nearly impossible to expunge it; something I knew all too well.

But I'd wanted him and we'd played phone tag for the last week, finally connecting today, the day of the auction. I'd thought about not letting him come tonight, but he'd sweet talked me, convincing me that he was worth all the trouble. I didn't have any gut reactions to him that led me to believe otherwise, so I'd relented, telling him that this wasn't the way I normally did business. He'd laughed, stating that this wasn't the first time he'd had someone tell him that. Vann seemed to roll with the punches, and with the chaos that infiltrated Brittny's life on a near-daily basis, she could use someone who could teach her how to wade through the crazy of life.

I spun in my chair and tapped out a quick email to Vann, including the contract, the wiring instructions for the ten-thousand dollar deposit, and the confidentiality agreements. He'd agreed to get those back to me well before tonight and that was the final piece I needed in place before I texted him the address to Trent's. Not that most people didn't know where the auctions were held, but that information didn't usually surface unless they were part of the inner circle I allowed to know that detail.

I checked my watch; it was still early and I had a lunch meeting with another prospect, then an afternoon at the spa to get ready for tonight that would hopefully scrub the rest of Odin's scent from my skin. I'd found myself thinking back over last night's events—a rarity for me—far more often than I would have liked today. Typically, I never gave men another thought once they departed, but Odin had managed to wiggle his way into my subconscious more than I preferred.

I made a few more phone calls, then leaned back in my chair, propping my heels on the edge of my desk.

Black Velvet was nothing to dismiss easily. Merely the location would add another 50K to the starting bids. Everyone knew the club's reputation—and I could still use Trent's, inviting the second-tier gentlemen to that. No one knew the final list of bidders until the evening's auction, as they were revealed. Some of them knew one another, but most of their circles never crossed. None of the bidders at Black Velvet would know who'd attended

Trent's and vice versa, unless they'd been to both, something I'd probably never need to do.

I'd been wanting to expand the direction of the auctions for some time now, and this would be the perfect way to do it. I had more than enough women for the rest of the year's auctions, and with two locations, I could double the frequency.

I couldn't ask Trent to close down his bar to accommodate the extra influx of women who'd heard about and contacted me, but if I could find my way into Black Velvet...

Thoughts swirled around my head. Even if I only did four exclusive events a year there. It wouldn't matter if the men from Trent's knew that I was doing them at Black Velvet, they'd be vying for the option to attend, and that meant they'd be more willing to spend more money at Trent's, most likely thinking that was the way into exclusivity. Unfortunately for them, what often worked in the real world worked against them in mine.

My gaze drifted to my phone. I wouldn't call him now, not when I had so much left to do to get ready for tonight's event, but I would contact him.

A surge of heat coursed over my body at the thought of him—and not just him getting me into Black Velvet. The man had left a mark on me, one that hadn't come off in this morning's shower, or during coffee, or in this sanctuary of my office where the only men allowed were ones who were bringing money and options for the girls.

I leaned over and spread the folders that contained the details of the men who'd attended Audrey's auction. Odin's sat at the bottom and I slid it free, pulling it into my lap and opening the front flap. His photo stared out at me, a recent one, making me feel like it had been taken this morning as he'd smirked and walked out of my home.

I ran a finger lightly down the list of his accomplishments, carrying over to the next page. I smiled; he hadn't been a match for Audrey, not even a little bit. I'd certainly let my own attraction affect my decision to let him come last night. He was far too sophisticated and worldly for her and I was almost glad that he'd called off the evening after I'd encouraged her to pick him.

Not that he wouldn't have been the perfect gentleman, but he almost would have set the bar too high for Audrey. No man would have been able to come close to how Odin would have treated her, both mentally and physically.

Even with me, he sharpened my wit by teasing me and pushing me, not something I usually allowed, but he found a way to sneak them in while distracting me with his looks or some mastery of my body.

On the second page, I found the list of his assets. They were all required to send such a detailed inventory to me. I wanted to make sure not only that they were who they said they were, but that there weren't hidden items in their past that would affect anything about the auction.

Which was why I hadn't been willing to let Vann's attendance slide until I had my hands on his details, even though everything else looked suitable—more so, in fact.

My attention drifted back to the folder, my finger poised against *Roderick Property* the old building downtown that held Black Velvet. Not that I'd not believed him when he'd told me, but I wanted time to process what this could mean for me. There might even come a day that I could hold fewer auctions, and only at Black Velvet. The women would be the ultimate prize and men would come from all over the country, giving the girls such a wider expanse of choice.

My phone chirped with a reminder that I only had fifteen minutes to get to the spa. I dropped my feet, closed the folder, and set it back on my desk. For tonight, I'd have to leave thoughts of Black Velvet on the back burner.

20

Ashley

Tonight was going incredibly well. Brittny had adjusted immediately to her surroundings, drawing the men into a bidding frenzy within the first half hour. They were captivated by her, as I'd known they would be.

Women like Brittny were the easiest to do these with. She understood what she had as a commodity and had no reservations about taking money for it. There was none of the immaturity that had plagued Audrey last night. Brittny was well-educated and well-spoken. She came from money and that helped her see her virginity as an asset.

It was only through luck that she'd managed to stay a virgin throughout college, to hear her tell it. She'd spent most of her undergrad years dating an older man who'd been overseas building his new business. They'd broken up before he'd come home and had a chance to deflower her.

Now she saw the advantage and had come to me after one of her co-workers became one of my clients. I'd made Brittny's friend a quarter of a million dollars and, as luck would have it, women talk.

It was one of the best parts to my program. I didn't have to advertise, didn't have to seek out women. I'd long ago found myself in a position that let me sit back and wait for them to come to me. I did my best to turn down a minimum of girls, though that was a growing challenge given my vetting process and time constraints of working alone. The demand had become so great that I was only able to work with one in ten women who contacted me.

Brittny had been an easy decision. And tonight she was going to make us all very rich.

Vann stepped up to me and I smiled, glad he'd come. "She's lovely." He kissed me on the cheek. We'd said hello when he'd first come in and he'd been pleasant and charming all night, getting along swimmingly with both the other men and with Brittny. She was quite taken with him and I told him so.

"It would be my pleasure to be your high bidder tonight."

I laid a hand on his arm. "I haven't talked to her yet, do you think she's taken with you?" I feigned concern. Brittny would have taken any of them home; I could tell she didn't care how tonight ended. She was in this for her bank account and she'd find a man to spend the rest of her life with later—if she ever did.

Brittny reminded me of myself. She was ambitious, gorgeous, and put herself first. Thankfully, other than the heartbreak that had come after ending a long-term, long-distance relationship, she was mostly unscarred, which would serve her well as she moved through life. By the way the men were throwing money at her, it was highly likely that tonight was going to set her up sweetly with a good nest egg to get started on the right foot. She didn't have the burden of debt that Audrey had; it was almost unfair that Brittny seemed to float through life unaffected, men and money falling at her feet.

But life didn't always stay on that trajectory. Hopefully it would be a while before heartbreak struck her in a way that left a stain.

"I'm willing to exceed anyone's bid by fifty thousand."

I eyed him and smiled. "No cap?" He had the money, so I wasn't worried about anyone outbidding him, but that was quite another thing when they were really paying millions for an evening with her. Some of these men were willing to go that high, but several weren't. As this was Vann's first, I wasn't sure if he really understood where the top might end up.

He glanced across the room where Brittny stood beside Wilder. A shadow crossed his face and he turned to me. "No cap. I want her."

A grin broke out on my lips. Vann was in for a hell of a ride if he thought there was a future for him and Brittny beyond tonight. She wasn't interested in any of them that way, but would probably lead him on and take his money tonight. The woman knew how to play to her audience. I admired how smart she was already at her age. It had taken me a lot of years and a lot of hard knocks to figure it out.

"All right, then. I'll keep you apprised of tonight's outcome as it progresses."

He kissed my knuckles. "Thank you."

He wandered away and I watched him circle slowly back to Brittny, letting Wilder have his time with her. Trent glanced over at me and winked. He'd been watching the men all night and knew how this worked. With as many as we'd had in here, he probably admired Brittny as much as I did. She'd needed none of his coddling or confidence building before the auction had started.

Wilder handed Brittny over to Vann, her last one-on-one of the evening, then came over to speak with me. I directed him toward the bar and asked Trent for a drink.

"And for you?" he asked Wilder.

Wilder shook his head, waving the offer away. "No. Thanks.

Too much money at stake for me to keep drinking. I need to keep my wits about me."

"What do you think of her?" I asked, taking a sip of my drink and pretending we were talking about which suit he liked better.

"She's stunning, provocative, amazing. What's the bid?"

I laughed softly. "It doesn't work like that Wilder, you know that."

He grinned and leaned in close. "Can't blame a guy for trying."

No, I couldn't. And I also knew that bending the rules always came back to bite me in the ass. "The question is whether you'd like to add another fifty to it."

He sighed heavily. "How much higher was it than my last one?"

"Substantial. Do you have a cap for the evening?"

He mimicked Vann's movement, watching Brittny over my shoulder and allowing the left side of his lips to curl up in a smile. "I probably should, but let's do this."

I chuckled softly. Brittny was reeling them in one by one. The girl would make a brilliant businesswoman no matter what industry she picked.

He left me and I smiled at Trent.

"She's having a hell of an evening, I take it?"

"Holy shit. Yes." I made the comment lowly so only he could hear me. We didn't often discuss the bids until they were over and I was paying him out. Tonight was going really well.

A twist reverberated through my stomach, making me wince slightly. Maybe too good. I was bound to have a hiccup that would throw my world off its axis. It was so rare that it made me wonder when the other shoe was going to drop and things were going to fly out of control. Because no matter how in control I thought I was, shit hit the fan when I least expected it.

21

Ashley

"Remember," I laid a hand on Vann's arm—the one not currently wrapped around Brittny, "dinner first, then on to your evening." I turned to face Brittny. "Call me in the morning."

She smiled and nodded, then gave her full attention to Vann. "I'll go grab my things."

She and I had already finished the contractual details a few minutes earlier and I'd told her that Vann would be her man for the evening. He'd given her nearly a quarter of a million reasons why. And she was very pleased. The money would hit her account within the next three days and she'd be a wealthy, smart woman with her whole life ahead of her.

Trent moved toward the front door, unlocking it, ready to let them out and re-lock the door after them so he and I could finish the evening in private before he reopened the bar to the public in a few hours. This wasn't a massive hit to his bottom line, especially considering what he made from the auctions. We all benefitted massively from his willingness to do private events. Vi held several of her after parties here after gallery openings, as well, quickly making Trent's the place to be. It was no Black Velvet, but he still had time.

Vann moved closer to the door and I gathered up a stray water glass from one of the tables.

The front door opened, startling all of us.

With a swiftness that terrified me, the one and only Carter—the man for whom I defined my life around, knowing only Before Carter and After Carter—walked into the bar like he'd been invited. Without missing a beat or noticing the minimal amount of people in the room, he walked up to Vann and they shook hands.

My mind raced to understand. Were they friends? Did Vann invite him here? And if so, did Vann know that Carter and I had a history?

Carter slapped him soundly on the shoulder. "I dunno, man, seems like a pretty weak party. You said it was something special."

My mouth opened and closed as my past collided with the present I'd worked so hard to construct. Carter swept the room, his gaze stopping on me. "Well, hello Ashley."

My hands shook and I did my best to hide them before anyone saw.

Vann looked at me and laughed. "I didn't know that was your name."

The room spun and my heart stopped.

It wasn't supposed to get out. My name was supposed to stay locked up, hidden away from those who would never know the meek little girl called Ashley.

My eyes darted between the men. This wasn't happening. I couldn't move. I couldn't get away from him—from my past. The muscles in my jaw locked and I couldn't open my mouth to tell him to leave, that he had to go.

Trent rushed forward and escorted Carter out, telling him that the bar would be reopened in a few hours. He locked the door behind him and rushed to my side. Vann looked from one of us to the other.

I couldn't speak. I sucked in air and couldn't quite process what had happened. In a rush, all the years I'd been Ms. M fell away. My life hadn't ever crossed Carter's—except in the courtroom. Now, he'd managed to break past the barrier that was once considered impenetrable. I didn't understand why he'd come and if it was just coincidence or premeditated.

I stared at Vann with unblinking eyes. Clearly he'd told Carter about the auction. That was the only conclusion I could come up with. It happened. It was how I got word-of-mouth clients and bidders, but never did I think that word would spread to the likes of Carter. And I certainly hadn't expected someone to bring a stranger in for one.

Those rules had been spelled out specifically in the non-disclosure and confidentiality agreements that I'd sent over to him today. Ones he apparently hadn't bothered to read.

Fury boiled up in me as the surprise and fear receded. I clenched my jaw.

Brittny walked out, none the wiser to anything that had just happened. Vann looked shocked, not realizing what he'd done. Not realizing that he may have just put my entire livelihood—and Trent's—and the auctions at stake.

Never mind my carefully constructed life.

Trent escorted Vann and Brittny to the door, taking over where I couldn't. He reminded Vann again about the rules, sent them on their way, and bolted the door. Then checked it again, watching the sidewalk until they made it to Vann's car.

He spun and raced back to me, grabbing both my shoulders. "Ash. Are you okay?"

I shook my head and clung to him. He drew me to him and guided me toward the office, glancing over his shoulder toward the door. What a shitty bit of luck, him unlocking it at that very moment, inviting my dark past inside.

But wasn't that the way Carter worked? Waiting until the perfect moment to strike.

It was how he'd raped me. It was how he'd turned my roommate against me. It was how he'd gotten off scott-fucking-free and was able to waltz into my life like he had tonight.

My body was cold and I felt sick to my stomach. I hated him with everything that I was.

This was supposed to be over. My life had moved on. I'd been able to push those thoughts that invited nightmares to keep me awake at night aside. But not now. Now, I'd be glancing over my shoulder wondering if he was there, wondering what he had planned for me next.

For all that Vi and Trent had tried so very hard to get me to a place where I could move forward after the mistrial of Carter's most recent sexual indiscretion and his subsequent release, he could still affect me with nothing more than a name-drop.

Even that was enough to send a course of shakes through my body. No one called me Ashley. That girl didn't exist anymore. Ashley died a long time ago, beneath Carter as he'd taken the very thing that Brittny had sold for six figures tonight.

Trent eased me down on the couch and stroked my arms. "I'm here for you, Ashley. Tell me what I can do. Should I call Elyse? Violet? I know they'd come for you. Let me call someone." He pulled his phone out of his pocket and pushed a button.

I shook my head. "I'll be fine." I fisted my hands. "I mean, not tonight, but some day. Don't call anyone. They're busy."

"Not so busy to come if you need them."

I slumped against the back of the couch, the lines of Ashley and Ms. M blurring further still as my clothes and posture didn't match each other.

Ms. M didn't slouch. Ms. M didn't let things rattle her. Ms. M was in command of every situation.

Ashley was a slob. Ashley got raped. Ashley paid the ultimate price for speaking up.

Ms. M was all that Ashley was never going to be because she'd been too scared to take life by the horns and direct it.

Ashley didn't exist.

Or so I'd thought.

Until Carter had walked in through that door.

"What are you going to do about Vann? Clearly he was the breach." Trent tried to change the subject, tried to get me back into the mode and persona of Ms. M. She'd have taken a breach like that in stride, shown the man the door, and nothing would have been amiss.

But this had been Carter.

"How in the fuck, Trent?"

"I'm sorry. I'm so, so sorry. Tonight had gone so well and I wasn't really paying attention. I should have seen him standing out there when I flipped the lock. I should have stopped him when he opened the door."

I gave his hand a weak pat, unable to do much consoling. He had been careless, but it had just been shitty timing. *Carter's* shitty timing.

"If you won't let me call anyone, at least let me take you home. You can come get the car in the morning. Or, better," he stood, "we'll take your car and I'll Uber back here."

I let him take my hand and lift me to standing. He pulled me into a sweet hug and held me, willing the uncertainty out of my pain-stricken heart. "I'm going to kill, Carter."

CONTROL ME, BOOK 2

22

Odin

I gave my phone an absentminded glance as it rang. Today had been one of those days filled with chaos and instability. Where I normally took them in stride, this one had me frustrated and ready for a drink.

I hit send on the email and gave my phone my full attention, finally caring who was bugging me. I smiled at the sight of Ms. M's name.

Took her long enough.

I'd expected her call days ago. After dropping Black Velvet I assumed I'd had her in my pocket and that she'd be angling for an invitation within twenty-four hours. That she was only calling now proved that I knew far too little about a woman who intrigued me a great deal. I'd have to change that.

"Hello, ma chérie."

"Odin. Nice to speak with you."

"What can I help you with, ma chérie?" Her voice sounded off and wasn't quite her usual lilt.

"I wanted to take you up on your offer regarding Black Velvet."

"Ah," I leaned back in my chair.

So that *had* been enough of an enticement for her to think about me. While I wasn't fool enough to think that how I'd pleasured her in bed would have been enough, it would have been a nice caress to my ego had she mentioned our evening before admitting to the real reason.

"You'd like to meet Sampson?"

"I've heard a lot about him. It's been a couple of months since I've thought about going to Black Velvet. I was thinking about acquiring an invitation for this weekend and thought if you could arrange an introduction to Sampson while I was there…"

"My pleasure. Except," I sat up in my chair and leaned my elbows on the desk. I pictured her sitting at hers, probably high in another penthouse suite, corner office, walls of windows, elegant interior design surrounding her own elegance.

"Except what?" There was definitely a tension in her voice. Something was bothering her or she'd had a rough day. I hoped it wasn't anything serious. My own day had been a straight up pain in the ass and I certainly wouldn't wish that on Ms. M.

"Except I'm headed over there in about an hour. Would you like to meet me tonight?"

There was a long pause on the other end of the line.

"Are you feeling all right, ma chérie?"

She sighed. "Yes. Just a long week."

"I am sorry. In that case, you must join me tonight. Let's drink away your blues."

"I'm not sure getting drunk with you is the best policy, Mr. Thayer."

"Perhaps not for you."

She chuckled softly. "Fine. I'll meet you. One drink."

"One is all it takes, ma chérie."

23

Ashley

The Uber dropped me off at the corner, as instructed, and I walked the remaining half-block to the building. Apparently once dark fell, the atmosphere around here changed and it became the exclusive haunt for the ultra-rich and their friends. Men in dark suits stood on the corner, watching.

Mishaps like what happened at Trent's the other night wouldn't occur here.

I sighed and slowed, taking in the ambiance of the night around me. It was a beautiful evening. The fog hadn't rolled in and I drew a breath. The first full one in a couple of days.

I didn't blame Trent. Honestly, I didn't. That was just how Carter and his life worked. He was on a constant trajectory to fuck up mine. Didn't matter how many things I had in place, he found a way in.

Two men flanked the door, both dressed splendidly in black suits and dark red ties. I smiled. "Please tell The Master that The Peacock has arrived." The men didn't act as if I'd said anything amiss, even though I felt like I'd said something ludicrous.

Apparently, one didn't get past the doors at Black Velvet without a suitable code name. Odin had given me all the details as we'd hung up and I'd agreed to come meet him. I didn't want to admit that this evening had excitement teasing the edge of my senses, both about seeing the man and the club.

The doors parted as they pulled them aside in perfect sync. "Welcome to Black Velvet."

Another man stood at the center of the opening, hands clasped at his waist. "This way, Peacock."

I smiled and followed him through the club. It was splendid. Everywhere I looked, class dripped from the surfaces; from the hand-carved tables and chairs to the inlaid dance floors, to the plexiglass bars and mirrored walls. As the name implied, black velvet draped many of the surfaces, complementing the dark wood and shimmering chandeliers. It was stunning.

We walked past doors that led to private rooms and—as a few opened—private dance floors. This was an incredibly intricate and intimate space. Rooms twisted into other rooms, hallways led to nothing, and yet it wasn't confusing. It was comforting, like the ultimate tree fort filled with magic and secrets. I didn't understand how the architect had done it, but they'd managed to create a grown-up maze of lust and desire.

On the left, my host stopped and his hand brushed a section of a mirrored wall. The section popped open and he pulled open a door that had been so perfectly tucked into the wall that I wouldn't have seen it had I walked by alone. I glanced over my shoulder at the bar we'd crossed since walking in, wondering how many of these rooms I'd walked past and had been completely oblivious to. My host said nothing, a secretive smile playing at his lips.

I peered into the room, noting Odin sitting alone in a dark leather chair that consumed the center of the room, legs spread, arms lanky and relaxed. I stepped inside and the door closed behind me, shutting us in together.

I wasn't scared.

A breath slid out of my nose, another big one like I'd taken outside. Odin was strong and competent and wouldn't hurt me. Not like Carter had, not ever.

My business brain went into overdrive, cataloguing everything about this room. It was big, yet intimate, furnished tonight with only the large chair. Did he expect me to stand all night?

Neither of us had drinks. Perhaps this was just where members greeted their guests. I didn't want to ask all these questions to quench my curiosity, but I had lots. If this room wasn't available to furnish differently, I could work with the one chair. This was all the more perfect for the clients who wanted exclusive evenings with certain girls. I hadn't done one of those in years—it took the right man and the right girl and most definitely the right price range. If everything wasn't perfect, then those felt a little too much like sex trades. I'd only done a few in my career and every one of the women had walked away with nearly a million dollars—and two had secured long term relationships with their bidders.

Odin seemed like the kind of man who might be interested in one of those. Maybe we'd have to discuss it later, after he took me to meet Sampson.

I walked around him, one finger trailing along the leather. He didn't move, content to let me peruse what I wanted, as I wanted.

"You look lovely, as always, ma chérie."

"Thank you for inviting me." His voice was mellow and kind, yet it still made my nerves stand at attention. There was no question that I was attracted to the man. If we'd met in this room before I'd let him fuck me, I'd have been thinking through all the ways I wanted to let him take me here.

His gaze traveled the length of my body, just apprising, not lecherous. He was a classy man, through and through, but I also knew that he'd take me with an animalistic need right here on the floor, or against the wall, or on his lap. I glanced at his lap and smiled.

He patted his leg. "Care to sit and chat?"

I smiled and shook my head ever so slightly. "No. Thank you."

"Mm. You tempt me, ma chérie." He rose and drifted closer, his fingers brushing against my hip as he circled me, mimicking my perusal of him and the room.

"I didn't come to be a temptation, merely to check out a new location."

He laughed softly and the sound lifted the hairs at my nape. He'd laughed like that while he'd been inside me, teasing me about something that I'd been so confident about. It wasn't mocking, and he would never press me on this item, or any of them, but it hinted that he didn't quite believe my bluff.

He stopped behind me, one hand trailing softly up my bare arm. I'd debated about changing my clothes before coming, but I'd been so purposeful about what I'd been wearing for the last few days. Carter had rattled me and the only way through it was to go back to the basics, back to where I'd started, back to the simple things like tonight's cream sleeveless dress that had cost me my first fortune and a loan from Trent to become Ms. M.

For the last few days I'd had to carefully construct my world from the ground up again, making sure that my foundation was stronger this time.

If I stayed in San Francisco, I'd reasoned, there were going to be moments when Carter's life slammed into mine. We didn't have any of the same circles, but as my clientele broadened, so would the paths that were potential opportunities to run into him.

I couldn't—I wouldn't—be a slave to my fear.

I'd conquered damn near everything life had thrown at me. Ms. M was a result of all that hard work and strength and courage and I wasn't going to throw it out because of one accidental meeting.

I'd already talked to Vann about the breach. He was apologetic that he'd only skimmed the contracts and hadn't thought it had been a big deal to mention the auctions to Carter. He'd apologized over and over for how much it had bothered me and that he could have potentially done any damage to my business.

His date with Brittny had gone incredibly well and they had another planned. He was grateful for the opportunity to come and wanted to make it up to me—he'd thought he had been by suggesting Carter swing by and possibly become a bidder.

I'd thrown up in my mouth at the suggestion that Carter was man enough to be one of my bidders. He could have been a billionaire and I'd have refused him regardless.

Carter didn't deserve to take a woman's virginity. He'd raped me. The entire premise of the auctions was to keep that from happening to another innocent young woman. He was the entire reason why I'd created them. I hated him anew.

Odin's fingers curled loosely around my arm. "You don't seem yourself tonight. Are you afraid to be in this room with me?"

I laughed gently. "No. Never afraid of you."

His lips touched the back of my neck. "Good. I would never hurt you, ma chérie. I hope you know that."

"I do." I wanted to sink into him, wanted to take a step back that would allow his chest to press into my back, wanted to feel his strong arms wrap around me and his voice whisper that it was going to be okay.

But I didn't.

Because I already knew it was going to be okay. Some way, somehow, I'd figure all this out. On my own, like I always did. Because there wasn't anyone to rescue me, no knight in shining armor, no hero to swoop in at the last moment to keep me from danger. I was all I had.

But for the moment—standing here in this room, away from the world and the chaos of my life—I could believe in fairytales, the same ones that kept those girls walking into my office, believing that a man and money could change their lives.

All money did was make for bigger problems. The real problems, the ones we all ran from, didn't go away. They just waited in the shadows until we thought we had life figured out, until we thought that we'd bought away all our troubles, purchased solutions for everything that got in our way.

For years, I'd been able to fool myself that money had solved every problem, but I'd only delayed them. Carter had already forced me into a court appearance, walked into a business transaction that wasn't exactly legal in the eyes of most judges, and turned my carefully constructed life upside-down.

Money hadn't done shit for me.

Odin paused his perusal of my neck, probably noticing that I wasn't responding like I had the other night. "Ma chérie, tell me what troubles you."

I shook my head. "Not tonight." It was a whisper, like the ones he trailed across my skin with his fingertips.

He let out a heavy breath, not quite a sigh, but not a normal exhale either. He was frustrated, and rightfully so. Most women probably tripped over themselves for a night with him. Everyone I knew would have been on their knees and sucking his cock the moment the door had closed behind them.

I wasn't most women. And he was going to have to get used to that.

"Then let me buy you a drink."

I turned and took half a step away, just enough to be out of immediate reach. I didn't mind his hands on me, they'd taken me to heights I'd enjoyed, but my head was a mess and I was feeling far too vulnerable to have the strength I needed around him. He was going to have to wait. At least for now.

24

Odin

She'd arrived right on time. The moment she stepped into the room, the room's energy transformed like she'd supercharged it.

Her eyes never stopped scanning. She was constantly taking in details, turning them over in her mind like she was trying to figure out how to capitalize on them. I enjoyed that about her. For all that she was stunning, her business mind was every bit as appealing to me.

I'd told Sampson to give me this room, the most exclusive in the building. I wanted to impress her.

And I wouldn't mind taking her against the wall in here, either.

No one would bother us. No one would interrupt until we chose to leave. I would let her lead the evening. I might do a few things to try and shift her thinking and entice her to take me home again when we departed, but I would not press her. Whatever had happened this week to upend her life had left a mark, a deep one by the guess of it.

I didn't like that. I missed her effervescence. I wanted to bring it back.

But I also believed her to be the kind of woman who didn't need others to add that into her life. She seemed like the kind of unique personality who could do that all by herself. I admired that.

Her perusal of the room was that of an owner. She looked at things the way Sampson did, judging every piece on its own merit, forcing it to stand on its own and not rely on anything else in the room to hold it up.

She was calculated like that. And I believed that also meant that she could cut the smallest thing from its spot the moment it was no longer serving its worth, a fact that both impressed me and instilled me with a twinge of fear. I would be the same in her life; the moment I stopped serving a purpose, I'd be gone.

I smiled and stepped toward her. Better to put as many ticks in the win column as possible, then.

"Come, ma chérie." I held out a hand to her and she didn't hesitate, settling hers into mine, the warmth sending a jolt of electricity up my arm. I liked her. Far too much for my own good.

We exited the room—it would be reserved for me all evening or until I told Sampson I didn't need it—and we headed toward the bar. I could have had drinks brought in for us, but I wanted her to see the rest of the club and to meet Sampson later. He was waiting for me and would impress her with whatever was needed.

We'd talked and I'd given him the gist of what Ms. M did for a living. He'd been impressed and had inquired as to how to become a bidder. We'd see if that conversation came up tonight.

I took her on a tour of the building, much like her initial host had, only this time I leaned over and whispered things in her ear, telling her who'd used the rooms and for what, leading her through the history of Black Velvet and all who'd come before her tonight. She asked questions, peppering me with comments and judgments about the building's interior. We discussed the architecture, the cost, my future plans. She was brilliant and met every single one of my answers with more questions to probe into my own business as well as that of Black Velvet.

I hoped Sampson was ready for her or she'd chew him up and spit him out, coming out as victor and new owner of Black Velvet if he wasn't careful.

I grinned and we stepped up to one of the alcove bars tucked into a recess. "Your usual?" I tipped my face toward hers, smiling at how caught up she was in the features of this room. Her face was alight with questions and inquiries. We discussed the number of bars in the entire building and she seemed pleased with Sampson's ability to serve all his customers.

We ordered—she a gin and tonic, me a Hennesy, neat—and I led her toward a collection of couches. She picked a leather one against the wall where she could watch the room. I slid in beside her, content to leave a small section of space between our bodies, hoping she'd close it as the night progressed.

"Tell me what you think," I asked, sipping on my drink.

"It's stunning." She looked around, her drink forgotten in her hands.

There was a childlike wonder to her in this moment and I devoured it, wanting to memorize this oddity about her. Perhaps it was just around me that she never let her guard down like she was in this moment; maybe it was the day coupled with being here, being with me, taking it all in for the first time. Whatever the right combination, I liked it.

"Do you think it could work for your auctions?" I stared at the room, picturing the events as they'd unfolded at Trent's. "You could use any of the private rooms, the one where you met me is the largest, or you could reserve these bigger rooms out here. Sampson is more than willing to work with your needs."

She swiveled, her knee brushing mine. "You talked to him about it?"

"Only briefly. I thought he should know what you might ask of him."

She bit her lip. "I suppose. There are just ways to approach the subject that can really turn someone off on the idea."

I cocked an eyebrow and tugged at a strand of hair that had come loose from her bun and caressed her cheek. "Do you really think me that crass?"

She shook her head. "No. I'm sure you handled it perfectly, it's just been a long week."

My fingers brushed her cheek, trailed along her jaw, and cupped her face. "I do hope there comes a day where you'll divulge these things to me, ma chérie."

Her eyes drifted closed and she let me play across the surface of her skin. This wasn't seduction, this was trust and I meant not to abuse it.

What I really wanted was to take her back to the room we'd just left and touch her like this on her entire body. We'd fucked the other night and she'd let me touch her as she'd wanted, but this was different. In this moment she felt unguarded, unbroken, unbeaten. I wasn't sure if there was something in her past that had come up to haunt her this week, or if it was just the same chaos plaguing mine, but I wanted to wash it all away.

I leaned close and paused before brushing my lips across hers. I hesitated, not wanting to take advantage of this moment. I shifted, settling a soft kiss against her cheek. "Ma chérie."

Her eyes blinked open and she smiled, straightening and putting all her walls back up as quickly as they'd fallen. "Sorry, I just got caught up in everything that is Black Velvet."

"I understand. I'm constantly getting caught up in everything that is you."

25

Ashley

I smiled and turned away, wrestling with the torrent of my thoughts and traitorous body.

Here, in this place, it was so easy to get caught up in the magic of Black Velvet. It dripped with luxury and the promises of needs met. Here, you could be anything, with anyone. It was truly the perfect venue for the auctions. I could hold them in tandem with what I did at Trent's, and even pull a few from him that were more suited for this locale and the upscale clientele.

Odin took a drink and watched me. "I hope you'll forgive my liberties, but I've allowed my business mindset to run away with options." He didn't pause to ask if I wanted to hear his ideas, or if I was even open to suggestions on how to change my business, plowing ahead after barely taking a breath. "While you've done a fantastic job, having another location will really allow you to scale the business, which is the true test of the viability of any business, especially if you want to bring on investors or sell it."

Neither of which I had any interest in.

"There'd be no reason to cease the functions at Trent's; those serve a certain clientele. But Black Velvet has the ability to catapult you into another dimension. You're already dealing with wealthy men as bidders, but the men who come here are a different cut—" He leaned close. "A cut above, if you will."

I wasn't sure about that. Most of the men who came to my auctions also came here. But I didn't say anything, content to let him wheel out his grand plans, as he'd clearly put a fair amount of thought into them.

And why wouldn't he? Any businesswoman worth her salt would want to be growing, expanding, looking to capitalize wherever she could. With anything else, I might be.

But this was different.

I didn't do this for the money—though it made me gobs. I did it—had always done it—for the freedom it gave the girls.

Yes, it paid me handsomely, but that was an aside. What I'd never wanted was a mill, churning out girls as fast as they walked through the door. That kind of indiscretion had gotten me a lawsuit and too many headaches.

"I know all of them, including the men who come in from overseas. While Sampson owns the club and manages the day-to-day, nothing happens here that I'm not aware of. Many of my good friends come here and I've made several good business contacts, thanks to the networking that goes on in Black Velvet. There are more than a few good options of people who could work with you, do the heavy lifting, especially vetting the girls and the bidders." He slowed long enough to sip his drink. "You could make the most of that; hold auctions every day, twice a day if you wanted. I could help you."

I coughed as I took a sip of the drink, liquid heading down the wrong pipe. Had he really just suggested that we become business partners? On an idea that we hadn't collaborated on? Maybe I'd heard him wrong.

"Odin this is really all quite grand." I patted his hand and situated my legs, scooting a few inches away. "But I don't want to scale the business."

He frowned. "Why ever not? That's foolish."

It was my turn to frown. "Not every business is built on capitalism."

He huffed. "Then you need me more than I thought." He swirled the liquid in his glass and took a sip. "I will make us rich."

I shook my head and stood, my glass forgotten on the table. This wasn't what I'd wanted out of Black Velvet. I didn't need a business partner. Trent was as close as I'd come and he only reaped the monetary rewards of the auctions. He had no say in who came—on either side of the auction, whether bidder or virgin. Sure, he sent people my way that he thought would be suitable, but never with any conditions. His suggestions came with the understanding that I always had the final say.

I had the feeling that Odin would not be the same. If he sent a bidder to me, I'd have to take him.

If those were the conditions to Black Velvet, he could keep them.

"Ma chérie?" He stood, sensing something was wrong, and came behind me, his presence towering over me—comforting, not intimidating. He reached forward, slowly, rubbing the backs of his fingers along my arm. "I did not mean to offend. If I did."

He palmed my back and I leaned into the pressure. I took a breath, getting my nerves under control. Odin hadn't demanded anything and I just needed to steer us back to how I wanted to keep things. I still wanted Black Velvet.

"I get possessive about this business."

"Understandable. You've done a phenomenal job, especially seeing as you've handled all of this on your own. I only wanted to augment what you've already built. That you've done such a job is the only way that it's scalable to the extent I believe it is."

"I get that." I turned to him and let my arms drop. His mimicked mine, arms at his sides, his gaze driving intently into me. "And I thank you for the compliment. I've worked hard to make this what it is, but not for the reasons you think."

His face softened and he drew me back to the couch. "Come. Sit. Tell me."

I hesitated, but only for a moment. He was encouraging and gentle and I wanted to discuss business with him, I just didn't want him thinking a discussion meant that he could take over what I'd built. Yet I also wanted to form an alliance with him in order to get to Black Velvet.

"The difference between what I've built and most businesses is that the girls aren't commodities. It's important to me that they make as much money as possible and that they have complete control over who the winning bidder is. I'm not their boss, I don't seek them out. I vet my bidders based on their personalities and the fit of the girls far more than their bank account. Getting into Black Velvet isn't about the access to the patrons; it's about the space, about how that will make the girls feel when they're somewhere exclusive that will accentuate all that this is and all that it's not. I've been particular about where I hold them and finally got to a point that I enjoyed working with Trent so much that I've stopped holding them anywhere else. But it's still a bar and there's something seedy about that. Black Velvet is different."

He nodded thoughtfully. "I see." He leaned forward and picked up his drink from where it sat beside mine. He leaned back into the cushions, sipping and watching me.

I wasn't entirely sure that he did see.

And I hadn't revealed another reason why I wanted Black Velvet—for their security. Carter's unexpected arrival the other night still had me rattled and had even crept into our conversations tonight, making me guarded and jumping to conclusions, which was something I rarely did. I could hold my own in the toughest of business discussions, but now I was twisted up with my past, making it difficult to be who I'd been just months ago.

Everything about Carter and my own situation was casting shadows on daily life.

I sighed and twirled my glass where it sat, no longer wanting the drink.

"I can order you something different. Wine, perhaps?"

I shook my head and looked at him. He was so strong and sure sitting here, like nothing bad had ever dared shine its inky blackness on him. I was sure that wasn't true; everyone had their own share of issues and obstacles. I'd just let mine affect me to the point that I'd built a whole business around it.

I'd never really gotten over it. I'd powered through it, used it as a catalyst to fuel my life, but I'd never done anything to truly rid myself of the poison that still lived inside me. It must be there or Carter's appearance wouldn't have rattled me as much as it did. He was a horrible person, but that didn't mean that I needed to continue to let him control areas of my life. Even now he was impacting my interactions with people who had nothing to do with him.

I wanted to be free of him, once and for all.

But I didn't know how to do that.

"Ms. M?" Odin's knuckles brushed my cheek. I missed his pet name for me and smiled, genuinely attracted to him, even still. Not quite enough for him to call me by my name, but the nickname had been a nice middle ground for us.

"I'm sorry I'm not quite myself tonight."

"Will you tell me about it? I'd like to know. Not to help, just to know more about you. You intrigue me and I want to learn you."

There was a slow simmer to his voice that curled around my nape. The man was sinfully sexual and his head for business was as intoxicating as the rest of him. He was the kind of man who could chase the remnants of Carter's effects from my life. But I had to do it on my own or they'd just reappear once Odin's massive stature departed.

"I want these women to have complete control over everything

—save the location. I give them choices that I think will be good for them, but in the end, they get to choose, and can say no to any of the men."

He grunted. "That's a lot of control that's not in your—the business owner's—hands. I don't like that."

"You don't have to. I told you that not all businesses are built for the sole intent of making money."

"Then it's in the top two. Some businesses choose to be environmentally conscious, and I applaud that. But, at the end of the day, if they're not making a profit, they're going to close."

"I make plenty of profit."

"The more you make, the more people you can help."

I admired his tenacity and his effort to make me see what he thought was perfectly sound reasoning. I appreciated it, as did my bank account, but that wasn't what I was after. Had never been after. I wanted that for the girls, and what I received in compensation was an aside. I wasn't sure that Odin would be able to understand that.

"Why? Why build a business like this when you can do it so it benefits everyone?"

"Because I lost my virginity when I was raped. I want to give these women a way to choose how they use theirs so none can ever take it from them. Auctioning off something so prized also gives them command over their lives and their financial future."

26

Odin

She said it so matter-of-fact that I wasn't certain I'd heard her correctly. "Raped?"

She shrugged. "It was a long time ago."

I spread my arms across the back of the couch and looked at her in a different light. She'd taken a monumental experience and turned it into something far reaching, far beyond anything I could have created. There were always catalysts in life, things that made you find your drive, propelled you forward, and gave you the courage to keep going when everything looked impossible.

But this, this was extraordinary. All that she'd managed was nearly incomprehensible. And I told her so.

She looked away and toyed with her glass again. It may have been a long time ago, but parts of it lingered, as with all catalysts. They left a residue, it was what kept you going.

I wondered if something had come up this week related to this revelation. "Did that impact your week?"

She shook her head and looked at me. "No. It was just a long week."

I nodded, understanding that our relationship wasn't to that point yet. She would let me flutter at the edges of her business, but her personal life was still off-limits.

We'd see how long that lasted.

For now, I would let her keep her boundaries. They allowed her to feel safe around me, and I wanted that more than anything else.

"But I hope that you understand a little better why I'm not interested in scaling the business. The way I do it was put in place for a reason, and I want to keep that structure. So much so that I'd rather forgo money to ensure that the girls get exactly what they need, how they need it."

I could not have been more wrong about her. I should have probed more and listened before suggesting what I did.

It was still a sound suggestion and I would not apologize for it —every business should be scaled to that point. But I would not have told her of my idea had I known her past. I would have kept quiet about it, letting her build her business how she pleased. I didn't need any more obstacles in the way of our future.

For there *would be* a future.

I wanted to soothe away her pain, her frustrations, and her past, ridding her of the bits that clung to her. She'd built this business to the point that it would continue on without the pain of her past and its lingering effects.

I ran a hand down her arm, easing her closer. She came willingly. Whatever lingered was enough to fracture her walls where I was concerned, and I wanted her, wanted to gentle her, seduce her, strip the pain away, if even for an evening.

Her shoulder brushed my chest and I gathered her to me, my lips gentling hers. She let me kiss her, allowing me to search her mouth, to suckle her lips. Her tongue made lazy circles around mine, but she let me lead, at least in this moment.

I trailed my fingertips through the edge of her hair at the nape, pulling sections out and twisting them around my fingers, then letting them spill down her neck. I kissed her cheeks, her jaw, the base of her ear. She leaned against me, comforted and relaxed.

Around us, the club continued to fill, people coming and going, dancing and drinking. I had no qualms about taking this as far as she'd let me out here in public. For now, she was letting me lead. Once I got her in private, I knew that would change and she'd want to be in charge again.

Now that I knew about the rape, I understood her need for control—both in bed and in business. I was certain I could change both of those, but it might take time. One thing I was very willing to give her.

She tipped her neck, allowing me more room to ply her. "Should we go back to your private room? Or a different one that's a little more comfortable?"

"What did you have in mind? I can have a bed taken into that one. Or handcuffs."

She smiled and let her eyes drift closed. "You'd let me restrain you?"

I chuckled and bit her neck. "Hardly. I was thinking it was your turn to be tied up so I can tease you."

"Mmm." Her hand caressed my face. "No one gets to tie me up." Her whisper held steel and I pocketed the insight. She had every right to say no, but I also knew the power in allowing yourself to let go. It might take some time, but she would relent. One day. One day soon.

"How about a bed? Or a couch?" She ran her other hand up my arm, and my cock twitched.

I wanted her and I didn't much care where or how. I would take her on the chair that still sat in the room, if we needed. "I'll need a moment to get it prepared."

"Fine." She stood, holding out a hand to me. "I'll go powder my nose. Meet you back at that room?" She glanced around, in the area toward the hidden room from where we'd come. "If I can find it again."

I stood and kissed her, my hands cupping her elbows. “I’ll have an attendant ready to escort you.”

She melted into me, allowing my hands to roam across her back and cup her ass. God, she was so sweet and delectable. I wanted to devour her.

With much effort, I lifted my lips from hers and turned her, sending her on her way. “Don’t keep me waiting.”

27

Ashley

D*ammit.*

I took my time in the restroom, checking my makeup and shaking out my arms after peeing. This wasn't how I'd wanted tonight to go at all.

It had been a long time since I'd told a potential partner that I'd been raped. That wasn't my style, nor was it anyone's business. That was in the past and had nothing to do with why I held the auctions anymore. If anything, it tainted them and made it sound like I was looking for retribution for what had happened to me in the past.

Odin had handled it well, but the last thing I needed was more information for him to use as leverage. He wanted things from me beyond what we did in bed.

In bed.

What the hell was I thinking, breaking rules for someone like him?

If I was smart—which I wasn't feeling very lately—I'd walk out and leave him hard and wanting in his private room.

If.

But I was feeling emotional.

Which was never a good thing.

Ever.

I sighed and leaned forward, hands on the counter, eyes direct and staring in the mirrored image three inches away. “Damn you.”

“Everything okay?” A brunette exited the stall and stopped at the sink beside me, washing her hands. “Guy problems?”

I laughed. “You could say that.”

Her gaze drifted down my body. She was half my age and stunning. She’d also had plenty to drink tonight, but she seemed to still have control of her faculties. “You’re gorgeous. Leave him and go find a better one.” With that, she wiped her hands and walked out, leaving me to ponder my reflection once again.

Was that what I wanted, a better man?

Definitely not.

I didn’t want a man at all; not for anything beyond the bedroom. And I’d already had Odin there. We’d had a great time and I’d let my greed for Black Velvet keep him around longer than I should have. So now what?

I washed my hands again and reapplied my lipstick, then watched Ashley move on the other side of the mirror. *What would she do?*

I laughed.

What would Ashley do? Ha! Ashley would ask for advice from everyone she could, not take any of it, and be paralyzed by indecision, eventually doing not a goddamn thing.

I was not Ashley.

I blew my reflection a kiss and grabbed my clutch, striding out of the bathroom and toward Odin’s room, silently following the attendant who made no mention of where we were going, but simply led the way. I still wasn’t entirely sure what I was going to do when I got there, but with every step my resolve stiffened.

Black Velvet was important to me. More importantly, it was

crucial to the girls and their success. I'd have to work closely with the owner—Sampson—to make sure that he was okay with me bringing in non-members for the one-time events. They wouldn't need to be members here, not before or after. That would allow me to vet who I wanted, culling the top. The top bidders, the top girls. The events here would be ridiculously exclusive.

I smiled. No matter what happened between Odin and me, Black Velvet would remain a potential opportunity. Odin would not withhold it from me.

I followed the attendant through the club, past the overflowing bodies and smell of expensive alcohol. For all that this was a high-priced club that catered to the upper set of wealth, it was still a club.

Which was perfect. I wanted it.

The attendant barely paused at the hidden door, and I took a deep breath. It was just one more night with him. So what if that made him a two-night stand? He was fantastic in bed, he'd proven that he was willing to let me lead, and this wasn't at my house. This was in a club, which made the stakes totally different.

Totally.

The door opened and Odin sat in the same chair he'd been in when I'd come in the first time. The door closed behind me and I didn't take my eyes off Odin. Didn't look around the room, didn't check to see if he'd bothered to bring in a couch or a bed for us to fuck on. I didn't care. I'd take him right here in the chair if I wanted.

Did I?

Leg splayed, he sat with his arms resting on his thighs, his very strong thighs. I slowed my stride, taking him in, letting him look, letting him watch. He inhaled slowly, drawing my scent deep into his lungs. Then he smiled and lifted a hand, beckoning me closer. "Come, ma chérie."

I didn't pause at the edge of his chair, setting one knee on either side of his hips and straddling him. His hands lifted from his thighs, allowing me room to move closer. My skirt slid up my legs and his gaze never wavered from mine.

He smelled good. Had I not noticed that earlier or was I only just becoming more attuned to him now that I'd decided to sleep with him? His hands slid around my waist, resting gently in the swell above my hips. "I thought you were getting us a couch. Or a bed."

He chuckled. "Is that what you really wanted? I know that's what you said, but you're not a bed fuck, ma chérie."

"Oh?" I laughed and leaned closer, barely brushing my breasts across his chest. "That's not what you thought last time."

"You were in charge." He gave a cocky shrug. "I relented."

"Bullshit." I whispered the word against his ear, sliding my thighs tighter against his. "You don't relent for anyone." His fingers tightened on my hips and he yanked me close against his hard cock. "Who's in charge this evening?"

He ground his hips into mine. "Always me, ma chérie. I am always in charge."

I laughed and bit his neck. "No. I am always in charge. You'd better learn that."

"Or what?" His hips pressed up into me.

"Or I'll leave."

His thumbs slid forward, dipping beneath the hem of my skirt and pushing it up my thighs. He palmed me and cupped my ass, rocking me back and forth.

I bit my lip and watched him. His lips were sex-hooded and full of lustful desires. One finger slid beneath my panties and into my wetness.

I tightened my hold on the back of the chair, shifting my hips forward and grinding into his hand. I needed to take control, to tell him what I wanted, but as his finger moved inside me, his thumb moving against my clit, I had no power to speak.

"And how about now?" His voice was a low growl. "Will you leave now? Could you leave now, ma chérie?"

"Not before you fuck me."

He laughed, low and rich. "You think to tell me what to do again this time?"

His fingers moved expertly inside me, making me crave more, making me need the impending orgasm.

My breath came quick and I sucked in air, unable to get enough as his hands moved in rhythm with my hips. The air in the room was warm, causing beads of perspiration to erupt across my skin. He leaned forward, kissing one away, trailing his tongue across my skin, tasting my collarbone, my cleavage, the base of my throat. The air kissed the trail, lifting the tiny hair on my skin and making me feel the orgasm across my entire body as it claimed me.

My head fell forward and I pressed my temple into his. "Fuck me, Odin."

He didn't answer, his own breath coming hard and hot as he continued to move inside me. His thighs were hard beneath me and I could feel the press of his cock against my bare thigh, nothing but his dress pants separating us.

I wanted him inside me. Wanted him to take me right here on the chair. Like this. Bent over the back. Legs draped over the sides. All of the above. I didn't care. I only wanted him, needed him, inside me.

The orgasm shook me and I trembled, sagging into him. His hands continued their perusal of my body, sliding up my thighs, across my legs, up my back, down my arms. They were everywhere and nowhere all at once. I needed to take control, needed to get command of the situation before he did.

I wanted control.

And yet...

I wanted him to take it from me, too. Wanted him to show me I could trust him with it.

"Fuck me, Odin."

"Say please."

I laughed and slid off his lap. "Those words are for you."

I stood on trembling legs, trying to find my footing both in this room and in this situation. I wanted him. More than I should. More than I'd wanted a man in a long, long time. My being here a second time was testament to that. I didn't like it. Didn't like how much I wanted him, how much I craved the feel of him.

His fingers were still wet, glistening in the shallow lighting of the room. He lifted them to his mouth and put them both in, sliding them slowly past his lips. He smiled around them as he tasted me. Sucked clean, he pulled them out slowly, dragging them down his lower lip, making it pucker.

I wanted to pull it into my own mouth, taste us both. I wanted to get on my knees in front of him and take him in my mouth, make him explode at the back of my throat. Wanted to taste him like he'd just done to me.

Damn him for making me weak like this. Damn him for being here, in Black Velvet. Damn him for being able to draw secrets and desires from me.

"Ma chérie."

I didn't answer. I crossed my arms over my chest. We squared off, neither needing control, both wanting it. He would relent again tonight, if I pressed the issue. And I would.

I would.

Really.

In a matter of seconds, I would demand what I wanted from him. I would not drop to my knees and undo his pants. I would force him to stand, to take them off himself. And then I would not slide my hands down those thighs, stroke his hard cock against my cheek, run my tongue along the bottom, cup his balls and taste them.

I would not.

My arms trembled and I squeezed them tight. "Odin."

"Ma chérie."

I laughed. "One of us is going to have to relent."

"Yes. I believe you will. It's your turn." He stood, stalking slowly toward me. I held my ground and squeezed my arms tighter. "Or is this why you only sleep with men once? So you don't have to be the submissive."

"I'm never the submissive." Never mind how close to the truth he was.

"I wonder why you've allowed me the pleasure of your pussy twice now."

"I wanted Black Velvet."

He laughed and came closer, circling me, touching me with the softest feather touch on the most unintimate spots—the meat of my forearm, the blade of my shoulder, the tip of my fingers. "You already had Black Velvet before you walked in this room. Do not take me for a fool. I know you," he leaned close, his breath at my ear, "Ms. M."

I shivered, hating myself for reacting to him. My name burned the tip of my tongue, but I couldn't let my past come up here. Couldn't let it interfere tonight when I so badly needed to cling to Ms. M and the courage she evoked.

"You expect me to ask you permission to fuck you? To beg you?"

There was a teasing edge in his voice and I tugged at it, raising an eyebrow but remaining silent. I wanted him to play with me. Wanting him to draw Ms. M out and leave Ashley forever in the shadows. I wanted him to eviscerate her without ever knowing her name. I wanted him to murder a girl that he'd never met, never known, would never know. I wanted him to draw out her last breath as I came with him inside me.

I wanted Ashley to never leave this room.

He circled me, his stride long and powerful. There was an intimidation there that I would not cower to. Ashley would have. She would have run from this room barely able to catch her breath and would have cowered in her bed beneath the covers, wondering what in the hell she'd ever been thinking to step into the same space as Odin.

I was not Ashley.

I would not cower.

I would not simper.

I would match him word for word, stride for stride.

I let him circle me one more time and then I turned with him, no longer giving him my back. He laughed. Threw back his head and laughed. The sound reverberated off the walls, the padded ornate ceiling, the lone chair in the room.

That chair was one more attack at my instructions. He'd not done as I'd asked and had them bring in somewhere soft for us to fuck. He'd left the chair, exactly where he'd had it positioned before my arrival, planning to either fuck me against the wall or that chair or take us to the floor and have his way with me there.

We'd see about that.

28

Odin

The woman was like no one I'd encountered. She had the wisdom and heart of a man, but the body of a goddess. She matched me in everything, not cowering to take my business advice—advice most men would kill for.

Then she climbed off my lap while my fingers were still damp from her and stood outside my reach asking me to beg for the chance to put my cock inside her. Again, most women would have been on their knees the moment they'd walked in the room. They wouldn't have given me a single chance to shun them, to send them packing.

Damn I liked her.

I liked everything about her from her brain to her tits. She was a fantastic specimen, both in mind and body. She made me hard. And she made me work. I'd never met an adversary quite like her, and while I had no intention of ever being on the other side of the table from her, I did like that she hadn't given in to any of my suggestions. That alone gave her a space as my equal. The woman was bold and fiery and self-assured.

But damn if I was going to ask her *please*.

She turned with me and I dragged a finger across her belly, just above her belly button. Her eyes flashed, full of desire and need. I wanted to make her crave me. Wanted to make her cave, wanted to make her beg. I wanted her to ask me with sweet words to put my cock inside her and make her come.

But first I was going to give her a slow, slow torture that built her orgasm to the point that she thought she'd never survive it once I allowed her to come.

I might let her be in charge tonight, I might let her take the reins and be in control, but I would not give her the release she was about to crave with a wanton desire.

There were so many things I wanted to know about her, so many things I wanted to discover. Right now, I wanted to hear her scream my name as waves crashed over her, threatening to drown her.

She stepped into me, blocking my move and stroking her fingers along the length of my cock. I was so hard and ready for her. If she was any other woman, I'd walk her backwards three steps, bend her over the back of the chair and fuck her until she trembled beneath me.

But this wasn't any other woman. This was Ms. M. This was the woman who refused to give me her name, who refused my help, my advice, my expertise.

Save here.

Here, she would let me fuck her with all the skill I possessed.

As long as I asked for permission.

Her touch was strong and bold across my cock. I wanted her skin on mine. I wanted her hand wrapped around my shaft. I wanted her making me come. I wanted to explode on her, spilling myself across her fingers. I wanted to watch her lick my come off her fingers. I wanted her to dip her fingers in her mouth, her pussy, sucking them clean. Then I wanted to devour her mouth. Tasting both of us. She was so goddamn beautiful and sexy.

My hand wrapped around her waist and I pulled her to me, snugging her ass against my cock. My lips traced the line of her neck and I bit her shoulder. One hand cupped her breast and I circled her nipple, forcing it into a tiny bud that I wanted between my teeth. She circled her hips against me, brushing her sweet ass back and forth against my erection. A bead of come wet the tip and I clenched my teeth, needing to be inside her. Wanting her nearly bad enough to ask permission.

But she was not a woman a man asked for.

She was a woman a man took. She was a woman that a man plundered, buried himself in, got lost in. She was a woman that made me want for things that I couldn't name, for desires so strong they overrode all the sense in my brain.

Her ass changed directions, circling the other way, grinding against me. I thrust my hips into her, sliding my cock along the cleft of her ass, driving into her with a need that threatened to make me weak in the knees.

I bent and picked her up, carrying her toward the chair. Why in the fuck had I not had them bring a bed in? How stupid was I to think that taking her against the chair would be enough? I wanted to lay her down. Wanted to bury my face in her pussy and lick her to the first of many orgasms tonight.

But I'd fucked that up by letting my pride and power keep me from having something brought in where I could have my way with her.

I turned her and lowered her to the chair, sitting her in it like I'd been when she'd come in. I lowered to a crouch in front of her, my hands on her knees. With a gentle pressure, I spread her legs, lifting each one to settle them on my shoulders. She bit her lip, drawing it tight between her perfect white teeth. "Relax, ma chérie. I'm not fucking you yet. You'll get your permission." That was a lie, but I wanted her believing that I was willing to beg.

One of us would be, of that I was certain.

She threaded her fingers through my hair, tugging on the ends and making my scalp tingle. I kissed the insides of her thighs, nibbling at the sweet spots, rising higher and higher toward the sweet smell that beckoned me. I wanted to devour her, wanted to dive into her and not take my time. But this was part of the seduction, part of what I needed to make her beg me to put my cock inside her.

I neared the top of her thigh and she squirmed, wanting me to taste her as badly as I did. I shifted, moving to the other thigh and starting over at the inside of her knee.

"Odin." It was a curse and a command.

But not a plea.

I chuckled against her skin, tasting her, spending a luxurious amount of time swirling circles against her inner thigh. Her fingers found her pussy, sliding inside and working her juices. I removed her hand and placed it firmly on the chair. She pushed back, and while I did not move from the spot on her thigh, we got in a tug of war; she trying to use her own fingers to ease herself toward her orgasm, me firmly holding it away so she would beg me to give it to her.

I trapped her hand against my chest, lifting my head from her leg to slide one finger inside my mouth. I scraped the edge of it along the side of my teeth, sucking it hard to the back of my throat like I wanted her to do with my cock, licking it the same way I'd treated her thigh.

She moaned and relented, allowing me to put her hand back on my chest. I returned to her thigh, an inch closer to her pussy, and she tugged at my shirt, trying to command me with her body as her words failed her.

I slid one thumb inside her and moved closer, nibbling the skin, tasting the sweetness of her legs and forcing myself to slow before tasting the treasure I truly desired.

I ran my nose across her soft skin, dragging it from one side of her pussy to the other, inhaling her perfect scent and kissing the far side of her leg. She squirmed and dropped her hand to her clit.

I moved it, pushing it up to her breast and kneading the tender mound with her hand beneath mine. She moaned and arched her back, gripping her other breast and tugging the front of her dress down, forcing the tight nipples free from her green lace bra.

While she was distracted, I licked her slit, once, hard from bottom to top. She bucked into me, smashing her pussy against my face. I laughed and gently bit her lips, forcing her to still. She slapped the top of my head. "You'd better do it right."

I licked her again. "Or what?"

She squirmed and I pulled away, making her wait and still before I touched her again. Two could play this game.

"Or I'll leave, Odin." She drew in a shuddering breath. "I don't want to, but I will."

"No you won't." I whispered the words against her skin, each one punctuated with a swipe of my tongue across her most delicate parts. I wanted to taste her until the sun rose in the morning. I wanted to kneel before her all night and make love to her pussy until she cried out for release.

"I will." Her own words held little conviction but I would not press her. I could feel her buckling beneath the pressure of my torment and this was not—I realized—how I wanted her.

I did not want her broken. I wanted her to come to me, bold and sure and positive that she wanted me. Needed me. Craved me with the same desire that made me want her.

I kissed her gently, then rose above her, bending her legs and leaning forward to take her full lips the same way I'd taken the others. Gently, I brushed our mouths together, breathing her air, smelling her scent. She watched me, wary and wondering what I would demand of her.

And if she'd have to leave.

29

Ashley

I had hoped he'd relent by now, asking me for the pleasure of fucking me. Mostly so we could get on with it and I could get home.

My pussy was wet and hot and demanding. I twisted my nipples as he kissed me, feeling my pussy clench and send a wave of desire through me. I wanted his cock there, right against my sweet spot. Wanted him plundering me and pounding into me. I wanted him spilling himself against the back wall of my pussy, wrapping his arms around me tight and calling out my name. I wanted him to make me come and gasp for breath.

His tongue slid inside my mouth, carefully and cautiously probing the depths. He tasted like me and I sucked his tongue, wanting it to be his cock. We'd get to that, but first I wanted him to eat me and do it right. I wanted him back between my legs, then I wanted him asking to fuck me.

I would not relent on this. I needed it. Ashley needed it. Ms. M demanded it.

He kissed me sweetly, our bodies barely brushing. It was a virginal kiss, a delicate caress. It was oddly satisfying.

He drew back and looked at me, locking his gaze with mine. His body hovered inches above me. "I'd like to make love to you, ma chérie."

I smiled. "Close. Try again." I drew his lip into my mouth, holding it tight between my teeth and nipping him.

He smiled and kissed me back, hard. His tongue demanded, his body pressed down onto mine, his hard cock digging into my thigh. I canted my head, allowing him to take the kiss even deeper. My hands didn't leave my breasts, squeezing them as he trapped them between our bodies.

He bit my lip as he pulled away, mimicking mine. "I'm going to fuck you, ma chérie."

I laughed and squirmed, pushing around him to get up. "Almost. But I can see that this is no use."

He shifted to trap me and I made my move, squeezing my body out from under him and standing, my legs nearly toppling me. He sat back on his heels and reached for me, his hand sliding between my thighs and cupping my pussy. "Ma chérie."

I leaned into the pressure. Why was this so hard for him? Why, tonight of all nights, couldn't he just do as I asked and be a good boy?

I sighed. He wasn't really that kind of a guy. I wasn't drawn to men like that. Especially not for a second night. Sweet men were fun for an afternoon, but they barely made it to the darkness.

Men like Odin didn't ask, didn't wait for their pussy. He demanded, he took, he plundered. He fucked the way he did everything—and I'd seen his business style earlier tonight. He claimed, he came boldly, he left his mark.

Men like that didn't ask permission.

And yet I needed him to. Just this once.

"Thank you for this evening." I pulled my dress up to cover my breasts, not turning to look at him, making no move to remove his hand from between my legs. I wanted him to finish me off, wanted him to give me the orgasm he'd been so expertly building. I wanted him to force me to turn and follow him to the ground while I sat on his face and rode him to my orgasm. I wanted to touch him, claim him, leave my own mark on him.

I was tearing in half. My past was taking over too much of my body and I needed him to send Ashley packing, once and for all. I knew he was the man to help me get there, to take back my body and my life, but in order to get me over this hump and to lay claim to more of me than she had, I needed him to ask me. To pretend that I was Ms. M and only Ms. M, the kind of woman who didn't lay down for any man, who demanded men ask to step into her space, who was so worldly and intimidating that men—even strong men like Odin—needed to ask.

"Ma chérie. Will you let me lay you down on this floor and fuck you senseless?"

A sigh tumbled across my lips. "Yes." It was a whisper that barely carried to where he sat, waiting, expectant, hand still between my legs.

But he did hear me.

His hand began to move, slowly, one finger circling my clit, one sliding along the wetness and testing at the opening. He pulled me closer, one step at a time, making me back up until I stood in front of him. He shifted his hand to my hip, brought the other up to meet it, and slid my skirt higher. I reached behind me and unzipped the dress, letting it fall and pool at my feet. He held it while I stepped out of it, his breath coming faster and skipping across my skin. Shivers trailed in the wake of his breath and he tossed the dress over his shoulder. I stood in nothing but my bra, and that came off easily.

Tears stung my eyes and I blinked them away quickly. Ms. M would not cry. She expected men to behave like this. Expected them to kneel at her feet, awed by her beauty and the grace of getting to lay with her.

Odin may not be the kind of man to worship a woman—and I sincerely doubted he'd ever let one get away with what I had tonight, a thought that made me smile somewhere deep inside where girlish treasures still hid—but I knew that we might also be on the verge of something new for both of us. Unchartered waters that terrified the fuck right out of me.

I wouldn't take us there.

After tonight we would be all business, all the time. But I needed the comfort of him in this moment. And for the rest of the moments until I left him in the morning.

He planted a soft kiss at the top of each thigh, then laid his cheek against my belly. I threaded my fingers through his hair, overwhelmed at the sweetness of the moment.

It left in a flash as he tugged me hard, making my knees buckle. I landed against him and he rolled to his back, taking me with him. Our bodies were an instant tangle, limbs and lips locking and weaving until all my perfect parts fitted into him. I tugged at his clothes and he stripped, tossing his shirt and pants in the direction of my dress. He slid me across the polished wood floor, bringing me beneath him and pausing, arms locked and keeping our bodies separate. "May I?"

There was no joking tilt to his mouth. In this moment, he'd given in to my demands. Which made it easy to give my answer.

Not that I'd have turned him down, not with the head of his cock poised at the entrance of my pussy just waiting for the word.

30

Ashley

"Yes." He entered me slowly, filling me one inch at a time, his gaze never leaving mine, as if he was still asking permission.

I took him in, holding his gaze, my hands cupping the curve of his arms, feeling the heat of him seeping into me. With the same measured movements, he withdrew and we began the dance we'd started the moment I'd walked in tonight. He, so sure that we'd end up here. Me, knowing with a surety that we wouldn't. My confidence came back with every thrust and I wrapped my legs around him, holding him tight against me.

He sped up the rhythm, then slowed again, teasing me to a soaking orgasm. Our bodies moved together and he repositioned me as he pleased, moving both legs to one side while he thrusted deep, and putting them over his shoulders when he changed it up again and barely entered me.

There wasn't much need for me to direct him; about the time I wanted to tell him what to do he sensed the shift and guided us to a new place, extending my orgasm over and over.

Depleted and sweaty, he came, growling into my ear as it overtook him.

Heaving for breath, we sank into each other. He showered me with kisses, trailing them across my face and down my neck. Our bodies slid against each other, still warm and slick with sweat. "Thank you for the pleasures of your body."

I smiled and kissed him back. "You're very pleasurable, Odin."

He kissed me thoroughly, swirling his tongue over mine, his cock still buried deep in my pussy. His hips began to move again and I stroked his back. He rolled us over and I felt him swell inside me, hardening again, ready for more pleasure.

I smiled and sat up, my hair damp and sticking to our bodies. My thighs pressed against his chest. This was Ms. M's domain: A man beneath her, in a private room of one of San Francisco's most elite clubs, riding him to another orgasm after having multiple.

My body moved over him. We were insatiable and compatible together, something I always looked for in a lover. It might take me a few to find someone so attractive on every front as Odin was. But I wasn't after a man with the full package; I was after a man who was fantastic in bed and who didn't expect anything of me after I left it.

That was Odin's flaw. He still wanted something beyond our fantastic sex.

His large hands roamed my body, palming my thighs and my breasts as I dragged my fingertips across his chest. I swiveled my hips, pumping against him as our bodies moved to a song only we could hear.

Beyond the room, the deep drum of the club's music pounded through the walls, but the only sound in this room was his panting breath and my soft commands for him to move beneath me. My frail attempts at controlling tonight ebbed and flowed as I struggled to maintain control of Ms. M and leave Ashley behind. Odin hadn't managed to remove her completely, which, I supposed, was an unreasonable thought. Much as I wanted to leave my past behind, she would always be a part of me and there was nothing I could do about that other than move on and hope I'd seen the last of Carter, once and for all.

Odin slapped my ass and gripped my hips, drawing me back to the act like he'd known that my thoughts had been fading. They shouldn't have been, he was more than enough man to keep me entertained. It was too bad about my beliefs that men were more trouble than they were worth and that relationships were worthless. What we'd had this time and last was perfect and fit into my life.

He drove hard into me, his thumb working against my clit as he built my orgasm from the inside and out. I pumped him, clenching his cock as I rode him, slowing and extending this—our last time, once and for all.

31

Odin

I held her elbow and kissed her cheek softly. "Goodbye, ma chérie. Until we meet again."

She smiled, cinching her jacket around her waist in a last effort to ward off my attraction. "Yes. And next time I should probably meet with Sampson."

I smiled and leaned forward to kiss her neck. "I could have stopped after your first orgasm and taken you, but you seemed eager for another."

She smiled and it was probably a trick of the streetlamp, but I could have sworn that a blush played at her cheeks. She wanted me and I knew it.

We'd stayed in the room long after the club had closed and I'd walked her out to her car where we stood now, the cool pre-dawn breeze kissing strands of her hair and lifting them into the air. I held her door, closing it gently after she got in, and stood watching her brake lights disappear in the distance.

As I walked to my car, parked on the other side of the lot, I wondered about the new information I'd gleaned about her tonight. Lingering wisps of pain clung to her. She might say that she'd gotten over the rape and had used it as fuel for the auctions —making a phenomenal business out of it in the process—but the memories haunted her. Maybe not all the time, but something had happened in recent days to bring it to the forefront again, that much was certain. The first two times I'd met her, she'd held no hint of the pain I'd seen tonight. There was a frailty to her that had surprised me—along with my need to protect her and take it away any way that I could. I'd settled for loving her, but that hadn't been enough.

The woman needed something more.

She needed Annika.

I started my car and drove home, thinking of the similarities of the two women. Annika, my friend with whom I'd shared all but the ultimate intimacy, and Ms. M, of whom I shared so little intimacy beyond the physical kind that I didn't even know her real name.

The highway stretched blank before me, doing nothing to stem the flow of my thoughts. Annika had shared many perspectives on the subject of rape, she herself being a product of rape when her mother was attacked and held at knifepoint while her rapist inflicted hell on her. I shivered. Every time Annika had shared a piece of the story with me—usually after a fresh visit to her mother—I'd been caught up in the atrocities that were committed against women. Which had made it easy to be one of the first investors to contribute money to Annika's rape center and organization that helped battered women with ongoing therapy.

I pulled beneath the overhang of the building and left the keys for the valet when he'd arrive in a few hours for his shift.

Perhaps arranging a meeting between the women was in order. I was well aware that Ms. M didn't want my meddling. With any part of her life—business and the incidents that got her there foremost on the top of the list.

But I knew what Ms. M didn't. I knew that ridding one's self of their past didn't eradicate the drive or passion that made businesses successful. Those carried on well after we'd managed the pain of our pasts.

Granted, I'd done just as Ms. M had, clinging so tightly to the things that had made me into the man I was, but through a very fortunate series of events—in hindsight, of course, no one thinks those types of catalysts and transformations are enjoyable while they're going through them—but I was through them now and that was the point. I had the advantage of being on the other side of my past, and I'd seen first-hand what happens once that space becomes opened up to other things in lieu of clinging to the pain and torment of memories.

As had Annika. Being around rape victims day in and day out would have consumed her had she not been able to move beyond the knowledge that her conception wasn't a beautiful pure wanted activity between two people who loved each other, but the result of a violent act committed on her mother. A mother who had become the beacon and reason for Annika to start her organization in the first place. Not only had she given her own life meaning, but she'd managed that for her mother, as well. The women were powerful and spreading their knowledge and experience far beyond the pain of their circumstances.

I wanted that for Ms. M for many reasons, but mostly, I felt like everyone deserved to live their own lives as they wished, not as reactions for events that happened to them.

I stepped out of the elevator into my own penthouse and undressed, setting my keys and watch into the long leather bowl that sat on the edge of the large dresser in my closet. I tossed my clothes into the hamper, not caring if they made it to the drycleaners. My maid would sort through all my clothes when she tidied up tomorrow.

For now, I wanted a shower and a way to cleanse Ms. M's lingering scent off my body. Not that I wouldn't bathe in it every chance she gave me, but I needed to get back to work with a clear head and a soft cock. Thinking about her would do nothing but distract me and keep my thoughts from focusing on where I needed them to be.

32

Ashley

I flattened my hands down my red skirt. Today was just another day, just another day prepping for my next auction.

Mikayla was the girl I'd chosen for the one next week. She was a friend of Audrey's and had come to me in the same way—wanting to get ahead on her way out of college. Mikayla's bills hadn't piled up the way so many young women's did, but she was still ready to put her virginity to work.

I was surprised at how many college girls were hanging on to that these days. A thought that made me think that maybe I was going to have to start requiring medical releases from them.

I sighed and slipped my cream cashmere sweater over my head, pairing it with gold earrings and a long string necklace. Today was several meetings with prospective bidders, some that I'd like to use at Black Velvet.

The thought of Black Velvet sent a jolt of electricity through me. It had been two days since my evening there and my thoughts had returned much too often to Odin and his body and what he could do to mine. I'd hardly ever recalled a lover past the next morning. There were so many others to experience that pining after one seemed like such a waste of energy and brain power.

But Odin…

He was different. There was a magnetism about him that had attracted me from the beginning, but I'd also felt comfortable enough to tell him about my past and how I'd started the business. I'd rarely shared that with a prospective business partner. And certainly not with a lover.

What was it about Odin that had released my tongue? And not just sexually. A smile played at my lips and I thought of all the places I'd put my tongue on his glorious body.

That was another thing; it wasn't like his body was exclusively decadent. I'd been with other lovers who took fantastic care of their bodies, from body builders to models to porn stars. But something about Odin's stature was handsome and elegant and so very sexy. I liked the way he moved around me and over me. There was an extreme protectiveness about his movements and I liked it.

He made me feel safe.

I picked my keys out of the bowl on the table, grabbed my purse, and headed out the door, slipping my sunglasses on as I went. Today's first meeting was at one, followed by back-to-back meetings into early evening. It worked perfectly so that I could swing by a few upscale bars tonight and see if I could meet any other prospective bidders that I could set meetings with later.

With the option of Black Velvet on the table, I wanted to increase the amount of bidders I had in my existing pool. All the current men had been vetted for Trent's—today's notwithstanding—and yet, I wanted a slightly different clientele for Black Velvet. Only a few of the men I had on the current roster would be ones I'd take up there.

If we could pull it off, I wouldn't mind having Mikayla's

auction up there as the first one. She was the perfect type of girl and she'd please those men and their pocketbooks very well.

At some point, I needed to see both Odin and the club's illustrious owner. Perhaps seeing Odin didn't need to be part of the occasion; lord knew I'd met other men on my own before. Every meeting today didn't require a chaperone. Just the fact that I wanted him there was reason enough to force him not to.

Whatever this strange attraction to him, I needed to get it under control, and fast. I had pending auctions and plenty of things to hold my time and attention without throwing a man into the mix. Sleeping with him a second time had clearly been my undoing. That rule had been created for a reason and I was foolish to have undone it just for the sole purpose of being with him again. There were plenty of men who could have given me a suitably good time that night. Now that we had business pending, I was most definitely never going down that road again.

No matter what.

I slapped the steering wheel for good measure and to instill the missing bit of steel into my thoughts.

Maybe tonight's agenda needed to include finding my next fuck.

Traffic slowed and I caught the tail end of a news story about a legal case that was wrapping up—having nothing to do with either rape or Carter, but my thoughts went there none the less. I quickly changed the channel, but the damage had been done. My palms got clammy and I felt beads of sweat pucker on my lip.

This had to end. I had to get back to how things had been before his recent mistrial. But I didn't seem to know how.

Maybe Odin's suggestion of doing more auctions and scaling the business was something to consider, maybe that would keep me so busy I'd have no time for either of the men.

The cars ahead of me picked up speed and I made it to my appointment with a few minutes to spare.

Inside, I was greeted by a lovely blonde who welcomed me

into a private meeting area. While I waited for Taylor McKenney, I examined the surroundings of his office. He'd come well recommended and I'd been looking forward to adding another real estate investor to my portfolio of bidders. Taylor seemed like the perfect match for one of the girls following Mikayla's and I was really hoping today's meeting wasn't going to reveal any of the red flags that prevented me from bringing a guy on.

Lord knew I had some serious making up to do after botching the scene with Asher at Audrey's auction. Never mind Vann not being trustworthy and committing the ultimate breach of contract.

But I'd known better with Asher. That wasn't his first rodeo. I'd let him get away with too much before, ignoring my keen instinct to let him come back. On paper, he'd been perfect, but I always gave credence to the intuition that had guided me on so many occasions. When I didn't listen to it, it cost me. And it most certainly had that night with Asher.

Vann was another story. There had been no red flags. I wouldn't beat myself up about that one.

Taylor walked in and I stood. He was dark and sultry. His fine features belied any of the ancestry that had given him a Scottish name, part of the reason I'd been so eager to meet him. He had Arabic qualities, a lean face, shadowed already with dark stubble, strong shoulders and long legs. He moved with the grace of a cat, stalking the room as he moved toward me.

We shook hands and he held my gaze. I was caught off guard again by the depth of his dark brown irises. He was captivating—and on first impression, I thought that if I had Black Velvet auctions opened for business, he'd be the first Dom to awaken a young woman's sexuality.

Maybe Odin was right. I needed him more than I realized. Together, we'd be unstoppable.

33

Ashley

My next three meetings went swimmingly. Taylor was an absolute YES, the other two were maybes for Trent's, depending on how their financials and background checks shook out. I still needed one more for Mikayla, but I could always send in one of my regulars, like Wilder or Ryder. Bringing in new men was such a wonderful experience for the girls and I liked having the perfect complements for them. Wilder would work if I needed him, but I needed another exotic man, like Taylor.

My last meeting was only a few blocks from Black Velvet. When I was finished for the evening, I took a circuitous route toward the highway, driving by just to see if I knew anyone who was outside. Honest.

My belly swirled at the lie, knowing that I was hoping to catch a glimpse of Odin. But he wouldn't be outside; the man probably had a private entrance and an entourage. Only the people who hadn't been invited stood outside.

I slowed as I turned the corner, my eyes scanning the patrons, men and women chatting in groups trying to pretend like they didn't care if they got in or—

I gasped, spotting Odin's tall figure near the main door. Head bent and listening intently to a beautiful woman leaning against the brick wall, smoking a long cigarette. They looked perfectly content and mesmerized by each other.

A pang of jealousy spiked through my stomach.

What the hell was that?

I sped away, blaming the ache in my stomach on my lack of dinner and hurried home to fix the issue. I'd forget looking for more prospective bidders in bars tonight. I'd be useless after seeing Odin giving another woman the look I thought was reserved for me.

34

Ashley

After a night of tossing and turning, I threw the covers off and stormed to the kitchen. The coffee pot malfunctioned, spewing hot water all over the counter and floor. I dipped the front of my robe in it while I was trying to clean up, and the fire alarm wouldn't quit chirping.

Thirty minutes of that had me pulling out my hair and ready to scream. I gave up on trying to get work done, closed my computer, and made my way into the master bath, turning on the shower and stepping beneath the steaming spray.

What right did I have to be jealous? I'd flat-out told Odin on the first night that there would be no future for us. Why *wouldn't* he take the time to talk to a beautiful woman, one who might want more than a single one-night stand from him?

I wondered who she was. She was gorgeous, decked out in a tailored dress that fit her perfectly and heels that had shown off her tight legs that were drool-worthy. There had been tons of beautiful women in the club when I'd been in there with Odin, but he'd had eyes for none of them.

Dammit!

I slapped the tile, frustrated that I cared, that I was giving him a second thought, that I wanted to know a single thing about a woman that had nothing to do with her virginity status. The way he'd been hovering over her, it had seemed like he'd been ready to divest her of any needs that hadn't yet been claimed.

I sighed and ducked my head under the stream of water, letting it pour down my face while I held my breath. If I was going to waste time thinking about him and who he was doing, I might as well give myself a fantasy and spend the time doing something pleasurable.

I wanted him here, opening the door and letting the steam roll out and around him. I wanted him reaching for me, telling me that he wanted me and no one else.

This was unchartered waters for me, needing someone. I hated how much I needed him and I let it wash over me like the water, soaking my skin with the craving of him. I wanted him hard and ready for me, stepping into the shower with his hard cock leading first. The steam would dampen the thick mat of hair on his chest, flattening it against the contours of his muscles, outlining the thick pads of his chest, the multiple stacks trailing down his belly to where his cock stood proud, straining against his skin to be inside me.

My hands played across my own skin, skimming lightly over my wet breasts, sending rivulets of water down my body, rushing across my clit and down my legs. I tweaked my nipples, envisioning Odin's strong hands, his arms wrapping around me, his body pressing into my back. I spread my legs, feeling the press of him between my thighs.

I was hot and ready, much as I always was when my thoughts turned to him. The water poured over me, steaming my body from the outside, while I took care of myself from the inside.

My fingers slid inside, found the ridges of my g-spot, and I eagerly brought myself to orgasm, thinking of him being inside me, against me. My body trembled, seeking and searching for him, needing him to be here instead of in my fantasy.

I leaned my forehead against the cool tile, rolling my head until my cheek felt the shock of the cold and brought me back to reality. The water was nothing more than normal, not a lover's embrace, not a man come to hold me and keep me safe from dangers that swirled around me, every day now.

My breath came in great gulps and I stepped out of the direct spray and turned the heat down on the water. Steam poured over the top of the door and I was reluctant to leave but I had things to do. The more I could focus on work, the sooner I could evict Odin from my thoughts.

I managed to keep my thoughts on the upcoming auction, and the men I'd invited, all the way to Trent's. I left a message for Odin, asking for a meeting with Sampson, but that was strictly business. He texted back that he'd get it setup for tonight.

For now, Mikayla's auction was scheduled at Trent's—a detail that could change up until the morning of the auction when I sent out the time and location.

I was doing my best not to anticipate another evening with Odin as I parked and thought about going to Black Velvet tonight. I avoided thinking of him as either businessman or lover, pushing the naked memories from my mind. There was no way we were having sex again, so that wasn't even a consideration. But I did want to get Sampson's approval to hold private events at his luxurious club.

If not, Trent's would work fine, just as all the auctions before Black Velvet had worked perfectly. Location was less important than the people attending; they made all the difference and I could put them all in a McDonald's parking lot and manage to pull off a remarkable feat that sent us all home with the riches we wanted.

But the opulence of Black Velvet made these more than auctions; they made them trades of power.

I used the back door of the bar, slipping through the hall and pausing at the door to Trent's office. Further into the bar, a TV chattered, breaking up the heavy silence of a bar like this that held so many secrets, from both the people who worked here to the ones who came in to play.

He sat hunched over his desk, papers spread out before him, one pen behind his ear, another in his hand. A pair of reading glasses sat just out of reach on the corner, making me smile. He continued to pretend that they were someone else's every time I asked about them, but they were on his desk so often that I'd finally quit teasing him about getting old. He worked so hard and gave so much that it didn't feel right giving him a hard time about something he obviously felt much too young to need.

Trent was a good guy. One of the best. He'd survived the death of his first wife and had managed to find love again. He was the kind of person who could make almost anyone believe in love.

Anyone but me.

"Knock, knock."

Trent looked up, startled. Then smiled and leaned back in his chair. "Morning."

"Hey." I walked in, set my purse on one of the couches, and settled into one of the large comfy chairs that faced his desk. "How's your day?" I glanced at the scattering of papers on his desk and he sighed.

"Another day in paradise. How's yours?" He tipped his head to one side and studied me, a crease forming in the center of his brow. "What's going on with you?"

I smiled and blew off his concern. No way was I going to tell him the thoughts that were currently swirling through my head, no matter how many lattes I'd inhaled to push my brain into overdrive and through my work.

We chatted of nothing, catching each other up on both business and personal matters. I held a soft spot for Trent and his amazing woman, Elyse. While Trent had been my rock for as long as I could remember, Elyse had been his, and together they'd become a solid foundation for me. Elyse knew the entirety of my past, having heard it all through Trent when he'd been troubled about how to help me during the trial. I'd tried my best to keep him out of it, leaving him to his own worries of being newly married and navigating ghosts of his own past. But he'd known something was up—as always—and had reached out to make sure I was okay. We'd made it through, Elyse had been a tremendous support and help for both of us; phenomenal considering that our business dealings had nearly been the undoing of their relationship before it had barely started.

"So the new business venture with Vi is going remarkably well and they're having a blast together." He sighed and looked off wistfully. "It's also a major boon to have the main women in my life getting along so well."

I smiled, genuinely happy for all of them. They were my family.

His attention returned to me. "And you? What's new in the man-department?"

I shook my head and checked my nails, splaying my hands in front of me and ignoring Trent's inquisition. "Same as last time we talked. I'm always looking for my next fuck."

He laughed. "Ah, Ms. M, you're always such a pleasure."

I smiled. "Well, I guarantee she's better than Ashley."

"Not so sure about that." He leaned forward, crossing his elbows on top of the desk. "I happened to like Ashley."

I grunted in a most unladylike and un-Ms. M fashion. "Well, don't plan on seeing her anytime soon."

"I miss her." He said it softly, looking intently at me like he knew I'd been lying since the moment I'd stepped in.

"I don't." I stood and paced the length of his office, pausing at pictures of him and Elyse—camping, hiking, beneath the Eiffel tower. They were scattered amid pictures of him and his first wife.

Elyse had been married once before and she knew the pain of

being a widow. They'd bonded over the deaths that had marred their lives, finding solace in each other.

I reached up and touched the frame of one photo, then the one beside it. It was almost not fair that he'd been able to find two loves of his life. Not that I didn't want him to enjoy life and have all the wonder of fairytales. It was just that…some weeks, like this one, I wondered why I'd missed out on any of the good and had only managed to collect the nightmares.

He stood and walked around the desk, stopping just short of where I stood. "You sure you're okay?"

I drew a breath. "Fine. Let's finish planning the auction."

He let me walk past him and take up residence in the chair again, pulling documents out of my bag.

His fingers trailed over my shoulder as he walked back to his desk. "We'll talk after."

I handed over the documents without comment. We would not talk after, at least not about what was bothering me. I wasn't talking to myself about that, let alone him.

35

Ashley

"All looks good to me. I like who you've picked." Trent signed the contract that sealed his take and the use of the private facility. We'd tweaked it a little since our initial one, but for the most part, it was the same contract we'd had since the very beginning. It released him from any liability surrounding the auction and spelled out exactly what we were doing here, lest it be considered prostitution or any level of the sex trade. These girls were willing participants, had sought out our counsel and his location in the process of auctioning off their virginity.

Trent didn't get a lot of say in the final choices of the men, but I was always open to his advice. If there was someone he knew—and he knew a lot of people—then I'd gladly take someone off the roster based on his opinion.

I smiled. Well, everyone but Jackson Morgan. He and Trent had never gotten along, and if I'd have been in charge of Kim's auction back in the day, I'd have listened to Trent instead of letting Jackson leave with her that night. A mistake that would have cost them both the time of their lives. And Trent and I the biggest payday ever.

This wasn't an exact science. A lot of times I only had the personalities and weaknesses that the participants showed me, which was never everything. We all hid parts of ourselves, and I knew that all too well.

"Now tell me what's going on."

He'd asked me that a dozen times while we'd been working through the paperwork and details for the auction. I'd told him that there was a possibility that I might be changing the venue and when he heard that he was losing out to Black Velvet he took it well, asking only for a ticket to the show. There was still some figuring to do regarding the dates and location, but for the most part, the event would be the same no matter where it was at.

In the other room, newscasters rolled through the afternoon news and we caught random snippets of stories while he stared at me, waiting for me to tell him what he already knew.

I put the papers back in my briefcase and tried to think of a way out of this conversation. I could just get up and walk out, but this was Trent. He knew things, he knew me—the real me, not just the Ms.-M-me that everyone else knew. If I didn't answer him today, he'd badger me about it the next time we saw each other, which would be the auction, and I had enough stress on those days.

Or he'd send his sister, Vi, after me to find out what was going on. And not that I didn't want to see Vi, but I didn't need them talking about me when I wasn't there to defend myself.

"I'm seeing Odin tonight."

"Okay." He drew the word out, like that required more explanation, and I supposed it did. He didn't know that we'd slept together—twice. And that made things different than if I was just seeing Odin tonight.

"He's my introduction to the owner of Black Velvet."

Trent leaned back in his chair. "Okay." He said it the same way and it was getting irritating.

"It's just that I'm thinking about him. We've had sex a couple times and I'm kind of looking forward to seeing him tonight."

He didn't say anything, just looked at me, watching me with those intent eyes.

"It's nothing. It's business."

His lips remained closed. If I was smart, I'd stand and walk out, bidding him good day. But I wanted to talk, to reason my way out of this, out of my feelings and why I continued to be distracted by Odin. Even today, my mind could not stay on task. Every movement by Trent was enough of a reminder of Odin's. He was a constant afterthought, a running shockwave though my body at all times. I hated that he had such power over me and my thoughts. I didn't want to allow him to consume so much of my space.

"Business has never bothered you quite like this before."

I growled and shifted in my seat. "No."

"Ash…"

I shifted nervously again, linking my ankles together and tugging the hem of my skirt. "I like him, Trent."

"Not a crime, Ash."

"It is in my life."

He studied me. "Do you really believe that? Really think that a relationship is the end of the world?" His eyes drifted to the picture of Elyse on the corner of his desk. "Maybe it's the beginning of the world."

"Ha! That's ridiculous. And why would I give up one-night stands for something stale and predictable?"

"Steadfast and always-there-for-you when the days get shitty, you mean?"

I snorted. "No one is there for you when it gets shitty."

He flattened his palms on the table and swished them back and forth, realizing I was a lost cause. "I don't want to tell you what to do. I know your history. I know why you sleep around without getting attached. I get it. But what if…" he looked up and stilled his hands, "what if you give this guy a shot and see if maybe he doesn't add a little strength to your days, a little sweetness to your nights. He's obviously got you in a state already; why not pursue it a little? You can always go back to where you are now."

"Seems risky."

He laughed. "It's just a date, Ash. You're not getting married. Try it out. Maybe he can cleanse you of some of your past that's come up lately." He leaned forward. "I just think it's worth a shot."

I ran a finger back and forth on the hem of my skirt. Out in the bar, the TV voices increased in pitch and Carter's name tweaked my ears. I stood rapidly and hurried out to the bar. "Did you hear that?"

He followed and grabbed the remote that sat on the edge of the bar, turning up the volume on the story and rewinding it to the beginning. The heat drained from my body so fast that I clutched the chair in front of me to stay on my feet.

Bits of the story pierced the fog of my brain. He'd been brought in for questioning… allegations of rape… new victims… mistrial. My head swam and I couldn't believe this was happening, not again. I wanted to be rid of him, wanted him gone once and for all.

Trent turned to me and pulled me into his arms. "I'm so sorry. We'll figure this out, we'll get all of this put behind us, Ashley."

I collapsed into him, beaten and distraught. Much as I wanted to believe that I could strip myself of my past, it just didn't seem possible. Here I was, an accomplished businesswoman, successful by every right, and a mere news story could rip the rug out from underneath me.

Trent smoothed my hair and rubbed my back. I clung to him, needing someone to support me on this very worst of my most recent bad days.

In the moment when I should be thinking that I was going to

endure and power through, I had a fleeting thought that this was a time when I wanted Odin's strong purpose to enfold me against him and hold me.

Dammit. I didn't want to have bad enough days that made me consider having a relationship. All I wanted was to get past this point of my life.

The problem was that man. Carter Ridley. I had to make him stop.

CONTROL ME, BOOK 3

36

Odin

I pulled the door to Trent's bar open, a little early for my rendezvous with Ms. M. I'd been eager to see her all day, thoughts of her consuming me since her call.

It looked different tonight, set as it was for a regular evening of patrons instead of the night I'd been here for the auction. On the far wall, a TV ran a news show and—

My feet stuttered to a stop: Ms. M in the arms of the club's owner, the man who'd poured my drinks the night I'd been here.

His hands roamed her body, his face tucked into her neck. A green haze clouded my sight and I clenched my fists together. What was he thinking manhandling my possession as he was? The woman was mine. Had been from the first night I'd met her. She might not know it yet, might not be willing to capitulate, but she was my woman and I didn't like his hands on her. A growl burned in my throat and I wanted to rip his hands from her body.

The usurper's head lifted and he smiled, jutting his chin to motion me over. His hand on her back lifted and he waved me closer. She buried her face in his chest, clearly craving his attention.

I cleared my throat and she glanced up at me. Trent spun her slowly toward me and gave her a small push in the back. "You're just the man she's been waiting for."

She sniffed and I got my first good look at her face: red, puffed from crying, and tracks of makeup marring her beautiful complexion. I gave Trent a worried glance. Clearly I'd misjudged the situation.

But he'd looked like a man with no qualms about putting his hands on her while she'd been distraught and I wasn't sure how much I liked that. He gave me a nod and disappeared from the room.

She came to me with no resistance, no hesitation. The TV clicked off and music surrounded us, easy jazz that probably wasn't what they played in here all night, but music that sounded right for whatever was going on.

I wanted to ask, but didn't dare make things any worse. All I knew was that the moment she felt like she could tell me, I'd find the man who'd destroyed her innocence and charm and beauty, and he'd pay for what he'd done to her. I hated seeing her this way. I wanted, now more than ever, to fix what had happened, to ease away her hurts, to protect her forever more from having this happen again.

"Ma chérie…" I did my best to comfort her, holding her and wrapping her against me tightly. She cried into my shirt, the warmth of her tears spreading out across my chest. I wanted to take her from here, take her back to my lair and lay with her, soothe away this pain with strokes on her body. Not sex, just… well, cuddling.

I smiled inwardly at that thought. It had been ages, maybe decades, since I'd wanted something other than sex with a woman. But Ms. M made me feel that way, made me feel like a young boy in love with a mysterious older woman. I probably had her by a couple years, but perhaps not. There was a timelessness about her that drew me in.

Except in this moment. In this moment she felt like a child, a hurting, abandoned little girl who so desperately wanted to be loved and protected.

And I wanted to be the man she came to in those moments. Not Trent, not someone else. Me. I wanted to be her safe harbor, her stronghold, her warrior. I wanted to fight for her, to protect her, to keep this moment from ever happening again.

I wasn't sure what she had on the agenda after our meeting. She'd done her best to keep her message very businesslike and that was why I'd chosen to text her back instead of calling. I hadn't wanted to accidentally reveal how excited I'd been for tonight, lest I scare her away.

But the truth was, I was still over the moon about getting to spend the evening with her. Even if it meant my need for a new, dry shirt.

"Do you want to talk about it?" I asked softly.

She shook her head vehemently and clung to me, a new wave of tears drenching the cloth beneath her face. I didn't care. I'd stand here all night if it meant comforting her. The patrons could come and go, swirling around us on their way to the bar. Trent could sweep around our feet and I'd still be holding her.

My hands spread wide across her back and I pulled her against my body. She melted into me and I glanced up as Trent walked across the hallway. He didn't make eye contact, content to leave us alone in this moment. I wished for a moment that she'd come to me and we weren't standing here. I wanted to take her away.

"Ma chérie. Can I take you someplace? Home, perhaps?"

She shook her head. "I'm not sure I want to be alone."

She lifted her head and swiped at her eyes and nose. She looked a fright. And yet, stunningly beautiful in her vulnerability. Of all the things I thought I'd get to do with her, holding her while she cried was not on the list. While I was honored, it hurt me that she was hurting.

"I'm sorry." Her voice was small, timid, so unlike the woman I knew.

"Please, ma chérie. Please don't apologize to me. I am happy to be here with you. I wish I could do something to fix this for you. I wish you'd talk to me." I pushed a strand of hair off her face and tucked it behind her ear. "Will you trust me with it? Will you let me take you to my home and sit with you? No sex," I quickly added. "No sex. I know you don't want that, but I agree that maybe you shouldn't be alone right now. I'd like to stay with you. We can go to your place." I didn't want that. I wanted her at my home where I knew where things were in the event she needed more comfort than what I could provide.

She sighed into me and tightened her arms around my back. I rubbed her from her spine to her shoulder blades, keeping the touch the most platonic I'd ever been with her—with any woman really, besides Annika.

Her eyes darted everywhere but to meet mine. Her attention strayed several times to the television. Had something been on that news channel that had affected her? I hoped not; I hoped she'd merely had a bad day or something menial. I hoped more that she'd tell me.

Her face tilted back and she looked at me with a searching, soulful gaze. "It's been a long day. I probably do need to be fucked."

I smiled. "Happy to oblige, I just didn't want to pressure you," I whispered, and brushed a few flyaway strands back from her forehead, letting my hands rest at her temples. Hers were still around my waist and I wanted to trap them there, to take them and lead her to my car that waited out front. Sampson was expecting us and he was easy enough to reschedule, but I didn't want her to not get what she wished from me.

"I'm sorry—" She swallowed and looked away. "It's been a long day. Maybe reschedule Black Velvet for another day this week?"

"I can call Sampson right away, but I don't need to reschedule our time. I'd like to stay with you, whether that's me taking you back to your place or us going to mine." I leaned in and kissed the tip of her nose. "Purely platonic. Or not. Whatever you'd like. I worry about you."

She swallowed again and I didn't miss the quick glance at the television. "I'm sure I'll be fine. I'll call someone." There was no confidence in the statement, which steeled my decision not to leave her tonight, not until she got her feet back under her, anyway. And she didn't need *someone*. She needed me.

Trent came out and paused a few feet away. His voice was quietly apologetic. "It's time to open. Most of the staff is in the back giving you privacy, but they've got to come out and start prepping drinks. You guys okay?" He watched Ms. M while he asked the question, not caring about my well-being, as should be the case.

She sighed and curled her fingers tighter into my shirt, filling me with another rush of pride. She was allowing me into her space more than she'd ever done prior to this evening and I didn't want to take that lightly. I'd taken my only misstep with the auction and Audrey, tonight would be different. Tonight I would not fail her.

Finally, she nodded and took a step out of my arms but let my fingers linger on hers. "I'll be fine. I'll have Odin see me home."

Trent gave us both a nod and walked back into the hallway. Low voices rumbled as he probably passed on the news to his staff that we were done hogging the room and they could actually get to work.

I tugged Ms. M to me and brought our linked hands up to my chest, cupping her face with the other. "Will you allow me to take you to my home? I'll cook you dinner and then give you my driver to take you home when you're ready."

Her gaze flickered across my face, as if trying to figure out my motives. I meant what I'd said; she would be cared for then seen home, no trickery.

I wanted to care for this woman in ways that confounded me.

37

Ashley

Trent had been one of my most trusted confidants, and sharing a comforting hug had happened on more than a few occasions as we'd seen each other through rough spots. I felt comfortable with him, I always had. Having him there for me in the moment of more news about Carter had kept me from devolving into a terrible depression like I'd suffered after the trial. He'd been my rock in so many ways and today had been no different. I'd felt safe in his arms.

But Odin…

Odin felt like coming home. Home to a place that hadn't existed for me since my childhood. Odin was expansive, big, extending a largesse that towered over me and all my problems—but in a good way. All women probably felt that way around him.

Thoughts of the woman he'd been with at Black Velvet surfaced but I quickly shoved them aside. No matter who he'd been with last night, he was here now. I needed his strength. We'd made no commitments to each other, quite the opposite, to be truthful. He didn't owe me any loyalty any more than I owed him mine. We were separate units, coming together here and there when our paths intersected.

That I'd let him fuck me twice was extraordinary, and if I let him take me back to his place there was a high probability that we'd end up in bed together again, no matter how platonic he thought we could keep it. There was a magnetism that drew me to him and it was the same for him.

No one else mattered beyond the two of us. I licked my lips and smiled. "Shall we?"

He turned and offered me his elbow, glancing over my shoulder at Trent who'd appeared in the doorway to see us off. He winked at me and I gave him a small wave, then directed my attention at Odin. "Thank you," I said softly, realizing I hadn't really given him much feedback about him showing up and changing our plans after he'd gone to the trouble of setting up yet another meeting with Sampson. "I'm not usually so poor at my scheduling."

He patted my hand and drew me closer into his side. "Life happens, ma chérie. There is no harm in putting your own self first."

"I don't do that. Work comes first, always."

He held the bar door and escorted me out. His driver waited at the curb and Odin held the door again while I slid in, then he climbed in behind me. The interior of the car was darkened, and soft light filtered through the windows. Odin gave the driver directions quietly, then leaned back into the seat, his shoulder brushing mine, our thighs pressed together.

He was strength and beauty in this moment, so far removed from the sexual space we'd been in since the beginning. I was seeing a different side of him tonight and it was intriguing.

Granted, he'd always been the utmost gentlemen, that aspect wasn't new, wasn't surprising, but this willingness to move us into a platonic space, even if just for the night. I wasn't sure where this fell in the boundaries of my rules. I'd never needed to have anything in place regarding relationships. I didn't do them. Period.

Yet here I sat with a man who had no intentions of fucking me tonight.

I glanced over at him to find him staring down at me. In the deep interior, his gaze was unreadable, yet I felt completely comfortable. His fingertips brushed my cheek and slipped down to hold beneath my chin, tipping my face up to his. "You look more relaxed already, ma chérie. No?"

I smiled and licked my lips. "Better. Thank you."

He lifted his arm and put it around my shoulders, companionable and kind. The rhythm of his breathing was solid and put me at ease.

As the car moved through the blocks of buildings, I let my mind stop fussing over what we might become to each other. The truth was, I liked him, plain and simple. Trent and I had managed to be friends without ever having sex. He was one of my most trusted friends, one of my preferred business partners, and a man I admired.

I was beginning to wonder if I would find myself saying the same things about Odin all too soon.

...If I continued to spend time with him.

Going to his house was one more crack in my carefully crafted life. I never—ever—went to a man's house, for the very reason they wanted me there—control. At my place, I controlled every element, from the music to the booze to what time he went home.

I liked control. Control was safe.

And yet, Odin was also safe.

Strength and power rolled off him. Which was why I trusted him to take me to his house and not demand control.

I smiled and laid my hand on his thigh, content in the moment. His arm tightened around me and I allowed him to pull me closer. There was a sweetness about this moment and I could almost see why Trent and Vi had both longed for more than just sex. There would not be a point where that would become truth for me, but this easygoing camaraderie was buoyant, and after the day I'd had, it was a welcome harbor.

For the first time in my life, going to my own house didn't feel safe. With Carter invading every part of my life—and not just Ashley's life, but *my* life, coming into the bar the other night during an auction, and "showing up" again today, even if only through the news story, and upsetting everything that I'd so carefully constructed in my life.

Thank goodness Odin wasn't willing to leave me alone tonight. I'd have been a wreck in my own home, furthering the instability and lack of feeling safe. I hated that Carter had that much control over my life. Hated it. I'd never given him control after that night, and now it felt like he had his hands all over everything.

But my home was still my fortress. There was no way for Carter to find me there… could he? Would he?

Surely he had enough tangling his life with the other women coming forward that he wouldn't pay me any mind. He'd had his chance to affect me the other day at Trent's and he'd done nothing out of the ordinary. Had he not been my rapist, I would have welcomed him in as just another gentleman and potential bidder.

But he was Carter. Nothing about him was as it seemed on the surface. My heart squeezed and I fought for control.

"Ma chérie?" Odin curled into me, seeking my gaze and offering comfort.

I drew from his strength, from the concern lacing his voice.

The car slowed and we stayed staring at each other. "Let's go in, ma chérie. We can discuss more inside."

I drew a shaky breath and let him pull me from the vehicle and back against his side. Night covered us like a warm cloak, and for the first time in weeks I felt like I was leaving my past in the car as it pulled away.

38

Ashley

Odin's building mimicked the man. Tall, dark, safe, welcoming. I was drawn to it, getting lost in the lines and the magic of the interior.

He led us toward the elevator banks and I was mesmerized by the dark color choices interspersed with glass and metal around the lobby. The doorman's alcove blended seamlessly with the entrance for the residents, turning the entire foyer into something that looked like the entrance to a stunning mansion instead of the lobby to a sky-scraping building. Dark wood paneling stretched around the room, broken by beautiful blue walls decorated with white molding and decorative sconces. The effect created small sitting and conversation areas, furthering the feel that this was a room in a home instead of the industrial and commercial feel of most apartment buildings.

Much like Odin, it felt like coming home.

"This is quite beautiful. Thank you for bringing me."

He smiled down at me. "Thank you for trusting me and for

coming. This building is another pride of mine, much like Black Velvet."

My feet stuttered to a stop. "You own this building, too?" This was one of the most sought after addresses in all the Bay Area. I'd tried to get in here before acquiring my own penthouse, but they'd been snapped up within the first few hours and that had been before I had the connections I did now. I turned to him and curled my fingers around the lapels of his jacket, sweetly smiling up at him. "You are far more integrated into the landscape of this city than I realized."

He rubbed the sides of my arms, not allowing his hands to wander anywhere inappropriate, in keeping with his promise to be platonic tonight. "I can list all the buildings, if you'd like."

He'd played so coy with me, giving me only the details of his net worth that I'd needed to know while vetting him. Clearly he had a few holding corporations that he'd forgotten to list. Had this building been listed as any of the assets, there would have been no question about using him as a bidder—as my top bidder. He'd purposefully left a massive chunk of his fortune out of the qualifications, and I wondered why. Most men beefed up their net worth, tossing in potential earnings as the numbers I was supposed to be using as factors.

I was fascinated by him, by his omissions as much as what he revealed. I was no stranger to secrets and dark places, I just never expected them from him, especially when he'd been so forward and forthcoming from the very beginning. I wanted to know why and what else he was omitting.

He detoured before going to the elevators, drawing me through the back side of the "living room" and taking me through the empty bar. The wood extended through here but not like in the commercial bars I'd frequented. Here, again, the homey feel made it feel like this was just another room in a giant mansion meant to host lovely parties and events for the owner's favorite friends. The designer had sacrificed table spaces in lieu of individualized seating areas, couches and big chairs—things never found in bars, lest the patrons use them sexually.

But here, they didn't seem to worry about things like that, trusting their residents to treat this as if it were their own home. It was a risky move, but one that had paid off tremendously. Now, more than ever, I wished this was my own home and this was a place I could host friends. Or whatever man I was entertaining for the evening.

"This is so lovely."

"Thank you. I wanted to create somewhere that felt like an individual home, not a hotel."

"Well, your designer accomplished all that and more. You should use him more."

He smiled and tucked me against him. "Thank you for the compliment. Designing them is almost as fun as buying them."

I couldn't hide my shock. My gaze flickered between his face, looking for the hidden joke, and taking another look around the room to see his signature fingerprints. "You did this? You came up with this design?"

"Do you like it, then?"

"Like it? I think it's the most stunning building I've ever seen. I tried to get in here and was denied."

"You should have come to me."

"I didn't know you."

He smiled and touched the tip of my nose with a finger. "Trust me, ma chérie, there is no way I would have denied you anything, even without knowing what a wonderful capable woman you are."

I felt the heat of a blush rise to my cheeks. There was something sweet and charming about tonight and I wanted more of it, never wanted to let it go. I didn't want to ruin the night with sex.

What a strange moment for me.

I took a breath and sank into him, warming to the moment and letting my reservations go. Odin was proving to be the kind of man who had no boundaries and who was going to push at mine no matter how firmly I wanted to keep them in place. If we weren't having sex tonight, then that meant technically we weren't breaking my rule…the same rule we'd already plowed through.

Thank goodness we weren't breaking it again.

I smiled and he curled his fingers around my nape, leaning in like he was going to kiss me. I tensed, not wanting the magic of the evening to fade. His breath was a caress against my lips. "Shall we retire to my home?"

I nodded, not trusting my voice.

We didn't move, staring at each other for another long stretch of moments like we had in the car. A silent conversation passed between us and I wasn't sure what we were saying to each other—or rather, I wanted to be blind to what he wanted to say to me. I wasn't ready, not quite yet. Nonetheless, I answered him in kind, letting him find what he wanted in my side of the conversation.

Finally, he pulled our bodies apart and led us back around to the elevators, whisking us away to the top floor.

I smiled at him. "No wonder I couldn't get the penthouse."

"I might have shared." He held the elevator doors with one arm and swept me into his home with the other, not allowing me to drop his hand, linking our fingers as the doors swept closed behind us, sealing us into his home.

I let the sharing comment drop, not wanting to take us there just yet.

"Would you like a tour of what could have been your home?"

I shook my head and tugged free of his grip. He let me go and I circled the massive couch taking up the center of the living room. It faced the expected floor-to-ceiling windows and a beautiful view of the Bay and the Golden Gate Bridge. I'd intended to sit and set the tone for our conversation, but I was drawn to the view beyond the glass.

I lifted my fingertips to the cool smooth surface and drew a breath. The morning's fog had lifted, leaving a clear view far into the sea. The sun would be setting in a few hours and I could only imagine what that show looked like every day. "This is spectacular."

"Yes." He stood a few feet behind me, and I was certain he wasn't looking at his everyday view through new eyes. I was certain his gaze was glued to my ass.

Which was fine. We'd skirted the boundaries of places I didn't want to go, and while I didn't want to have sex with him, I didn't want a relationship either.

I was a conflicted mess.

The brush of his fingertips was light on my shoulders. "I'm here if you want to talk, ma chérie."

I sighed. He'd been so kind, so understanding. "Thank you." I glanced over my shoulder and tried to catch his gaze, but he was engrossed in the lines of my shoulder. I turned back, watching him in the reflection.

Did I want to tell him, reveal my past? So many dangers lurked there and I'd been working so very hard to shake off my past and leave it behind me.

Maybe talking through it with someone like Odin could give me the roadmap to the future I'd been craving. Maybe he could shine some new light on it that no one had been able to before now. It was a lot to put on him, but he had pretty broad shoulders, so there was a chance that he could shoulder this. And me.

"It wasn't just the rape that affected me. My roommate—and best friend—had been his girlfriend." I drew a shaky breath and his hands slid around my waist, light and careful. I drew strength from him and leaned back into him. "She refused to believe my story. He lied to her." The weight of the past rose up and I let Odin lift it. I kept talking, too scared to stop, too terrified that the power of it would crush me if I didn't finally release it. "She hated me. Hated me from the second it happened, and in a second I went from having everything to losing so much of my world."

His breath was soft on my shoulder, covering my skin like

armor. In that second I felt like he'd protect me against anything. I drew one of the deepest breaths I'd had in a long time, letting the weight of his strength flow deep into my belly.

"Carter wasn't ever charged for that rape." My voice shook. "Then today…" I turned around and waited for his gaze to meet mine. "Today, I found out that he's been taken in for questioning in another case."

"Another girl?" The shock booming beneath his voice steeled me and I continued.

"Yes. And not very long ago, I had to testify in a case against another girl."

"Two? Two *plus* you?" He turned me in his arms, his fingers firm against my jaw as he searched my gaze. "I'm so sorry. Why didn't you tell me this?" His jaw clenched and he looked away. "I'm ashamed at the thoughts that went through my mind when I saw you with Trent earlier. I thought…" He swallowed. "It doesn't matter. I'm ashamed of what I thought and I'm sorry. I hope you'll forgive me."

I smiled. "There's nothing to forgive."

He simply stared at me, taking all of me in. "You are a wonderful woman and I want so many great things for you. I would give you everything. Tell me now what you'd have from me."

I shook my head and turned back to the glass. "This. Just this for tonight."

He pulled me tight against his chest and tucked the top of my head beneath his chin. "All night."

I drew another shaky breath and folded my arms over his, hugging myself through him. "Carter got off in the trial I testified in. A mistrial. Twice now he's gotten off while I—and the other woman—haven't. We've lived every day with the destruction he wrought. It's not fair. I was so alone and the injustice of it weighed on me. Not even my best friend believed me, why would a DA? They never even charged him, let him off without so much as a warning and any scars to bear." My voice trembled. "While I've borne all of mine." I was quiet for a moment, watching the shadows lengthen across the city, the sun making her slow descent into the sea. "I keep thinking something is going to happen that will allow me to move past this. I've done so well for so long...starting the business, keeping it going, making my life. This new resurrection of all these feelings is taking its toll and I don't know what to do to shake it and go back to normal."

He listened, careful and quiet, not saying anything, not trying to seduce me, just there. It was nice.

"And I saw him the other night." His arms tightened around me as I continued. "He walked right into Trent's. I didn't know it, but he's an acquaintance of one of my bidders, one who breached all kinds of rules and told Carter about the auction and that he should show up and check it out. I was furious." Heat bolstered my words and I felt a little strength returning to my backbone. "I was fine for so long. Nothing came overnight. I had to fight every day to win, to be better, to not succumb to the past and the fear. I thought I had it all under control. But now, having him free—in my own city, nonetheless, a city where I am queen and rule the night—it's unnerving and I feel like it's slowly seeping the life out of my days." I sighed and leaned into him, then did something completely out of character and kicked off my heels, tossing them to the soft carpet beside us. I resettled into the hollows of his body, warring between being Ashley and being Ms. M, neither confident and strong in this space tonight.

"How can I help you?" He held me so close and I kept waiting to feel the firmness of his erection in my back but it never came, like he was completely fine standing here, looking out across the Bay.

39

Odin

I would have done anything in this moment to free her of her pain. I had no idea—absolutely none—that she was under this kind of scrutiny or self-investigation. It worried me and I was, again, so glad that I'd pushed to let her bring her here.

To listen to her, there hadn't been anyone to help her get through this and I was getting the feeling that there might not be anyone else even now. Beyond Trent.

And I'd forsaken her that, coming in earlier tonight being jealous of the one man who'd become her family and support. While I probably should cut myself some slack for not knowing—the woman wasn't exactly forthcoming—I still should not have jumped to such conclusions.

But she was mine.

Whether she knew it yet or not was of little consequence. I would give her the time she needed to heal, but I would also speed her to her healing.

Already, a conversation with Annika was forming. I knew that she could give Ms. M the tools to get her past this dark spot. She'd been very agreeable to meeting with Ms. M, telling me what services she offered at the center, what women she could put her in touch with, everyone from therapists to doctors to other women who'd not only survived, but had flourished, much as Ms. M had.

In fact, I was amazed at what she'd managed to create without a support system. My admiration for her grew and I was fascinated that such a tumultuous event could have spawned such amazing things in her life. I hated that something like that was the catalyst behind her success, but at the same time, we all had things like that in our past.

I hated that, though. Hated that anything—or anyone—could cause her such pain. This jackass was not a man, he was a creature that needed to be locked up for all his transgressions; not just the ones he'd committed against the wonderful woman in my arms, but for all the women he'd accosted. I hated him. More than I'd loathed even the people who'd wronged me across the years of my life. I would pull every string I had, call in every favor, to see that he was not allowed to walk freely.

The pain of her situation was far from over. If he was currently being brought up on charges, I assumed that meant that there was a likelihood that they'd come to her for assistance in finding details of her own past. I wondered if there was a chance that he could be charged with her rape since nothing come of it at the time. So many advancements in DNA and evidence had happened since her rape, surely there was something to be done.

I didn't want to inquire, didn't want to make tonight about anything that she didn't want. I would stand here all night with her in my arms if that was what she needed.

But I wanted to help her move past this. It felt so much like she was stuck in quicksand, unable to get back to where she'd been, or to create a new future for herself.

I liked who she'd been when I'd first met her. I liked who she was now. But I could feel the pain and weakness in her. Could feel that she hated her weakness.

If she would let me, I would be her strength.

"There's one other thing." Her voice shook and I held her. She twisted, her bare feet silent on the rug. Space cushioned the air between our bodies.

Tonight was not sexual, though she was still stunning. Tonight was soft, easy, comfortable. Even talking about the horrors of this topic, I still felt a camaraderie with her that I liked, that I wanted.

Clearly she wanted it too, much as she didn't want to admit it. And I was fine with that. I would wait for her. She would figure this out soon enough and I wasn't about to let her have too much time away from me to forget how well we were together even in these soft moments. I waited for her to continue, to tell me what else she held deep in her secret chest.

"My name—" She glanced away, watching the clouds spin across the sky. "My name isn't Ms. M."

I smiled softly, not wanting to startle her away from telling me this most important thing that I was fairly certain she didn't reveal to a lot of people. You don't come up with an identity without keeping your real self from nearly everyone. Not that I didn't understand a little more fully now why she'd done it, but it was still curious that she'd been so adamant about keeping her truth silent even after we'd had sex. It was a matter that I hadn't pushed on, realizing even then how much her privacy meant to her. Now, so much more.

"Ashley. My name is Ashley McGrath." Her voice was so quiet I could barely hear her. I knew that this was a massive step for her.

And maybe for us.

Pride and passion swelled in my chest. I drew her to me in a hug and whispered against her ear. "It's a beautiful name. For a beautiful woman."

She snorted. "A stupid girl."

"No." I shook my head and drew her away from me so she

could see the sincerity in my face. "Not a stupid girl. A brilliant woman. A smart, inventive, survivor. Ashley is the woman I met that first night, the woman who captivated me, the woman who stunned me from the second I saw her. That's Ashley."

She shook her head and let me draw her to my chest again. "No. That was definitely Ms. M."

"They're one and the same, ma chérie. One and the same."

She blew out a huge breath. "I don't want to believe that. I want to believe I'm smarter than Ash was, stronger, braver, unwilling to let men control me."

Ah! A light blinked on in my mind as I realized how much she'd controlled every aspect of our interactions, from the auction to the first time we'd had sex, to every time that I'd tried to bend her to my will in the smallest of things. This woman existed off control.

I smiled softly and tucked a loose lock of hair behind her ear. "Not all men want to control you. Some want to watch you shine, want to stand beside you in awe of everything that you manage to accomplish. Everything Ashley manages to accomplish."

The corner of her mouth turned up in a disgusted smirk. "Ashley manages to screw up most everything. This is really for the best."

"I doubt that. Ashley is you, ma chérie. Whether you want to believe that or not, it's the truth." I drew her over to the couch and sat, taking her with me and settling her beside me. Our thighs brushed but it was in the camaraderie of the night. I liked this companionable space we'd been able to carve out tonight.

Another reason why I'd wanted to come here. Here, I could maintain a non-threatening atmosphere, loosely holding her until she was ready to go, yet able to comfort and caress her until then.

40

Ashley

I woke early, curled in Odin's arms, both of us fully clothed and tangled together beneath a blanket on the couch. The night had ticked away in stretches of silence and the occasional long conversation. He told me of the challenges he'd faced both as a young man and some of the more recent business hiccups.

He'd hesitated in sharing them, telling me that they far from measured up against what I'd dealt with, but I'd assured him that to each of us, our challenges are struggles, real to us without comparison to what anyone else is going through. Trent had taught me that. I'd always had such a hard time talking to him about things while he'd been working his way through Paige's death.

After a couple months of me telling him that everything was fine, he'd sat me down and made me spill the issues that had been plaguing me. I'd realized that he'd been right, that through our own lenses, life looks shitty sometimes and we think we'll bend under the weight of it.

Odin had finally relented and taken my opening, telling me stories about himself. I was coming to admire and like the man. He was charming and funny and humble, even with all the holdings that he'd amassed across his life.

It was his humility that was still kind of shocking. I spent so much time with wealthy men that it was refreshing to find someone who didn't flaunt it all over.

I was finding a lot of things about him refreshing.

The evening had drifted into night and I'd fallen asleep curled into him, comforted and safe in his arm. The man had a mesmerizing way about him and I'd never experienced anything quite like him.

I eased my way off the couch, tucking one blanket around him and pulling one around my shoulders.

I padded into the kitchen. We hadn't managed to get to the tour of the place, forgoing it for cuddling on the couch and talking.

Wow.

Talking and cuddling.

If that wasn't a relationship, I didn't know what was.

Dammit.

I'd gone and gotten myself into the one thing I'd sworn off my whole life.

I opened cupboards until I found coffee and started the machine, eager for a bold cup that could jumpstart my mind and get this relationship crap out of my brain.

What was I thinking? *A relationship.*

Clearly I'd been so void of platonic touch that I was ready to dive into something that broke every rule I'd had since that horrible night with Carter.

What in the fuck?

The coffee pot filled and I searched for cups and creamer and sugar, finding them all behind the door beside the stove. I loaded my cup with all three and cradled it against my chest, wandering toward the back of the house in search of Odin's closet and a comfy set of clothes to change into.

I should go.

Thoughts bombarded me as I padded silently down the hallway. Rich artwork hung perfectly-spaced along the white walls of the wide hallway that led toward a couple of guest rooms. I kept going, assuming his room was the one looming at the end of the hall.

Each room I passed was decorated as tastefully as the rest of his home, all a reflection of what I'd seen in the "living room" downstairs. The man had impeccable taste. Not that I should be surprised; he exuded class and style from every part of his being.

The master bedroom was quietly tasteful, much like the man himself. A massive four-poster bed stood in the middle of the room, flanked by equally-imposing nightstands and a chair beside his walk-in closet. I set my coffee cup on the dresser and walked in, perusing the selection and deciding on a well-worn t-shirt and a pair of his boxers.

I set my clothes on the arm of the chair, chiding myself that I was clearly planning on spending the day with him when I should be slipping out and leaving him a note.

But something about last night's sweetness kept me tethered here, wanting to spend more time with him. I had plenty of work to do and he probably did too, but I wanted to spend the morning with him.

I was such a moron.

Dammit.

And I'd told him my name. My real name, like some dumb teenager wanting to reveal secrets and share emotions.

What was I thinking? It wasn't like I hadn't earned these rules the hard way, putting them in place for things that needed structure.

I picked up my coffee, took a sip, and wandered back out to the living room, peeking into the other rooms along the way, finding a beautiful study and an office, along with another guest room. This penthouse was substantially nicer—and larger—than mine. It was lovely. And it suited him perfectly.

As mine did me.

I found him sitting up on the couch, wiping the sleep out of his eyes. He watched me walk toward him, noting the change of clothing. His eyes were sleep-hooded and sexy, his hair rumpled on one side and a nice shadow of his beard caressing his cheeks and jaw.

All the emotion of last night served to strengthen me. He was a good man. A safe man, a man that I could have sex with one more time without danger of losing myself in.

I set my cup on the table and made my way toward him. He shoved the blanket aside and opened his arms for me. I went willingly, wanting to share more of what we had last night, as well as get us back into a place where we left all that sweetness in the past. I'd shared my secrets, now it was time to be who I wanted to be for my future, some strange mashup of Ashley and Ms. M.

Words weren't needed in this moment. We'd shared so many last night and this part was easy between us. This part didn't need anything but our bodies.

He twisted and pulled me beneath him so I was laying on the couch, legs extended and tangled with his. I lifted a bare foot and caressed his calf.

Somewhere throughout the night, he'd taken off his belt and unbuttoned the top two buttons of his shirt. I caressed the skin peeking out and leaned forward to kiss him there.

His skin was warm. My fingertips toyed with the rest of the buttons on his shirt but he trapped my hand. "Are you sure, ma chérie? We don't have to do this if you'd like to have a platonic morning before you go."

"I'm sure." I leaned up and kissed him gently. "Thank you for last night." I brushed the crease at his forehead. "And no, that's not what this is about. I like you. I'm mostly naked. I'd like you to fuck me."

He pressed his hips into mine. "No fucking this early in the morning. I will make love to you, ma chérie."

I shook my head. "No way. Definitely none of that!"

He chuckled into my neck. "No? Maybe we should try it first." He swiveled his hips and trailed kisses along my skin.

"I've tried it." I bit him and scraped my nails along his back, then tested several of the buttons, slipping them through the fabric and revealing his sculpted chest. I tugged the shirt free and slid my hands over his muscles. "Fuck me, Odin."

He nibbled on my earlobe, tugging it into his mouth and scraping it over the edge of his teeth. I moaned and shifted beneath him, wrapping my legs around his waist. He ran his fingers down my thigh. "Tell me what you want, ma chérie."

"I thought I did."

"No. I want details, darling. I want you to tell me very specifically what you want and where you want me."

I smiled, liking that he was so agreeable this morning.

"Take your pants off, Odin."

He pressed into me, shifting our hips so I could feel his erection. He felt good this morning, every bit as good as he'd felt last night when we hadn't been sexual at all. It should have troubled me that he was becoming a wonderful well-rounded man who I enjoyed hanging out with. If I wasn't careful, I really was going to find myself in a relationship.

He pushed up off the couch, taking his sweet time and leaving a trail of kisses along my skin. I watched his every move, liking the sleekness of his body, the breadth of his shoulders, the lines of his muscles.

Taking his time, he unbuttoned his pants, letting them slide down his thighs and puddle on the ground. I licked my lips and shifted, propping my head on one elbow to watch him. I was still barely-clothed in his boxers and undershirt. There wouldn't be much time to get me naked—if that was what I wanted.

I thought about how I wanted this morning to go and there were so many possibilities. I wasn't opposed to having a tender morning, as long as it was scripted as I wanted it. We may have shared some magical things last night, but I wasn't ready to give up control.

Not just yet.

He stripped, standing naked and proud just out of reach. Staring down at me, he stroked himself, filling out his hard cock as he watched me, his gaze touching my breasts, the vee of the boxers, the length of my legs. "Tell me, ma chérie. I'd hate to think that you don't know what you want to do with me."

"Oh, I know." I lifted my hips and slid the boxers slowly down my legs. "I want you to fuck me, Odin. I want you right here between my legs. I want your hard cock inside my pussy. I want you making me come. I want all of that right now, Odin."

He knelt between my legs, stroking my skin. "Your wish is my command." He yanked me closer, running my ass along the cushion and sliding my t-shirt up my stomach, revealing the curve of my breasts. His eyes widened and he growled. "Take your shirt off."

I smiled. "Are you trying to tell me what to do?"

"I want you naked."

"What if I don't want to be?"

"Oh, you do." His voice was low and strong. There was a hint of humor to it and I liked that he didn't immediately acquiesce to my demands. He was a strong man, and taking orders from me wasn't easy for him. Not even in bed.

I liked that he did it anyway.

I smiled and tugged my shirt over my head and tossed it to the floor. "Better?"

He grinned and spread my legs, putting my thighs on either side of his hips. I hooked my ankles and tightened my hold as he stroked the entrance of my pussy, already wet and ready for him. I moaned and arched up into him.

He held off, teasing me.

"Dammit, Odin." I growled and writhed beneath him, needing him far more than I'd realized. The last several days had taken its toll on me and it had been far too long since I'd been able to have a release. Odin had been my last partner and we'd gone too long since the last.

He entered me slowly, watching me and inching his way to filling me. It was a tender moment and, coupled with everything that we'd shared last night, several emotions that I didn't recognize surfaced. I let them come, adding them to the desire and passion that already simmered throughout my entire being.

He moved at a leisurely pace. This wasn't fucking, but something far sweeter. I wasn't sure that I minded. The words to chastise him and make him take me harder died on my tongue, dissolving like sugar. He wasn't in control, but neither was I. We were somewhere in the middle, giving and taking. It was strange, and I was in danger of letting all the rules slide.

I lifted my knees and tapped his shoulder, making him pause and reposition us, my ankles resting on his shoulders. His desire changed, becoming more feral and without words. He followed my lead, no longer challenging me for control, but giving it over willingly.

I might have little control over the other spaces in my life, especially where Carter had his filthy paws on places, but there were places and moments like this one where I held a firm hand on the events as they unwound.

His hands gripped my hips as he drove deeper into me. We moved as one unit and this was the first time in over a decade that I'd willingly taken a man for a third consecutive time.

And I was starting to wonder if there was going to be a fourth.

41

Odin

The woman was wild and free. There was so much about her that I wanted to know, and one of these days I was going to make her give me control and take her the way I wanted.

But not this morning. This morning I would let her have her control so that she could begin to knit her life back together.

Annika would be a huge resource for her, would be able to give her some of the stability she needed to get past this place. I wanted that for her.

She looked so beautiful in the early morning light, here on my couch, moving wordlessly beneath me. I brought her to orgasm a handful of times, and when she got up to leave I let her go.

In all honesty, I had been surprised to find her still in the house. When I'd woken without her, I'd assumed that she'd flown back to the safety of her own nest.

I didn't want to look too far into her actions this morning, so close to what she'd shared with me last night. She needed to find her equilibrium and I understood how unsure a person could be so fresh on the heels of a trauma being reopened. I would give her whatever time she wanted.

After I showered and made my way through the house, I called Annika to see if I could further a meeting between the two women.

"Good morning!" Her voice was light and bright, the opposite of what she could have been.

Annika had worked hard—just like Ashley—to make her mark in the world. I had so much confidence that she could give Ashley exactly what she needed. I suffered no delusions that I wasn't the person to give her that—at least not in this. I could give her other things though, of that I was certain.

I quickly updated Annika on what I'd learned about Ashley last night and we chatted through some options.

"I'd really like to meet her. I think I can get a better read on what the best next step is if we have some time to chat through where she's at. With the allegations coming out, she's having to rehash things that she thought she'd handled."

Annika had confronted her past so quickly, being honest with herself and everyone around her about her conception and what it meant to be a product of rape. She'd found power in the truth and had always done her best to encourage other women to face it head-on. *You can't beat what you won't face,* she'd told me so many times as I'd battled the demons of my own past.

"She'll be fine, Odin. You're such a huge asset to her."

I shook my head. "No. She's strong. She can do this on her own, I just want to see if I can give her resources. I knew you'd be able to help her out."

"Glad to. It's been a while since you've seen the operation and what we've accomplished with the organization. Why don't you come by later today? I obviously can't let you interact with any of the women, but I'll see if I can carve out some time for you to meet with our therapists, get some information on how you can advise and help her. What you really want to do is be a support—

the support she wants, not what you want. A lot of people want to speed victims through this part, get them 'over it' and on to the next thing, but everyone processes this at their own pace."

"Thank you for that reminder and perspective. What's the next step for her at this point? I don't want to startle her, don't want to demand that she do this with you. She's in a vulnerable place right now, and the last thing I want to do is send her in the wrong direction."

"If she's strong, like you say, then she'll be okay. Give her time to go through this at her own pace. I know it probably seems like she should be past this by now—"

"No. I get it. We all move at our own speed. I don't want to rush her."

"The best thing is to tell her about the organization but don't force her to seek help."

I sighed and rubbed my head. "Thank you. What can I do for you?"

"Nothing. Nothing. You're such a tremendous resource to me, too. Thank you for chatting the other night, and I'm looking forward to getting to meet her. Is she special to you? I guess I should have asked that in the beginning."

"She's very special. I like her quite a lot. But right now I really want to focus on getting her what she needs. It's been a rough week for her and I don't like seeing her so beaten down. This thing has been hard on her."

"It's hard on everyone. I get it. You're a good friend. Or boyfriend. Or lover. Whatever you are to her."

I smiled and dodged the question. Annika was always wondering what was going on with my love life and had set me up on more than a few blind dates. It was her life's mission to get me something permanent—whether I wanted it or not.

Until Ashley, I had most certainly not.

42

Ashley

I left Odin's feeling…strange. The night had unfolded far differently than what I'd anticipated.

He'd been kind and thoughtful. Overall, I was happy that I'd let him take me to his house. The sex, of course, had been phenomenal. I couldn't believe that I'd told him my name, and yet there wasn't much of a surprise there, either. I'd shared so much of my past with him, and the more he'd heard, the more he'd allowed me a safe space to tell him other things. Telling him about who I'd been as Ashley had seemed like a natural progression.

Surprisingly, I didn't regret it like I thought I might.

I didn't regret any of the things that had transpired between us.

I pulled into the garage and parked, glancing around with a nervousness that hadn't existed for me in far too long. I hated that Carter had gained space in my mind and fears. I hated him for so many things.

I shook off thoughts of him, already intent on researching everything I could about the most recent allegations. I wanted to know about the other women and what he'd done to them. I wanted someone to figure out a way to stop him.

I caught a whiff of Odin's cologne as I stepped into the elevator and the air conditioning swirled around me. I smiled and ducked my head, pulled into thoughts about my last few interactions with him.

Black Velvet was still a very viable option for everything I wanted to pursue going forward with the business. I wasn't sure what that would mean for Odin. He clearly wanted to be involved…though perhaps after last night and what he'd learned about me those desires had changed. Perhaps now that he understood what truly drove me he would allow me to continue on my own path instead of the one he wanted.

The elevator doors opened and I paused, listening to the soundless emptiness that stood on the other side of the metal box. I wanted to believe that Carter couldn't find me here—wouldn't find me here—but my mind was a little too good at thinking up possibilities, what with him being foremost on my mind.

After a few rapid beats of my heart, I stepped into my home and let the doors close behind me. I hated this feeling of being trapped, like my every move held a risk of running into Carter.

"Dammit!" I tossed my purse and keys onto the table and marched into my home office. I was not going to let him control anything else.

I tapped the keys on my computer, bringing it to life and sitting heavily in my leather chair. For a moment, I considered making some coffee and settling in for a serious research break, but reconsidered, thinking this wouldn't take too long.

After all, how many women could there be?

43

Ashley

Vi opened her door to me, a stricken look on her face. She hugged me and drew me inside. "I'm glad you called."

What I'd found during my research had rocked me to my core.

The more I'd read, the madder I'd become. There were multiple women—nearly a dozen. I was pissed. For so many reasons. Reasons that had swirled inside me like a wild tornado that I had to get rid of. That was when I'd called Vi.

"Tell me what you found, what you couldn't tell me over the phone."

I sighed and sat heavily on her couch. She brought over two glasses and a wine bottle, pouring healthy doses for both of us.

"It wasn't just me, Vi. There were a bunch of women. He's a serial rapist." I took a drink and settled against the back of the couch, letting the alcohol flow through me and warm the cold icy ball that had been in the pit of my stomach since reading the first story.

"And he's gotten away with all of them?" She was shocked and leaned forward, patting my knee. "I'm so sorry. I really wanted all of this be over for you."

"I know one of them."

Her eyes widened. "Seriously?"

I nodded and took another drink. "Her name is Daphne. She's a personal shopper at one of the boutiques where I shop. I couldn't figure out where I knew her from when I first saw her photo, but then on the drive over it clicked. She's so brave, Vi, talking about this, sharing her story. I'm such a wimp."

She moved to sit by me on the couch, stripping the glass from my hands and setting it on the table and pulling me into a hug. Her hands stroked my hair and I did my best to bat down the emotions as they came surging to the surface.

"That's not true and you know it, Ashley. You're strong and amazing. Think about all the things you've done since Carter. You're so much better than he is. I don't know how that fucktard has gotten away with what he has, but we'll figure this out."

I nodded and sank into her, letting her hold me. I was fascinated at how empathetic she and Trent—and now Odin—were being about this situation. It had made sense back when it had happened, and even with the recent mistrial that had brought all the emotions back to the surface. I really did have spectacular support and I appreciated it. I lifted my head and told her so.

She hugged me and handed my glass back. "I just have to remind you who you are. Carter makes you forget."

I smiled and took a sip. "True. How? How does he do that?"

She glanced at the television, off and blank. I wondered for a second if she'd seen any of the news stories about Carter. He was hardly big news, but locally they'd covered it far more than I'd wanted. "Because you let him."

I shook my head. "I don't want to. I don't want him to have any more impact on my life. I thought that I'd moved on."

She sat thoughtfully, then took my hands. "Do you think talking about it helps them?"

My stomach clenched. "I've talked to you about it." As the words left my mouth I knew she was talking about something more, something terrifying, a very thought that had occurred to me while I was writing down names of the other women that Carter had raped.

"I'm proud of you for doing that." She squeezed my fingers. "But I'm thinking that maybe there's more power in telling other people."

I stood jerkily and paced the floor, holding my arms tightly across my stomach. "Other people?" I thought about how hard it had been to tell Odin. She was talking about telling people I didn't even know.

"Unless you like being here and you want to keep wallowing in it."

She was such a shit sometimes. An honest shit, but still a shit. "Damn you."

She smiled. "Just trying to help."

I paced the living room, rolling through the thoughts that had come up all day.

"What about talking to this Daphne. Does she know you?"

I nodded. "I see her every week. She's fantastic and thoughtful and I'm sure she'd be open to talking to me. Especially if she knows that I was one of Carter's victims."

"How long do you want to wait?"

I sighed. "Not sure. I keep thinking it's going to go away." I looked at her. "It's not going away, is it?"

She shrugged and stood, coming to stand beside me, rubbing her hands up and down my arms. "I'd tell you if it would, right? And I've never led you down a bad path either, right?"

I made a face. "There was that one Tuesday—"

She laughed and hugged me quickly. "Glad you can still have a sense of humor. We'll figure this out. But seriously, I've always had your back. Right?"

"Yes." She had, she and Trent both. I'd had their support from the very beginning of wanting to take my life back. And here she was again, ready to give me whatever support I needed.

"Will you trust me to help you with this, to help you finally put it behind you?"

"God, yes." I was so ready. "Let's call Daphne."

She hugged me. "I'm so proud of you."

"And there's one other thing." I couldn't believe I was about to say this. I swallowed and stared deeply into her eyes, summoning all my courage.

"What?"

"I think I need to confront Carter."

She blinked. "Are you fucking kidding me?"

44

Ashley

The shock rolled off Vi and I understood it. I'd had the same reaction when I'd first thought about it, but the more I'd tested the idea, the thoughts had become a fantasy of all the things I should have said to him back on that fateful day, things that I'd thought of since then, things I'd only come to in the last few hours. "I want to do this. I need to do this."

She took a step back and shook her head. Now it was her turn to fold her arms protectively over her stomach. "It's a bad idea."

"What's he going to do?" I laughed bitterly. "Rape me?"

"There are other ways to hurt someone."

I shook my head. "No. Not anymore. Once, maybe, but he can't hurt me anymore."

She weighed my words, studied me, looked beyond my current posture to figure out my intentions.

"I'm fine. Really."

She pursed her lips. "No you're not. But I understand what you're saying. You will be okay. Eventually." She shook her head and stepped closer, taking my hands and rocking us gently. "And if talking to him is what it's going to take to speed you toward it, then let's do it."

Tears burned my eyes. I knew that I could count on her and I was trusting that I could also trust some inner knowing that was guiding me toward this decision. "I know where he is. They finished questioning him and he's at his place."

She arched an eyebrow. "And you know where that is?"

I nodded. I'd looked it up. I had his address, along with the names and numbers of all the women he'd hurt.

"Let's go." Her voice was quiet and she slipped her arm through mine. "I'll drive."

I couldn't speak the entire time, thinking through all the different ways this could possibly go; all of them ending in me getting what I wanted—the last word.

Now that he'd been questioned again and all these women were coming forward, surely he was starting to realize what he'd done, how many lives he'd destroyed. I wanted to hear him tell me that. To hear him admit he was wrong.

Vi sped us through the roads toward his apartment, glancing over to check on me every couple minutes. I let her take my hand and she squeezed, comforting both of us.

The car slowed and she parked, resting her hands on the wheel. "We're here."

I took a breath and got out of the car, unwilling to pause and lose my nerve. "Let's go."

We marched arm-in-arm up the stairs to the apartment building. It was a mediocre brownstone that held no originality—so much like the man himself. I knocked on his apartment door and took a step back, leaning against Vi for support.

The door swung open, Carter's laughing face appearing from the darkness. He wasn't shocked at all to see me, his face lighting up and leering as he stepped forward. "Well, hello, Ashley. Figured I'd be seeing you soon. Sorry we didn't get much of a chance to chat last time." He grinned and looked Vi up and down. "And who did you bring me?"

I stepped in front of her, summoning all the strength Odin had imparted to me last night. "I came to talk to you."

He leaned a shoulder against the door. "I'd invite you in, but sounds like you don't want to bother." His gaze dripped down my body and I fought the urge to tremble.

"There's nothing for me beyond these steps. But I do want to talk."

He shrugged. "Fire away."

Vi took a small step back, giving me space to have this conversation. I'd been surprised that she hadn't wanted to discuss my strategy or any of the things that I wanted to talk to him about. She'd let me take the lead, following where I'd wanted to be silent, leaving me to my thoughts. I'd compiled them carefully, ready to lead him right where I wanted.

"How'd the cops treat you?"

"Fine. They're a bunch of dicks. I expected that. My attorneys are handling it."

"How long before they bring you in and question you about all the other women that have come forward?"

He laughed. "Get real. Half those women are lying, some of them aren't even attractive enough for me to consider. They'd be lucky if I raped them. It'd be the most action they'd see all year." He laughed again, winking at Vi.

Heat bloomed in my stomach at his answer. He hadn't changed at all. So many conversations from college came bombarding back, ones I hadn't even thought of before this moment. He'd always been such a horrible human being and now he was showing his ugliness again.

"You never came forward. You're proof that you liked it. Those other women just needed a good fucking and I gave them what they needed. Then they got pissed because they weren't getting it from their other boyfriends. That's the only reason they made a squawk about it now. Fuck those bitches."

He leered at me, taking power from the conversation and being able to justify what he'd done to us. I'd thought there would have been some remorse, some inkling of the damage he'd caused. Rage steeled my limbs. He was nothing. He was no one. I couldn't believe that I'd given him so much power over my life.

No more.

"You know what, Carter, I came to thank you."

He balked, straightening and leaning forward. "I knew it."

"Thank you for being such an asshole, especially today. I'm an amazing fucking woman. I'm brilliant and strong and there is no way you're ever going to get away with raping another woman. I'll see to it."

I turned, grabbed Vi's arm and marched us back to the car. His laughter followed us and all it did was fuel my resolve that this was going to be over for good. I wasn't sure how, but I was going to figure this out.

As I pulled Vi to the car, I spat out my true feelings. "The world would be a better place without him."

45

Ashley

"Are you okay?" Vi reached over and took my hand. "Because I'm not. I don't know how you could be. I can't believe what a fuck he was. No remorse. None." She glanced over and slowed to take a corner. "Sorry, I'm rambling."

"It's okay." I stared out the window, trying to piece together my plan now that he'd completely torpedoed it. I'd thought for sure that he'd have been able to say something worthwhile, something to let me lay my past behind me for good. I was reeling.

And realizing that yet again I'd allowed him to control the outcome. Everything I'd said to him was true; I was amazing, I had pulled myself up from the gutter of where he'd left me, and I'd had some unbelievable accomplishments in my life.

But I'd still banked on getting some resolution from him.

Foolish.

"Now what?"

I pulled out my phone and thumbed to where I'd left Daphne's number, quickly dialing her, not wanting to lose my courage. It had slipped so much while I'd been standing there talking to Carter.

"Hello."

"Daphne, this is Ms. M, one of your—"

"Yes! Hi! How are you? Are you at the store? I was off today. I can run down though. Are you going to a party tonight? I have some great ideas."

"No. Thank you." I paused and tried to figure out how best to frame this. "I have something I want to discuss with you. It won't take much time. Can I meet you somewhere? Is there a coffee shop close to where you are? It will just take a few minutes." I wasn't entirely sure that was true, but if we made it past the first five minutes and she chose to share more with me, then we could stay and chat through things.

"Sure. Yes!" She gave me the name and address of a little bakery, one that was open for a while and that apparently served great pastries. Vi said we were thirty minutes out and Daphne was happy to meet us there. I hung up and let out a sigh.

"You're a champ."

I rang my hands. "I don't feel like one. Not at all. I feel like a fraud and a loser."

"You're neither. You're strong. And wonderful and powerful and amazing. You're all those things that you said to Carter. He wasn't worth those words, he wasn't worth your time. You were big to give him such precious commodities. You're better than he is."

I sighed. "I used to know that. There used to be a time when he didn't even cross my mind. It's been years. Years. And now this."

She nodded and got on the highway. "I know, babe. We all go through deserts, but maybe this is finally it for you. Maybe this is finally your time to cut him out of your life for good."

"I can't keep doing this, Vi. I can't keep riding this rollercoaster."

"Then let's dig in. Let's do this once and for all. Let's tackle this motherfucker and never look back."

I loved her. I grasped her hand and held it to my chest. "I couldn't do this without you. Thank you."

"You could. You totally could. But thank you. I'm always here for you, babe. Always."

We pulled up to the side of the curb and she put the car in park. "I'll wait in the car?"

I chewed my lips. "Yeah. Maybe." I swallowed and my fingers tightened on the door handle. "Keep your phone on."

She nodded and squeezed my arm. "I'm so here for you. You need anything and I'm running in. Promise."

I blew her a kiss and got out. My stomach tightened and I imbued Ms. M. I couldn't be Ashley right now. Not here. I needed Ms. M's strength, not Ashley's weakness.

Maybe that was part of what had broken me, standing there on the stoop at Carter's; maybe hearing that stupid girl's name, the one who'd made awful mistakes had plunged me back into the despair of what I'd been instead of who I was.

But that wasn't the case with Daphne. She only knew me as Ms. M. Knew me only as the strong, confident, rich woman who didn't balk at dropping a grand on a skirt. That was who I needed to be from this point forward.

I drew a deep breath, threw my shoulders back, and walked through the door of the shop.

Daphne sat at a corner booth, delightedly sipping coffee, and when she saw me she waved gaily. Ah, youth. She gave me a huge hug and I clung to her for a few seconds longer than I should have. "Thank you for seeing me on such short notice like this. I promise to only take a couple seconds."

She sat and waved the waitress over. "Oh my gosh, no problem. You're one of my favorite clients. I'm so glad you called. What's going on?" She took a sip of her frothy coffee, eyes wide like she was ready for me to reveal something exciting and wonderful.

I wished.

I ordered and smiled kindly at her, breathing the power of Ms. M and who I'd been in my best moments, who I was every time Daphne and I related to each other. "I have a little bit of my history to share with you." I pressed my lips together. "Not a lot of people know this..."

She reached over and grabbed my hand. "Oh my god, do you have cancer?"

I smiled. "No. Nothing like that." Her perspective was refreshing. I didn't have cancer. I didn't have a terminal disease. I didn't have a family member who'd died.

I had a past.

My resolve to see her was strengthened as was my decision to tell my story. Vi was right, sometimes we have to go through the dark to get to the other side. I was pushing through, and the people around me were going to be the light.

I let the story unfold and she listened intently, barely moving, barely talking. She reached over and took my hand in the middle, to strengthen me but not to sway my words.

As I came to the end, I let out a huge breath. "Thanks for listening. For coming to meet with me. I guess I wanted to know how you've been so strong through all of this. How you found the courage to come forward and press charges."

She shook her head and took a sip, thinking through her answer. When she looked up, there were tears in her eyes. "It wasn't easy, I'll tell you that. Worse than just getting raped by him, I'd fallen for him prior to that. I'd bought all his pretty lies and had believed that we were something special. The night he raped me I'd said no and that I wanted to slow down. We'd gotten so intimate so fast and I'd been on a break with my boyfriend and he and I were working it out. But Carter was so demanding and yet so sweet when he wanted to be." She swallowed and squeezed my hands. "He's a master manipulator. It took me a long time to figure out that I'd been played, that there wasn't much I could have done to see through him. He's a genius. Most importantly, I finally got to a point that I knew—I *knew*—that none of it was my fault. Carter is a douche and a manipulator and a complete asshole. I hope he fries."

I laughed. "Me too." I was quiet for a moment, thinking through all that she'd said. "It's too late for me to press charges for my rape, it's been too long, but I want to do whatever I can for the rest of the cases. I'm willing to testify or be a character witness." It was my turn to squeeze her hand. "I'll do whatever you need."

She smiled. "Thank you. I'm not really worried about it. I don't give him that kind of power over my life. I'm past all that. But I don't want anyone else to get hurt; that's what drives me now."

I nodded. "I'm sorry I couldn't do that for you."

She smiled. "Not your fault, Ms. M. Not anyone's fault but Carter's."

A wave of forgiveness came over me—not for Carter, but for myself. I understood what Daphne meant—and realized how long I'd been punishing Ashley for something that had never been in her control.

We said goodnight and I hugged her, making sure to remind her that I wanted to do whatever I needed for her.

"And I for you. This takes a while. You might feel good and like you've got this now, but there are going to be mornings where it's going to be the opposite. I'm always just a phone call away. And get some counseling. Some rape counseling. Those people know what this is like like no one else does. It makes a difference." She squeezed me in a hug again and whispered in my ear, "You can do this."

For the first time in my life, I believed it.

46

Odin

I hadn't been positive that she would agree to another night with me at Black Velvet. Her eager agreement had pleased me and it was my hope that having her come as a customer and not as a potential partner would set the tone for our evening. And perhaps, our relationship.

Annika had called again today, confirming the therapist names she'd given me during my visit and asking if I'd had a chance to talk to Ashley yet. I'd promised that I'd keep her in the loop.

My trip to the organization had gone well and I'd gleaned a new perspective about women who'd been put in that situation. It had been impossible not to compare my own hardships, ones that I'd thought so large without the perspective of what these women had endured—were still enduring.

So much of my young life had been shaped by my father's leaving, by my mother's own hardships—shaped differently of course, but still inflicted by a man. She'd allowed that to beat her down.

It was interesting as I'd read the files and listened to the counselors talk about their clients—no names to protect their confidentially, of course—how differently a similar situation could impact two women, how one used her anger and frustration at the situation to fuel her comeback and how another woman struggled to move even inches forward. And I understood that, too.

Over my career, I'd met more than a handful of people who'd been abandoned by one parent or another, some who'd risen above the adversity and some who'd been crippled by it, blaming their circumstances on the atrocities of their lives. I'd wavered between the two, only occasionally allowing myself to wallow in anything other than success. The loss of my father had driven me, and while I understood that that in no way compared to what these women had undergone, I understood the difficulty in having to take responsibility for how we reacted to something that was beyond our control, hard as it may be some days.

While I'd been there, I'd pondered what I would do in Ashley's situation; she'd done her best to move past it and not have to think about it only to be forced to face it again as her attacker had come front and center into her life. In that, I'd been lucky. My father had made a clean break, escaping us for all time and never returning, not even the occasional phone call or card on a birthday or at Christmas. When he'd walked out of our lives, he'd gone for good.

Perhaps inundated as Ashley had been, I wouldn't have been able to move forward as completely as I had. Maybe his ability to leave us for good and never look back had been a stroke of luck instead of the awfulness I'd thought.

I wasn't sure that was true for my mother and sister. They'd both been dreadfully impacted by my father's leaving, Mother most of all. Alice had been so small and I'd done my best to be a fatherly substitute, but I understood a longing for something she'd never had.

Which brought me back to Ashley and what I'd learned today from Annika. She'd given me such wonderful access to so much information and I'd been grateful for her time and thoughtfulness.

Annika's triumph over her situation was bold and sure, confidently moving beyond her circumstances. While on the outside it seemed as if Ashley had done the same, the simple act of not being able to use the name she'd had when the event had transpired made it clear there was some residual hurt and grief.

I understood so much more about her now, why she behaved the way she did, why she held the auctions, why she chose the women she did and the bidders she did. I'd been so stupid to disrespect the rules as she'd laid them out, thinking that they'd been there as guidelines instead of boundaries she's put in place for good reason.

But I hadn't been able to sleep with Audrey, that much had been so apparent from the very beginning, from the moment I'd seen Ashley, really. That woman had become the center of all my desires from the moment I'd seen her. Watching her do business had only solidified my need for her. The woman was complex and amazing and fascinating. I admired everything about her, and that admiration was part of what was driving my desire to find opportunities to assist her in moving past this, for good this time.

It was understandable how she'd been thrust back into the trauma and how much that had affected her adversely, having buried it instead of dealing with it. According to the counselors, there was still a chance for her to make those inroads.

If she wanted.

The fleeting thought of Audrey reminded me that I wanted to do something to apologize properly, understanding now what it had cost her. Understanding so much more about what she'd truly committed as a participant in the auction now that I had a better handle on who Ashley was and how and why she picked the girls that she did. Audrey had been smart and beautiful, able to capitalize on her assets where others hadn't. And what a different situation from the girls that Annika helped. They each stood so boldly in their spaces, serving women the best they could with their histories. Now, if I could do anything to help

Ashley blend her past to her present, she'd be that much farther ahead.

I looked up, noting her arrival into the club. I walked down the short flight of stairs and took her from the host.

"Thank you for coming." I pressed a kiss against her cheek.

She slipped off her short jacket and I laid it over my arm, stepping a few feet to the left and exchanging it for a claim ticket. "Thank you for inviting me." She stepped close and curled her arm inside my elbow and tipped her face up to me. "And thank you for the other night."

"It was my pleasure. As is tonight. I wanted you to get to see the bar as a patron instead of as a partner; get a feel for what your people will experience."

"Thank you for the perspective." She paused and watched a trio of couples walk past us. "I continue to thank you, but it's true. I really appreciate all you've done for me over the last couple days."

"I know how much you want to use Black Velvet."

She shook her head. "No. Not just that. I needed you as a companion and you were there in fine form."

I blinked, taken aback by her words. I'd expected her to enjoy tonight, but not quite to that point. I smiled and led her deeper into the club, pondering the best way to spend tonight. I'd expected her to be her hard-exterior self, wanting to challenge me at every turn. She seemed subdued, gentled, and maybe a little timid. I wanted to help her and I wasn't positive how to do that.

"Would you like a drink?"

"Of course." Her voice had a smile and I tipped my head closer to her. "I'm glad you came tonight, did I mention that?"

"You did." Her breath was warm on my face and I could get lost in her eyes. I wanted tonight to leave a mark on her, something that she wouldn't have such an easy time forgetting.

We ordered drinks and I took her around the club to places we hadn't visited last time, letting her enjoy them and peruse them at her leisure. "Is there any particular area you'd like to see?" I ordered us drinks while I waited for her answer.

She smiled and toyed with the rim of her empty glass. "Oh, I can think of one place." When she looked up from beneath her lashes, there was the smolder of the Ms. M I'd met on the first night. I wanted all of her, unconcerned with which version of her she wanted to play, what version she needed to be to feel comfortable with her entire world.

Our drinks arrived and were left unattended as I watched her, waiting for her to finish her statement. We would move at her pace tonight, whatever she wanted that to look like. I knew what I wanted, and that was mostly her naked and with me. I wasn't picky about where or when.

"Take me to your room, Odin." She smiled wolfishly, bold and sure of herself.

I took a slow drink and set the glass down. Tonight I would let her be in charge for a bit, but she would also get to learn to trust me, to feel safe with me, and I would build on what I'd created in the last days.

With slow, measured movements, I stood and set my glass on the bar. "There are more parts of the club to see."

She shook her head. "No, thank you."

"Are you certain? I want to ensure that you get everything you want from this evening." I made no move to close the distance between us.

"Have you ever known me to not be certain when asking for something?" Since coming in, her demeanor had continued to increase, ratcheting up bit by bit until she was this tiger standing beside me.

"I have not."

"Then I'm curious to know why you're hesitating." A hint of a smile played at her lips, lips I wanted to kiss and taste and have on my body.

I held out a hand to her and she put hers in, squeezing my

fingers. I brought them to my lips, touching the warmth to my mouth. "Your wish, ma chérie."

"Don't make me ask twice, Odin."

I chuckled softly, scooped her up, and tossed her over my shoulder. She squealed softly and I slapped her ass in an attempt to quiet her. We'd been at the bar merely around the corner from the room we'd used last time. I'd made several requests for the room, not quite certain what she'd be in the mood for.

A host opened it for us, closing and locking it behind us to keep prying eyes out. I felt her fidget on my shoulder, trying to look around the room, probably searching for the chair that had been here last time.

Last time, when she'd asked me for the very things that were now in the room.

I laid her on the edge of the bed, following her down as she fell from my shoulder. I gave her no chance to protest, smothering her body with mine and devouring her mouth. I wanted her, wanted all of her, the darkness, the troubled times, the curves, the passion, the fire.

She was and had always been an amazing woman. She was a woman to be prized and treasured. I wanted her to feel whole, to feel cherished, to want those things from me. Never had I wanted so much approval from a woman.

A moan drew my attention back to her. I kissed her deeply and passionately, letting her feel all the things I wanted from her. She was magnetic and beautiful. "I want to take my time with you tonight. Want to shower you with attention."

"No. Fuck me, Odin." She reached up and pulled the satin shirt off, ducking her head and sliding it over her arms. I helped her off with her skirt, wanting her naked for how I wanted to pleasure her. She tugged at the collar of my shirt. "And get naked."

I straightened, sliding her skirt off her legs and tossing her shoes over my shoulder. "I can fuck you with my pants on."

She laughed lightly. "True. Then get on with it."

I yanked her closer, drawing her legs up and over my shoulders. My hands played over her skin, smoothing across her belly and stroking her soft, white breasts. Her hard nipples against the insides of my palms made me groan. She was so sexy and every time I got closer to her, the more her sex appeal expanded.

My tongue swirled through the middle of her belly, making her squirm. I was going to take my time with her before we got to the fucking. I wanted her realizing all too well that she was someone I wanted to treasure, well beyond the bedroom. Tonight would be something larger than pleasure.

I admired who she was outside the bedroom, now more than ever. Her ability to take her adversities and turn them into the business she had was extraordinary, but I also wanted her to know that I was there for the tough times too, like I had been the other night. She was coming to mean a great deal to me and I wanted more than just sex from her.

I leaned up and took one of her breasts in my mouth, rolling her hard nipple between my teeth. She moaned and raked her nails down my back, pulling me closer. I took my time on that breast, palming it and sucking it deep into my mouth. She rolled her other nipple between her fingers, tugging it in concert with what I was doing. We moved in tandem, pleasuring her together.

My hands played over her body, sliding around her back, palming her ass and lifting her against my body. I held my cock away from her, not wanting to push us to that point just yet. I would pleasure her as she'd asked, but on my time.

Every time with her could be the last, depending on if she got her way, and this would make the fourth time, which was three beyond what she'd wanted to give me. I fought the smile that played at my lips, liking that I was challenging long-held rules that constrained all the parts of her life.

Those rules were important and had served her well, but there were bigger things for her on the horizon. I wanted to be a part of all of those, and I would be if she'd relinquish a bit of her control.

Her body curved and moved beneath me as she pleasured herself, lifting her belly to rub against me. I moved to her other breast, taking her fingers in my mouth first, suckling them until she withdrew and pushed them through my hair, moving my mouth to her open nipple. I treated it like I had the other, biting and licking it as she moaned and writhed, her hands tugging at my hair, adjusting my angle and shoving her breast deeper into my mouth. She was aggressive and needy tonight and I liked it.

Up to the challenge, I lifted my head from her breast, palming them and moving lower, licking the curves and planes of her stomach, swirling around her navel and heading lower, lifting her legs to my shoulders and kissing my way down her legs, tasting the bend of her knees, the sweet softness of her inner thighs, before pausing intently before licking the wetness between the folds of her lips. I touched gently, softly, making her hips buck wildly as she sought my tongue again. I brushed the scratch of my beard against the inside of her thigh and she squeezed both legs against the sides of my face. "Stop that!"

I bit her, unwilling to take all of her commands tonight. I would take her as I wanted, making her squirm and wait and building her desire.

"Odin, this is not fucking."

I laughed and bit her again, scraping my teeth along her body. "Maybe not from where you are, but this is very much fucking in my book."

"I want you in me." Her voice was husky and strained. We'd been so wonderfully intimate such a short time ago, so much passion and vigor. I loved that here she was again, searching and straining for me.

"And I want to be inside you, ma chérie. Do not mistake my leisure for lack of desire." I brushed my lips softly against her thigh, first one side, then the other.

"Odin, do not test me tonight. Please do as I need." Her voice broke at the end of her request and I licked her once, from bottom to top, quelling her words and making her gasp for breath. Her fingers tightened on my hair, tugging me hard against her pussy. I shifted my hands, palming her ass and lifting her into my face so I could pleasure her properly, swirling the tip of my tongue over her clit, sliding in and tasting her sweetness. I dipped my fingers inside, seeking to feel her tighten around me, and she did, shifting her hips. I felt the tremble of her skin and I did not release my plundering of her.

I twisted her, pulling her closer, drawing her upward at an angle that no longer allowed her to move her hips as easily. If I got my way, she'd stay just on the edge of getting to control tonight.

Her orgasm built and built and I lowered her just barely to the bed, sliding my fingers in farther, curling against her tightness. "Come for me."

She moaned and twisted against the pressure, tossing her head back and forth, grabbing for my body and trying to pull me forward. As the orgasm claimed her and she arched her back off the bed, I pushed deeper into her, holding the orgasm as the waves passed over her, taking her farther. "Odin." She slurred my name and it broke my control.

My other hand worked my belt and the buttons of my pants, shoving them off my hips. I grasped her legs and yanked her toward me, nudging the head of my cock against her wet pussy. She opened her eyes and came back to consciousness and awareness, smiling broadly. "Are you ready to fuck me yet?"

I laughed, squeezing her hips and tugging her another inch closer. She bit her lower lip and wrapped her legs around my waist, flexing and creating a tug of war. "I'll fuck you when I want. You're not my boss."

She propped herself up on her elbows. "Odin, you either put your cock in me right now or I'm getting dressed and walking out."

With one quick move, I flipped her over onto her belly and

lifted her ass in the air. She tossed a glance over her shoulder, giving me a look that she was ready to be taken.

And I would take her. Take her well.

47

Ashley

He was demanding and, once again, wanting control. I was losing control around him. I was losing control of my entire life and I wasn't sure what I was going to do about it.

I wanted him in me. I wanted him fucking me and turning me inside out. I didn't want to think anymore.

Seeing Carter and Daphne and learning all the information I had was wearing me down. I wanted an escape. I didn't want to have to put energy into making tonight run like I wanted. I just wanted it to happen. I wanted him to not fight me for control. I wanted him to give it freely and completely.

But that wasn't Odin. It wasn't what had drawn me to him. It wasn't why I was currently naked with him. I liked his strength. I liked his confidence.

I still wasn't sure that I was ready to relinquish control. Carter had taken so much from me and when I'd tried to gain it back yesterday, it had slipped again. I didn't want to relinquish what I had with Odin. I liked being in control.

His teeth grazed my ass, biting me lightly. And as his fingers tightened on my hips, I felt the thick hardness of his cock and strained backward. "Odin."

It was the only request I needed to make. He slid his cock inside me, pushing slowly until he filled me. I twisted my hips, taking him fully and dropping my head forward and breathing deeply. He stroked in and out, making me crave more of him. "Deeper, Odin. Fuck me."

He moaned in pleasure and his fingers tightened on my hips. I was glad he'd brought a bed in so we could be like this. I liked him from behind, taking me deep, leaving his mark on my body.

Orgasms swirled and retreated around me as he changed up the rhythm. I pushed back into him, slapping the meat of my ass against his hips, feeling the scratch of the hair on his thighs up against the smoothness of my own.

He drove into me, leaning forward occasionally to lick the length of my spine. "I want you, Ashley."

I froze and scurried away from him, pulling the sheet off the bed and wrapping it around me.

After a moment to get his bearings, he blinked and reached for me, a confused smile playing at the corner of his lips. "Playing hard to get?"

He walked around the bed, his cock still proud and straining toward me. I couldn't quite process him calling me Ashley. No one had called me that after I'd created myself as Ms. M. Now I regretted ever telling him. I wasn't ready for my lives to collide like that. I wanted Ashley staying in the past, not climbing into this fucked-up future that I was struggling to get under control.

Odin slowed, the smile falling off his face as he realized that I wasn't playing as much as swimming through the emotions trying to overtake me. "Ma chérie?"

I shook my head. "You can't call me that."

He frowned. "I thought you liked it when I called you ma chérie. It is an endearment. I mean no harm by it."

I shook harder. "No. Ashley. You can't call me that. I'm Ms. M."

He drew me carefully against him, his cock flagging but falling comfortably against my thigh. "But you are Ashley."

I shook my head again, feeling like I couldn't stop physically denying all the things surging up in me. "Not tonight. Please."

He hugged me, his arms wrapping around me. "I am so sorry, ma chérie." Carefully, he drew me back to the bed and laid down with me, keeping me tight against him. "Tell me what troubles you. Tell me what comes up for you as your demons when I call you that. Tell me what I can do to help you."

I sighed heavily, the warmth of my breath tumbling across my chest. "I saw Carter yesterday."

He looked up, startled and shocked that I hadn't mentioned this before now. "I'm so sorry, ma chérie. Had I known that, I would have approached tonight differently."

I shook my head, soft waves of hair caressing his arm. "This was what I wanted. I didn't want to talk or think about him anymore. I wanted to get lost in you."

He kissed my forehead tenderly. "Let me take you home."

I thought about it for a moment, but there was something about being here in this place that changed the dynamic of who we were together. When I'd come in tonight, I'd spent a moment searching out the woman I'd seen him with as I drove by the other night. Now, with my entire life upended, I wasn't sure that I could lean on him like I was, knowing that there were other women doing the same thing.

But if I mentioned it, we'd be treading into territory that seriously felt like part of a relationship.

A thing that I knew I didn't want.

48

Odin

There was something else going on with her, something more that she wanted to tell me. I wanted to ask questions that the therapists had given me, wanted to see if I could draw out important points that would help move her forward.

But I wasn't sure that this was the right time or place. Especially after what she'd encountered yesterday, seeing her attacker again. I wanted to tell her about Annika, about the resources that were available if she just asked.

But I wasn't sure if she was ready to go there just yet.

She chewed her lip, a surprisingly out-of-character slip for her, and I noted her willingness to let down a few walls around me. Then her demeanor shifted radically and she swiveled, giving me a hard look. It was the most steel and fire I'd seen since coming in tonight. I smiled. "Yes, ma chérie?"

"Why would you want to take me home? When you had that beautiful woman from the other night at the club?"

The passion of her jealousy made me swell with pride. Was the illustrious Ms. M coming to care for me? Want me?

Oh yes, this was fantastic.

I'd not expected Annika to come down and meet me at the club the other night but she'd been out this way having dinner with a prospective partner who was going to help with the marketing and media end of the organization. It had been easy to run over after her meeting. She hadn't wanted to come inside the club and I didn't blame her, so I'd run down to meet her.

Was that when Ms. M had driven by? Had she been on her way to see me and the thought of me being with another woman had chased her away?

I wanted to roar with pride at the thought of her thinking me hers. The pain of the jealousy I'd experienced when I'd walked in and spotted her with Trent had been intense. While I didn't want her to experience anything unpleasant, there was something about knowing she cared enough to spend time and emotion on jealousy that made me feel like we had a chance.

I leaned in and kissed her softly. "There are no other women for me, ma chérie. Only you. And if you'd like, it would be my pleasure to introduce you to Annika, the woman with whom I was speaking outside Black Velvet the other night. She counsels rape victims."

49

Ashley

Never. Never in my life have I ever asked a man about another woman. Not even the time I'd walked in on him fucking one. Men didn't matter to me. Who they fucked didn't matter to me—certainly not who they talked to.

I hated that I'd been unable to get the image of Odin and the woman talking out of my head. Hated even more that I'd said a word to him. This emotional rollercoaster had to go. This was a perfect reason why no one could call me Ashley—it messed with my head and I couldn't think straight. I hated it.

But even with all those emotions, there was one playing louder than the rest, one my goddamn heart had responded to. He'd gone above and beyond my question, admitting that I was the only woman he was interested in. That statement made me feel things that I wasn't ready to look at just yet. But it stirred something deep in my chest that was equally alarming as it was warming.

Now the question was whether or not I wanted to go back to his place or if I wanted to take my own advice that I'd been ignoring for too long and run back to my own home, hide there until I found where my true self had been hiding.

His fingers ran leisurely over my arm, waiting and looking a bit worried. I hadn't yet answered his remark about either going to his home or about the woman.

A woman who counseled rape victims.

My entire life was colliding. And I didn't know what to do about it.

If we went back to his house, I knew I could distract him, which meant that there'd be no more talk of this woman—or what she did for a living. I leaned in and kissed him gently on the cheek. "Let's go."

He watched me for a moment, then smiled. "Yes, ma chérie."

We dressed, the emotion and intensity of the earlier passion dissipating on the thick air. The use of my name, followed up by this woman who counseled rape victims, was too much for me to regain my desire for him. I wanted comfort…and probably sex later once I managed my emotions.

I must get them under control.

While I stressed over my mess, the night fell away. Before I knew it, Odin was escorting me into his bed. Our sex was easy and pleasurable, me not asking for anything more than what he wanted. I maintained control by not giving in to my desires.

It was a little step in regaining my sensibilities, but one in the right direction. I'd never been this off-balance before, and though I didn't want to believe that Odin had anything to do with it, I had to admit that he'd been a phenomenal assistance to me in the days that had passed. Even tonight, he'd wanted only to care for me—something I never would have allowed under any circumstances.

He was getting to me.

I slipped out of bed in the middle of the night and stood at the windows, watching the moon crawl across the black sky. Who was I anymore?

I didn't want to be Ashley, but there was truth in what Odin had said. She was me, much as I didn't want to admit it, much as I'd tried to ignore it for vast swaths of time. What was the danger in allowing that?

I lifted my hands to the glass and traced a design. The danger, of course, was that I would lose all of the confidence and business acumen I'd worked to build over the years since my rape. I tipped my head—losing my brains didn't seem that likely—but the confidence was a factor. I'd already slipped where Odin was concerned.

Dammit.

Odin.

What was I going to do about him? Tonight should not have happened. We didn't even fuck tonight. Tonight was the closest I'd come to making love in all my sexual experience.

And the problem was that I'd enjoyed it. Immensely. And the curling up afterward, the soft discussions that had become so much of my norm. I didn't want to enjoy the man as much as I did.

Every time I thought that I had begun to rebuild my walls, he did something sweet and gentlemanly. It was charming. Everything about him was endearing. And we had a lovely connection. One that I'd wanted to keep firmly in the world of business. Black and white, that was how I liked my life. Clear boundaries. Defined rules. No gray. Only black. Only white.

Odin had spilled paint across my entire canvas and there would be no cleaning this up. Not easily, anyway.

After an hour and no answers, I returned to his bed, slipping in beside him and turning away my worries for the moment. They'd be back soon enough in the morning. His big arm curled around me, tugging him tightly to him in sleep. Before I bothered to question the last time I'd done such a thing with anyone else, I closed my eyes and let the dream-world take me.

We woke together, each coming awake slowly, aware of the other. His hand spanned my back, my thigh resting between his. He watched me, but said nothing. A heaviness weighed down the silence like he had something to say—no big mystery since I'd worked to avoid the real topics he'd been pushing.

"What did you think of Black Velvet last night?" He tucked an errant lock of hair behind my ear, then trailed his fingers down my cheek. Though this was clearly not the real subject he wanted to discuss, I appreciated his attempts to spare me of it, even if only for a little while before he brought it up again.

"It is still lovely. Thank you for the tour and for giving me a new way of seeing it. If anything, I'm more certain it will work perfectly for the auctions." I ran my fingers through the mat of hair on his chest. "I do think I should meet Sampson."

He lifted my fingers and kissed them. "And you will." He fell silent again, smoothing his hand over my head and hair, comforting me gently though I'd not awoken with any sense of the dread and worry that had plagued my days. He had things to say and, much as I wanted to pretend he didn't, I had enough on my plate without having secrets and mysteries between us.

I leaned close and kissed his chest, pressing my lips against the hard peak of his nipple, then biting it—no point in sending him into conversations if I didn't have to.

His fingers touched beneath my chin and pulled my face up, bringing it to his mouth and devouring my lips with a punishing kiss. He kissed me with passion and desire and all of the heat we'd been missing last night.

And yet...I could nearly taste the unsaid words on his tongue. I let him finish and pull away, gentling my lips with a kiss. My hands cradled his cheeks. "Odin, what's on your mind?"

He kissed me gently. "Am I that transparent, ma chérie?"

I laughed softly. "A bit."

He sighed and rolled over, taking me with him so that I lay across his chest, his hand spanning my back. "I know it upset you last night when I mentioned Annika, and I don't want you worrying that I was talking to her again after the night you saw me with her at the club."

There was no surge of jealousy, but I was curious. "No need to worry. I can handle it. I'm a big girl." I playfully twisted his nipple and he caught my hand, bringing it up to his lips.

"I know you can handle anything life throws at you, but that does not mean that I won't do everything I can to keep from hurting you."

"Odin," I chastised him sternly. "Tell me."

He stared at me, then smiled kindly. "Annika's mother was raped." I flinched and he held me until it passed, then continued. "Like you, Annika used her situation to better the world. She formed an organization that has grown to be one of the largest centers for battered women in the state. She's truly remarkable. As a woman who's seen so much trauma and sadness, I turned to her for counsel."

"About me?" I propped up on one elbow. Had he really gone out of his way to find someone who knew about rape simply so he could ask them questions?

"Of course, about you."

"And what did you learn?" I wasn't sure how I felt about that. Or this conversation.

He gave a half-hearted shrug. "Much. I talked to therapists, I took a tour of her building. It was all very informative. I gained a new understanding of, not only what a woman goes through, but the long-reaching impact."

I rolled over on my back, completely confused. "I'm not going to flip out or anything." I threw my arm over my eyes. "You don't have to worry."

He kissed my arm. "I do worry." There was a long pause and I could feel him staring at me. "Have you visited with a therapist about what happened?"

I grunted. "No."

"Why not? It's very helpful."

I shook my head. "I managed just fine until recently. Even now it's hard to say I'm not an accomplished woman who's risen above her circumstances. I'm not those women in the shelter. I took a shitty thing that was out of my control and turned it into an empire."

He didn't say anything and I felt the uncomfortable need to justify myself. "I couldn't talk about it. Back then, everyone vilified me and said I was a slut. Then it didn't seem like the kind of thing to tell prospective bidders. Hell, I've only barely said anything to anyone about it." I peered at him from beneath my elbow. He was staring down at the mattress.

"I think you should talk to a therapist. I met some nice ones—"

"No."

He rolled to his side, mimicking the posture I'd had earlier, his hand settling between my breasts. We lay there for a length of time, our breath coming together, our bodies warm and easy beside one another. He was just so damn easy.

"I'm just not ready, Odin," I said quietly.

"I understand, ma chérie. It is not my intent to push you somewhere you're not ready to go. I understand better now than ever that this journey is each woman's. Some move quickly and others take longer. I want only to help you, to comfort you." His hand roamed side-to-side in the valley of my breasts, not moving farther into anything sexual. He really did want to talk about this, and secretly, I appreciated every ounce of his compassion and all that he was willing to do for me.

50

Ashley

He parked the car and leaned over, taking my hand. "Are you still sure about this?"

I swallowed. We'd talked at length about Annika and what she had here at her organization. He'd been kind, listening and not pushing me. It seemed that with every interaction we drew closer to each other. Again, I told him things that I'd not told anyone about my fears surrounding the rape and what that would mean for me to bind the two halves of my life. He'd reassured me that no harm would come, rather that I would be able to grow and move past what Carter had done to me. I wasn't so sure about all of that, but I was intrigued by Annika—if for no other reason than she'd done what I had, turning a tragedy into something amazing. I wanted to know if she'd not encountered anything about her father or if she was one of those rare people who'd simply moved past it once and for all and hadn't looked back.

One like I thought I'd been.

In the end, he'd been able to convince me to go and see her, no strings, no promises, no therapists attached.

Now that we were here, I was hesitant. If I went in, wasn't that like giving control over to Carter again? Admitting that he'd had something to do with my life and that I was still reeling from the impacts? I wanted to go back to ignoring what had happened and just get on with living my life.

But I also wanted him to pay.

I was so conflicted.

Odin squeezed my hand. "We don't have to do this today. We can come back another time if you'd prefer."

I opened the door. "No. This is fine. Let's do it."

He got out and quickly walked around, holding out his elbow for me and escorting me across the street. Nerves swarmed up in my belly and I wasn't completely sure about this idea, but there was still a strength about Odin that made me feel like I could get through this.

After all, this wasn't anything other than talking to his friend.

The building was rather large and seemed like it had apartments above the main portion that resembled a clinic. I wasn't sure if they were all part of Annika's organization or just coincidence. Either way, it intrigued me. I was beginning to be able to look at this situation like any other research into one of the people I worked with, it just so happened that Annika was on the other end of the spectrum from where any of my girls or bidders started.

He took me past the main entrance, around a beautifully landscaped corner filled with benches and lovely floral planters, down a lesser traveled street. Three simple doors allowed back access to the building and I assumed they were for staff. We walked past the first two and I tried not to question where we were headed, trusting him even in this moment. He made me feel safe and I wasn't sure anyone had ever given me that much stability in my life. Trent was a good friend, a confidant, and someone who'd give me anything in his power to give, but we'd never traveled all the way inroad with this situation—mostly because I'd never allowed it. He'd supported me to the fullest where I'd let him.

Odin stopped at the last door and knocked. I looked up at him, still not sure that I was ready to go through with this. I glanced down the block. Everything seemed so peaceful, not like this door could be the entrance to a world of hurt.

As we waited for the door to open, my eyes caught sight of someone all too familiar rounding the next block, coming our way. He was on his phone and didn't even notice me.

But that didn't matter. He was still in control.

Odin looked down at me just as the door opened. I could feel his gaze on me but I had eyes for only one person. "Ma chérie?"

"Come in," a voice said. I yanked my gaze away from Carter and stepped inside. How in the fuck did he seem to be everywhere lately? I didn't understand.

Odin's fingers curled around my upper arm. "Ma chérie? What's the matter?"

I shook my head and distracted myself with the lovely interior of the offices. I wouldn't speak Carter's name. I wouldn't give him even more control than he already had over me.

I held my hand out to the same beautiful woman who I'd seen with Odin that night at the club. "I'm…" I cleared my throat, trying to decide what name to give her. If I was going to do this, then I had to go back. I had to go back in time to when I was someone else.

Odin's fingers squeezed mine, as if understanding the pause. "Ashley. I'm Ashley," I said in a shrill voice, fearful that Carter would be the next person to walk through the front doors, trapping me inside.

CONTROL ME, BOOK 4

51

Ashley

"Annika." She shook my hand firmly but gently, a practiced gesture that offered both comfort and reassurance. She smiled broadly as if she knew what internal war waged inside my head. "Please, come into my office so we can talk. Can I get you anything? Coffee? Water?"

"I'd love a water." I set my purse down beside the chair and rubbed my temple. Maybe I'd been mistaken. Maybe it had just been someone who *looked* like Carter on the street.

Odin and Annika spoke quietly and she left to get our waters. I needed to put this away; it was nothing more than a freak thing. There was no way he could have known that I was here since we'd only decided to come less than an hour ago. I needed to rationalize this and stop letting my mind run away with things, coming up with scenarios that weren't going to help me get past all this.

Annika came back and handed me a glass of ice and a water bottle.

"Thank you."

"Please, sit." She motioned us toward a set of couches and chairs. Odin took the couch, patting the cushion next to him, which I took. Annika sat in the chair to his left, rounding out the sitting area.

"I appreciate you coming," Annika said, taking a drink of her tea and setting it on the coffee table. "Odin's told me so much about you and it's always nice to meet another businesswoman in the Bay Area."

She and I settled into a short conversation about business and the obstacles that we'd both experienced with building our legacies into what they'd become. I liked her right away. She was easy to talk to—like a female version of Odin. I could see how they'd become friends. We drifted into conversations about people we both knew and wondered how it was that we'd managed not to find each other sooner. She was an amazing conversationalist and it was such a nice treat—sometimes talking to college-aged girls and rich, intimidating men got a little old.

"I'll admit," she said, "when Odin first told me who you were, I was a little intimidated. It's not every day you get to meet one of the top up and coming women in San Francisco."

I smiled and took a sip of water. "I'm just a woman."

She lifted her mug in a toast. "Well, from my seat, you've accomplished some incredible things."

A soft silence fell between us and Odin leaned over, patting my thigh. "If you're okay, I'm going to run some errands I've been putting off, let you two work through whatever you'd like. Call me when you're ready and I'll meet you outside." He leaned over and kissed me. "Or I'll come in."

I nodded and waved him off, thoroughly at ease with Annika now that we'd been able to break the ice and I didn't feel like she was going to bind me and send a therapist in to question me. He left and Annika smiled at me. "I'd really like to help you with anything that you think is hindering your progress with your past."

I took another sip. "How much did Odin tell you?"

She shrugged. "What he knew. But that's hardly the entire story. There's always more."

It was a bold statement, one I could handle in one of two ways, depending on what outcome I wanted.

What outcome *did* I want?

"Were you ever at this crossroads?"

She tipped her head to the side. "Which one is that? I've had a couple."

"Thinking you'd buried your past and finding out you did nothing of the sort."

"Ah. That." She set her mug down and came over to stand beside the couch. "Do you mind?" She pointed at the spot Odin had vacated.

I inclined my hand. We might as well do this thing, I'd come all the way down here.

She sat on the edge of the couch, took a deep breath, and leaned back, staring up at the ceiling. "Because of my situation, I've never encountered the type of trauma that you and my mother did. I cannot even begin to understand what that's like, the terror, the helplessness. But I do know what it feels like to be more than a mistake—to be the product of a violent assault. They each have their own burdens and I've done my best to keep from minimizing either. No matter what any woman goes through when it comes to rape, it is horrible. We are all victims."

I took a drink to clear my suddenly-dry throat, but did not interrupt or add anything to what she had to say.

"My mother didn't see it that way, though. From the time I can remember, she always had a positive outlook on life. On the rare occasion that we talked about my conception, she would smile, pat my cheek and say how fortunate she was to get me as such a blessing in her life. It took me a really long time to understand how she could be so forgiving. She never pressed charges. We never spoke my father's name. But I swear to you there were days that I'd see her staring off into space, and I could only imagine that she was making up some story about him and what their horrible interaction had become for her life. She even told me that if she had the choice to change the events she would choose the same." Her voice broke and she looked into me. "Because of me."

I swallowed and fought the tears watering in my eyes.

"I was angry for a long time, furious at that man—I never referred to him as my father—for what he'd done to my mother. It wasn't until I matured and left college that I found a place to let go of the past. That was when I started this." She spread her arms and indicated the building around us. "My past has never risen up against me since that moment that I made a choice."

We sat quietly and I thought about what she was saying. I'd thought that had been the case for me, too. Until the events of the last several months.

"I do not ever expect a woman to get to that place. My mother was extraordinary."

"Yes. She was. Was she like that about everything, or just this event?"

She shrugged. "Everything, really. She believed that everything that we encountered in our life was put there to make us better." She swallowed. "She got cancer last year and she tackled it with the same grace and courage. I am constantly amazed by her." She took another drink. "Would you like to know something she told me that helped me to release the anger that I'd carried my whole life?"

"Please."

"She said, *forgiveness is merely giving up the hope that the past could look any different.*"

The tears I'd been holding back fell, unable to be contained any longer.

52

Ashley

Annika listened as I told her about Carter, not holding anything back now that the tears had begun to flow. I told her of that night, how he'd lied to me, and then after, when he'd lied again, turning everyone from my best friend to our college community against me.

She let me talk, offering encouragement and tissues, passing no judgment. It became easy to understand why she'd been able to build such a massive community and help so many women. I was sure that she wasn't able to talk to all of them herself, but she'd probably put great managers and people in place.

"And what's happened lately that's brought your past crashing into your present?"

I told her about the trial, about the new allegations against Carter, and about talking to Daphne. The more I talked, the more Annika's shoulders lifted and the less she smiled.

After I finished, she leaned in and gave me a long hug. A real hug, the ones I craved from Trent and Vi—and now Odin. There weren't very many people who I allowed into my space like that.

Intimate is different than sex, and Odin was making that line blur so much. I could see it already blurring in this space, too. Annika had drawn out pieces of the story that even I hadn't remembered. But that didn't help me with anything…I was still in this same tortured space.

When she pulled away, there was a fire in her eyes, one I'd not seen since coming in. "I have people inside the court systems. I'll make some calls, we'll see how many of the accusations can be brought together all at once. That will help." She squeezed my hand. "We'll make him pay for this. Maybe not for yours, but he'll pay for everything we can exact."

I nodded, still feeling raw from divulging everything.

"Let me talk to Daphne, see what she can tell me. I'll keep you posted—" She looked up. "I mean, if you want."

"I have to work my way through this, I think. I've ignored it for too long."

She smiled. "That's the best first step. Don't be too hard on yourself. There are a lot of steps. You've managed to do some incredible things. You've managed to build an amazing business. This was the fuel. You have to separate yourself from the fuel, from the past. That made you, but now you're you. It was just a catalyst. You get to own what you did with that. A lot of people curl up and choose to opt out of life. Which is fine, it's their choice. This is hard. This has the ability to take the wind right out of your sails. I've had women who are in your same position end up losing everything, unable to get their feet back under them. Don't short-change what you have accomplished just because of a couple minor setbacks. You get to choose your future. Everyday."

I smiled. Normally that kind of bullshit went in one ear and out the other. I'd heard it all and had circumvented all of that and had lit my fuel on fire and burned a path that set me up at life. But apparently that method had also burned through the bottom of everything that I'd erected.

Today, I wanted to hear it, wanted to smooth it over my

wounds like a salve. I liked hearing it, wanted her to keep going, wanted her to repeat herself a dozen times. I took a deep breath.

"And you have access to any of my counselors, any time." She squeezed my hand softly. "But you don't have to. This is still proceeding at your speed, no one else's. And you can slow it down or speed it up or bring it to a complete stop at any time. You are always in control."

I laughed. "That's the one thing I've felt like I've had so little of lately. My life has been so carefully controlled, I thought that nothing could shake me. Today helped." I paused and smoothed the leg of my pants. "Today helped a lot, thank you. I'd like to be involved as much as you can tell me as you find things out from Daphne and your people. I'll give the counseling some thought." I stood and gave her another hug. "Can I see your operation? Can you tell me about how it all came about? You said you were impressed with me, but the admiration is mutual. I'm amazed and awed. You've given me hope. I feel like once Carter has paid—for anything—that I'll start to feel like I have control and like I'm finally a new person without my past hanging over my head."

"Maybe. Don't put so much pressure on one thing, though. You have to find that peace within yourself. That was a lesson that took me a long time to learn."

I nodded, understanding what she meant. And yet, I still felt like that would give me so much closure and peace about my own situation, even if it came for another girl's trauma.

Closure in any sense would help me to finally move forward.

And I was so ready to move in any direction after being stuck for so damn long.

53

Odin

The location of the safe house had given me the idea to swing by and check in on my mother. After seeing Annika and Ashley getting along so well—as I knew they would—it had been easy to leave them alone so that Ashley could begin the big step of putting her life's pieces back together. I wanted her to find wholeness, and Annika had all the tools if she'd just be willing to use them. If this turned out to not be what she wanted, I would not begrudge her the lessons, and I would know that we'd given her the best possible option to work it out.

And I would still care for her and would still want her in my life. Very much.

I knocked on Mother's door and walked in, expecting to find her home. I often meant to come visit, but we were both so busy. It had been weeks since I'd been able to see her, though we talked on the phone nearly every day. "Mother?"

"In here." My sister's voice met me.

"Alice?" It was odd for her to be here during the day with her work schedule. I'd gotten her into the real estate game early, but she'd made her own name as one of the best commercial realtors in the area.

I found them in the back room, the air around them heavy. I hugged Mother and kissed her cheek, then sat beside Alice, pulling her against my side and kissing her temple. "What's up, Buttercup?"

She gave a half-hearted laugh at our usual teasing. "There's no easy way to put this..."

I frowned, my stomach lurching. I didn't want to hear bad news about either of them; they'd been my foundation for so long. I needed them, much as I needed Ashley.

"Your father's back." Mother spit the words, her heavy accent giving them hard edges that could have left bruises.

I blinked and stood, pacing the small room. "I don't understand. What do you mean, *back*?"

"He called me." Alice shifted on the couch, drawing up her legs, her slender arms curling around her knees. She'd never known our father. He'd left when I was barely a boy. He wasn't a father to either of us, so why start now, when we were adults? Neither of us needed him, we'd given up on him so long ago and I was troubled by this resurgence. "Asked if we could grab lunch."

I blinked. "Just like that? Did he say where he's been? Why he left?"

She shook her head. "No. I was too shocked to ask. I'm sorry, I should have gotten more information from him."

I returned to the couch and sat beside her, putting my arms around her. "I'm sorry if I made you feel like you should have handled it differently. I'm sure I would have done the same. What did you tell him?"

"I just told him I'd have to call him back."

"When did this happen?" I felt like I'd been out of the loop on all of this. Mother hadn't mentioned it when we'd talked yesterday, but I also realized that maybe this wasn't the sort of thing you talked about on the phone.

"This morning. On my way to work. I came over here, took Mom to lunch, and we've been talking about it since then."

It bothered me that neither of them had called me. I frowned. "Would you have told me?"

Alice leaned her head against my chest. "Of course. I was just so shocked, that's all."

"I'm sorry he called you first."

"He asked for your number."

My heart paused. I wasn't sure if I wanted to talk to him. Not just yet. I needed to figure out why he'd bothered to come back now. I didn't want him messing up any of our lives. He'd chosen to opt out years ago.

I looked at Mother. "How do you feel about this?"

She pursed her lips and stared out the window for a long moment, then turned toward where Alice and I sat on the couch. I could remember so many afternoons just like this, her meting out our punishment for something we'd done, us waiting for the judgement. This was only slightly different, in that the punishment would come for our father, one she'd probably wanted to issue long ago. He'd walked out on all of us, but she'd never quite been the same after he'd left. I'd always wondered if she thought he'd come back, if she thought that he'd make his way home after all his wandering.

And now, he'd chosen to call Alice—not me, not his wife—the little girl he'd hardly known.

"I cannot fault him for wanting a relationship with either of you." She smiled. "You're wonderful children." She stood and I rose, coming over to escort her into the kitchen. "Are you hungry?"

And that was that. Once Mother started cooking, the discussion was over, her punishment served and onto bigger things. I wasn't sure what would come of this stuff with our father, but as far as she was concerned, we were done discussing it. I'd have to get Alice alone later and work our way through it, decide if either of us wanted to talk to him.

54

Ashley

I waved goodbye to Annika as she stood in the doorway and watched us go. I'd spent over three hours with her—far longer than I'd anticipated—and Odin had seemed pleased when he'd picked me up, giving her a healthy hug and escorting me to the car.

"Well?" he asked as he turned onto the highway.

I beamed and squeezed his hand. "You were right."

He leaned over and kissed my cheek. "This wasn't about being right. Tell me about your afternoon."

I divulged most everything, telling him how we'd talked, how marvelous of a listener Annika was, what we'd discovered with just a little more digging on Carter, and that I'd agreed to consider counseling.

"That's wonderful. I want you to be happy."

I watched him watch the road, shifting the car into another gear as he pushed the gas, speeding us home.

"We're meeting with Daphne tomorrow, and Annika is certain that we can push that case through, especially if I agree to testify, which I will. Then we're going to get a hold of the rest of the girls who've come forward lately and do the same thing; sit down, talk to them, and work within Annika's court contacts to ensure that Carter goes away for a long, long time."

"Mmm." He glanced over and gave me a small smile. "Sounds like you two conquered a lot today." His voice hid something. I wasn't sure where he'd gone while I talked to Annika, but something had either gone wrong while he'd been away, or he'd gotten bad news, or he hadn't wanted me getting along so well with his friend.

That last one was so far-fetched that I tossed it immediately. For one, I wouldn't be attracted to a man who didn't want to further everyone's relationships around him. Something was defiantly eating at him, though.

"Do you want me to take you home?" He didn't look at me, tossing the question over softly.

I frowned. That was a first. Odin never wanted to go to my place, not once we'd started down this weird path that was continuing to look like a relationship. "Either place. We can go to your house." I patted his hand. "Are you okay?"

He nodded and shifted, pushing the car faster. I didn't question him all the way to his house, or in the elevator, letting him muddle through his thoughts. I wanted to ask what was bothering him, but without our clearly defined boundaries, I felt like our conversations were blurring through all the possible lines.

He made us glasses of wine and we sat on the couch, curled together while he asked me more questions about my day, attentive and yet something was definitely still bothering him. His hands traveled over my neck and shoulders, lightly caressing me while we drank and talked.

As I finished my glass, he set it down and stood, taking my hand and leading me back to the bedroom. "I should probably go. I have work in the morning."

He didn't answer, drawing me toward the bed and laying me

down, kissing my neck and the bare curve of my shoulder. I laid back into the mattress, expecting him to come with me. He held up a finger and asked me to wait. I didn't mind, we'd had more than enough sex at this point to know that whatever he was bringing tonight would make for some great sex, even with his mood in such a somber place. I'd hoped that the wine would help. Maybe I should start with giving him a blow job.

I sat up on the bed, fully intending to unbuckle his pants and pull his cock out. When he returned, he held a silken strap in each hand. I smiled, recognizing the ones that had been on his bedpost the first night we'd been here. I'd nearly tried them on him, but now I was excited to get to do it, especially after the breakthroughs I'd had today.

"Scoot up to the headboard, ma chérie."

I laughed. "You'll not be tying me."

"Tonight I am." He swallowed and looked away, then drew his gaze up my legs. I was in a better place tonight than I'd been in a long stretch, finally seeing some progress and the possibility of a light at the end of the tunnel.

I drew my shirt over my head, releasing my breasts for him to touch. I hadn't bothered with a bra when we'd first gone over to Annika's, and now I was glad. I held my wrists together and out for him.

He shook his head. "No. Not like that. Lay on your back and put one toward each corner of the mattress."

I did as he said and a thrill shot through me. I'd never trusted anyone to be in control. I could see the need for it creasing the corners of Odin's eyes. Whatever had happened to him today, he needed to feel like he had control over something. I certainly understood that. If this was enough to give him back a semblance of control, then I would let him tie me.

He kissed my arm, taking his time, working his way from my elbow up to my wrist, nibbling the skin, scratching it with his beard, tasting it with his tongue. I allowed him to slip the satin around my wrist and he tied the knot quite snug. I liked that he was a man who knew how to dominate.

That was one of the biggest reasons I'd never let any of my other lovers do this to me—none of them could have successfully pulled off the dominant role. That was one of the reasons they were drawn to me—I controlled and dominated every situation. Even Odin had liked that part of my personality, even though it had clashed with his own need for control.

So here we were, working our way through what it looked like for him to be calling the shots.

He crawled up on the bed, slowly working his way across my body, both legs on one side, then straddling me, then moving to the other side, his lips never leaving my body. As he moved over me, I lifted up, licking his stomach, but he pulled away, slipping his fingers deftly over my wrist as he bound the second part of my body.

I smiled. "Now what?"

He kissed my fingers, taking his time with each one of them, drawing them deep into his mouth and nipping at the tip. I curled my fingers into his mouth, touching his tongue and dancing with him. We were so in tune with the others' body and I liked that part of our sexual encounters. Odin kept it fun, and I had a feeling tonight was going to be one to remember.

55

Odin

I hadn't expected her to relent, controlling as she was. Perhaps this day had been good for us both.

I wanted to control at least one thing today. I'd gone from—much like Ashley—having all my ducks in a glorious row, everyone marching along as they should, to this news of my father, sending everything scattering.

I'd enjoyed getting to question Ashley, asking about her conversations with Annika and anyone else she'd met, learning about what she'd seen, being able to picture it all, thanks to my recent tour. She'd talked excitedly and animated, buoyed by her entire day. I was so glad, wanting her to get along with Annika, needing them to get along. Annika had been such a good friend to me through the years, and there had to be a way for her to help Ashley, there must.

And it had worked. Not that I'd had any intention of manipulating Ashley, but there were so many things I wanted for her and this had seemed like a natural next step.

Now I wanted to work through my own healing, grasping as I was for the threads of my carefully constructed life.

Seeing Alice so dejected and lost after a mere phone call had me in a twist. I didn't want any of the women in my life hurting. My mother hadn't been much more lively as I'd gone to leave. This news had affected her. Far more than she'd wanted to let on.

I understood that, not wanting to reflect on my own feelings. I'd been devastated as a boy as he'd vanished, leaving me to care for the two women who'd been my whole world, my mother, my rock, and her new baby, my little sister, a child I'd vowed to care for until my last breath.

When he'd gone, those vows had become so much more real. I was the only man they'd had as we'd grown up, and now that was all a mystery.

I trailed kisses across Ashley's skin, wanting to taste all of her, wanting to get lost in her body, her sounds, her scents. I wanted her to carry me away from my brain tonight. Wanted to escape these thoughts.

I tethered her arms to the bedposts, drawing them tight and spreading her arms wide. This was what I needed; her submitting to me. I'd wanted this from the first moment I'd met her and I'd been happy to let her lead, happy to get us to this point when I could be the one in control of her.

"You're a beautiful woman." I paused before using her name, not wanting to get us back to that place where we'd been at Black Velvet. Though she'd used it today with Annika, I was still wary. I was already walking into unchartered territory by dominating her.

On any other night I would have pushed her boundaries, but tonight this was for me, this wasn't about her and what she needed to move forward, this was about what I needed to stay together.

I leaned over the bed, withdrawing a riding crop from the

nightstand. She smiled and licked her lips. "Why Odin, you have quite the talents."

"You just wait." I trailed the leather tip across her body, making her squirm. She didn't test the restraints, leaning into the pressure like a good girl. I told her so.

"You make a good Dom." She purred and stretched beneath the leather as I moved it across her stomach, swirling it once around her bellybutton, then bringing it down with a hard smack. She moaned. "Yes."

Her voice was a husky whisper and my cock twitched to life, wanting more of her noises, needing them. I moved the crop between her legs, skimming over the wetness in her panties. She spread her legs, and her fingers clenched into the satin binds. I rubbed the crop over her clit, letting the moans soak into my skin. I leaned over, tasted her nipple, felt her squirm.

I should have blindfolded her, but again, I didn't need her to learn anything tonight. This was for me and only me. I would pleasure her, of that she could be certain, and in her pleasure and her orgasms, I would find myself. That was such a common misconception about the need to dominate: It had nothing to do with selfish loving. Quite the opposite, in fact, which was why I'd never had a problem with Ashley dominating me. I knew that I would get my own pleasure.

I trailed the crop past her pussy and onto her thighs, slapping her gently once or twice, then drawing it back up to her clit and smacking her hard. She arched into the feeling and my cock tightened. I leaned over, kissing her skin, tasting all of her, then lifted her hips and drew her panties off, revealing her freshly-shaved pussy.

The woman was gorgeous. I'd had beautiful women before, but it was her spirit that so completely captivated me. Even today, fresh from a crying jag with Annika, she was vibrant.

I spread her legs, the crop laying unused beside me on the bed, my cock hard and wanting her. With a quick flick of my fingers, I undid my pants and withdrew my cock, smearing it through the wetness gathering at her opening.

She strained against the binds, wanting to touch me, wanting to control my movements.

I entered her slowly, watching her body respond.

Another wonderful point of pleasure with bondage was that with so much of her response restricted, I got to receive the truest parts of her reaction to me, how her body arched into me, how her pussy clenched so tightly around me. This was a turning point for both of us, one that would leave us changed in the morning.

A change I very much wanted.

56

Ashley

Lingering thoughts of last night followed me through my morning; into my own shower after leaving Odin, the entire drive to pick up Annika so we could meet Daphne for lunch.

The morning had stretched into a massive space filled with my thoughts. Odin had performed spectacularly and he'd made me feel safe enough to allow what he'd wanted. The pleasure of the bondage and allowing him to take charge had been more exciting than I'd imagined, always having been the one in charge. I still had been far from letting go, but it was a huge step to let him tie me up.

And that crop!

My belly clenched and my mouth watered at the memory. I eased through traffic and let my body swim in the thoughts of how expertly he'd wielded the leather wand across my body, making me tremble in anticipation of the next strike—and ultimately—the feel of him inside me. I wouldn't be allowing that with anyone else, and I still didn't feel like Odin and I should continue on with this relationship. Lines had been getting blurred since the very beginning and it was no surprise that they were still being obliterated left and right.

I sighed and took the exit, checking the clock and speeding up to make sure I wasn't late. For now, I needed to focus on what was coming next. Daphne had been gracious to meet Annika and me on such short notice, especially since I'd already bugged her about the situation with Carter. But that hadn't been enough, and Annika had been so kind about helping me and getting me through this, no matter the cost to her. She had so much going on in her own life, with the organization and the crisis center and the constant stream of women in and out of her life. Yet, she'd still been willing to help me.

She was waiting for me on the curb and slid inside. "Doing okay?"

I nodded and she patted my hand.

The conversation quickened the moment we met with Daphne. She was gracious and hit it off with Annika, as I knew she would. The waiter filled our drinks and took our orders and Annika launched right into the matters at hand. "Carter? How do we put him away?"

Daphne sighed. "She has to testify. We need everyone to come out against him."

I swallowed, my throat suddenly parched. "Are you certain?" I had promised I would, but only in theory. This was real.

She nodded. "I'm afraid so. It's as it was the last time you participated in a trial against him; it's the character witness statements that override the evidence and it should have been enough in that one. The more you can continue to remind everyone of what he did to you, even though the statute of limitations has expired on your own case, the better chance of him finally paying. You can still make him pay, you can still be impactful."

That was so easy for her to say, having already gone public, having already testified, having already moved past the pain and into her new life. I still had so much work to do. Last time, I was in a closed room. I didn't even have to come face-to-face with Carter.

Now she was asking me to do this in front of the world.

Annika reached over and took my hand, Daphne laid hers over the top. "You can do this," Annika whispered.

"You can," Daphne agreed.

With the two of them at my side, I almost felt like they weren't completely lying to me. I certainly didn't feel 100% confident, but I was closer than I'd ever been. "I'll do it."

57

Odin

My phone rang and I shook hands with my potential client, agreeing to touch base with him later today after he'd had a chance to look over the figures. The limo door closed behind him and I picked up the call.

"Odin?"

"Yes. Who's this?"

"This is Vi. I'm Ms. M's friend."

I frowned, an unsettling feeling swelling in my belly. "Is anything wrong?"

"I'm just…Fuck…" She cursed beneath her breath. "I shouldn't have called you. I don't meddle. I just…"

"Please tell me."

"I'm worried she's going to do something stupid."

"What does that mean?" The heat in my stomach hardened, making me worry. I knew that Ms. M and Annika were meeting with the other woman they thought would help in the pursuit to put her attacker behind bars. Everything seemed like it was moving toward her health getting renewed so she could move past this point in her life. I didn't think there was anything to be concerned about.

And now a friend of hers was calling me out of the blue telling me otherwise.

"I wouldn't be worrying if she hadn't already confronted Carter. And now, with things looking like they're not going to progress like she wants, I'm just worried that she's going to take matters into her own hands. She wants justice and Carter showed no remorse when she talked to him. I know she wanted that so bad."

Fear rose up in my chest, squeezing my ribcage until breathing became difficult. I wasn't sure if I could trust Vi, but Ashley had spoken of her often. They were friends. We'd met at a gallery opening organized by Vi.

"How do you know about her speaking with Carter?" Ashley hadn't exactly been forthcoming with me about it and we'd been together nearly constantly since then.

"I was there. She made me take her over to his place. It didn't go at all how she wanted. It affected her. I wouldn't be contacting you if this wasn't serious. I've been thinking about it for the three days since we went there. But I don't want her to do anything...stupid."

This wasn't good. Now that she was on the path toward making things right, there was always a possibility that she'd take matters into her own hands.

But this was Ashley. Surely that wasn't truly an option for her.

But this was her friend, and if she was worried, then I should be as well. "Thank you for calling. I'll speak with her about it. I'm sure it's nothing. I'm sure she wouldn't go to such lengths."

"Maybe." She sighed. "But she's put up with a lot regarding Carter. His freedom has eaten at her for a long time."

"I thought this was only recent."

"I thought so too, but the more I looked at her actions, the more I listened to what she said, it was obvious that even though she wasn't dealing with any of it, the pain has been festering inside her. Listen, Odin, I know you don't know me, but I don't do drama. I wouldn't be involving you if this was something I could handle. I wouldn't be bothering you if I thought she wasn't going to do something extreme. She's not the kind of person to key someone's car. If she's going to bother, it's going to be with irreparable damage—possibly to both of them." She paused but she didn't sound finished. I waited for her to continue. "She said the world would be a better place without him."

"What do you wish for me to do?" I didn't like the panic that lay in Vi's voice. She'd known Ashley far longer than I. Clearly, Ashley trusted her as well, taking her to confront Carter.

I didn't like that she'd not only not told me that she was going to do that, but hadn't confided in me immediately after, either. There had been no red flags for further action on Ashley's part when she'd told me that she'd seen Carter. Just when I thought she was growing more comfortable with me, I find that she is still holding parts of herself back. That it was on this topic troubled me, this topic that I'd devoted so much time and energy and resources to helping her work through. Both Annika and the therapists had told me that she needed to work through it her own way and that I would need to be patient, and yet to be left out of something so critical was bothersome.

"Confront her about it. I think she'll listen to you. You can make her see reason that she needs to let this go, that she needs to move on and stop hanging her success and failures on who Carter is and whether he goes free."

"She will not listen to me. I've already given her access to therapists and a friend who counsels rape victims. They're talking today."

"Really? She didn't tell me that."

"It seems she's keeping things from both of us."

We hung up and I pondered the conversation and the new revelations about Ashley. I agreed with Vi's assessment that she wasn't the kind of woman to do something incidental; if she were to take action, she was going to make it count.

Had I made a mistake in encouraging her to confront her past? I'd only meant for her to move past the obstacles that were hindering her, not create new ones that could jeopardize her future.

She was supposed to come back to my home after her meeting with Annika and Daphne so we could talk about it and discuss plans for the evening. I'd hoped to arrange a meeting for her to sit down with Sampson and organize her first auction at Black Velvet. Now, I felt like we needed to put that on hold for a while until she could work her way through these parts and be free of it once and for all.

The front door opened and she swept in, looking a mixture of excited and terrified. I drew her to me and held her against my body, wondering what the best way to broach the conversation with Vi was. "How was lunch?"

"Goodness. Scary and good, I guess. Daphne says I have to testify in this upcoming trial. Annika made a few calls to the court. I have a deposition later in the week and then I'll be one of the witnesses once they set a trial date. I'm so scared. I wish it would all just go away."

Her words were a knife to my heart. "Listen, Ashley, you've got to let the court handle this, let the prosecutor do his job to put Carter behind bars. Trust the system."

She pulled back and looked at me, confusion on her face. "I know that. I'm just not looking forward to having to talk about it. Again. In public."

"I understand and I'll be with you the whole way, along with Daphne and Annika. It's just…"

She frowned. "What's going on, Odin?" She pulled free of my arms and took a step away, crossing her arms over her chest in a defiant pose.

I sighed. "Your friend Vi called me. She told me more about

you seeing Carter. All you told me was that you'd run into him. But you sought him out, didn't you? Vi said you told her that you wanted him off the earth. She's worried you're going to do something stupid."

"Stupid like testify against him to put him away for life? Stupid like that?" Her voice rose with anger and indignation. "Stupid like take charge of my life? Stupid like not letting Carter have any control over my happiness anymore?"

I reached for her. "We're merely concerned for your safety."

"Or for what it's going to do to your reputation if you're with someone who's a public rape victim?"

"What are you talking about? I couldn't care less what others think of me. You know that. I don't want you getting hurt."

She huffed and marched to the window. Clearly her emotions were all over the board, and I couldn't blame her. This wasn't easy. "Tell me about lunch."

She shook her head. "It was fine."

"Ashley."

She hunched her shoulders. "I should go. I have work to do."

"I was hoping you'd stay, that we could talk, that you could meet with Sampson."

"Don't hold that over me! Just because you're my access to Black Velvet doesn't mean you get to control any part of my life. I'm going to handle this however I want."

"I'm not asking you to do anything different, Ashley. I'm asking you to stay safe."

"You don't get to ask me to do things, Odin. We're not in a relationship. We just fuck and we did that far too many times already!" She marched through the room and back out the door she'd come in. I let her go, not wanting to say anything that would do more damage than I'd already done.

I walked to the window and stared down onto the street far below, thinking I could see her from this height. My forehead rested against the cool glass and I mentally kicked myself for broaching the subject. I should have known that she wouldn't like me meddling.

Now my fear was that I'd sent her headlong into the direction I was trying to keep her from going, adding fuel to her fire.

I wrestled with work in my office for a half hour before giving up and making myself a late lunch. I'd planned on an early dinner with Ashley before meeting Sampson. Both were now thrown out the window.

I ran a hand through my hair. Today had not gone as expected. I'd already tried calling Annika, but her phone had gone to voicemail. Nothing about this situation was going according to my plan and that was unsettling. Everything went as I wanted it.

I finished making lunch and sat at the table, a whisky tumbler beside the plate—today had been a day that would require drinking into the evening. I'd thought about calling Ashley, but had hesitated, wanting to let her cool off until she felt like we could discuss this further. My chest pinched and I hoped that she wasn't going to do anything stupid in the meantime.

A knock at the front door startled me and I frowned. She wouldn't have knocked. Perhaps it was Annika, coming over instead of calling. I really wanted her take on lunch and how it had gone.

I opened the door to find my sister standing there, tears streaking down her cheeks. "Alice!" I gathered her in my arms and drew her in, taking her to the couch. "What's happened?"

She shook her head and I gave her a box of tissues while she tried to compose herself enough to speak. "Can I get you anything? A drink? A blanket?" She was trembling, blowing her nose and blotting her eyes.

"No. Just give me a second."

I leaned back into the couch, rubbing her back and waiting.

She sighed and turned to face me, her back resting against the arm of the couch. "It's our father."

I grunted and crossed my arms, angered that he was still affecting Alice like this. "What's he done now?"

She shook her head. "He called again. I stayed at Mom's last night. We talked. A lot."

"How is she?" With everything going on with Ashley, I hadn't had enough time to really think more about my mother and how this was affecting her.

Or about my father and how it was affecting me.

"She's lonely. If he's coming back to make a go at reconnecting to all of us, she's willing to listen to him. I just don't understand what he wants."

"Well, first, there's no way I'm letting him near her until I talk to him." I patted her knee resting against my thigh. "Or you, for that matter."

"He asked for your number again."

I frowned, only delaying the inevitable. "Give me his, I'll call him."

"What are you going to say?" She fumbled through her purse, coming up with her phone and sending me a text with his contact information.

"I don't know. I want to know what he wants."

"Do you think it's because we've built such successful lives for ourselves? I mean, he's no slouch, he's still CEO of his company. Does he want something from us? I just...why now?"

I shook my head in confusion. "I guess there's only one way to find out."

"Don't do it yet." She laid her hand on mine. "Let's talk first."

"What are your concerns?"

"That you'll tell him to stay away from me and Mom." She stared at me, a pleading look in her eyes.

I grunted and crossed my arms. "I won't determine your relationships. But I do want to know his intentions. Is he coming back just to leave again?" The pain of his abandonment when I was a boy still hurt. I'd long ago given up the need for his approval or communication, but that was an easy stand to make when he wasn't around to challenge it. With him back in my life, would I forgive all his past transgressions and open myself to the hurt again?

Which was exactly what I was asking of Ashley—to forgive Carter so she could be in a relationship with me, to possibly be hurt again. I groaned and focused on Alice and the conversation at hand. I would need to think long and hard on what this meant for Ashley and how I could be helpful.

"And Mom? Will you determine her relationship? What if he still loves her? Or she loves him? She's been single since he walked out, no matter how many times I've tried to get her to date, or even go out to dinner with someone. She refuses. She pines for him. That's some of what we talked about last night. He was her true love. I don't want her to be alone forever."

I grunted. "We'll see." It was a terrible idea. It was a horrific idea, letting him back into any of our lives, let alone Mother's. He'd treated her well enough…until the leaving. I'd never gotten over what he'd done to her.

She'd cried for months, lost pounds she couldn't afford to lose, stopped going out, stopped letting her friends come over. She'd retreated into our family, becoming a shell of the woman she'd been during my younger years. Alice had never known the woman I had. She knew the one who'd had to work multiple jobs, who yelled too much because she'd lost the beauty that had been in her life, who took whatever jobs she could to make sure we had a roof over our heads. My first paycheck had gone to her, and half of all the ones since. Yet, still, she lived in that house, that home that he'd turned into a shell when he'd walked away.

Damn him. I hated everything about the idea of having to allow him even the space to talk to me. To Alice. To Mother.

Anger bubbled up in my belly. No, I should definitely not talk to him now, not if Alice wanted a chance to know him.

And I meant what I'd said; her relationships were hers to have, whether I agreed with them or not. "I only want to protect you."

She patted my thigh. "I know. And you've done a fine job. It's just...he's my father and I never knew him."

"Not everyone gets a happily ever after, Alice."

"But I can want one for everyone, can't I?"

I sighed. "Yes. But at what cost?"

She made a face and laid her head on the back cushion. "I want her to be happy."

I touched her cheek. "As do I, but do you want to risk it with a man who's already hurt her so deeply that no one could come near her?"

The side of her mouth tipped up. "I guess not."

"I promise I only want what's best for you, for both of you."

58

Ashley

I slammed the file down on my desk and marched to the door, looking for Tiffanie, my assistant. She'd gone to lunch over an hour ago, and goddammit, I needed her.

Fuck that.

I marched back to my desk, pushing the files around. I didn't need anyone. The more I leaned on people, the more they let me down.

Look what happened with Odin, he'd become such a huge part of my support system through all of this and then the moment I tried to do something on my own, he punished me for it, yelling at me for taking risks. I was so glad to have seen that side of him now! Dammit, we were not in a relationship. What did it matter how he behaved outside the bedroom?

We'd gotten to such a fantastic place, I'd felt comfortable letting him dominate in the bedroom, and for what? To have him strip me of all my power, like he'd given me a semblance of control, when he'd been controlling everything from the very beginning.

Anger pulsed through me. This was why I didn't do relationships. I had repeatedly tried to keep from being in one with Odin. At every turn I'd taken three steps back, refusing to let it be anything more than sex.

I sighed and sat heavily in the chair, refusing to think of him anymore today. I had three auctions to put together—Mikayla's creeping up—and I wanted all new bidders at each of them. I was culling my list and, dammit, I should be setting up one for Black Velvet. Damn him for taking that away from me. Not that he'd been the one in control of that; he just made me think he was. I could call Sampson myself.

I wrote a note and stuck it on the edge of my computer screen. I'd do just that. I didn't need Odin. I could handle Black Velvet all by myself. Just like I did everything.

I couldn't believe that he took Vi seriously. I needed to call her and give her a piece of my mind! Of all the underhanded things for her to do! We'd had a code our whole lives—we didn't meddle. She didn't see me calling Trent when her engagement had blown up, or when she was fucking everything with pants.

She'd been behind me the entire time during the confrontation with Carter. She'd been supportive—or so I'd thought. What in the hell had she been thinking getting Odin involved? She didn't even know him, didn't know anything about how he'd react to being called like that out of the blue. She had no business.

I was so furious. At all of them. Especially Carter for putting any of us in this position. My life had been perfect before he'd shown up again. Before he'd raped again, before he'd walked into Trent's like nothing was amiss, before he'd laughed off the attacks, truly believing that he'd done those women—and me—a favor, giving us what we'd wanted. He needed to disappear, and not just into the jails where he'd get out in a matter of months because they were overcrowded with murderers and drug dealers; I wanted him wiped off the earth so I'd never ever have to hear about him hurting anyone else again.

My phone rang and I jumped, then I checked the screen, slightly disappointed that it wasn't Odin calling, then furious at myself for wanting it to have been him. I needed a day at the spa. And maybe some therapy. I made another note to call Annika's therapists so I could get started on putting myself back together. Clearly I had some work to do.

"Hello?"

"Ashley? This is Margaret Choy. I'm Daphne's lawyer. I wondered if you had a few minutes to talk?"

I swallowed and nodded, then found my voice. "Yes. Thanks for calling. How can I help you?"

"Daphne says you're willing to testify in the upcoming trial against Carter Ridley. I wanted to set up a time for your deposition. We can talk first if you'd like, but I've found that the best cases are the ones where you tell the story for the first time to the court reporter. I'll be there to make sure things don't get out of hand. Do you think you can handle that?"

"I did a deposition once before."

"Yes, I pulled it up. You did a fine job. This will be like that. You'll do the deposition and then they'll use that to determine if we have enough of a case to go to trial. I need you. You'll be a big part of what I'm mounting against him."

My throat was suddenly dry. "Y-yes. I can do that. When?"

We set the meeting for tomorrow morning. That gave me the rest of the day to get my shit together, get these bidders vetted, and stop thinking about Odin. Work had been my salvation before, it would be again, if I'd let it.

"Hi!" Tiffanie rushed in, my dry cleaning and bags of lunch in her hands. "I'm so sorry that took longer than I wanted, but I got him!" She beamed and I suddenly remembered that I'd asked her to swing by an architectural firm to see if she could get a meeting set up with a potential bidder. His name had come to me through a couple of bidders weeks ago and I'd been unable to capture him. A small twinge of guilt snapped across my gut and I let it go.

There was no reason that I couldn't be intense here, ready to get to work.

She hung my clothes in the closet and held up the bags of salads. "You want to eat here or in the conference room? I'm starving!"

I smiled and stood, some of my tension from earlier dissipating. "Conference room. And thank you for all your hard work. He'll be a great add." She was a good girl, one who'd originally come to me for an auction and I'd denied her, wanting her here instead. We'd spent hours discussing her future and she'd quickly seen the advantage of working behind the stage instead of standing on it for one time. With what she made on the auctions, she'd more than tripled what she'd have taken home that night.

She'd also realized the benefit of being single as she met and flirted with the men who would become my bidders. I didn't have any rules or restrictions on who she slept with and she'd worked her way through several of them, enjoying the spoils that came with entertaining rich men.

For the most part, we didn't overlap on our tastes. The men I took home weren't her style, and vice versa. On the occasion that we had, I'd bowed out, wanting to keep her happy, and unwilling to let something as inconsequential as a man come between the stellar work she did here.

I followed her into the room, bringing two bottles of water, setting one at her spot and taking the chair beside her. She laid out our lunches and sat, beaming and proud of her accomplishment. "Are we all set for Mikayla then?"

I frowned and tossed my salad aimlessly with my fork. There were implications from Margaret's call. If I was going to be testifying and an active participant in the trial, that was going to take some time, not to mention an emotional toll. I hadn't had time to think it all through. "What do you think if we postpone it?"

Her eyes widened. And rightfully so. I'd never done such a

thing in all the years she'd been with me. "Why?" she whispered. "Is she having second thoughts?"

"No. No, nothing like that. I have some personal things coming up that are going to take my time but I'm not sure how much."

"The news didn't get a hold of another story, did they?" Alarm rang through her voice. The last run-in with the press had affected her as much as it had Trent and me. While I did my best to shield her, that journalist had been far too effective for my liking.

"No. This is something from my past. When I was younger." I pressed my lips together and set my fork down. Maybe I should tell her, lest she get blindsided by it.

She was another of the people who knew that I'd been raped. She'd asked plenty of questions before coming to work for me and I'd seen no reason to keep that from her, considering it was such an integral part of why I did what I did. It gave her a different perspective on the auctions, one she'd not only appreciated, but admired. "The man who raped me in college is coming up on charges." She inhaled swiftly. "And I've been asked to testify."

"Oh my god, Ms. M!" She rose from her chair and came around, stuttering to a stop before swooping down and hugging me, realizing what she'd been about to do. We weren't physical, and while I appreciated the sentiment, I wasn't sure I wanted to skew our working relationship like that.

I leaned forward and patted her hand where it rested on the table when she'd come to a stop. "It's fine. Thanks for your concern."

She leaned a hip against the table and folded her hands at her waist. "Are you going to be okay? When does all of it start? Yes, of course we should postpone the auction until you're done with all that circus. I'll make the necessary arrangements."

"I'm hoping I'll be fine. Talking about it is new to me, but I finally feel like it's important, like by keeping silent I'm telling him that it was okay."

"It's so not okay." She huffed and returned to her chair. "Not okay at all." She lifted her gaze to me, tears shimmering in the corners of her eyes. "I'm sorry."

I smiled. "It's fine. Thank you. And thank you for handling everything. I'm hoping this won't be disruptive, but now you know in case it is."

"I'll do my best to make sure it isn't any more disruptive than it has to be."

In that moment, my already high opinion of her rose and I made a mental note to buy her something special once this auction was over.

59

Ashley

The next morning was a true San Francisco morning, overcast and dull, gray and damp. It matched my mood perfectly. I dressed in a gray silk suit, gray heels, and swept my hair back in a tight bun. No jewels, no drama. Today I wanted to be invisible. Today was about Carter and what he'd done.

I checked my phone, answering texts from Annika and Daphne, who were both meeting me at the courthouse to sit in the room and support me.

Vi was coming, too. I'd called her last night, berating her for involving Odin. She'd explained her worries and I'd yelled at her. It had been the most tense conversation we'd had since becoming friends. And while she understood my place, I'd had a hard time seeing her side. She'd hurt me and she'd begged me to let her come today and support me. I'd hesitated, but in the end I'd relented, knowing that I'd need my entire team with me. Trent would have been there, too, had I asked. But I hadn't. There would still be time for his comfort and support after today; we still had a trial to get through.

I parked and drew a breath, then got out of the car and hurried toward the big main doors of the courthouse. It was now or never and I'd done my best this morning to steel myself—clothing and weather included—for what was to come today.

My biggest concern was that my new hatred for Carter would bubble over into my deposition and I wouldn't sound like the victim, but an attacker who hated him and wanted him gone—for good. I knew that it was important for me to sound like I'd had no way out of the attack, that he'd been the pursuer and had done everything in his power to control me, to rape me, to make me pay. All of that was true.

If the defense could twist my attitude to suit them, I knew they'd stop at nothing to get Carter off. He'd walked before and they'd see to it that he continued to get off.

I hated him so much.

That anger fueled me up the steps and into the courthouse. Vi, Daphne, and Annika waited for me outside the room, surrounding me in a hug. "Have you all met?"

They nodded. "We got here a bit ago and made introductions."

"Sorry I'm late." It was only a few minutes before the deposition was supposed to start, but my intent had been to get here early enough that I could take a couple of breaths to compose myself.

"You're fine, dear." Annika took my arm and led me through the doors into the small meeting room, letting me walk deeper into the room without them as they took seats toward the back. I'd had to request special permission to have them here, but Daphne's attorney had said that it wouldn't be a problem; most people testifying on topics like this needed people with them and the judge hadn't had any issue with my request.

"Ashley." A slender dark-haired woman moved toward me, hands outstretched in greeting. "I'm Margaret. Thank you for coming."

We made small talk until the judge called the proceedings to order and gave us instructions on how today was going to go. I remembered most of it from last time and was ready to get this behind me even though that meant I was that much closer to a public trial.

I threw my shoulders back and drew a deep breath. Margaret set her hand in the middle of my back, covering the space between my shoulder blades. "Don't worry. I've got you."

Emotion rushed through me, tears gathering in my eyes. I wasn't sure if it was the protective position of her hand or the words or that I'd simply felt like no one had had me in far too long—maybe all of the above. I blinked the tears away and gave her a watery smile, which she returned, and we took our seats, me at the head of the table, beside the court reporter, Margaret to my left.

We began with the basics—name, age, occupation. We moved through how long it had been and why I'd never pressed charges. As I was explaining my reasoning and what it had been like at such a young age, Margaret's assistant rushed in. "You have a call."

The judge banged his gavel. "We're in the middle of a proceeding."

"It's urgent, Sir. I'm sorry." She looked at Margaret with pleading eyes. "It's the defense; he said it was urgent."

Fury contorted her features. Clearly she didn't appreciate the interruption or being made to look like her help was incompetent. I flashed through what I would have done to Tiffanie in the same situation and there wouldn't have been much left of her.

Margaret turned slowly toward the judge. "Five minute recess, Your Honor?"

He huffed and gave a curt nod. Margaret patted me on the arm as she stood. "Sit tight. This will only take a second while I castrate him for this bullshit tactic. They knew I was meeting with you today." She marched from the room, and as the door closed I saw her lean into her assistant and say something under her breath, probably the same disapproval I'd have given Tiffanie.

Minutes ticked by. I swiveled in my seat to check on my support crew in the back. Annika was on her phone, probably dealing with a crisis, Daphne and Vi were engaged in a quiet conversation. I turned my chair back toward the judge, rifling through papers on his desk, possibly ones pertaining to the case but they could have been any of the other dozen he probably still had to deal with today. I checked the clock, five minutes already.

With a frown I checked the door.

As I was spinning back around to rest my arms on the table, the door eased open and Margaret walked back in, her face a sickly shade of pale.

The judge looked up, then started and half-stood. "Margaret, are you all right?"

Daphne rose and the rest of us looked on, confused.

Margaret came to stand beside me and looked at me for a long moment. "He's dead."

I blinked. What was she talking about? Who? The defense attorney?

"Margaret," the judge said. "What's going on?" He turned sharply toward the court reporter. "This is all off the record."

She nodded and turned a switch, presumably turning off the recording that went with her notes.

Margaret put her hand on my shoulder, then turned to the judge. "Your Honor, it's my understanding that Carter Ridley is dead."

I blinked. The room swam.

Daphne stood. "What? What are you talking about, Margaret. Is this true?" Annika put a hand on her arm to keep her from walking forward. Vi stood and came over to my side, knowing I'd need extra support. She was right. I didn't know what to do, couldn't process the information. How could this be?

"What happened—"

The judge smacked his gavel hard against his desk. "This proceeding is called to a halt for today. I'll get with the defense attorney and discuss the next steps. If this is indeed true, we'll need to call a mistrial as he's clearly unable to stand trial."

I stood. My legs trembled and could barely hold me. I leaned against the table for support. This wasn't happening. "I don't..." I looked to Margaret for direction. What was the protocol for something like this?

"Go home." She gave me a short hug. "I'll get this sorted out and call you."

I stood and looked at the faces of my support system. Annika was taking it all in stride, unaffected by the specifics of this case, especially when she was so inundated by so many others on a daily basis. I was glad she'd been here for me, though. I was grateful that they'd all come.

"Thank you." I moved toward Annika and Daphne, wanting to hug them before they left. I was assuming that Vi and I would go get a drink or an early lunch. We needed to talk. We said our goodbyes, and as the women were leaving, Daphne asked Margaret how he'd died.

"He was struck by a car this morning walking across the street. A car hit him. He died instantly."

I gasped and lifted my hand to my mouth. Everyone made comments, and when I turned to ask Vi if she was ready to go, she was studying me with a wary gaze. "A car? When?"

Margaret was putting things into her briefcase and half-listening to Vi while addressing her assistant. She straightened and slid the briefcase strap over her shoulder. "Right before the deposition, I guess."

I didn't glance at Vi. I knew the story brewing in her head and I wasn't going to discuss it here. It bothered me that she thought I was capable of running Carter down.

Daphne grinned and hugged Annika and then me. "I'm finally free. Free." She smiled broadly and twirled once. "I know I shouldn't be happy about his death, but he killed a part of me, a part I never thought I'd get back. And now—now that he's gone—

I'm my own person. I can finally be free. He's never going to walk around a corner, never going to set foot outside a jail to attack some other innocent woman who falls for his bullshit." She grabbed me. "Ashley this is wonderful! Don't you see?"

I nodded, not feeling at all like she did. I understood, of course. I'd thought that if he was just gone it truly would be better.

And she was right; there was no way he'd hurt anyone ever again.

But I wasn't sure the outcome made me feel like I'd thought it would.

The room emptied and I went to stand beside Vi. "Do you want to grab a mimosa and brunch?"

She stared at me, looked around the room, then leaned close. "Did you have anything to do with his death, Ashley?"

CONTROL ME, BOOK 5

60

Odin

I closed the door to Mother's house quietly and followed Alice through the living room. We hadn't bothered to call before coming over. She was our mother, after all.

After getting Alice to understand that I wanted the best for our mom, that I'd seen things that she hadn't, and that I, too, wanted our mother to have something amazing and wonderful and perhaps not our father who'd abandoned all of us, we'd parted ways, promising to reconvene at Mother's house the next day. We all needed space to figure this out alone before we could move forward together.

That was true for Ashley, too, I realized, who I still hadn't contacted since she walked out on me yesterday.

"We simply cannot let him back in our lives," I'd told Alice on the way over after I picked her up. "We've made a life for ourselves without him and he doesn't deserve to be a part of it. Mom worked her ass off to give us what we have. You and I both got her amazing work ethic. We made it, not with anything from him."

"I know," she'd agreed. "He made the choice to leave when you and Mom needed him."

"And you." I looked at her as I drove, the conversation ended, both of us lost in our thoughts about what it would have been like to have had a father growing up. I'd at least had one for a little while, but not Alice. She'd only ever had our mother—our changed mother, not the one I'd had when I'd lived in the fairytale of our perfect family.

Alice and I were now on the same page about our father having lost his rights to our family. He had to live with the consequences.

"Mom?" Alice poked her head down the hallway as Mother came out of the back bedroom. "Hello! You brought Odin with you? Come, sit, I'll cook for you."

"No, Mama. I'm fine. I ate a late lunch."

She drew us into the kitchen, pulling dozens of dishes out of the fridge and reheating them. Alice and I pulled up chairs at the table and waited, knowing there was no use in resisting. "Did you talk to your brother, Alice?"

"We talked, Mama." I scooped a heaping of vegetables and meatballs onto my plate and remained silent. "We talked."

She turned, a large smile on her face. For a second, she looked ten years younger, youthful, and vibrant. For a second, I nearly rescinded my decision to let our father back into our lives if the mere thought of him was enough to make her beam like this. The possibility of him being in her life for good could transform her.

But only if he was as good as we all remembered from the good times.

I wasn't so sure.

The danger was that he'd destroy the bits of her that were left.

A danger I wasn't willing to risk.

"I think we owe him a chance to try." There was a hopefulness in her voice that I couldn't ignore.

"I'm not sure." I finally spoke.

"Alice, I thought you talked to him."

"I did. We did talk." Alice wouldn't meet my gaze. And that was fine; Mother had sent her with a mission and she'd clearly failed to accomplish it. I'd been the one to turn her over to my thought process. I would tell our father that he'd missed his shot and was no longer welcome. But I understood how telling our mother that might be difficult.

"Mother." I stood and walked over to the counter where she stood. "I don't want you getting hurt. None of us have really talked to him. Who knows what his intentions are?"

She frowned and moved away from me. "It's not that simple, Odin. You and Alice were kids; you don't remember all the things that happened before he left. You don't know the details."

"It doesn't matter. I know what you've been like for all the years that he's been gone. He broke you. He walked out on us. All of us."

"And now he's back. Forgiveness is a virtue, Odin. I taught you better than this. I taught both of you to forgive no matter what's been done to you. Most especially when it comes to family."

"He's not my family!" I clenched my fists, unsure where the words had come from. Never in all my life had I yelled at my mother, never even raised my voice, never disobeyed her. And here I was, doing all three. Never mind that I was a grown man; she was still my mother and a woman to be respected.

Alice gasped and sat back heavily in her chair, dumbfounded at what I'd just done.

Mother stepped up and poked me in the chest. "Unacceptable Odin. You have gone too far!"

"I'm sorry." I bristled at her tone and the tip of her sharp finger, not that I didn't deserve it, but it was still challenging to accept that she didn't want to see my side—our side. I didn't want her headed toward heartbreak, I didn't want her going around us either. I wanted us talking about this.

"You don't get to decide, Odin. You don't know." Her voice

shook and I wanted to hug her, but she was a little porcupine, ready to stick me with a thousand needles.

I couldn't stay. So many emotions were raging inside me, turning me inside out. I knew I didn't have a right to make this decision, and yet, I was the man of the house. I'd filled that position quite well, keeping them both safe. We'd grown up just fine.

I walked away, stopping at the door to the kitchen and leaning against the wall, touching one of the photos of the three of us that she had hanging on the wall. "I only wanted what was best."

"As did I! Don't you see, Odin, that's all I ever wanted for the two of you. I hung on far longer than I should have. I made your father stay months longer than he wanted. He wanted to go before Alice was born, but I begged, I pleaded for him to stay. And then he couldn't take it anymore and he did what he'd wanted from the beginning."

"So why let him back in?"

"Because forgiveness. Forgiveness wins every time. A lot of years have passed since he left. A lot of time and regrets and mistakes. All of those thoughts that we've had about him? Maybe he had them about us, too. Maybe he wants to fix it. Don't we owe it to him to give it a try?"

"I don't think so." I said it quietly, but I meant the words, meant the sentiment. I didn't want him hurting any of us.

Maybe me most of all.

"I've hated him for a long time."

She walked over to me and put her small hands on my chest. "I know, Odin. You think I didn't hear you crying in your room all those nights? You think I didn't call your father and plead with him to come back for you?"

My heart constricted at the admission. Had she really?

"Yes," she answered the unasked. "I did. I stood at your door all those nights, listening to you, wanting to comfort you but also understanding who you were becoming as a young man; not wanting a mother's pampering anymore. I hated that your father had left you at such a vulnerable age. And yet, he'd tried far earlier, when it would have been so much easier for you to adjust. You would have been littler. Alice would have had zero memory of him, even less than she does now. You wouldn't have taken it so hard, wouldn't have blamed yourself so much. But I couldn't undo what had been done. It was as it was. He was gone."

"And now he's back." The words came out harsher than I'd intended. My voice was rough with the emotion she'd drawn out with the story. I didn't know she'd heard me all those nights. I knew that she cried herself to sleep, for I'd stood outside her door, listening, wanting to be able to say something.

And neither of us had, both believing that the other was so much stronger than they'd let on, neither one needing the other, both wanting to be tough for Alice.

But that didn't change anything. He'd left. Left us alone, left us to fend for ourselves. And we had, dammit. We'd made it, we'd survived. And now look at us.

"I just don't think I can forgive him for walking out on all of us."

"Forgiveness is the greatest virtue, Odin. Nothing else will come of your life if you let this poison you."

"It's been this way for years, why not let it be as it is?"

"I already told you, it's not your decision."

"I can't stay and watch him hurt you."

"So you're walking out, too?"

I shook my head. "That's uncalled for."

"I forgive you." Her voice was slight but steely.

I touched Alice on the shoulder on my way out. We'd figure this out, but I couldn't do it right now, couldn't talk this through. My head was a mess. We'd come to the perfect solution and I didn't want Mom twisting it so that we'd all have hope again. Hope was dangerous. What we had, worked.

I got in my car and sat there for a long time, unable to drive away, but unable to get up and walk back in the house. I drummed my fingers on the steering wheel and thought about what Mother had said, about how that made me feel. Would it have made a difference if she'd have come in on those nights and rubbed my back, told me it was going to be okay, promised me that she'd try to call him?

And was I making another wrong decision now? Should I be supportive, giving her the latitude to do what she needed, what she thought was best?

I sighed and started the car. I wasn't sure where I wanted to go, just that I needed to be in motion for a bit, driving my way through the problem. I considered calling Ashley, but thought better of it. I knew she wasn't through with me and would reach out when she was ready.

At least, I hoped she would.

My phone rang and my heart leapt, thinking it could be the one person who could make me forget about the problem I was facing. I frowned, the car not picking up the number and telling me who in my contacts was calling. It wasn't Ashley.

I wasn't sure that I wanted to conduct business right now, but it would be a distraction.

"Hello?"

There was a long pause on the end of the line and I strained to hear if the caller had hung up. "Hello?"

"Son? Odin? Is that you? It's…it's your dad."

61

Ashley

Vi's question reverberated through the room though she'd merely whispered it, asking if I was responsible for Carter's death.

How could she? What had happened to our relationship? How had we gone from having such a close friendship to her thinking I'd murdered a man?

I measured my breaths and my words; my voice still shook. "Really? After our conversation last night?"

"That was before he showed up dead!"

"He wasn't dead when you involved Odin!" My hands fisted at my sides. "You had no business bringing your fears to his attention. They were unfounded then, they're unfounded now. I cannot believe that you think I would give up my freedom to eliminate Carter. There's no way to get away with something like that without spending the rest of my life in prison."

"You've already given up your freedom to him, how would this be any different? You're in a prison of your own making. Every time I think you're past this, you backslide into that girl who couldn't think for herself, who was terrified of everything, who didn't think through consequences, who OD-ed on the weekends without caring about who she hurt or who had to take care of her. Yes, that's exactly what I think you'd do: take him out given the chance and never think about it again. When it comes to Carter, you don't have any sense. You fly off and do things that are dangerous—like going to his goddamn apartment! That was so stupid. But I supported you, because you needed it. And goddamn it if I need to call your boyfriend because I'm worried, then I'll fucking do it. If that keeps you from doing something stupid, then I'd do it again in a heartbeat. You can't blame me for wanting to keep you safe. That's the kind of friend I am, take it or leave it."

"You're as bad as Odin; accusing me of being capable of something like that. I can't believe you think I'm so awful."

"Not awful, just careless." She looked away, then back. "You get so consumed with the righteousness of your desires that you don't think about the possible consequences. If you didn't do it, then I'm sorry. I'm sorry for ever thinking you could do something like that, I just know how passionate you are, how badly you want to be past this, and I really thought that you'd do whatever it took, that you'd finally reached your breaking point, that it didn't matter what happened to you as long as he couldn't hurt anyone anymore."

She threw her hands up and took a deep breath. "And I wouldn't have blamed you. He fucked up a huge part of your life. So much that you didn't even want to be you anymore. I don't have any idea what that's like. I mean, sure I've had some rough bits, but I've always known they were a part of who I was, part of the machine that guides the shape of me. I've never had anything so awful that I wanted to be a whole new person. And I feel like I've done a pretty shitty job of being a friend for not understanding that better than I did. When I thought you could kill Carter, it fucked me up really bad, because I thought I could have prevented it if I'd have just tried to be a better friend and less consumed with myself."

She shrugged and looked genuine. Apologies weren't Vi's thing, and I understood that what I'd just gotten was as close as she was going to come to giving me anything like a normal one. But that was one of the things I'd always admired about her, one of the ways I'd shaped Ms. M, actually—she didn't bend for anyone. She stated how she felt and you could love it or fuck off. I'd just never been on the receiving end before.

"You were probably right in thinking that, really. I've been in a dark place for a long time and, truthfully, I have thought how wonderful it would be for him to just disappear, awful as that sounds." I lowered my voice and looked around the courtroom, now empty, our voices echoing softly off the high ceiling. "I keep thinking that he's going to lose his hold over me, but he's like a virus, some awful, deadly, debilitating disease, one that's completely taken over my body."

"I know," she said softly, taking a step closer. "I've watched it happen. I was there in the beginning, Ashley, I was the one who thought this whole Ms. M thing was a terrible fucking idea. But you wouldn't listen to me. You had Trent telling you all the things you wanted to hear. So I let you run with this thing, knowing at some point your past was going to do exactly what it fucking did and run over the top of you." She grimaced. "That might have been a bad choice of words, but stick with me here—you simply can't outrun your past, Ashley, much as you thought you had, much as you created a woman who is exceptional in every way, I'll admit, but now we're here, with me thinking you offed a guy."

I had a feeling we were going to keep talking in circles, with her thinking that I'd done it, but coming around to the possibility that I was telling the truth. I wasn't sure how else to convince her.

I took a shaky breath, wanting to figure out how to get us past this with our relationship still intact. I loved Vi, loved her so much, and didn't want anything to come between us, most especially Carter.

Carter's death had given me what I'd wanted from the very beginning, what I'd longed for when Trent and I had gotten drunk one night and I'd said I wished I could just kill Ashley and become someone else. To which he'd asked why I couldn't. Ms. M was born.

No one would ever control the way I felt or the status of my relationships. Vi had every right to be concerned, and I appreciated her worries, misguided as they might be.

But that was neither here nor there. She was Vi and I loved her. Carter would not take anything else from me ever again, most certainly not the woman I considered my sister.

With every minute that passed since hearing the news, more chains and baggage from the past fell off me. I smiled and put my hands on her shoulders, stepping close. "While I'd like to think that I could have gunned the gas had he been standing in the middle of the road, I'm just not quite that much Ms. M. Somehow, some way, I'm still Ashley."

Tears gathered in her eyes in a most uncharacteristic display of emotion from Vi. "Maybe now she can learn to live again."

"Maybe." We hugged but there was still some tension between us. This wasn't a complete reconciliation and I probably needed some time to really ponder what she'd said and why she'd thought it. She probably needed to think about what I'd said about not killing Carter—but that the thought had been there.

To break the silence before it grew more awkward, she asked how things were with Odin while we gathered our bags.

"I'm not speaking to him currently."

"Hmm. Wondered why he wasn't here."

I didn't respond to that, sighing. "It's a big mess."

She nodded and we walked out, agreeing to meet up again soon. She gave me another hug and I kissed her cheek, thinking maybe it was time to go find Odin and make things right with him.

He'd only been doing what Vi had—protecting me from myself.

62

Odin

My father's voice reverberated through the entire car like a gunshot. Much as I'd tried to ready myself for this moment, the sound of his voice disturbed me. I didn't have anything to say to him and words failed me.

The thought of hanging up crossed my mind. I knew Mother was obviously ready for us to return to being a family, but Alice and I were going to need some time. I drew a deep breath and was about to tell my father exactly that.

"I'm sorry for calling like this, unannounced and without your permission. I just, well, I've been trying Alice and she's letting my calls go to voicemail. I just wanted to try you and see if it went to voicemail, and then I was going to leave you a message with all of this, but if you don't mind, I'll just let you know why I was calling. First, let me put one huge thing to rest: If it's a concern, I don't want anything from either you or your sister, other than to get to know you. I've been out of your entire life and I realize that was my choice. I just...I'd like to do what I can to remedy that and catch up on your life. I'd like for you to get to know me, too." Silence stretched for a moment while I searched for words. "I was wrong, Odin. I made a mistake. I'm asking for a chance to try and remedy all the years I've missed. If you don't want to, I'll walk away. I'll stop calling both of you and I'll try to resolve myself of this grievance that you're unwilling to forgive me for. Luckily, if that's your choice, I don't have long."

What the fuck did that mean, he didn't have long? Was he pulling a game on me, trying to guilt me?

"Sorry, that came out wrong; I'm not dying or anything. I just took a job assignment that's sending me overseas. I turned down the advancement that would have kept me over here, where I could see you both on a regular basis, I mean, if you'd even be open to that. Like I tried to say earlier before I botched it, I'll be gone before long and I really wanted to see my kids before I go. After I leave, I'm not sure there will be much reason for me to come back very often and I'll be making my home over there until I retire, so this really is kind of the last chance I felt I had—"

"Fine. Yes."

There was a long pause. "Yes? Really?" He paused a second time, and when he started again his throat was thick and clogged. "Thank you, Odin. I don't expect this was easy for you, don't have any expectations of what it will look like when we get together, but thanks for allowing me this chance."

"I'll call you in a bit, after I've had some time to digest this. We'll arrange a meeting."

"Yes, fine. Thanks again. Talk soon." He hung up, probably before I could back out.

What in the fuck had I been thinking, agreeing to that? Some of Mother's words still floated around in my mind, enough apparently to make me consider allowing my father to come back into my life.

Which wasn't what I'd agreed to, I told myself, forcing my pounding heart to simmer down. I'd merely agreed to think about meeting with him and, at worst, I had to endure such a thing one time.

But that also meant that I'd just opened the door to him meeting Alice and Mother. After I'd so vehemently told them both that I didn't feel good about that.

I groaned and pulled into the exit lane, taking the turn to get me back to the house where I could explain to both of them what I'd just done.

I doubted they'd begrudge me, especially after I told them that he was leaving the country. For all we knew, this was going to be a one-time thing, closure for all of us.

Hopefully.

And not a reopening of old wounds.

I couldn't have exactly said no to him. Neither of them would forgive me if they found out that he'd told me that he was leaving the country for a possible indefinite amount of years and I'd told him to go fuck himself.

Truthfully, the more I'd thought about it, the more I wanted to hear what he had to say, wanted to hear what had been going through his mind when he'd walked out on us, if he'd been purely selfish or if he'd cared at all about the damage he'd leave behind on his kids' little hearts—or his wife's.

Though I wasn't sure there was anything he could say that could really explain his actions.

I slowed through the neighborhood, not quite ready to barge in and tell the girls what I'd done until I could explain it with some confidence. I'd negotiated multi-million dollar deals, had gone toe-to-toe with some of the toughest bargainers in the industry, had smooth-talked my way into meetings I'd had no business being in. But when it came to being tough on the man who'd walked out of my life when I'd been just a boy, I'd been reduced to that shaken little guy whose world was turned upside-down one Tuesday morning when I'd gone into the kitchen as my father had been walking out.

I'd called after him and he'd looked back, but hadn't stopped like he usually did in the mornings, coming back in the house with a smile and a hug. No, on that day he'd not given so much as a wave, briefcase in one hand, suitcase in the other. I'd assumed he'd been going on a business trip and had forgotten to tell me, but why then wouldn't he have come back for a hug or two?

That had been my last memory of him, for decades.

Not that I'd thought about him much, barely thinking of him at all after the first couple years, actually. But in that first year I'd replayed that morning every night when I'd gone to bed, trying to figure out what I'd said to him that had made him leave.

I'd never told my mother, and Alice had been too little. Even when she'd gotten older, we'd rarely talked about him, Mother and I choosing to simply accept that we'd done something to push him away and that he was never coming back. By the time I'd become a teen, my father had been a shadow of a memory, someone who'd seemed to exist only in the barest of thoughts, more of a ghost walking through pictures and memories than someone who'd not only been real, but my hero in those early years. He'd been unable to do anything wrong in my eyes and I'd always hoped to have the chance to make up for whatever mistake had pushed him away.

Though I rarely admitted it—even to myself—he was the reason I'd driven myself so hard, hoping that one day when he walked back through our lives, I'd be able to prove that he'd been wrong to give up on us and walk away, that I'd been a son worth loving, a son worth sticking around for.

But I'd never gotten that chance. Even after all the scholarships and good grades, the exemplary letters and recommendations to get into the top colleges that he'd always wanted for me, the job offers that had come piling in and the money that had followed, none of it had been enough to bring him back around. And somewhere in there I'd forgotten who I'd been doing it for and I'd begun to ride the wave of my success simply for the pleasure of it.

Somewhere I'd stopped doing it to prove myself to him, but rather to myself, to prove that I could do anything I believed in and that no one's approval mattered.

Until I'd heard his voice.

Then all that baggage that I'd stuffed away so tightly into that teeny dark space had come rushing up to the point that it had robbed me of the ability to speak. All the speeches that I'd shouted and cursed and memorized in my room had failed me, all the questions, the beseeching needs, the hurt had rocketed up from the depths and paralyzed my tongue. I'd simply been able to listen as he'd spelled out whatever he'd wanted with barely any comment from me.

I pulled over a half block from Mother's house and pondered not only what I'd done but how I was going to explain it. How would they react? When would they want to meet with him? Were we all going together or would we do it separately? I wasn't sure I could be there when my parents saw each other again, wasn't sure I could endure the hope that would light up Mother's eyes and put a spring in her step. Alice would be the same, not having any memories of him but what she'd been able to dream up as she'd though about a man so wonderful and amazing as her little-girl mind had been able to conjure.

And what would I do when I saw him for the first time? When I overlaid the image of his older self with that one who'd walked out all that time ago? Would I find my voice? Would I say the things that had nearly burned through my esophagus when I'd spit them out in my room, night after night? Or would I listen like I had today, be rational and thoughtfully contemplative, open to hearing him out before jumping to conclusions?

No matter what happened, this was going to leave a mark on all of us.

There was only one person I could imagine having by my side as I embarked on this journey. And she was the one person who wasn't speaking to me.

63

Ashley

I let myself into the penthouse. I'd thought about calling but had decided to just show up and get on with it. I was fired up about everything, all the emotions creating a vile stew of a hot mess that I had no idea how I was going to sort out. Diving right in seemed like the best way to get on with it.

I found him in the kitchen, drink in hand. He lifted it in salute and took a drink. "Like one?"

"Please." I dropped my purse on the table and walked over to the couch, curling up on the end and expecting him to come over and join me. He did, sitting down with some space between our bodies, making no move to kiss me hello. We'd left on such disagreeable terms it made sense that he wasn't quite sure what to make of me.

He handed me the drink, I thanked him, and took a slow sip of the Manhattan, savoring the flavors. I sighed and leaned back into the cushions.

"I've missed you." He took a sip. "Though that's not quite accurate. I actually haven't been able to stop thinking about you since you left and I owe you an apology. I'm sorry for the way things went and I should have been much more understanding. I hope you'll forgive me." He finished his drink and stood, stepping closer until he towered over me. "I somewhat hope that's why you've come, to tell me that I was an ignorant ass and that, even knowing that point, you're still willing to forgive me and spend some time with me."

I swirled the alcohol in my glass and took a breath. "I'm not sure why I came, actually. My head is a complete mess right now. The day started with me going to the courthouse to testify against Carter." He lowered himself to the coffee table, one leg on either side of mine, his hands on my knees.

"I'm sorry I wasn't there. I wish you would have told me." I shook my head and continued, afraid that if I didn't get all this out it would end up poisoning me. "Moments after I sat down to testify, we got a call that Carter had been killed."

His fingers tightened on my knees and I could see the concern flash across his face, those fears that Vi had planted rearing their ugly heads. Nevertheless, I plunged on, telling him what had transpired in the room this morning, what Vi had asked, where we'd left things.

He let me talk, not interrupting even when it looked like he had questions. I finished my drink and he took it, setting it beside his on the coffee table at his hip, his fingers quickly returning to my legs, as if he had to hold on to me lest I rise to the ceiling like an untethered balloon—a thought that wasn't far off from how I felt. I drew a breath, opening space for him to speak.

"Admittedly, I'm a little shocked at the timing of Carter's death. I'm sure most everyone was. How are you handling it, knowing he's gone?"

I swallowed. "Like the heaviest weight in the world isn't holding me down anymore, threatening to drown me. I didn't even know it was there until it was gone, now I realize how amazing it is that I've managed to get anything done with it on me. Hearing that news felt like the ultimate release." I met his gaze and said the words that would condemn me forever if he believed any of what Vi had told him. "I feel so relieved, to be honest, horrible as that makes me sound, to be glad that someone's dead. That's a horrible reaction and I'm sure I'll eventually feel bad that he's dead. I'm sure there was some good in him somewhere, maybe somewhere later in his life when he could have rid himself of his own demons, but for right now, I'm just so damn happy that he's gone."

"I think it's perfectly normal to feel like that, ma chérie. I can think of many enemies that I'd like to be rid of; some I would probably relish their extinguishment. Do not be so hard on yourself." He rubbed my knees, moving higher up my thighs. Again, it was a comforting touch, not sensual. I liked that we were finding spaces like this to exist.

Even though it made us feel like we were in a relationship.

A feeling I was starting to think I wasn't going to be able to avoid where Odin was concerned.

I relaxed into it this time, feeling a freedom in that place that had come from Carter's death. How strange that something that only involved one area could impact so many parts of my life. The words began to flow, much as they did around him, and I took a deep breath, releasing it and relaxing into his touch.

"It didn't help that I almost lost my relationship with you and with Vi. I'm still so mad that she told you those things, those untrue things about what she thought I was capable of doing." I gave him a hard stare, a little of my fire returning. "I didn't kill him."

He nodded and I felt—unlike what I'd felt with Vi—that he really did truly believe me. "I know, ma chérie. My worry was never that you'd injure him, but that you would endanger yourself —either knowingly or unknowingly."

I gave him a small smile. "I'm sorry that I was so upset about you thinking that. This," I waved a hand through the air between us, "is so new to me and I'm not sure I know how to interact with someone caring about what I do or what I think."

"I'm not sure I want you changing how you do either, certainly not to please me or to avoid an argument. Much better to say what you think and stay true to yourself than capitulate because you'd prefer not to have an honest conversation with me."

And just like that, I found myself in a relationship for the first time in my life.

I blinked and lifted one of his hands to my cheek, flattening his palm against my face. We held each other's gaze as we pondered the move that I'd allowed. He smiled and swished his thumb across, then returned it to my knee, content to leave us where we were for a moment so I could continue purging not only the day's events but the ramifications.

"The entire process was terrifying."

"Why?" His question was soft, understanding that I wasn't talking about simply the act of being around Carter, but something much bigger.

"It put everything at risk. I managed to stay out of the spotlight the last time I testified against him. But this was so different. This was me going public; this was me showing my face to the world and voicing what he'd done to me. And I don't exactly run a business that needs much public attention. I could have destroyed everything that I've built. This trial could have been the end of me, of Ms. M, of my entire existence. My business isn't exactly looked on in a good light in most circles."

He pursed his lips but didn't say anything, leaving the probable comment about Ashley and Ms. M silent for the moment.

I left unsaid the implications that had arisen with Carter's arrival at one of my recent auctions. Vann paid big time for that breach of contract. He would never set foot inside one of my auctions again, and he forked over a steep fine. That was when Carter came barreling back into my life and set this whole circus in motion.

And now it was over.

It was strange, this freedom that seemed to pervade my entire soul. I wanted to open myself to it, lean into it. I felt like I could fly, literally. People had made that stupid statement over the course of my life and I'd always mocked it. Clearly, it had been such a ludicrous thought that the chains around my ankles wouldn't allow me to entertain.

Now, I understood it completely, wanting to experience it to the fullest. I shook my head, amazed at what I'd truly been able to step into, fears and all.

"And yet you testified anyway, knowing all that?"

I sucked air deep into my lungs, feeling parts of me opening like they hadn't had oxygen for decades, and perhaps they hadn't. "I had to. It was time, and after talking to Annika and Daphne, it seemed like going public was how they'd both managed to put this whole thing truly and forever behind them. Losing everything in my business—my outward life—didn't seem like such a big deal compared to the possibility of losing Carter's hold on me." I shook my head. "And now that he's gone—really truly gone and not just locked away for a little bit of time in jail, but truly gone—now I really know just how much I've lost over the years." I looked up, looked into his eyes, and trusted him. "I lost a whole person, Odin. I lost—" My throat closed and tears rushed to my eyes. "I lost Ashley."

He moved to the couch, pulling me onto his lap. "No, ma chérie. That's what I've been trying to tell you. She's always been with you. She's just been waiting for you to have the courage to let her take on this life that you've created for her. She's never left you." He pressed a kiss to my temple. "You are still Ashley. You have always been. She is you."

His breath was hot against my ear and I let the tears fall, let them track down my cheeks. He didn't rub them away, just let them fall, didn't wipe them like they didn't belong. They fell onto our clasped hands where he held me and continued to talk, telling me over and over that I'd not done what I'd always thought and gotten rid of that silly girl who'd made no mistake at all, but who'd been taken advantage of by a horrible human being who'd done it to several women—smart women, women like who I'd built Ms. M into. None of this had been Ashley's—*my*—fault. This had been Carter's fault. Always Carter's fault.

And it was only now, through his death, that I could really see that. Once and for all.

Odin held me, cradling me and rocking gently back and forth on the couch, stroking my back, my hair, my arms, comforting me as I needed it. Like I'd never allowed anyone to do before.

When his lips found mine, I didn't resist.

64

Ashley

Nor did I resist when he lifted me from the couch and carried me toward the bedroom.

Nor when he paused at the dresser, setting me atop it and pulling open the top drawer to reveal a delightful display of handcuffs, whips, and blindfolds. I smiled and kissed him, my hands cradling his face. "What do you have in mind tonight, Odin?"

He grinned and pulled one of each collection from the drawer, sliding it silently closed. "I suppose you'll have to wait and see."

"Who will be wearing them tonight?"

He laughed. "Oh, you, to be certain."

I raised an eyebrow, perched as I was on the dresser, my toes dangling above the soft carpet. He lifted one leg, flipping off my shoe and tossing it over his shoulder, repeating the process with the other. "You are so sexy, Ashley."

I smiled, letting the word settle into my heart. "Thank you," I whispered.

He leaned in for a kiss, dipping at the last moment to lick the side of my neck. I let my head fall back, let him taste me at his leisure, in no hurry for the night to get on to anything else.

Tonight felt almost virginal, like my first time experiencing sex as Ashley.

At the thought, tears sprang to my eyes. Odin lifted his head and cradled my face. "Tell me." His words were a whispered caress across my skin.

The words tumbled out and he watched me, intently holding both my gaze and my body. "How do you want your first night, Ashley? Tell me what you want."

I shook my head. "No, Odin. You tell me. Take me. I'm yours tonight. You lead me wherever you want to take me. If this is truly my first night, then I want to experience all of it as you would take a virgin." It was his turn to show the emotion welling to the surface as the reality of what I was giving crashed over him.

What an interesting gift Carter had given me in the end; he'd given me back the one thing he'd taken, the only thing he could have given me. And while I wasn't exactly thankful, I could be grateful in that moment that I had Odin to give my "virginity" to.

His touch turned tender and he lifted me off the dresser, carrying me over to the bed and laying me down softly. His fingers played at the edges of my clothing, grazing the tiniest bit of skin before slipping beneath to explore further.

As my clothes came off, his kisses deepened and grew longer, expanding the space between the moments of my becoming fully naked. Then he took his time exploring my body, his lips and tongue wandering slowly and deliberately across me, watching my reactions and gauging his movements off them, not asking me if I liked anything, just exploring different ways to touch and caress me until my breath hitched and he found the ways that I'd always enjoyed him before now—except that there hadn't been a before now. This was his first time making love—

My breath caught.

The air pressed out of my lungs.

I focused on his kisses, forcing my brain to quiet for a moment as I avoided any semblance of truth in that thought.

His tongue stroked the bottom edge of my ribs, traveling higher until he took my nipple in his mouth. He suckled it, then paused and lifted his head, tipping it a bit to the side as if he'd heard my thoughts. He watched me, waiting for a reaction out of me. "Ashley?"

My smile took a few seconds to warm, then it broke the surface and bubbled out in laughter.

He bent his head again and took my other nipple. "I'm glad you're enjoying yourself, dear."

"Thank you for knowing what I needed."

He shrugged and moved between my legs, then let his head travel lower. "We're not even to that part yet."

I sighed and waited for his tongue to slide inside me, but he kept moving away, trailing his fingers down my legs, past my toes until he was no longer touching me. I lifted my head and watched him walk back to the dresser and gather the items he'd removed from the drawer off the top.

He set them on the bed at my hip and began unbuttoning his shirt, slowly disrobing as I watched. I sat up and reached for him but he brushed my hands away. "Not yet, Ashley. I'll let you know when you can touch me."

I smiled and lowered back to the mattress, content to watch. He was a beautiful man. The soft lighting of the room accentuated the planes and curves of his body, making his muscles stand out.

His shirt slid to the floor and then his pants followed. The hard curve of his cock stood out against the tight boxer briefs and my mouth watered at the sight. I wanted to roll forward onto my knees and take him in my mouth.

But I also wanted to let him lead. This was becoming very enjoyable—freeing. Every time before—and with every partner—I always stayed several steps ahead of the action, sure of what I wanted, what I needed, how best to please the person I was with, and how to get the most pleasure from them.

Tonight was different. Tonight was about nothing more than this very moment.

Perhaps that had come from Carter, too; a knowing that there is only this moment and this moment is the only one when we're truly alive. By thinking too far into the experience, I robbed this moment of its joy and pleasure. By setting expectations of what was to happen next, I robbed the next moment of its surprise.

Another smile played at the corner of my lips as I allowed the next moments to wash over me.

Odin eased me toward the head of the bed, not yet restraining my wrists to the hooks that had held me tight the last time, only cinching the handcuffs down until they were firm, but not too tight, around my bones. Still, he didn't hook the cuff to the bed, trailing his fingers down my body as he moved to the other side of the bed where he repeated the process with my other hand.

The blindfold came next, but he didn't slide it on from the position where he'd stood to handle the handcuffs. He knelt on the bed, easing forward, my eyes trading between the huge bulge in his remaining piece of clothing and the satin between his fingers.

I licked my lips and watched him, eagerly soaking every possible ounce of life from this moment. The satin kissed my body, sliding over my skin as he moved it higher, between the valley of my breasts, across the beating pulse on my throat, across my lips, over my eyes, through my hair, dropping it at the crown of my head.

His hard thigh brushed my shoulder and he picked up my far arm, scooting it a little away from my body and creating a space. A space he then filled with his knee so he straddled my body, his ass hovering a few inches above my breasts, less as I sucked in air, his cock straining against the fabric within licking distance of my mouth. I bit my lip and he watched me.

I knew full-well the punishment that came from doing things before they were allowed. Punishment was one of my favorite forms of play and I'd often wielded it on my own lovers when they'd been too eager to move to the next thing.

I breathed into the moment and felt my chest move higher, closer to Odin's firm ass.

His hips began to move, bringing his cock within a breath of my lips. I watched him watching me, wondering what he wanted me to do, if he preferred the punishment, or if he preferred my obedience. If he kept this up much longer, he'd get both.

His hands hung at his sides and I lifted my fingers to lace with them. He brought them to his stomach and flattened them just below his bellybutton. I stroked his skin, moving my hands upward and outward, smoothing them across the hard ridges of his body and back down, skimming the waistband, but not dipping lower.

His hips continued to move, side to side, back and forth, mesmerizing me. He pushed my hands lower and I cupped his cock, the chains dangling against my forearms, the only other sound in the room beyond our breath. I arched my back and pressed my tits up into his ass. He shoved his boxers down and set his cock free. I moaned, wanting to taste him, wanting him in my mouth so badly.

I licked my lips again and reached for his bare cock, but he caught my wrists, spreading them toward the bedposts, hooking my right and then the left. I turned my face so his cock caressed my cheek and he paused for just a moment to let me. Then he pulled away, watching me watch him. The blindfold came next and I was instantly robbed of the vision of him straddling me and about to fuck my mouth.

Dammit, Odin!

I knew better than to call out and invoke more punishment. I'd seen the ball gag in the back corner of the drawer and I did not want to forgo the taste of him.

His finger brushed against my lips, pressing my mouth open. I drew him in, craving any part of him inside me, any part that he'd give me. He ran the pad of his finger against my teeth, along the side of my tongue. I sucked him, swirled my tongue so hard and fast against his body that I could already feel the orgasm building inside me. I took his finger deep, tasting him at the back of my throat, wanting his cock there, fighting the urge to slip beyond this moment. He moved in and out of my mouth, as if training a virgin for the first time how to take a man all the way to his entirety.

I moaned, wanting more of him.

His body weight shifted and the warm hardness of his cock brushed against my chin. Then he pulled his finger out, trailing it across my lips. I opened, wanting it back, needing him.

His cock slid gently past my lips. I opened for him, felt the weight of his body against me, and he pushed deep. I took him, letting the thickness of him expand my throat. My tongue swirled against the underside. I strained against the handcuffs, wishing I could wrap my fingers around him and stroke at the same time, bringing him to orgasm like the one building in me. He was going to make me come simply by fucking my mouth.

He moaned and slowed down, withdrawing past my lips, then pushing in again. I fisted my hands, my nails cutting into my palms, the metal cutting into my wrists. This was the most frustrating and erotic thing I'd ever experienced. No one had bound me, no one had proven that they could be trusted with my body.

Let alone the rest of me as I'd give over to Odin.

"Ashley…" He moaned and I took him deep, wanting him to come in my mouth. But he didn't yet, stroking slower and slower, maintaining his control, winding us both up into an orgasm that would prove to be explosive.

His hands brushed against my skin, my face, my hair. He stroked me deep and fast and slow and shallow, changing the stroke as we both neared the edges of our orgasms. I wanted him. Wanted him more than any lover I'd experienced.

And yet, I felt like I'd never know sex beyond this moment.

He withdrew, trailing his cock down my body. I wanted to be able to watch him, to see the look on his face as he rubbed his cock against me, stroking against my breasts, touching my nipples with one hand and stroking himself with the other. I heard his quick intake of breath and then he rubbed against me again, trailing the hot head along my waist, across my hip, along the edge of my knee.

I'd never been touched like this before.

Robbed of my sight and touch, I was forced to see him through my skin, feel his position, see what he was doing in my mind. It was an overwhelming experience, especially coupled with what the day had brought before we'd come to his bed. My entire being was experiencing a complete overhaul, a transformation. It was like a rape all over again, but one that destroyed the evil, the dark, the bad, pushing into me with a fierce possessiveness that I wanted to give myself over to.

He moved between my legs, his lips trailing against my skin, touching the places where his cock had traveled, mapping me with his body, creating a maze in my mind that I could barely follow. Then his hands brushed my shoulders and he settled between my legs. I lifted one leg to curl it around his. He lifted it higher, bringing it up to his hips.

I waited, eager, wanting, needing, ready to experience this possession of him from my virginal state.

"Ashley…"

"Mmm." I was no longer capable of words. I wanted too much, too hard, too fast.

"I want to take you. I want to push myself inside you. I want you to wrap your pussy tight around me."

"Yes."

"Are you sure?" His voice trembled and a wave of emotion overtook me as I realized what he was asking.

He was asking permission to have sex with me, to take my virginity. Here, in this moment, with me bound, naked, and so completely wet and wanting him, he was still pausing to ask if he could enter me.

A tear slid from the corner of my eye and beneath the blindfold. I let it go, not trying to take it back. "Yes."

"Yes, what, Ashley?"

"Yes, I want you to make love to me, Odin. Please."

He entered me slowly and again I teetered between wishing for the ability to watch him and enjoying the blessing of being robbed of my vision, trusting only the feel of him as he entered me, reading my body, adjusting as I wanted, moving in the spaces that I craved. He lifted my other leg, wrapping them around him. Again, he moved fast, then slow, mixing up our loving as he anticipated my every need.

His thighs moved against mine, his chest rising and falling, brushing against me and then being stripped away as he lifted off me, changing our position only slightly as to drive deeper into me.

I was expanded in ways I'd never imagined possible.

My thoughts tumbled over each other, trying to make sense of what was happening to my body as he stroked me. His hand slid up my thigh, palm flat, pressing into the meat of me, coming to rest at my clit, stroking me in a slow, pleasuring circle that expanded my space into more shapes than I'd seen in my lifetime. I'd been touched by a lot of men in a lot of ways, but yet again, Odin was taking me places that even I, with all my experience and one-night stands, hadn't been. It was amazing, it was heady, it was intense.

I'd never been freer. I'd never had such an experience.

The orgasm built slowly, gathering from my toes and fingers, traveling up my limbs to converge at the center, but not in my pussy where they'd all originated. This continued to travel higher, leaving a smoking trail of heat as it went, consuming all the darkness, imbuing me with a heavy light that filled all the spaces, some that I hadn't known had existed before this experience.

A sob tore at my throat.

This was what I'd always wanted for all of the girls. This was what I'd wanted for each of them. This was why I went to all the trouble to put the auctions on. This was why I went to all the trouble to find the bidders that I did.

This was what I'd wanted for Audrey when I'd paired her with Odin.

This was what I'd lost.

What I'd known I'd never get back.

What Odin had found, brushed off, and given me back like a diamond buried beneath rubble. And it was more than anything I could have ever thought I'd deserve.

65

Odin

We lay curled in each other. I'd uncuffed her after that first orgasm, letting her ride me to the second. The connection between us had gone somewhere differently than times past, deepening as she'd allowed me into her space, trusting me more and more.

Not that I hadn't earned her trust, but still, to receive it had been a remarkable moment. And I knew what that meant, the giving of such a thing; for Ashley that was the ultimate commitment. She was mine, and as long as I didn't screw up again as I had in the beginning—and those few times since—her trust would be mine to keep and maintain.

My fingers trailed over her arm, her palm soft against my stomach. As we lay in stillness and quiet, the situation with my father returned to the forefront of my mind, try as I might to keep him from intruding on this moment. "Can I share something with you?"

She moved, shifting her face to look at me. "Of course."

"I've said little of my father, for good reason. We didn't have a relationship after he left when I was young. He's my catalyst, much as Carter was yours."

"I'm sorry."

I shook my head and continued to stroke her arm, reveling in the soft feel of her skin. "It's no matter. Like you, I used it to create something bigger and better than what I'd been. But he's returned."

She lifted up on an elbow and stared into me. "Are you okay?"

I touched her cheek and let her head return to my chest. "I'm not sure. My sister was the first one to tell me of his return, he'd called her and was trying to get to me and my mother. At first, I didn't want anything to do with him; after all, he'd made his choice when he walked out on us."

"And now?"

I sighed. "I'm struggling. He called me, a restricted number that I answered. I listened to what he had to say, much as I didn't want to. I guess he's leaving the country soon and wanted to settle things before he went. I don't understand why he's waiting until now to begin a relationship."

"Does it matter?"

"I suppose not. It's just that I have so much unresolved about him and the impact his leaving had on my life."

"Then why not talk to him?"

"I haven't stopped thinking about him. When I have sex with you is the only time my mind quiets about him, about my mother, about what it will mean for Alice now, having a father in her life for the first time. Already, even with you here against me, my mind is a tumble of thoughts and memories. He was my hero and then he walked away."

She was quiet for a moment, her hands stroking me from chest to hip. I liked the feel of her fingers against my skin. She was good for me. Clearly, the way she quieted my mind, the woman had a perfect effect on me. Which was why I wanted to talk to her about this.

"Did he tell you why he was contacting you now, where he's been?"

"Not where he's been. We didn't get into any of that. And all he said about why he was contacting me now was simply that he was running out of time."

She glanced up again, a worry creasing her brow. "Like he's dying?"

I shook my head. "No. At least not that he says, just that once he leaves the country he might not be coming back."

"That is curious, that he's waiting until right before he goes to make any attempt. Has your sister or your mother talked to him?"

"Not yet."

"So what's the next step?"

"I told him that we'd meet up at a later date."

"What are you waiting for? He's already left. There's nothing more he can do to impact your childhood. The damage is already done."

I chuckled softly. This, from the woman who'd spent her whole life reeling from damage inflicted years ago. "Yes, you're right of course. He's just a man, what can he possibly do to me now?"

She settled against me. "I'll support any decision you make." She paused, taking a long breath. "I mean, not that that matters. I just, it's, you were there for me, is all."

I palmed her head and held it against me, wanting to pause this moment and keep her safe, leave all the world outside here, away from us. "Thank you, ma chérie."

Again, I understood the depth of the gift. There were few people she would willingly back. We'd traversed a massive length of space, and while I'd been optimistic that she would eventually relent and allow me into her life, it was still a surprising turn. She was good and truly mine.

We would be good together; a power couple. I was still optimistic that she would allow me to wield some ideas in her own business. And perhaps, one day, we would discuss mine and she could give her perspective. I respected and admired everything about her.

"I suppose I should set a date to meet with him. Waiting serves me not at all."

"Trust me, waiting doesn't do you any favors. Get in there and manage all the emotion at once. Don't let it fester. You've already got plenty from when you were a child. Work through it now so you can be done with it."

"Solid advice. I sat up and pulled on a pair of jeans, walking bare-chested and bare-footed to the living room to retrieve my phone. I brought it back in the room and sat on the chair by the window, staring out over the skyline. My fingers selected his number after only a moment's hesitation. The phone rang once—if that—and he answered.

"Odin?"

"Hello."

"I didn't think I'd hear from you so soon."

"Yes. Well, I've been doing some thinking. I'd like to meet for lunch tomorrow if you're free."

"Yes. Yes, I am." He paused. "Will your mother be joining us? Or Alice?"

"Just me."

"Fantastic." He blew out a long breath. "I'm looking forward to seeing you."

"See you tomorrow." I hung up, feeling awkward about the transaction. I wasn't sure how I'd wanted it to go, but that had seemed weird and clinical.

Ashley sat on the bed, legs crossed, breasts bare, the sheet piled around her waist. She twisted her fingers in her lap, then stilled them when she saw me glance at them. "That was it?"

I shrugged and crawled back into bed beside her. "He agreed."

She smiled. "It will be fine."

I stared at my fingers, thinking about what Ashley had said

about not waiting. Wasn't that true for my mother and Alice as well? What good would come from making them wait any longer than tomorrow? I frowned as I thought through what could come of tomorrow if they went. And what if they didn't. And how little of either I could control.

I dialed Alice, smiling as she answered. I filled her in on what I'd done, asking if she could join us, holding my breath as I asked her to see if Mother could as well.

"We'll be there." Her voice was breathless and excited. I hung up.

"I'm not sure what I've done."

Ashley leaned forward, putting her hand on my knee. "You've done the best you could. No matter what happens, no matter what your father says to any of you, no matter how tomorrow starts or finishes, you did what you could and you've given this a shot. That's all."

I tugged her forward and rolled back, landing with her on top of me. "I'd like you to come."

She lifted up off of me, startled. "Serious?" She bit her lip

"I know you've yet to meet my mother and sister, but I need you there with me. You said you supported whatever decision I made."

"Yeah, but that didn't include me coming."

My face fell. "Will you really not attend?"

She shook her head. "No, I'll come."

"No you're not, or no you are?" A smile played at the corner of my lips. If she was being this unclear, it meant that she was definitely coming. If not, she'd have been adamant and decisive.

"No, I'm coming."

I hugged her and buried my face in her neck, rolling over and pinning her beneath me. I could get through anything with her by my side.

Even my father.

66

Ashley

I'd not expected Odin to ask me to meet his family. Family was such a strange and unfamiliar concept to me. My own had been estranged well before my trauma in college, and they'd wanted nothing to do with me after, worried that my rape would tarnish their standing in our small Baptist community back home. My younger sisters hadn't bothered to check on me from that day forward, and while I'd checked up on them from time to time, I'd never bothered to reach out. From what I could see on social media and the internet, they were content and happy in their little bubbles, married and popping out children left and right, keeping their domineering husbands happy, as well as our parents.

And yet, to Odin, family was something quite different, something to be cherished and shared. It was a strange concept, and under any other circumstances, with any other man, I'd have not hesitated in saying no.

Yet, this was Odin, a man who had me thinking so much of the rules and boundaries that I'd had my entire life, ones I'd put in place to keep me safe, to keep from getting hurt. He'd proven that those weren't needed with him. Being with him was like starting my whole life anew. How fantastic that I was getting to do it out from beneath the burden of Carter and all the baggage I'd inadvertently carried with me for so long.

I allowed myself to wonder about his mother, what she'd think of me. I'd never cared before now, not needing anyone's approval or bothering to waste time on what anyone cared to think about me. People were of no consequence and I had no need for them. My bidders and girls were the only people who ascended to a level that caused me to offer concern for them. Obviously, Vi and Trent were exceptions, and now their respective partners. But in the everyday interactions of my life, I did what I pleased and people could think as they wanted.

I'd never had a relationship, so there'd been no family to bother about, no one to influence or impress. But Odin...

I wanted—for the first time in my life—to make a good impression on the people who mattered in his life. I wasn't sure if he'd thought any of that through where Trent and Vi were involved, or if he even considered them like I did. To him, everyone was probably someone who mattered to me, from the girls to the bidders to my acquaintances, not understanding how much I'd held people at arm's length, not realizing perhaps how choosy I was when it came to who I allowed in my inner circle—far more than who I slept with.

Odin had received such a peculiar view and perspective of who I was, seeing me first from the business side, and me having no intention of allowing any other side. Then he knew me from my very closest inner circle, far beyond any man I'd ever allowed there.

I was still somewhat unbalanced, having to recalculate with every interaction with him, expecting to behave as I had with all those who'd come before. Yet with Odin, nothing was as it had been before. He was so very different, in ways that surprised and pleased me constantly.

And now he was asking me into his own inner circle, where his most treasured people resided. And his father, of whom I was interested to see how that would manifest in Odin's life.

I knew that so much of what he'd created had been as a result of his father's departure from their family. While my parents had been strict and domineering, they'd been there for me until I'd left for college and had the world open up to me, showing me how blinded I'd been in our little town and beneath my own father's rule. It had taken me a few years out here, but after the rape, my parents had shown their true colors and I'd been able to cut my ties with them easily. Severing my relationship with them had been a release of all that had been my childhood and the lies and rules they'd inflicted on me.

I'd been much more successful in letting that go than I had Carter's impact on my life—no wonder, really. What Carter had done to me had affected my future, they were nothing more than moments in my past.

I'd made my own family, hand-picking the people I'd wanted, ones I knew I could trust, ones that proved their devotion and commitment to my own success as well as their own. Trent and Vi had been in such a similar situation, both without their parents—though for different reasons—it had been an instant bond between us, a vagabond collection, hell-bent on making it on our own.

Truly, Odin was the perfect complement to what I'd been able to create as an adult woman.

When he'd first asked me if I'd come to meet his family, I hadn't been sure how I felt about it, nervous that those weren't people he'd hand-picked and a flash of my own childhood and the constant judgment had risen up. For a moment.

Then, a well of emotion that I'd been resisting suddenly

bubbled to the surface and I was overcome with a feeling of love for him.

I loved him.

Truly.

I blinked and glanced away, sorting through the truth of it. I really wanted to meet his family, the family of the man I loved.

What a strange and unfamiliar place to find myself in. And so soon after such an amazing shift from this morning with everything that had happened with Carter.

I looked at him, watched the reflection of him in my eyes. He was so strong and kind and good, all the things I'd never thought to want in a man. And yet he was all the things that I'd liked to surround myself with, rich and talented in bed. There was so much to him and he seemed to like me.

And he supported me. Even to the point that when my closest friend had involved him, he'd not thought twice about doing whatever he could. Prior to that, he'd gone out of his way to speak with Annika, to go to her organization, to find out all he could about rape, talking to therapists, figuring out how to support me.

The man was amazing. To say nothing of his business acumen. He was brilliant and well-connected, willing to share his knowledge and angles. I'd like to reconsider the ideas he'd had for the business. I had to reconsider every decision I'd made to this point, having seen it all through the lens of being one of Carter's victims.

Now I was free and there were so many ways that I could see things, could shift the outcome of what I wanted to do, all the things I wanted to pursue. Now I was open to any suggestions that could better the business—and subsequently, the outcomes for the girls.

The girls.

I let my thoughts wander toward the ones who'd found love, the ones who'd moved their auction-relationships into something more. When I'd talked to them about it, they'd been so confident that love was going to see them through, would overcome any differences they'd had in the beginning. Life lay before them like a buffet, and while I'd been happy for them, I'd also known that love didn't exist. It was a product of fairytales and would only create turmoil and heartache for them later. So far, they'd all managed to stay in love and happy, even some of the girls from the very beginning.

Now I understood.

Now I knew love.

I looked at Odin, lying on top of me, asking me to meet his family, telling me that I'd been his safe space, the only place he'd been able to use as an escape to quiet his mind. I could certainly understand that. How many times had I trusted that I could lose myself in him? I'd told him so many things that I'd never offered to anyone and he'd proven over and over that he would be steadfast and stable. We were such an interesting pair, both with such turmoil in our pasts. I'd not guessed that his had affected him so. But here we were, standing for each other.

"I'd like to meet them. Thank you for asking me to join you. Are you sure, though? I mean, maybe I should meet them all after you've had a chance to settle into having a dad."

He shook his head. "No. You're going to be a part of my life for a long, long time. He needs to know about you from the very beginning." He leaned up and kissed me softly. "You're as much a part of my life as my sister is."

I blinked, taken aback. That was pretty serious.

But then, so was me being in love. I touched his cheek. "I love you, Odin."

He drew a quick intake of breath, then covered my mouth with his, kissing me deeply. I wasn't sure why I'd said it aloud, but I'd wanted him to hear it in this moment. And I didn't care that he didn't say it back. That I loved him was enough. I knew how deeply he cared for me.

His tongue traced my mouth, moving over my teeth and my tongue, sweeping deeper across my lips. I opened for him, not just in my mouth, but my entire body and soul, giving myself over to him like I'd never done before. I'd allowed him spaces I'd never offered anyone, and I'd do it again. This feeling of freedom and opportunity was startling and yet so very exhilarating.

His fingers roamed my skin, touching trails he'd explored so thoroughly earlier. I wasn't sure who was getting tied up tonight, but it didn't matter anymore. We knew that we could trade control back and forth seamlessly.

His thighs were hard against mine, his cock settled between my legs, but not quite at the entrance, not yet. He seemed perfectly content to take his time and kiss me like he didn't have anywhere to be. I savored the feel of him, luxuriating in this moment of simply being together.

His hands traced my body, running slowly from my shoulder down to my hips. I gently scratched the length of his back, running my hands across his skin as he kissed me.

My mind quieted and I was overcome by the silence. Normally, I could not exist separate from all the thoughts that flooded my mind every waking moment of my life. He managed to quiet me, all of me.

I kissed him back, enjoying the simple pleasure of it, feeling the softness of his lips with no expectation that I needed them anywhere else. He smelled delightful, like spice and wine. I inhaled, letting the scent of him fill my lungs and letting the feel of his body fill my heart. Without the typical noise bombarding me, his heartbeat was easy to hear, the thump of it resting a few inches above mine.

While I hadn't known it in the beginning, it had been his kind heart that had probably attracted me to him in the first place. It had been his heart that he'd offered for Audrey when I'd asked, his kind heart that had kept him from sleeping with her on that very first night, his heart that had looked after me, had wanted things for me, was resting with me now.

He was the ultimate safety net and he'd proven it time and

time again. Even when he and Vi had made me so very mad, it had been easy to walk away because I'd known that he'd be waiting for me if—and when—I'd ever wanted to come back, even though in that moment I'd been most definitely not coming back.

Yet he'd waited, knowing that the decision had been mine to make and he respected whatever I decided. It would have been so easy for him to pursue me, to chase me, to convince me that I'd been wrong. But he hadn't.

And that was because of his heart. This heart that I liked so much. This heart I loved.

He moved over me, trailing kisses down my neck and the swell of my breasts, moving quietly from one to the other, smothering them in delicate kisses that barely brushed my skin. The next set of kisses circled my nipples, dozens of the lightest touches, careful caresses that made my skin quiver with the attention.

His tongue flicked out to taste my nipple, hardening immediately beneath the wet warmth. He tasted all of me like a man robbed of food for weeks, drawing the tip between his teeth and tugging gently, licking the teeth marks, dipping to kiss my cleavage, then back to care for my nipple. I'd never been loved in such a way.

Mostly because I'd never allowed it.

That had all changed.

Some because of Carter and the freedom that had come from his death. Most because of Odin and who he was as a man, as a lover…as a friend.

This was a freedom unlike anything I'd ever known, most especially in this space. There was no longer a need to dominate him, to keep him from taking us somewhere I didn't want to go—because I'd go anywhere with him. I could trust him. He'd proven that he could be trusted with anything I was willing to give him, from my heart, to my business, to my well-being.

His mouth moved lower, trailing more kisses down my belly, moving slowly as if he feared missing a single inch of skin. I traced the curves of his shoulders, the indentation of his biceps, the swell of the muscle rippling at the back of his arm as he moved over me. This was a luxurious lovemaking, taking us back to a time when there was no press of obligations or trials or places to be. I'd never had such a luxury.

Again, Carter had given me a gift I hadn't known that I'd needed. And thankfully, Odin had been here, ready to embrace the bits of me before they'd scattered to the wind as I figured out what came next for me.

I sighed and relaxed into the movements of his lips. He was so talented and caring, a combination that made for explosive lovemaking. I ran my fingers up his sides, testing the indentations of muscle. He squirmed, chuckling against my skin. I did it again and he bit my stomach just above my bellybutton, then scratched his stubbled chin across the soft skin. I squirmed and tickled him again—something I'd never, ever done with a lover, nor allowed done to me. How peculiar to be finding so many places that were new and exciting and exhilarating in a place where I thought I'd gone everywhere there was to go.

His bites turned more intense as he moved lower, scraping his beard against my thighs, nibbling the edges of my pussy as he stroked me with his tongue. One finger slid inside and I grabbed a handful of hair with one hand, the other moving to circle my clit as he moved inside me, making me arch my back. Desire filled me from my heart outward.

I'd never made love before, never loved a man to allow us to take me here, and it was a heady experience. I'd never have thought that something could change the dynamic of sex, that there was a way to make it more intoxicating and fantastic, but this was it, this was the part everyone craved, everyone went looking for, the feeling people weren't willing to walk away from.

I understood it now. For the first time in my life.

He brought me expertly to climax and moved over me, stroking my side and rolling me over beneath him. I arched my back and glanced over my shoulder, wanting him, looking at him to make sure he knew how much I wanted him. He growled, stroking himself hard and fingering me, stretching and readying me. "I'm going to take you hard, ma chérie."

"Yes, Odin." I wiggled my ass, pushing back toward him, wanting him. Wanting him hard and fast and raw and real. I wanted him to love me with a fierceness that could splinter me. His fingers moved in and out with a slow deliberate stroke. I glanced at him again, my fingers fisting in the bedsheets. "Odin, fuck me."

"Don't boss me, woman."

I laughed. "I will."

"You're not in charge tonight."

I backed into him, moving with his fingers, rubbing my ass against his cock. "Want to bet?"

He continued to stroke me, ignoring my attempts to get him to hurry. "I do not gamble when it comes to what I'm about to do to you."

"Then get on with it."

He slowed his stroke, withdrawing, pausing and entering me again. "I'm not taking your bossing. Not tonight."

I pushed back, hard, rocking him backward, his head falling off the edge of the mattress, his hands flying out to steady himself. I quickly twisted and straddled him, sliding onto his hard cock. His fingers latched on my hips, holding me tight against him. His face was stern and the muscle bulged in his jaw. "Ma chérie…" His eyes dropped closed as if he were trying to maintain his control. I clenched my pussy around him, and he growled, tightening his hold on my hips. Ignoring his resistance, I began to move, taking control. My hands roamed his chest, pinching his nipples. He slapped my ass and I began to move, swiveling my hips and moving against the pressure of his hands, resisting his attempts to keep me from riding him.

I raked my nails down his chest and wrapped my hands

around his wrists, tugging them free and pinning them to the bed. The movement tipped me forward, letting my nipples rake his chest. He turned his hands over, trapping my fists, pushing his fingers between mine and linking us. He pushed up on his elbows, lifting both our hands, giving me leverage to move.

And move I did.

He watched me, staring deeply into my eyes as I swiveled my hips, grinding against him, stroking him long and hard. His hips moved with me, pushing deep into me, wanting control, but relinquishing it one thrust at a time. We moved together, our bodies as in tandem as our hearts. I brought him to climax and he called out my name as he came, his fingers tightening on mine. I came after, squeezing him tightly and falling against his chest as the orgasm overtook me, depleting all my strength and energy.

He curled me against him, wrapping me in his arms and tugging the sheet over us, loosely shrouding us against the air conditioner as it blew across our sweaty bodies.

He pressed a kiss against my ear, a gentle, tender reminder of what we'd shared, what he'd given, what I'd allowed.

It was perfect.

67

Ashley

"You look lovely, ma chérie." He stood at the entrance to my bathroom, watching me dress. We'd come back to my place after a short nap, readying for drinks tonight with everyone over at Trent's bar. Vi and Elyse were coming tonight, as well as Gavin, Violet's man.

It had been Trent who'd suggested the get together as soon as he'd heard the news from Vi about Carter's death. I'd readily agreed, needing my support system and wanting to be with them now, out from beneath the baggage I'd shed with this new freedom. I wanted to see if my long-standing relationships with everyone were as affected as this one had been with Odin.

Trent and Vi were my closest friends—my only friends, really. I'd shunned them during this ordeal, not because I didn't want their support, but because that was how I was. When things got tough, I retreated, working to handle things on my own.

And because this had been related to my rape—something none of them had, thankfully, ever had to deal with. It was one of those things that made it awkward for them to know what to say or how to act. I'd seen it so many times over the course of my life, especially in those early days. I'd realized early on that it was easier to just go it alone than put someone in a position where we all felt uncomfortable.

But none of that mattered tonight. Tonight was about friends, about people who'd become my family.

I glanced in the mirror, catching Odin's eye. What would he become, given the chance? Friend or family?

He walked into the bathroom, pausing behind me, his hand finding my stomach, palm flattening against my dress. I'd decided on a red sleek sleeveless dress, one that I'd never worn as Ms. M, thinking it more attention-drawing than my usual. It had nearly been a bygone conclusion the moment I'd seen it hanging in the closet. I'd paired it with silver strappy heels and simple diamonds at my ears and throat. "Thank you for bringing me with you tonight."

I smiled at his reflection. "Thank you for agreeing."

We kissed gently, Odin careful not to smudge my makeup. It was sweet.

He took my hand and led me to the car, then escorted me into the bar when we arrived. They were at a table in the back corner and Trent had roped off the entire section, giving us plenty of privacy. There weren't many people here yet, it was still early, but Trent's was becoming quite the popular place.

I hugged everyone and introduced Odin even though he'd met everyone but Gavin and Elyse. He was, of course, the perfect gentleman. I could feel the heat of Trent's gaze. We really hadn't talked about Odin for a while, I hadn't seen him to update him. I wasn't sure what he thought of me bringing him, and hadn't said anything when he'd offered the invite. Truly, I hadn't really been thinking about it, having gone nearly everywhere with Odin since the drastic change to the events of the trial. We'd been inseparable ever since, and I wasn't sure that I wanted that to change for a while.

He held a chair for me and I sat, looking up at him while he took the chair beside me, draping his arm across the back of mine. It was surprisingly easy to stay in the space of Ashley that I seemed to curate around Odin, even when surrounded by everyone else who knew me as Ms. M.

They didn't seem surprised at all.

I leaned back in the chair and watched them interact, thinking about my relationship with each one of them. I guess they'd always known that I'd still been Ashley, just like Odin had. They'd all known long before I had, but had trusted that I'd figure it out, content to keep the faith and let me come around.

We laughed and talked and drank throughout the evening. Food showed up at some point, a random selection of pub food that Trent's was known for. It was good, and hearty, and the drinks flowed.

I hadn't let myself enjoy an evening quite as much as this one in a long time. I had no one to impress, no one to vet, no one to worry about. This was just about me and my friends and the man I'd come to love.

Trent and Elyse caught Odin in a conversation, leaving Vi to come over and take Odin's seat. "Hi." Her voice was confident and yet small, like she was waiting for me to blow up. It was a strange place that she and I hadn't ever been. I didn't like it.

I reached over and grabbed her hand, putting it to my heart. Life was too short to have any animosity. What she'd done, she'd done because she cared about me. "I love you, Violet. You're my sister and nothing you could do will change that. What you did pissed me off, make no mistake." Her eyes watered and she squeezed my fingers. "But I understand why you did it." I gave her a smile. "And, if I'm honest, I'm glad you did it. I'm glad you care that much. I'm glad that you love me as much as you do, and that you worry about me. I've been in a bad place." I pressed my lips together and looked away, glancing at Odin and drawing a deep breath. "Maybe worse than I was willing to admit, to be honest.

But sometimes I think we can't see that when we're in it, right? Remember how bad you were after the engagement broke?"

She nodded.

"And?"

"And you freaked out and called Trent and told him that you were worried. And then you called Kim and then you got Jackson involved."

We laughed softly and she laid her head on my shoulder. "I've missed you, Ms. M."

I kissed her forehead and nuzzled my cheek into her hair. A sigh settled in my chest. This was how life was supposed to work. "You can call me Ashley."

She stiffened and held her breath, then let it out slowly and lifted her head. "Are you sure?"

I nodded. "Yes. Odin's been pretty instrumental in getting me to realize that I've always been Ashley, that she's never gone away like I wanted her to, I just made her fierce and gave her some backbone that I started calling Ms. M. But she's never gone anywhere." I smiled and glanced at Odin again. "She's just been waiting for me to get my shit together."

Vi leaned over and kissed my cheek. "Glad to have her back." We stared at each other. "Glad to have you back." She pulled me into a giant hug and I felt the surety of her heartbeat against my own.

"Thanks for waiting on me."

"You're worth it." We separated a little. "Now let's go dance!!"

"No!"

"Yes." Elyse had pulled away from the men and was within earshot. She grabbed one arm, and Vi the other, and we headed out to the dance floor.

Ms. M hadn't stepped foot on anything as silly as a dance floor in decades, maybe ever. She didn't dance. The music took over and I let my body begin to move. As Ashley, I'd loved to dance, danced every weekend. It was one of my most favorite things to do. I used to dance in the kitchen while I was making breakfast, dance in the bedroom, dance through the hallways. I spent so many nights in the club.

Until Carter.

Really, that Ms. M was kind of a stick in the mud. She might have been sophisticated and rich, but she didn't have any idea how to have fun.

Maybe Ashley could teach her.

We danced until we dropped, then made our way back to the men. Hunger burned in Odin's eyes, and probably the other men's but I didn't have eyes for them. I wanted my man. Wanted him so much. We kissed and he pulled me into his lap, running his fingers up my thigh. "I want to take you right here, ma chérie. Watching you dance was enough to make me very hard, woman."

I stroked his cock, wrapping my fingers around the length of his hardness. I bit my lip, wanting him. "There's an office in the back."

Trent nudged my shoulder as he walked by. "I heard that!"

We laughed and I turned, settling in beside Odin on the big couch. He nuzzled my ear, then put an arm around me and I shifted, settling my back into his chest, my hand on his thigh. Trent had Elyse were next to him with Vi and Gavin finishing out the circle. We were a contented, happy group, this family of mine.

"So, what's the latest?" Trent asked. "Are you ready to schedule a couple more auctions now that you're done with all the trial crap?"

I nodded. "I've been thinking about adding another venue. Odin knows the owner of Black Velvet."

"Black Velvet?!" Elyse leaned forward in her chair and elbowed Trent. "I would love to go over there and check that place out!" She turned sheepish. "I mean, I love this place, but Black Velvet, Trent!"

He laughed. "I know. I know."

"Holy cow, girl, you really should have auctions over there.

Your clientele would love that. It's so their kind of place. And I would imagine the girls would be more at ease over there, too. I mean, you do such a great job of making them feel good about the sale, but I have to assume that every little bit helps."

"For sure. I'm doing a better job vetting them lately. I've had to turn quite a few girls down." I'd be interested to see what kind of girls I attracted from this point on. I wondered how much of their own insecurities were a reflection of what mine had been. I had a feeling that those relationships were going to be just as different as everything else.

Trent grinned, watching Elyse get so excited about the venue. Truthfully, I hadn't given it much thought—how strange that for the first time ever I'd let work slip to the wayside. I was so excited —exuberant really—to see what would come next for me. So many things had changed already that there was sure to be more amazing shifts on the horizon. Trent winked and touched my arm. "I'm happy for you. Really. I'm totally open to still having them here, but for sure you need to do some at Black Velvet. That place is wicked." He bumped Elyse. "So I've heard."

"Trent, if you've been in there, so help me God." Elyse laughed.

He kissed the back of her neck. "You really think I'd go in there without you?"

She smiled and they shared a tender moment. A week ago I'd have rolled my eyes and thought they were crazy and oblivious to the real world and the problems that existed there.

Now, I was a changed woman, so changed that when I turned to Odin, I went looking for the same sweetness and he didn't disappoint. His kiss was gentle and full of promise. I liked it. "Black Velvet is yours, ma chérie. You have but to ask."

I smiled and settled my palm against his chest. "I want far more from you than Black Velvet, dear."

"Oh?" His smile vanished and he trapped my hand beneath his. "You have but to ask."

"Just you." I snuggled against him. "I just want you, Odin."

68

Odin

If there'd been a moment prior to now that had caused me more anxiety, I couldn't think of it. I'd done billion-dollar real estate deals, multi-national deals, had million-dollar deals fall through. None of them had me more stressed than meeting my father.

Ashley had done her best to comfort me, but she'd eventually left me to stew in my own anxiety, promising to meet me at the restaurant in enough time to walk in with me. I hadn't wanted her to leave, but she'd convinced me that some time alone to deal with my thoughts would benefit us both.

Dammit, that woman had captivated me. All of me.

And when she'd told me that she'd loved me I'd been too stunned to reply.

I'd loved on her with my body where words had failed me.

It wasn't that I didn't love her, quite the contrary. I felt so deeply for her that it scared me. I wanted to protect her, to keep her safe, to keep her for always. She'd become so instrumental to my happiness, to the constant contentment that surrounded me at all times.

Except today.

What did I care how today went? My father hadn't been a part of my life for more than two decades, there was nothing he could do to me, nothing he could take from me.

It was my mother I was worried about. And sweet Alice.

They were the ones he could hurt. Though I'd warned them not to, they were both coming with expectations today and that was never a good way to start a meeting. He'd failed all of my expectations, even the small ones that I'd tried to rid myself of, knowing he could never come through for me. I knew if they had even a tiny expectation of him, he would let them down. I didn't know what today was going to bring and I'd second guessed my decision to allow them to come with me before I had a chance to feel him out and find out his motives.

I needed him to be the man we all needed.

But I wasn't stupid enough to expect that he'd come through now when he hadn't been able to before now. Part of me felt like this was an attempt to assuage his sins before he left the country, rid himself of the obligation of us while he still had the chance, then have a fresh start overseas after he'd been able to meet his singular demand as a father. As far as we were concerned, he'd have done his duty, met with his adult children, noted that they were doing fine, and then he could get on with his life.

Breaking Mother and Alice's hearts as he walked out.

I pulled into the parking lot and dialed Ashley, spotting her as she got out of her car. I shouldn't have let her drive; now we'd have to leave her car here or take it back to her house before going to mine. I pushed the thought away. I didn't want to have to think about anything other than what was about to come so I could head any issues off before they touched the women in my life.

Ashley included.

She saw me and waved, hanging up before I could hear her voice. I hugged her to me. "Thank you for coming."

She kissed my cheek and threaded her arm through mine. "Thank you for inviting me. I'm excited to get to meet your mother and sister. A little nervous, too."

"Not my father?"

She shrugged and patted my cheek. "I'm what you are where he is concerned. I don't want to be overly eager to meet him if you've not adjusted to the idea."

I kissed the back of her hand. "I'm not sure what I am, to be honest."

"You don't have to decide right now. Or ever. You can meet him and still be perplexed."

"I'm just worried about Alice and my mother." We'd reached the doors to the restaurant.

"I know. And I'm sure they're worried about you because they know you're worrying."

"It's a vicious circle." I opened the door and scanned the room, looking for the man I used to know. He was seated in a far corner and half-rose as we entered. Mother and Alice pulled the outer door as we stepped inside and I moved back to hold the door and kiss them hello.

Mother patted my cheek, much as Ashley had done. "You'll be fine, dear."

I didn't repeat the phrase back to her, knowing she wouldn't settle for it. Alice stood behind her, looking timid and excited. I winked at her and Ashley moved beside her, striking up a conversation about shoes that seemed to put Alice at ease. They chatted comfortably as I escorted the three of them into the restaurant and toward my father's table. Mother's fingers tensed on my arm and I covered them, stopping just short of where my father stood.

"Hello, Reginald." Mother's voice shook.

He stepped closer, nodding at me and holding out a hand to her. "Suzanne. You look lovely."

Her hand released from my arm and she let him take her fingers. I tensed as he drew them to his mouth, kissing them softly. She melted, her shoulders relaxing, like decades of sorrow and tension were falling away.

I tensed, catching all of it and holding it, not allowing it to go too far, not allowing her to give any power to him so that he could use it against her. Dammit, today was going to take a hell of a toll on me. But I didn't care. These women were worth any amount of distress to me. I could take it.

He escorted her to a seat and I took the one beside her, Ashley next to me, Alice rounding out the table, putting her on my father's right. We spoke of small talk, the weather, Father's new position. He kept us entertained with stories and, as he did, I remembered this at the dinner table each night, him making Mother laugh, teasing me with funny bits of stories that hadn't related at all to his day at work, carrying them into the nighttime as he tucked me in. My heart ached at the memory and I blinked away a sudden rush of emotion.

Damn him for being able to play us all so easily.

I glanced at Alice, she was captivated, mesmerized by every word falling from our father's lips. I remembered that, remembered the feeling of being in awe of him. She was so much older, wiser, a brilliant businesswoman, yet still a girl who'd never had a father, a girl given a chance to have something she'd ached for, a chance to fill a hole that I'd never been able to.

The sensation of how I'd failed her expanded, pinching my stomach. I'd done my best, but I never could have been a father to her.

Nor had she wanted me to be.

I stayed on the fringes of the conversations, watching Alice and my mother, cautiously gauging their adoration and commitment to a new relationship. He didn't bring that up, didn't mention when he'd be able to see us again, and I realized that this would probably be the last we saw of him. This was closure for him, truly.

He and Mother reminisced about times they'd had together. He made her laugh and, again, I watched parts of her heal.

While the two of them talked, Ashley talked to Alice, engaging her in deep conversations. They were genuinely hitting it off and that soothed some of the wounds being inflicted by the other side of the table. It would take some time, I feared, for Mother to get over this visit. I could feel her hanging hopes on his words and actions tonight.

I leaned back in my chair, watching two separate relationships. Alice and Ashley, two of the most important people in my life now, as an adult. And my mother and father, the two most important people of my childhood.

There was so much I hadn't known. What could have made him walk away? What could have made her pine for him for years and years after he deserted his entire family, leaving her with two small children, never to return again?

I half-listened to their conversation as it turned soft. He apologized for any trauma he'd caused her.

"I made it fine. You left me with two wonderful children. They were easy to raise."

He glanced at me and winked. I diverted my attention to my plate, clearing my throat and taking a drink.

"You raised them wonderfully." He turned his attention back to her. "I'm sorry I wasn't there for all of it."

"Please don't apologize," Mother said, a sternness in her voice. "We did just fine. They've turned out like they did because of the hardships and the turmoil. We have no regrets. I do hope you'll be able to spend time with them now, now that you know what exceptional adults they've become."

I didn't say anything, fearful of rebutting her offer, and a little bit interested to hear how he would respond. On the other side of the table, Alice and Ashley's conversation ground to a close, probably for the same reason.

"I would." He cleared his throat and folded his napkin, putting it beside his plate. "I hope you all know that." He lifted his gaze to me, then to Alice, then to Mother. "I've wanted for so many years to contact all of you. I've watched from afar for a long time now, gauging your successes, trying to figure out the perfect moment when I wouldn't cause you any grief. But you continued to skyrocket, your own success moving ever forward as mine did the same. We've all been on an upward trajectory and I didn't want to do anything to derail that."

Here it comes, I thought darkly, *the bomb that he's been planning on dropping from the first moment when he called Alice.*

"I was afraid," he said, his voice trembling.

The honesty of it caught me off guard. I pulled my hands into my lap and clutched them tightly. Ashley's hand found mine, covering them. I didn't dare look at her, my emotions roiling in my chest.

"What do you mean by afraid?" Alice asked.

"I was worried that you'd refuse to see me, refuse to let me explain and offer an apology."

He still hadn't explained, and yet, I wasn't sure that I wanted him to. I understood enough about relationships and the challenging dynamics of kids that maybe I hadn't known everything that had gone on beyond the parts of their marriage that they allowed me to see. Mother's refusal to let him apologize for what she'd been able to pull off as a single mom stuck with me. I'd liked getting to see her own what she'd done—because she'd been incredible. She was still incredible.

And while the tension and sorrow had managed to fall away, and it had scared me, maybe I'd read it wrong. Maybe this was closure for her, too. Maybe this was what she'd needed, a chance to say goodbye, a chance to lay her past to bed, a chance to acknowledge just what a miracle she'd been able to pull off, raising two amazing kids into tremendously successful adults. It was because of her, her work ethic, her commitment to our family, that Alice and I had busted our asses like we had to make it in the world, to give back to our mother, to make sure she was cared for like she'd cared for us.

I had a new respect for my mother—not that I hadn't had immense amounts of it prior to now—but there was another layer of it. I was proud of her. So, so proud. And, for the first time, I knew she'd be okay.

I also knew that Alice would follow our lead. If we made it through this with a closing of the chapter of our childhood, then maybe we could leave the past behind us.

I looked at Ashley and squeezed her hand. Maybe we could all find a way to forge a new future, one that had nothing to do with the past.

69

Ashley

"You look beautiful, Darling." I set one of Mikayla's rich red curls over another, layering the effect of her shimmering hair. I'd never seen a color like it before and I knew the men I'd selected for tonight would appreciate the richness of it.

"Thanks. I'm a little nervous." She tugged at the hem of her silver mini-skirt. I pulled her fingers away and trapped them between mine.

"Nothing to be nervous about." *What a lie,* I laughed to myself. Tonight was the first auction at Black Velvet and I'd been a mess for the last several days, wanting to make a stellar impression on Sampson. Odin had opened up an entirely new world to me where I cared of people's opinions. I wasn't sure if I preferred being a cold-hearted bitch.

Truthfully, Sampson had been delightful and had offered me the world. Had I not been involved with Odin, I'd have most certainly taken him up on his bawdy offers. As it was, I was delighted to be getting involved with him in the business sense. I wanted tonight to be wonderful because it would help all of us take my business to the next level. Odin had been kind and understanding during the meeting when I'd had him come to the office to discuss his ideas for the auctions, the same ones I'd dismissed so many days ago when I'd been uninterested in doing anything different than how I'd done it since the beginning. He'd been full of amazing ideas and ambition, deferring to me on everything, not forcing my opinions, merely accepting them and moving on to the next idea he'd had. There had been some phenomenal ones, and with my new view from beneath the freedom I was experiencing, they were good, they were sound, they would make bundles of money…not just for me, but for the girls. And now, for Sampson.

Trent hadn't been cut out completely; we'd decided to keep a monthly auction there, but with the way the scheduling worked, it was easy to add several more during the month at Black Velvet. They weren't open for business on Mondays and Sampson was looking forward to having the additional income from the extra day, not to mention the lower overhead since we'd only need a single bartender and a couple of bouncers.

Most of the men I'd selected to come to Black Velvet weren't trouble makers—like Vann and his frustrating oversight that had brought Carter across the threshold, never mind nearly derailing my entire business by leaking information that wasn't supposed to be shared. My assistant, Tiffanie, had been relentless and dogged in her research into the men. If they had a single blemish, no matter how long ago, she'd eliminated them from the options of bidders at Black Velvet before I even met them.

We'd added two more bidders beyond my usual number—one of Odin's suggestions—to raise the bids and the level of competition. According to Odin, men at these levels were all about winning, far more than the men I'd had before. And truly, while I did use the element of their competitiveness for everyone's benefit, I was playing with men of net worths far exceeding some of the highest I'd had at Trent's. I usually had one or two men with massive balance sheets, but here, tonight, they were the wealthiest men I'd entertained thus far. Several had come as introductions from Odin, all men he'd worked with and respected.

Sampson came in and kissed my cheek. "Everything ready?" He glanced at Mikayla and winked. "Gorgeous."

Tiffanie came up with the drink I'd asked her to get for Mikayla, giving me time to draw Sampson off to the side. "Is she here?"

"Just arrived, that was why I came in or I wouldn't have bothered you."

I put a hand on his arm. "You're never a bother. This is your place."

He drew me closer. "This is your event. I hope you'll consider this your place tonight."

"You're too kind." I glanced at Mikayla and Tiffanie, content that they'd be fine for a few minutes while I handled this bit of business. "Will you have her escorted to the room where I first met Odin? I'll go there now to receive her."

"Of course." He leaned forward and kissed my cheek.

Odin walked in as Sampson left. I smiled and walked toward him, not wanting to delay much before we started the auction. "Grab us a seat, I'll be with you in a bit." I brushed my fingers across his arm.

"Do you have a second?"

I smiled. "Of course. For you? Three."

"I'll barely need two."

This playfulness was unexpected and nice. I needed this to keep tonight's stress away.

"I made a few calls today, there was some unfinished business from my evening with Audrey."

I frowned, confused. "What?" The only thing he hadn't managed that night was having sex with her. A sudden surge of jealousy coursed through me. I blinked and held my breath.

"Nothing too grand. Nothing to worry you." He drew me closer. "Audrey had a desire to work at a firm I'm familiar with. I called Marcus Long, put in a good word for her. He's asked her to come work for him." He shrugged and looked away, seemingly embarrassed now that he'd told me.

"Odin..." I waited for him to glance at me. "Thank you." I hugged him. "There was no need for you to do that. Thank you."

He kissed my forehead. "I did it for her; it was the least I could do. Now, go tend to your things. Annika is waiting."

I blinked, unsure how he knew that I'd arranged for her to come and that she was the one waiting in the room for me. He didn't answer my unasked question, just stepped away, turning me toward the door and allowing me to go. I hurried along the empty hallways, toward the room where Annika waited. I could have done this after the auction, but truthfully, I was too excited.

Sampson stood at the door, barely pulling it closed. He looked up as I neared. "All yours."

I nodded and slipped inside.

Annika turned, a large smile on her face. "Ashley. So good to see you. Thank you for inviting me."

I hugged her. "My pleasure. Thank you for coming."

"Of course. The bouncer guy said you wanted to see me before I went to sit down at the auction. I'm so interested to see how these go. What a wonderful thing you're doing to get these women started on a great path."

I shook my head. "This is nothing compared to what you do, which is why I wanted to talk to you for a moment before the auction."

"Of course."

I led her toward the small loveseat situated along the far wall. "I make my living off the auctions, keeping a portion of the proceeds."

"That makes sense."

"I've done enough of them that my income has begun to

exceed what I can spend." I stopped and pressed my lips together. "None of this is coming out right."

She patted my hand. "Take your time, dear."

I smiled and tears welled in my eyes. "What I was trying to say was that I'd like to make a donation to your organization."

"You're so sweet!" She leaned forward and hugged me. "But you didn't have to tell me that tonight. We could have gone to dinner."

I withdrew the check from the pocket of my suit and handed it to her. "I was really excited. It couldn't wait—"

"Ashley!" She stared at the check, then lifted her gaze to me. "This is a million dollars."

I shrugged. "Like I said, it gets hard to spend money after a certain point."

She shook her head. "This is too much."

"No." I reached forward and covered her hand. "Never too much. What you do is amazing. And expensive. Find a way to spend it. You'll put it to far better use than I ever could."

We stood, my legs shaking, and she hugged me again. "Thank you." Her words were thick with emotion.

I shook my head. "No. Thank you. For helping Odin to help me, for helping the women that you do. For being there for me." A tear streaked down my cheek.

"He loves you, you know."

I nodded. "I figured he did."

"I don't think he's ever told anyone. Not since his father left."

I escorted her to the door. "I figured it was something like that. He gave me the time I needed to come to grips with my rape. I'll give him the same respect. It's enough that we have what we have. Getting to tell him was healing for me."

"You're healing for each other."

I agreed. Whole heartedly.

This is the end of Control Me. Thanks for reading! Click here and start reading my new Black Velvet series today!

BONUS BOOK

On My Knees

The Hollywood Nights Series Vol. 1

Alpha Billionaire Romance

CJ Thomas

70

Nash

She had the type of presence that filled the room.

Out of the dozen or so interns who marched their way onto my set today, she was the only one who caught my eye. She was beautiful, young, and had a strong, confident gaze that made my heart skip a beat the moment I laid eyes on her.

This semester's internship program was going to be just fine, I thought to myself before spinning back around in my director's chair. My arms bent and I adjusted the headset firmly placed over my ears. We were right in the middle of filming a scene—a very intense moment unfolding before us in a long, thrilling and action-packed story that I was in charge of directing.

The cop held the gun to the temple of the man he'd kidnapped. The man was bound to a chair and beaten by the cop. He'd pissed his pants. There was blood streaming down his nose and leaking from the corner of his mouth.

I sat forward, immersing myself completely into the scene.

"This is the last time I'm going to ask you." The cop pressed the muzzle of the gun deeper into the flesh of the criminal's head. "Where are my wife and daughter?"

The criminal's eyes were fire as he swished the pooling blood inside his mouth before spitting it on the cop's shoes. "I told you already." He winced when the cop applied more pressure to the weapon. "I don't know."

I stood and whispered inside the camera director's ear, "Good, good, zoom in on his eyes. I need to see the fear and anger in both their eyes."

He nodded, and a second later, both their eyes were on the screens.

"Perfect." I rubbed the palms of my hands together.

The cop pulled his hand back and brought it down like the swing of a hammer, crashing the butt of the handgun into the side of the skull of the criminal, crunching his face.

An intern gasped behind me. Much too loud for me to ignore it.

My hands planted on my hips as I twisted, giving the dozen or so interns a pinched expression.

Several saw me turn around and straightened their stance in response.

Fucking rookies.

The moment I found her, standing casually, still completely immersed in the scene unfolding behind me, I stopped breathing. She was the type of person I needed around. The person who got lost in the story, unable to hear the distractions around her, completely studying it all. And it didn't hurt that I found her utterly irresistible and all too easy on the eyes.

She was perfect.

My cock twitched as my eyes drifted down her body before rounding her delicious curves. She was a full bodied woman, and I knew exactly what I could do when she offered herself up on a plate. Because after talking to me, that was exactly what she'd do. I'd work with all that—I drank her in.

When I lifted my gaze up off her breasts—something I wouldn't mind getting lost in—I found her staring at me.

Her face flushed and she quickly looked away. I missed her Caribbean green eyes immediately.

"We're hunting your brother down," the cop whispered in the criminal's ear. "If we find him with my family, my guys will kill him."

I turned my attention back to the scene, but my mind was on her. I wanted to know her name, what made her want to study film, and if she was available for a drink. Anything to get myself buried deep in all that.

"And he will kill your family." The cop beat his victim to a bloody pulp. Blood splattered across the floor and flew through the air.

"Yes, yes, this is fucking gold," I said excitedly to my team working hard beside me.

The door burst open and the cop's partner dove across the room, wrapping the cop in a tight bear hug to restrain him. "Okay, that's enough."

The cop fought his partner and yelled at the criminal, still wanting to continue beating the life out of him.

My lips curled into a smile as I glanced back over my left shoulder, admiring more of everything that she was. Her lips were full and I knew they would be perfect for sucking my cock. She had loose bangs draped just above her brow and her jet black hair was pulled back tight into a flawless ponytail.

I bit my bottom lip and felt the heat move to my lap. So easily I could imagine wrapping my hand up in her long locks as I tugged it back while I punished her with my hardness. And I just damn near lost my mind when her pebbled nipples poked through her shirt as if calling me home.

"Fuck you. It's not enough!" the cop screamed, shaking his partner off his back.

I turned back to the set.

"Listen." The cop caught his breath and cooled down as he listened to what his partner had to say. "SWAT is outside the house. It's been confirmed. Your family is alive."

71

Alex

Breathe, Alex. Breathe.

I didn't know where to look and fought the urge to glance at the others to see if I was the only one he was looking at.

This was so weird.

We'd just got here and, somehow, I'd managed to get his attention despite standing in the back, well behind him. Like I wasn't nervous enough already.

This was big.

Today was huge.

I had everything riding on this and I couldn't screw it up.

He looked over his should and stared directly at me.

I shifted uncomfortably and couldn't help but feel that I'd done something wrong. No matter how hard I tried to keep focused on what we were *all* invited to come here and do, it was impossible. Not with how I could feel his heavy gaze constantly falling over me.

The moment he turned back around, I let out a weighted sigh.

I tucked my trembling hands inside my pockets so no one could see my nerves on full display.

I knew who he was. Our professor briefed us yesterday. I'd been waiting for this day for a very long time. Today was our first glimpse behind the scenes. Up until now, we'd read, studied, and discussed theory behind the film industry and now it was time for us to get firsthand experience at what it was like to direct and produce a movie.

The director stood and walked over to a cameraman, whispering something in his ear.

My class was part of the elite program designed by my professor. We'd be following this particular film and director over the course of several months. And somehow I'd managed to catch the attention of none other than Nash Brooks on day one.

The next time he glanced at me, I froze.

Apparently he and my professor went way back—like, forever kind of back. This wasn't new for Nash. He'd done these sorts of intern workshops before, and soon we'd all be divided up and tasked out different roles each week. Or at least that was what was supposed to happen.

I didn't move until he lifted his eyes off me.

I could breathe again.

It was one of those once-in-a-lifetime opportunities that I just couldn't pass up. Not even if I was guaranteed to win the lottery would I have passed this up. This was what I wanted to do more than anything. Getting a job in the industry—and working next to someone as talented and successful as Nash Brooks—would be the same as winning the lottery to me.

Everything he touched turned to Blockbuster gold.

It didn't matter how much money I could use right about now. I'd still do everything in my power to be here, making the most of this opportunity. And if anyone needed to see just how serious I was about making it in Hollywood, they could look at my bank statements—I was dead broke.

I had nothing, and put everything into making sure I was part of this group of interns.

I'd drained my savings and took out more loans than I knew how to repay over a single lifetime. I was so far into debt pursuing this dream, it wasn't even funny.

My parents, God rest their souls, tried their entire lives to make this their dream as well. Working hard, doing what it took, anything to make it big in Hollywood—except they didn't make it. Not before a car crash took both their lives.

This wasn't just my dream, this was my *family's* dream. Even with them gone, I knew they were still supporting me from Heaven. That was just the type of people they were.

The actors shouted and I stared straight ahead but wasn't paying much attention. I couldn't. Not with the way Nash scooped me up in his arms with those gorgeous ebony eyes raking over me.

Nash was devilishly handsome and completely out of my league. And the fact that I was even thinking about him in any way outside a working relationship was just stupid.

It would never happen.

I wouldn't allow it.

Especially if that meant risking everything I'd worked my entire adult life to get to where I was now. Forget about it.

Yet my heart fluttered every time I found him staring, and all I could imagine was wrapping my legs around him while he hovered over me.

Acting wasn't for me. I'd tried that first. Spent the last four years studying the art. Well, really ten if you considered my middle and high school years when I first gave it a try. And as much as I loved playing different roles, directing and getting behind the camera was where I really wanted to be.

I'd do anything to make my dream come true. *Anything.*

The next time I caught him staring, he winked.

Well, except maybe that.

72

Nash

"Cut! Let's wrap it up for today. Good job people." I stood from my director's chair. "This is fucking brilliant!"

"Mr. Brooks, good work," the camera director reached out and fist bumped me.

"You too. Keep it up." I turned to make sure she hadn't left yet. Thank God she was still there.

Professor Ted Fields, my longtime friend and master instructor of cinematography, wouldn't allow everyone to disappear so quickly. Not without first introducing me to them. After all, that was why they were here.

Now that I could completely focus on her, it was apparent just how much taller I was. Not like that wasn't the case with nearly everyone I crossed paths with, but I liked my women short and easy to maneuver around. And with an ass like hers, I bit my lip and grunted, well, let's just say that it had so much potential for me to find a variety of ways to get lost in it.

She stood there with her arms casually down at her sides as she laughed and talked with another intern. She had the most sexy smile—warm and inviting—and I could hear her contagious laugh from all the way over here.

I stood and stared, not bothering to act busy or hide the fact that all I could pay attention to was her. I wanted to know more, to be the one to make her laugh, and also to be the one to dangle her over the edge until her face twisted and her lips rounded.

Occasionally, she would glance in my direction as if keeping an eye on the man she knew was thinking dirty thoughts about her. Each time her eyes caught mine, there was a glimmer that made me believe she was the type of woman who might be willing to go home—and to bed—on a first date.

I moved to the corner of the tent, hung my headphones on the hook attached to the post, and let my assistant know that I wanted everything ready to go by the time I arrived at 6AM tomorrow morning. "Not one thing shouldn't be ready for me when I arrive. Do you understand?"

"Yes, Mr. Brooks." She gave a curt nod as she hugged her notepad to her chest. "Everything will be just as you expect by the time you arrive in the morning."

I stepped out from under the tent and planted my hands on my waist. These were my new interns. I bit the inside of my lip as I studied their faces. Already, they were looking too comfortable inside my house.

"Nash." Ted came up to my side and slapped me on the back. "Meet your new interns."

"They're just kids." I gave him a sideways glance.

"The best of the bunch." He crossed his arms.

"Let's hope so."

"An equal number of men and women."

We both stared straight ahead and I debated whether or not to thank him now for bringing the ponytailed beauty around. I decided against it. He knew me all too well and would advise me against doing what it was I was thinking of doing. So I kept my thoughts to myself. The difference between me and Ted was simple; I wasn't in the same position as he was and could do what I wanted with whomever I wanted.

"Well, let's go introduce you." He smiled.

"Don't bother. I'll take it from here."

He laughed.

I marched on over and said in a loud, firm voice, "These are my new interns." I rubbed the palms of my hands together and laughed. "Looks like there might be one or two future directors in this group."

Each and every one of their faces lit up.

When I stopped only five feet in front of them, they all shut up and their faces turned to stone. Perfect. They knew who was in charge and I didn't need to remind them of that, or why they were here. My gaze hopped on down the line until I finally landed on her.

She held my gaze when the others cast theirs away, diverting eye contact. I liked that she seemed to be the only confident one in the bunch, but I also didn't want to mistake it for what else it could mean—a challenge to authority.

"Who here wants to be a director?" I pulled away from her gorgeous, round face.

All dozen hands rose to the air.

I paced up and down the line before stopping in front of her. "Did you like my hook at the end of that last scene?" Her smell was intoxicating. A blended mix of spring water and fresh mountain flowers—so pure.

"I did," she said confidently.

"It was perfect? There wasn't anything you would have done to make it better?"

She remained silent for a moment as she thought how best to answer my question. And in the time between, I stared into those eyes that took me straight to the white sand beaches found in the Caribbean that had the ability to make even a celibate priest's cock hard. "Well?"

She tilted her head to the side, giving me the look like it was a trick question I asked. And I guess it kind of was. Except I didn't really care what she said, as long as she said something, so I could hear that articulate voice of hers again.

"Go ahead." I closed the gap between us. "Tell me." I was so close I could practically feel the heat radiating off her.

The other interns all held their breath, waiting to see how this played out. They were as anxious as I was to hear what she had to say.

"There was just one tiny thing I would have changed." Her voice swirled around me and prickled my skin.

My brows lifted high on my forehead. "And what would that be?"

An intern next to her shifted her weight and stood with one arm holding the other at the elbow, carefully studying my reaction.

"I would have had the cop kick the chair over." All the blood in my heart swelled my cock the moment she said it. "He's a badass cop."

"That he is." The corners of my eyes smiled.

"So he needs to finish the scene and give hope that he'll defeat this evil he's fighting."

Each word was music to my ears. Not once did she doubt herself. Nor did she shift her weight between her feet. There was a confidence to her that immediately roped me in. What she said was fucking brilliant.

But there wasn't a chance I'd let her know that. At least not in front of the other jokers she studied with.

My head turned to my right, and the moment my eyes landed on the next intern, her cheeks flushed and her knees shook. "What do you think?"

"About what, Mr. Brooks?" Her voice cracked.

"Her answer." I pointed at the sexy hourglass I wanted to bury my cock inside. "Do you agree?"

"I think it would really add to the scene." She nodded as she spoke.

My chin dropped to my chest as I shook my head and chuckled.

"Except we haven't read the script!" someone down the line said.

"Who said that?" I asked.

"I did, sir." A young stick figured man raised his hand. "We don't know what's coming next."

I moved quickly to stand next to him. "You're abso-fucking-lutely right."

He laughed, as did his buddies.

"The writers and I have been over this exact scene hundreds of time before today." I paused to see their faces. "I haven't slept, I've called off dates, and did anything to make sure that by the time today rolled around, I wouldn't fuck it up." I walked closer to her, stopping momentarily to pick up a script from a table nearby.

Everyone remained silent.

I took my time to stare into the eyes of each and every one of these rookies before stopping in front of her again. Her eyes teased me, luring me in and getting me hard.

"Go home, read the script, and next time, come back prepared." I threw the script at her beautifully-formed breasts.

What she didn't know about the script we were playing out, was that soon I'd make her mine.

73

Alex

All I did was answer the question he asked. He didn't have to cut me down at the knees. And especially not in front of my entire internship class.

Ugh, it was so humiliating.

When I saw the bus coming, I stood from the bus stop bench and slung my handbag over my shoulder. At least it was over. The bus stopped, opened the door, and when I stepped inside the driver smiled as I flashed my Metro card.

These buses were always packed. It was like the entire city was in my shoes. None of us could afford a car. Even when we all wanted one.

Traffic was awful, but who cared. At least then I could sit in the comfort of something that made me feel just a little bit successful and not have to worry about who I was next to, or who wanted to be next to me.

It was a trick question Nash asked. That was why it took me so long to respond. No matter how I answered it, I couldn't win. He had his eyes set on me the moment we arrived.

I worked my way to the back of the bus where I saw an open seat.

That was the thing—I'd always had that look about me. The look that invited confrontation. My entire life. From the moment someone stole fresh baked cookies from the lunchroom cafeteria in middle school and I got the blame for it, I had the look that said I was guilty. It had happened countless times since then, too. So frequently, in fact, I was nearly immune to noticing. Even though I was very rarely actually guilty.

And this latest incident was right when I wanted it most.

The seat was empty. Perfect. At least something seemed to be going my way today. I scooted my bum across the vinyl covering and snuggled up against the window, staring outside as the bus pulled away from the curb and began taking me across town.

Fuck, I sighed. That was the last thing I needed on my first day on set with Nash Brooks.

Unbelievable.

I cast my gaze down to the script—*When Darkness Fell.* That title . . . I wasn't so sure it was the best choice. It was a gritty crime movie where the detective, not always one to follow the rules, was on a mission to solve a crime when his family got abducted. The premise was good. The execution, well, there was no doubt that would be the best in the business—especially since Nash Brooks was at the helm.

My head hit the back of the seat when I couldn't look at the stupid script any longer. I hated that he handed it to me. I'd read it. Hell, Professor Fields made sure I read it before today. I'd thought everyone did until that asshole spoke out of turn and admitted that no one had read it. Apparently I assumed wrong. Yet, somehow, I ended up being the only intern, the one who'd already read it, getting told to go read the fucking script.

The bus wasn't so bad. It was slow, was filled with L.A.'s sketchiest citizens, and I got hit on, like, all the fucking time. No, it was good. Really. I rolled my eyes. Who wouldn't want to have this rich cultural experience day in and day out?

It wasn't like my idea on how to end the last scene was a bad one. In fact, it would have really finished the scene strong. Completed it. Instead, it just ended. Dropped off and fell flat. Nothing was worse than an abrupt ending that left the viewer a bit let down.

But who gave a flying fuck about what I thought? My friend, Kendra. That's who. I dug my phone from my handbag and gave her a call.

"Hey, what's up?" She answered right away. "You meet Nash Brooks?"

It was all she seemed to want to talk about these last few weeks. Or at least once I found out that I was selected to be part of the small group to work alongside him. Everyone in L.A. knew who he was. And not like how the rest of America knew him either.

Nash Brooks wasn't just one of the best directors of all time. He was young, in his mid-thirties, and struck gold when he was in his early twenties. You could say he got lucky, but I knew he was pure genius. That was what molded him to be the notorious playboy who roamed Hollywood's bachelorette population; all of L.A. knew that.

"Yeah, I met him." I closed my eyes and could see his messy hair that fit his style flawlessly.

Nash wasn't just a billionaire playboy who made kick ass movies. He'd been seen with actresses, rock stars, and even the princess of some small European country I couldn't pronounce the name of even if I tried. Oh, and never to forget, according to the tabloids, he was hung like a horse. And Kendra certainly knew about that.

"You don't sound too excited about it," Kendra said with more attitude than I was in the mood for.

Kendra studied law, and when she didn't have her nose buried in a textbook, she loved talking about her recent sexcapades. And when she wasn't doing that, she was fantasizing every waking moment about just how big she thought Nash Brooks's shlong was.

"Because he's an asshole." I slumped further down in my seat. We'd just passed the park, and that meant I had at least another forty minutes on the bus before my stop.

"What happened?"

"It's too long of a story for the phone."

"Okay." She drew out her word slowly, as if annoyed that I wouldn't dish out the details now. "Let's get a drink, then."

I debated whether or not I was even in the mood for that. He'd really killed my day, and I kind of just wanted to go home and take a hot bath.

"C'mon, I'll pay." Her voice was more inviting than before.

That was becoming all too common and I felt bad about it. She shouldn't have to pay for me to go out. But after the inheritance her grandparents left her after they died, she never had to worry about money ever again. I often wondered why it was she even bothered working. But law was her passion, just as entertainment was mine.

"I can't let you do that." My tongue swept across the front of my teeth.

"Don't sweat it. You're my girl. Plus, it's been a couple days and I could really use a good fuck."

I laughed. "Cool. Same place same time?"

"See you there."

Anything to take my mind off the disaster that unfolded today.

74

Nash

"You know she was right." Ted clasped his hands behind his head as he leaned further back in my director's chair.

I knew Ted wouldn't let this one go. That was the kind of guy he was. Always watching, looking out for the interests of his students. And that was what made him a better man than I.

But I didn't question her because I thought she was right or wrong. I questioned her because I needed to hear her voice blanket me in her sexiness. And that . . . that right there was something I wasn't about to tell him.

Not now at least.

"You could have at least given her some kind of recognition for having something intelligent to say."

I glanced in his direction from the corner of my eye.

"If I were in your shoes, I would maybe consider re-filming today's scene."

"You could help close up shop for the night." I stood and

turned to peer down at him. "Instead of telling me what I *should* be doing."

He laughed. "Just admit it."

I arched a brow.

"Her answer was brilliant." He jumped to his feet. "Go ahead. Admit it."

I straightened my spine and squared my shoulders with his. We both stood over six feet and were solid muscle. "What, are you sleeping with her?"

He chuckled. "She's the best in the group. And the only one I let read the complete script before today."

"I knew it." My hands rested on my hips. "You *are* sleeping with her."

A flash of anger tightened my mid-section. I wasn't one to get jealous, but the thought of him sleeping with her, the woman whose legs I wanted wrapped around me, made me really hate him right now.

"I see." He dropped his chin and shook his head as he stared at me from under his brow.

"You do, do you?" I challenged.

It was her voluptuous body I wanted spread across my satin sheets. Nobody else's. Only her. And the way I saw it, my good friend Ted, was the only obstacle standing in my way.

"Yeah, I do." His jaw clenched.

"You know I had no choice." I lifted my chin, never taking my eyes off his intense gaze. "Someone is always my first victim. Today, she was the unlucky one."

He chuckled. "You're a sick son of a bitch. You know that?"

My lips curled into a devious smile. "If I can't keep the rookies in check, then this will be over before it ever leaves the ground."

His hand lifted and squeezed my shoulder. "You seem wound tight. Everything else okay?"

"Everything is fine," I reassured him.

My stress was high. As high as it always was when I was in the middle of making a movie. There were so many tasks that needed to get done and we were on a tight schedule. Sleep came in short bursts and I survived off energy drinks. And through it all, I fucking loved every moment of the wild ride.

"Just like all the times before." He released his grip on me. "Quick to cut the ones who aren't cut out for the job."

"You mean weed out the losers." I laughed.

"Say it how you want." Ted moved behind a camera and started pressing buttons. "They're in school. They're students. They have a whole lot to learn still." He glanced over his shoulder to let me know he was serious about them being young.

"And that's why you're a teacher and I'm a director." My fingers grazed a script laying on the tabletop.

"Look, all I'm saying is that you didn't have to come down on her so hard."

I pointed at him. "You need to quit fucking your students."

He laughed. "Believe what you want, but I'm not fucking her."

My phone buzzed and I swiped it alive. "I have to take this."

Ted nodded and continued his slow prowl around my work.

"Mr. Reid." I pressed the phone to my ear. "What a surprise."

"Nash Brooks." I could hear his smile through the phone.

"What can I do for you, Wes?"

"You free tonight?"

"Why?" My brows furrowed. I knew Wes well enough that he wasn't just reaching out to have drinks with a buddy. No, it was always business with him and something was up. I could feel it.

"Nothing serious." His voice was calm and collected. "Just need to catch up on a few details. That's all."

He represented Ricky Moran, my star lead actor. It didn't matter what I had going on—when Wesley Reid wanted to meet, I fucking met. Without question.

Like the rest of Hollywood, Wes didn't give anyone a choice. Premier was the hottest agency in town and Wes was a goldmine of opportunity in L.A. This could be anything, but I could almost guarantee that it involved money. "Yeah. I'm free. Just closing shop for the night."

"Good," he said, friendly enough. "Meet me at Mojito. Eight, sharp."

"No details?" Ted was staring at me, wondering what it was Wes wanted. "C'mon, Wes. Shed some kind of light on the subject."

Silence hung on the line for a moment too long, just enough to get my nerves rattled.

"Let's just say that there's a quarter million different reasons you and I should talk."

75

Alex

"Damn, girl." Kendra gave me the once over. "And, here, I thought I was the one dressing to get fucked."

Suddenly my ears burned hot.

Kendra reached for my hand so she could twirl me around.

It was a party dress. I knew that. I'd chosen it on purpose. It was short. Like, halfway-up-my-thigh kind of short skirt that revealed too much. The way the southern California desert night air drifted up between my legs made me feel more exposed than what I considered comfortable. But I felt free flowing and I liked that.

Kendra whistled.

The back was open and I wasn't wearing a bra. Not with this dress. It didn't make sense. So my boobs were forced to support themselves tonight. I was also afraid of having my panty lines show through the thin fabric, so to eliminate that disaster I wore a thong. And now that I thought about what exactly I chose to wear tonight, Kendra was absolutely right—I *was* dressed to get fucked.

After the kind of day I had, maybe that wouldn't be a bad thing.

Like that would happen. Ha!

When I stopped twirling, Kendra stopped so we were standing face-to-face. Kendra licked the pad of her finger and pressed it against my bare shoulder. "Zizzle."

"Okay, stop it." I shuffled my feet. "Can we please just go inside?"

Kendra smiled and opened the door. It wasn't like I was the only one dressed to kill. She looked sexy as fuck, too. Once I stepped inside, I was surprised by how busy it was for a Thursday night. But then again, since this place opened up, it was the most talked about restaurant-bar on Rodeo Drive.

A tall man dressed in a designer suit couldn't take his eyes off Kendra. And who could blame him? She was a petite little thing who I'd heard was a vixen in bed. Don't ask me how I knew that, but people talk.

The hostess greeted her and before she said anything, Kendra turned to me. "Up or down?"

The bar appeared to be full up here and I wasn't in the mood for sitting outside on the patio.

"C'mon, what are you in the mood for?" Kendra was always so impatient. "To be on the top or bottom?" She wiggled her brows, giving a playful smirk. At least she found humor in all this.

I scanned my surroundings again. We'd been here twice before and had spent one evening up, and another down. The two levels had a totally different vibe. The top was lighter, upbeat; and down was a dark hidden bar that made you feel like you were stepping back in time when prohibition was in full force. "Down."

"Ohh, yeah. I like it." The words rolled off her tongue as she turned on a heel and told the hostess we'd escort ourselves down below.

"Like we're doing something illegal." I leaned my shoulder into hers as we both giggled. Because that was what it felt like when drinking downstairs.

"Let's drink the expensive shit." She hooked her arm in the crook of mine and together we began to move toward the staircase winding down.

My eyes dropped to the floor. I couldn't afford this place, even in my dreams.

"C'mon, hun." She pulled me tighter to her side. "Don't worry, I've got this."

My eyes softened and I said, "Someday I'll repay you. I promise."

She wrapped her hand around my wrist and tugged me downstairs. The air was damp and had a musky smell to it. Not quite like mothballs, but dewy. The light was low as I followed Kendra straight to the bar where she took two open seats on the far side. She ordered two whiskeys and I didn't want to know the cost. But it was safe to assume, because of where we were drinking tonight, they easily cost well over $20 per drink.

The handsome young bartender pushed two crystal glasses our way; one in front of each of us. I stirred with my straw before even thinking about taking a sip.

"So, you going to spill it or what?" Kendra took a sip and made a face.

"There's not much to spill." I barely looked at her when I said it.

"You made it sound way different earlier. Like you had big news."

"Did I?" I didn't know why I agreed to drink whiskey. There wasn't anything I liked about it. The flavor was just as harsh as the burn in the back of my throat as I swallowed it down. "It's just that the director ripped me a new one."

"Nash Brooks ripped you a new one?" Her brow formed a perfect arch.

I nodded and had a feeling where she was going to take this.

"God, what I'd do to have him do that to me." She gazed straight ahead as her daydream of Nash Brooks unfolded like a storybook inside her mind.

I rolled me eyes. Then snapped my fingers in front her face.

She blinked a couple times and giggled. "He's probably just feeling you out, Alex."

"This felt different." My eyes narrowed. I could still hear him belittling me in front of my colleagues. "Like he had his sights set on me the moment I arrived."

"Maybe he was just having a bad day." Kendra started scoping the room out for hot guys. "God, I'm so fucking horny. All day, it was all I could think about." She turned to me. "The only thing that gets me through the day. You know?"

"How's the job going anyway?" I wrapped my lips around the tiny straw. It was funny because I wasn't even sure this was how I was supposed to drink a drink like this.

She shrugged her shoulders. "It's good. Lots of bitch work. But hey! Livin' the dream."

I laughed. She was always so sarcastic, sometimes I couldn't tell if she really liked what she did or not. For all I knew, there was a hot guy at the office that made her want to stick around.

"What about him, would you fuck him?" She dropped her chin to her chest and gently nodded behind me.

He was tall, and dark, but looked a little rough around the edges.

"I bet he'd drive me home."

"He looks like a sketch-ball." I turned to scan in the opposite direction.

"Oh, no fucking way." Her jaw hit the floor.

I spun around to see what she was looking at. My heart stopped. The sip I'd just taken threatened to spill out the corner of my mouth. I knew him, even from all the way over here. He was instantly recognizable and impossible to ignore.

"Is that—" Kendra stumbled on her words.

"Wesley Reid." I set my glass down. Anyone who ever wanted to be an actor and was living in L.A. knew who he was.

"But who is that he's with?"

I twisted around and covered my face inside my hands.

"No way . . ." Kendra's voice dropped low. "You know him?"

"You do, too." I spread my fingers and peeked at her.

"Nash?" She mouthed as her eyes rounded.

"Oh God." My face planted into my palm. "We should go."

"No fucking way. You have to go talk to him."

"Go talk to him?" My expression was pinched.

"Flirt with him." She leaned closer. "Tell him you want him to take you home so you can—" Her brows rose high on her forehead.

"Kendra!"

"What?" She set her drink down and acted like it was nothing. "If you won't do it, I guess I'll have to." She slid off the barstool and was heading in their direction before I had time to stop her.

I had no choice but to follow or risk looking like an idiot.

76

Nash

"Wes—" I leaned forward on my elbows. "You've got to fucking believe me."

"It's plausible." He didn't flinch. "It's the same studio." He shrugged his shoulders and looked elsewhere.

I couldn't believe he was even asking me this. After what I watched happen to Blake Stone, no fucking way I would want to be associated with him in any way. "Look, Wes," I pleaded. "I can keep my eyes open and let my most trusted associates to do the same, but that's about it."

He shot me a wicked glare.

"It's all I got." I opened my palms. "Right now, I'm focused on the movie."

He didn't say anything, but he didn't have to. Wes was notorious for saying plenty with how he looked at you. Unfortunately for me, I was on the wrong side of the stick today. "I thought all that was taken care of anyway."

He swirled the ice in his drink. "Apparently there were some loose ends that slipped past the authorities."

I rubbed my forehead in an attempt to suppress the headache I felt coming on.

"Besides thinking that I already found it and am stashing it away for an early retirement," I laughed, but Wes didn't find it funny, "what do you want with it anyway?"

He stared into his drink long enough to make me believe he was contemplating his words carefully. Finally, he raised his glass and glared at me from over the rim.

No matter how much this conversation unsettled my nerves, I fought to keep face. There was no such thing as weakness when working with Wes.

Wes and I knew each other fairly well. He was well respected in the industry, and Ricky Moran, my star actor, was represented, not only by Premier, but by Wes himself. And until his latest woman came around, he let it be known he cared for only one thing—money.

That was why I didn't want anything to do with this. Because if what he was saying was true, there was no question it would trace back to him and Blake Stone.

I took a sip of my draft beer.

He never did answer my question. Instead, it was important I changed the subject without it looking like I was the guilty one. It would be tough to do, and even if I did manage to pull it off, he'd never believe me. At least, not until the truth finally did come out and he learned that I wasn't involved in any way, shape, or form. Just as I was trying to tell him. "I was really hoping you wanted to talk about Ricky."

He dropped his elbows to the table and closed half the gap between us. "What's up with Moran? Everything all right?"

"Yeah, yeah. He's fine," I calmed his worries.

He leaned back. "And you best believe that I have people on the inside watching your every move."

I sighed. This was going nowhere. I knew he was talking about Ricky Moran. I didn't have anything to hide, so fuck it. But Jesus fucking Christ, a quarter million dollars supposedly stashed away somewhere on my set? It seemed ludicrous. "Wes." My tone was more serious. "Does anyone else know about this?"

He dipped the end of his cigar in his bourbon.

If we weren't careful, this could blow up. Seriously explode and take a lot of people out with it at the same time. I realized that the only reason he was even discussing this with me was because he knew he could trust me.

"No one." He puffed his cigar. "Keep it that way, too."

I knew he meant business. "Yeah, of course," I whispered, staring down into the abyss of my glass. "I'll take a look around tomorrow, see if I can find anything."

Wes's face softened as it lifted and he looked over my shoulder.

I turned to see what stole his attention, and when I looked, I couldn't believe my eyes.

"Hey boys," the small woman teased.

"God damn, if I haven't died and gone to heaven." Wes was always quick with the women.

The woman's friend stared at me with large doe eyes and I casually looked away, acting as if I didn't recognize her.

"Thought I recognized you, so we thought we'd come and say hi." The small woman tugged on her friend's arm, making her stand by her side.

Wes's face scrunched, trying to place a face. "Can't say we've met, but I'm certainly interested in getting to know you." He held out his hand as if telling them to sit.

I slammed my drink down on the table. "You're interrupting a meeting."

Their faces dropped and Wes furrowed his brow.

"Now, if you don't mind, go back to where you came from." I lifted my drink and held it to my lips until I knew they got the hint.

"Yeah. Of course. Sorry." They turned and walked away, confused by my sudden outburst.

"What the fuck was that?" Wes asked.

"My fucking intern."

77

Alex

Kendra brushed off Nash's rudeness as fast as she found another table of guys to flirt with.

She had the confidence I could only dream of. Men devoured her free spirit. Even I did. What I'd do to have that very same carefree attitude that came so naturally to her. I admired it so much but it just wasn't who I was. No matter how hard I tried.

I spun the ice in my drink and watched her from a couple tables away. She sat in a guy's lap, twirling his long locks around her finger, luring him in nice and easy.

The way I felt was about the same as my glass—empty.

I knew she didn't mean to ditch me, but that was how it felt as I sat here alone with my thoughts. And after what happened with Nash Brooks and Wesley Reid, I just wanted to leave.

I mean, what was the point?

Kendra hadn't even bothered looking in my direction since she found him.

And Nash was such an asshole.

It was like he didn't even remember me. Like he didn't chew

me out and embarrass the shit out me today. It wasn't like I was really expecting much from him, but the least he could do was acknowledge my existence.

Tonight was such a mistake.

A big fat mistake I regretted.

I should have never let Kendra drag me to his table. Now I was so royally fucked it wasn't even funny. There was no way I was going to get through this internship alive. Let alone a position in the industry now that Wesley Reid knew my face.

I ducked my head and glanced over my shoulder to where Nash and Wes had been sitting. They were just finishing their drinks, getting up from their seats behind the table. I watched them as they made their way through the crowd and toward the stairs. Not once did either of them look in my direction, yet I was so paranoid they would. Like they had nothing better to talk about than me. I'd made a complete ass out of myself—they knew it and so did I—and there was no way I was that forgettable.

Or at least I hoped I wasn't.

When they weaved through the tables not too far from where I sat, I ducked forward, hoping that I was invisible. Against all odds, it seemed as if I was. Once they were headed up the stairs and out of sight, I could finally sit up straight again.

This was so stupid. I didn't feel like myself. Then again, I hadn't had so many big failures in a single day before. And when so much was on the line, too.

The bartender brought me another drink and said, "This one's on the house."

It couldn't get any more depressing than that. He even felt bad for me, sitting here all alone. No matter how much I wanted to act like I didn't need it, I accepted without hesitation.

Even though I knew the best thing would be to get home, go to bed, and forget today even happened, I reluctantly stayed, hoping something would go right for once.

I hadn't even taken my first sip when Kendra jumped on the stool next to me.

There was no point in saying anything because she had it written all over her face.

"See that guy over there?" She peered over her shoulder in his direction.

I acted like I hadn't been watching her get her freak on and played along. "I see him."

"What do you think?" There was a glimmer in her eye that allowed me to see clear into her future.

I glanced over my shoulder again. "He's all right."

"He's more than *all right.*" She leaned forward with a silly grin on her face.

I raised my brows.

"I'm going home with him."

"That was quick." My finger circled the rim of my glass.

"I told you I needed to get laid." She looked back in his direction. "And you should, too."

I rolled my eyes.

"He's got friends . . ." She leaned her shoulder into mine.

I didn't know why, but I looked over at the table again. It wasn't like I was going to go through with it even if I thought I had a chance. As my eyes drifted over the outliers, none of them were all that interesting. "Nah, I think I'll pass."

"Pass?" The word hissed as it rolled off her tongue.

"They don't portray the kind of confidence I need to convince me they'll last long enough to get me off." My face was expressionless. "I might as well take my chances with myself and fuck my vibrator instead."

Kendra laughed. "I see my sarcasm is rubbing off."

I smiled. "When life gives you lemons . . ."

"You make lemonade."

We both laughed.

The long-haired slim Jim strode over to our table and asked if she wanted to *hit it.*

Ugh. I wanted to gag. He was so gross. She really would try anything at least once. There was no way. Not my type. It didn't matter how desperate I was, I wouldn't ever stoop that low.

"Are you going to be fine getting yourself home?" Kendra's voice was filled with compassion as she hooked her thumb inside of her purse strap, pulling it in place.

"Yeah. I'm a big girl." I forced a smile.

We hugged and promised to text when both of us were home and safe.

He settled his bony arm across her shoulders and she clamped onto his waist. I watched them disappear up the stairs and waited a couple minutes before leaving myself.

I didn't bother finishing my drink. I wasn't in the mood.

Kendra's new man's friends were starting to look it my direction.

"Not gonna happen. Not now. Not tonight. Not ever," I said to myself.

Today was rough enough already. First, I woke up stoked to be starting the internship and getting my hands dirty on set. Then I got reamed by the director for something I apparently did wrong, only to be ditched by my best friend on the one night I really needed a shoulder to lean on.

Fucking brilliant.

I started to head up the stairs.

Typical Kendra to pounce on the first man who spoke to her in a nice voice. Maybe I was just jealous of what she had and I didn't. I, too, could use a good lay.

I moved swiftly through the busy upstairs and couldn't get outside quick enough. What a relief it was when I finally did step out beneath the night's dark sky.

I looked around, taking in the scene of Rodeo Drive. There were couples strolling hand-in-hand, laughing and enjoying the night. The air was crisp as it settled fresh in my senses, and since I was in a nice part of town with perfect weather, I figured it was as good as any night to take a mini-stroll and clear my head.

As I passed the shops and restaurants on Rodeo Drive, it was clear to me that this was the world I wanted to be in. Not with where I was now. Not broke and with no money. But at the top.

The lights. The cameras. The fame. The glory. All the reasons I'd come to L.A. in the first place.

It was everything I wanted but didn't know how to get. My career was in the hands of luck.

My arms wrapped around my body and hugged my stomach as I rounded a corner and hit a brick wall. "Oh, my God, I'm so sorry," I said, lifting my head to see who I just walked directly into. When I regained my balance, my heart nearly stopped—just my fuckin' luck.

He looked back at me, the corner of his lips tugging into a knowing grin.

I debated whether or not I should apologize or tell him to fuck off.

With how today went, and how he treated me like I was dirt, telling him to fuck off seemed like the more appropriate response.

78

Nash

I couldn't let her leave without me.

The moment I saw her walk outside, I downed my drink and exited out the back. The woman I was talking with yelled after me, but I paid little attention. I moved swiftly through the alley, hoping that I'd catch her before she caught a cab.

She was the one I wanted. The one I laid eye on first. The same sweet sexiness that I couldn't stop thinking about.

I straightened my shirt and ran my hand through my hair. My legs moved swiftly, and when I was about to turn a corner—*Bam!* —there she was, falling backwards from my brute force. My lips curled and all I could think about was how it seemed as if the universe was trying to tell me something.

She apologized before lifting her gaze to meet mine. Once she recognized who she was talking to, her lips pinched together and she narrowed her eyes.

Neither one of us said anything and time seemed to freeze.

"Look," she cast her gaze to the ground, breaking the uncomfortable silence between us. "I'm sorry. I don't know what I did wrong. If there is—"

I pressed the pad of my finger to her lips and silenced her.

Her gorgeous, tropical green eyes widened and it wasn't difficult for me to get lost in her beauty. My manhood swelled and twitched. Her lips were plump and were the type that stirred my imagination to awaken the dark desires I harbored—*oh the possibilities with this one.*

Slowly, I inched closer, closing the gap between us.

Her eyes darted across my face as she held her breath, waiting to see what I did next.

She was impossible to resist, and I knew from the moment I laid eyes on her this afternoon, that I had to have her. I leaned in and pressed my lips to hers.

She never backed away, nor did she protest. I held my mouth on hers and she closed her eyes as her mouth parted. My tongue plunged into her mouth with desperation.

She swished her velvety muscle over mine, wrapping her arms tightly around my neck as I pushed her back up against the wall.

My hands slid down her sides before coming back up and devouring her breasts. She arched her back and pressed her boobs deeper into my palms as they massaged her flesh.

The hum of car engines passed and echoed off the alley's brick walls and she sucked me in deeper. Pedestrians walked by without a care, and God damn, she tasted so nice—a mixture between sweet candy cherry and alcohol.

She fisted my hair and curled her leg around my thigh.

I thrust my hips deep between her thighs and was painfully hard. When I pulled back, breaking our kiss, I circled my hands over her wrists and pulled her arms high above her head.

Her eyes glossed over as she sucked in her bottom lip and gave me a *c'mon and fuck me* look.

I tightened my hold on her wrists with one hand and made it impossible for her to wiggle free. My head dropped to her neck as

I peppered kisses across her neck while I lifted her skirt with my free hand.

It didn't take long to find her hot mound, the dampness already seeping through the thin fabric of her nearly nonexistent panties. My cock swelled against my zipper the second she moaned.

"You're a bad girl." I nipped at her ear.

Her teeth found bare flesh on my neck. "Yes. Yes I am." She sank her teeth in.

I moved her panties to the side and slid my finger through her folds. She was so wet—wet and ready for my impending punishment. The pad of my thumb circled her swollen nub, and when I pressed it, her mouth rounded and she gasped.

"You want me to fuck you?"

"Yes." She tightened her leg wrapped around my thigh.

"Say it."

"Fuck me."

"No." I plunged a finger deeper into her hot cavern. "Say it like you mean it."

My lips crashed over hers and our tongues curled over and tied a knot. She was a killer kisser. The passion she had, I wondered if this was just how she was, or if I'd brought something out of her tonight.

"I want you to fuck me hard," she growled, fisting my hair.

My lips crashed over hers once again, and as she kissed me, I undid my belt, pulled my pants down to my knees, and freed my cock.

It ached and begged for relief.

I spun her around so her stomach faced the wall. I tore the foil wrapper open with my teeth, rolled on the rubber, hiked up her skirt, and plunged my thick girth into her dripping pussy.

She gasped at the suddenness of me driving deep inside her. Her sex clenched on my shaft and my fingers tightened their hold on her fleshy hips.

"Your. Answer. Was. Fucking. Brilliant," I said through clenched teeth, pumping fiercely into her.

She sucked in a breath and rode the wave.

I continued punishing her with my cock.

She mewed.

I unleashed a frenzy of quick piston-like bursts.

Her mouth opened and her voice vibrated in unison with my assault.

I thrust deeper and harder. My hand reached up and hooked around her throat. The tingle at the base of my spine intensified and I needed to see her face as I came inside her. I pressed her face against the wall and forced her to look at me.

A second later, I threw my head back and worked through the most intense orgasm I'd had all week.

79

Alex

I glanced over my shoulder to see if he was following me.

What the fuck just happened?

My hands flattened and smoothed down my skirt. The moment they brushed over my hips, I winced. They were bruised from where he'd sunk his claws into me. My fingers worked feverishly to try to bring some kind of normalcy to my frazzled hair.

Disbelief didn't even come close to explaining how I felt.

Nash Brooks just fucked me in an alley. Took me, claimed me as if I was his.

It was the hottest sex I'd ever had.

My shoulder brushed a couple I passed on the sidewalk. "Hey watch where you're going," the guy bitched at me.

"Sorry," I mumbled, hurrying along.

The walk signal flashed white the moment I hit the cross street. I scampered across the crosswalk with no real direction where I wanted to go. My head was still spinning. My sex throbbed, and the only thing certain was that I needed to call Kendra.

She wasn't going to believe what just went down.

Hot damn, the rumors were right. Nash was seriously hung. So fucking big. I'd never been with a man like him before. The way he stretched me to painful pleasure was so incredible. The intense heat that set my insides ablaze was unlike anything I could have ever imagined.

I picked up the pace without reason.

And how he took control over the situation—he was dominant, liked things his way, and my sex was still quivering because of everything he did. He had me coming quicker than anything I'd experienced before. Wave after wave of pleasurable bliss.

I tucked my phone back inside my clutch.

Kendra and I had set rules and only called when we were both home safe and sound. If I called her now, she wouldn't listen. No matter what it was I had to say. My story had to wait, and it was going to be a serious test of patience. There was still a lot of distance between me and my front door.

I kept looking over my shoulder, thinking he wasn't done with me.

It didn't matter that I saw him zip up and walk away. Because I also heard what he said. His words were seared into my brain. "This, between us, isn't over." He smiled and I quickly got lost in his sexy-ass dimples. "There will be more, and you should always be ready."

And maybe that was why I was walking in the opposite direction so fast. It wasn't because I was ashamed of what I allowed him to do. No, that was really fucking hot.

No, the reason I kept looking over my shoulder was because I was in utter disbelief. It was unfathomable to think this would happen only an hour ago.

My shoulders tucked and I worked my way through a crowd standing outside the bar entrance, smoking on the street.

Nash created mystery, hope, and somehow made it fun. I liked the excitement of not knowing exactly what he was going to do next. If he'd even do anything at all. Either way, the game he'd started had definitely turned my shitty day completely around—even if it was just a onetime thing.

My feet shuffled over the concrete as I scurried beneath the street light. I heard what he said. Clear as day. He knew exactly who I was. And *he liked my answer.*

My lips spread across my face into the largest grin I'd had in what felt like a very long time. And just as I rounded the corner, I looked over my shoulder one last time.

He wasn't there.

I'd just have to wait to see him tomorrow.

My toe jammed into a solid block, tripping me. I went flying through the air head over heels. Once I landed and pushed myself up off the cool pavement, I looked to see what I'd just tripped over.

What the—

I looked around, but I was the only one on this block.

Slowly, I crawled on my hands and knees until I hovered over the duffel bag. It was open and spilling bricks of hundred dollar bills out the top. Just when I thought this day couldn't get any stranger.

A shiver shook my body.

The sound of my heartbeat thrashed in my ears.

Gently, as if the bag was going to bite, I pinched the zipper cautiously and opened the duffel bag a little bit more.

Holy shit. My eyes bugged.

There was more money inside this bag than I'd ever seen in my entire life. Voices battled inside my head about what I should do. One side told me to take it and run. Pay off my debt. Move to a new apartment. The other side screamed for me to run. This wasn't mine. The money belonged to someone dangerous.

I looked around one last time.

The block was quiet and void of people.
My hand trembled as I zipped it back up.
Fuck me, I breathed.
My body shook uncontrollably.
Fuck it. I grabbed it and ran.

BONUS BOOK 2

On My Knees

The Hollywood Nights Series Vol. 2

Alpha Billionaire Romance

A Shot of Romance

CJ Thomas

80

Alex

Cash. And shit loads of it.

I looked over my left shoulder. My bedroom door was cracked. Only a little. But still too much to keep me from feeling comfortable.

I ran to shut it tight.

I bit the inside of my cheek as my fingers pinched the deadbolt. My chest rose as I inhaled a deep breath of stale bedroom air. Time seemed to slow as my fingers turned. My breath was trapped deep inside my lungs up until I heard the lock click in place—relief swept over me.

My forehead dropped to the door and I sighed.

I was home.

And I was safe.

At least for now.

My chest rose and fell as I took a couple deep breaths before finally turning around to face the reason I ran home as quickly as I could. I was hot and sweaty and still needed to kick off my flats.

My hands were still clenched tightly to the doorknob behind

my back, as if subconsciously I wanted to flee. Run away from it all. Forget I'd made this really fucking bad decision.

That would be the smart choice. But now I was afraid that it was too late. I'd made my decision and it was something I had to live with. No one could know about this.

And I meant *no one*. Not even Kendra.

My heart pounded irregularly in my chest.

I hoped that I wouldn't come to regret this.

My head fell back and crashed against the door in the same spot my forehead was pressed only a moment ago. I couldn't help myself. It was impossible to resist. My eyes were glued to the pile of cash.

It was so bizarre. So many questions swirled inside my head. Not one of which I had an answer to.

Where did it come from?

Whose was it?

Why was it there?

My face dropped into the palms of my hands and I struggled to swallow down the pain in the back of my throat.

This wasn't mine.

I should have just left it where I found it.

What was I thinking?

I rubbed my face and wondered how this could be real. There was no way. Any minute I swore cameras were going to pop out of nowhere and someone would tell me I was part of some reality TV prank. *The joke was on me.*

"Ha! Welcome to the big leagues, interns," I could hear Nash Brooks's voice saying.

My gaze fell at my clock sitting on top of my nightstand—after midnight—before falling to the floor, crumbling beneath the weight of my night. I pinched the bridge of my nose when they closed again.

And if it wasn't an initiation prank from Nash Brooks, then it would be the police who would come knocking. Or even worse, the rightful owners of all this cash.

My eyes popped wide open.

No one knew me or where I lived, I tried to reason with myself.

No one saw me take it. *Or, let's hope there were no witnesses.*

I was the only one who knew I had it. *Please God, keep this between you and me.*

There was no reason to worry—except I knew I wouldn't find a wink of sleep tonight.

I pushed off the door and marched straight for my bed. Slowly, I lowered myself to the edge, letting the mattress dip beneath my weight. My fingers brushed feather-light strokes over the green bricks before I finally had the guts to pick one up.

My fingertips peeled back the wrapper and time seemed to freeze.

I counted it carefully. As the number steadily increased, my head started to float. It was $100 bills in stacks of 25. My eyes widened when I realized that I was holding $2,500 in just my right hand. All cash. And I couldn't help but wonder, *how much money was actually there?*

I leaned over and pulled back the sides of the duffel.

One by one I counted the bricks inside. There seemed to be no end in sight. I kept going, digging through the pile without making a dent. I was sure the bag was bottomless.

Several minutes passed before I unloaded all of its contents, stacking each and every brick nicely on my floor.

I'd created a castle of money—100 bricks total.

I wiped my brow with the back of my shaky hand.

$250,000.

It wasn't chump change, but the kind of money people killed for.

My breaths came out in small shallow rasps. I was scared. Really fucking scared. Like, the kind of fear that penetrated down to my bone, kind of terror. There was no denying I was in way over my head without a clue as to what to do next.

No one leaves or misplaces this kind of money.

Shit. Fuck. Holy. Fucking. Shit. I began pacing my room.

When I heard the front door open, my heart stopped.

My head spun in the direction of the bedroom door.

The air I was breathing trapped itself inside my lungs the moment my throat constricted. I held my breath and listened.

Heavy footsteps moved across the floor. I could hear a couple muffled voices through the wall. Quickly, I stuffed every last brick back inside the duffel, zipped it up, and tossed it under my bed.

The footsteps continued my way before they stopped right outside my door.

My hands trembled and my face grew hot from the lack of oxygen.

I stared and waited.

Then someone knocked.

81

Nash

I tossed an empty box across the stage. "Fuck!"

My hands rooted firmly into my hips as I fought to catch my breath. I'd torn the place apart. And all for what? Chasing a hidden and lost treasure I wasn't even sure existed?

Fuckin' Wes.

He was the one to blame. He'd planted these thoughts in my head and led me to believe it would be here, somewhere on my movie set.

I should've known better.

It was probably his way of getting back at me for something I wasn't even aware I'd done. He was like that—ensuring we all knew who the big man on campus was.

All night, it was all I could think about. Well, besides what I did to my intern in the alleyway.

I bit my bottom lip and chuckled.

God. She was so fucking tight. The moment I slid my girth into her hotness, I knew that it wouldn't be my last conquest. There was so much potential. Her height, size, and roundness left every last possibility on the table for me to have. And after experiencing that little taste of what could be, I couldn't wait to explore every inch of her and make it clear she was mine.

My thoughts slowly drifted back to my conversation with Wes. The money was real. He wouldn't just call me up, out of the blue, if it wasn't.

What he did to Blake Stone left ripples across town. For the most part, the overwhelming majority were happy for Wes to take him on. Fight him for what he was doing to our industry. Yet, hidden behind all the praise, there were a handful of people who now swore themselves as Wes's enemies.

Blake Stone would get what he deserved. I was sure of it. But I sure as shit hoped that Wes wouldn't get what some thought *he* deserved.

As for me, I just wanted to stay out of the drama.

My mind was set on finding that money. I'd heard enough—through trusted sources like Julia Mabel—to believe that not all the money the DEA suspected Blake of making was accounted for. No one knew exactly how much was missing, but it was thought to be somewhere in the hundreds of thousands—the kind of treasure worth hunting for.

I let my eyes drift across the set.

It had to be here, hidden somewhere among all the clutter.

"What the hell happened here?" Ted's voice echoed off the walls behind me.

I turned around and found him alone. He walked slowly toward me with his hands in his pockets, scanning the floor I'd just made a mess of.

I moved across the room and joined him.

It was a war zone after my tirade. He probably thought I was drinking and had a moment of self-doubt. It had happened before on a movie I had been filming, but not for a while. And wasn't that something that happened to all creative types? Losing their cool when thinking what they created wasn't good enough?

"I, huh, I lost something." I ran my fingers through my hair.

He squinted at me. I could tell he was silently calling my bullshit. What could I have lost that was so important to tear apart the stuff hidden in the corners that hadn't been touched in years?

It was a stupid excuse. I knew it the moment I said it. You'd think I would have a few more tricks up my sleeve from constantly being surrounded by the world's best actors.

But I didn't.

My mind was too far down the rabbit hole, chasing this stupid dream of easy money.

"What's up? Don't you have class or something?"

Ted paced back and forth, picking up and turning over boxes, setting them back in their proper places. He took the time to read the script printed on the outside of each box before moving across the room and opening another chest.

As I kept my focus on him from the corner of my eye, I couldn't help but question his behavior. It was like he had also heard of Wes's theory and was looking for the prize himself.

"I thought more about how you treated Alex." He flipped a box inside his hands and glanced in my direction.

"Who's Alex?" My brows drew together.

He gave me a skeptical look. "The intern who answered your question perfectly. The one you treated like dirt. My best, and most promising, student. Remember her?"

"Oh, her." My words were as slow as my nodding head. "Haven't we talked about this already?"

He hung his head to his chest and clucked his tongue. "She's really good."

I knew that.

She was good. Yes. But I swore to myself that I'd make her fucking great.

My eyes closed. And when they did, all I could see were her amazing Caribbean green eyes and jet black hair; all I could fell was how that tight pussy of hers fit over my cock like a glove. "Why is it you're here?" My eyes opened and landed on Ted.

"I came by because I have a request."

I paced back and forth, wondering where I would hide stacks of cash if it were me smuggling drugs. There were too many nooks and crannies, too many props and other junk to know where to even begin to start looking.

If it were me, I'd hide it in plain sight.

I glanced over my shoulder in Ted's direction. "What kind of request?"

He put the box he was holding back down. "I need you to keep your distance from Alex Grace."

That was her full name—*Alex Grace.*

I liked the way it sounded rolling off my tongue. Smooth and sexy, just like my hands on her hips as I drove into her, punishing her with my pulsing cock.

Ted lifted his brows as he stared at me.

She would be impossible to keep my distance from. There were three things that consumed me.

One. *When Darkness Fell.*

Two. The supposed missing money.

Three. Her—Alex Grace.

"If you're interested in her, why not just come out and say it?"

He pinched his lips together. "I'm not having this same conversation with you again."

I laughed. "It's no secret."

He stared at me but couldn't find the same amusement I was having.

"And if you think you're doing a good job of hiding it, you're not." I waved him off, rolling through my laughter. "It's just that you keep talking about her."

"I'm asking you for this simple favor because I don't want to see you toss away someone who actually has talent."

My laughter dimmed. "What's that supposed to mean?"

He began to walk away. "Just do me this one favor." He sliced his hand through the air.

My gaze quickly landed on the one box Ted didn't bother stacking.

This wasn't over.

I'd have Alex Grace.

And I'd find the money Wes clued me in on.

Wes was one of those guys who just begged for competition. He invited me to play when he asked me if I knew anything about it. And now I wanted it—really fucking bad. The way I saw it, it was a race to find it first.

And the clock started now.

82

Alex

I met Kendra early for coffee. When she called, I figured she'd want to talk about last night.

We ordered our drinks and we found an empty table in the back, up against the windows looking out to the sidewalk.

She kept stealing glances at me between licking her lips and smiling, waiting for me to ask.

"What?" I giggled, playing dumb.

She shook her head, giggled, and swished her bangs across her forehead.

"How was he?" I asked. No use in dragging out the inevitable.

She sprang forward, straightened her spine, and slid her elbows halfway across the table. "He plays the *guitar*."

"Slim Jim. He plays the guitar?" My words were slow as my mouth slackened.

She nodded enthusiastically.

"What about . . . you know?" I rolled my wrist.

She slumped down in her seat. "He was okay."

Memories of him polluted my mind. He had that grunge look

to him. I knew that neither he, nor his friends, were my type. Lucky for me, I decided to leave alone and not take Kendra up on her offer of allowing me to sleep with one of his friends. That one decision allowed me to experience the exclusive, and massively hung, Nash Brooks. Which I was sure was a hell of lot better than the sex she had.

"He was a stub." Kendra narrowed her eyes and held up an inch gap between her fingers to show me his size.

I looked away, recoiled, and shook through a tremor.

That wasn't the last of her story. She continued on, going into much more detailed information than I ever cared to know. Slowly, my eyes glossed over, my ears muffled, and my mind drifted back to Nash as I stared at my friend, pretending to listen.

Nash Brooks.

My sex clenched just thinking about him. And if it wasn't for finding that money, he would have consumed me entirely.

"He was so tall; there was no way I wasn't going to not be on top." Kendra was still talking about her night rolling around with Slim Jim. "It was fun for what it was, but I won't be seeing him again."

I set my coffee mug back down after taking a sip. "Are you ever going to stop shopping around?"

She belted out a sharp pitched laugh. "Baby doll, please." She angled herself so that she was facing the counter. "The only way I'll stop sleeping around and be exclusive to just one penis, is if someone as famous and rich as Nash Brooks decides my pussy is the one his donkey dick wants."

Heat swept my face and I had to look away.

She stopped talking and eyed me. "Are you blushing?"

My eyes were all over the place, trying to find refuge anywhere but on her.

I wanted to tell her about Nash fucking me. But I couldn't. It didn't seem right. Like she'd believe me anyway. One minute he was pushing me away at the bar, and the next he had me pressed up against a brick wall, spreading my legs wide.

The entire night was too random for even me to believe that was what *actually* happened. Besides, it was probably a onetime thing anyway. I mean, if it happened to Kendra, I'd have more questions than I had time for. And that was exactly what I didn't want to happen—setting myself up for my own interrogation.

"It's my roommate." I changed the course of our discussion, knowing that she'd understand if I brought up my bitch of a roommate.

Her lips pointed and curled over her coffee mug. "She still squawking like a banshee when bangin' his brains out?"

My eyes smiled. Kendra always had a special way of saying things. "Yeah, but last night she came home and marched straight up to my door."

"What did she want?"

"She said that I needed to move out."

What I couldn't tell her was how scared I was that someone was after what I found. I wasn't sure what I was going to do with the money and I thought it was best to keep quiet about it until I had a plan. I was sure someone would be looking for it and I didn't want to entangle Kendra in my own mess.

"Fuckin' bitch," Kendra said under her breath. "What are you gonna do?"

My hands cupped my mug as I stared into the creamy abyss. "What *can* I do? I have to find another place."

"Doesn't she have to give you some heads up?"

"No." I looked up at her from beneath my brow. "I never signed a lease."

"Because . . . ?" She craned her neck like it was the weirdest thing she'd ever heard.

"I couldn't afford the first and last month's rent." I lifted my mug and sucked down a sip. "Or the security deposit," I said, swallowing down the hot liquid.

"But she let you live there anyways" Her brow tightened.

I nodded once. "I pay more per month. That was our agreement."

"And now she's kicking you out because the boyfriend wants to fuck her in your room?"

"Oh, God. Gross." My nose scrunched and I turned away as if I smelled something foul.

"What?" She shrugged her shoulders. "They probably already have. When you weren't there. She'd totally do that. You know it."

"Stop it." I leaned back and twisted my hair over my shoulder. "I don't know how I'm going to afford another place."

Except that wasn't entirely true. If only I had the guts to spend the money I found, then my problem would be no problem at all. I could live anywhere I wanted. If only it was that easy and I could brush off the guilt I knew I'd feel if I did spend even just one dollar of it.

Something about all this didn't gel.

"I know you're not going to like this—" Kendra lowered her chin and arched a brow. "But you could always come live with me."

83

Nash

"Alex!" I called her over.

Like I could stay away from something I desperately needed to have all to myself. Ted was naïve in thinking that his request, and our friendship, was enough for me to stay away from someone like her. He knew me better than that.

She ran over, and when she was within reach her chin dipped down. "Mr. Brooks."

I reached out and smoothed my hand down her upper arm. Naturally, she pulled away, like a flinch, but eventually settled into my warm embrace. "Alex, please. Call me Nash."

She eyed me with a set jaw.

"Easy tiger." I laughed. "If Nash is too formal, stick with Brooks. Just drop the mister. Got it?"

She nodded, giggled anxiously, and relaxed as she tucked a loose strand of hair behind her hair.

Her ears flamed red and I knew she was just as lost in what happened last night as I was. My gaze drifted across her delicious features all too easily, as neither one of us had the tenacity to talk about what happened.

Her black hair cascaded down her back. She was wearing a loose fitting guava colored blouse, matched perfectly with washed out jeans. Her earrings feathered a turquoise color that brought out her flushed cheeks and had me painfully hard.

She rocked back and forth on her heels, staring out over the busy set as teams marched from one task to the next. It was late in the afternoon and I'd been working them hard for a few hours now.

"I want you to work with Ricky Moran."

Her head tilted to lock eyes with me.

I knew what it was she was thinking. And, no, it wasn't that. She was doing just fine working with costume to get everything set for the next scene. "Is that a problem?"

"No." She shook her head, and when she did, her bangs swished across her forehead. "What is it you want me to do?"

"Anything he wants."

She lifted her hand to her mouth and tapped her finger on her bottom lip.

Fuck me; she was dead sexy. There was nothing I wanted to do more than tug down that same lip and slide my cockhead past it and over her satin tongue.

"Hey, Ricky." I caught him passing by. "C'mere."

He jogged over. "What's up Nash? You like that last scene or what?" He bounced on his toes like a MMA fighter and let out a booming laugh.

"There's someone I'd like you to meet."

His eyes landed on Alex.

"Alex, Ricky." I waved my hand between the two of them. "Ricky, Alex."

"Hi." Alex held out her hand. Ricky shook it.

"Ricky, when's the last time your trailer was cleaned?"

Alex's face reddened as she glared at me.

"A long time." He leaned back as he said it.

"Good. Show Alex the way. She'll be cleaning it now." I crossed my arms across my chest and smiled.

"Thanks Nash." Ricky flung his arm around her shoulder and leaned in to whisper something in her ear that I couldn't hear as they walked away.

I knew she'd hate me for it, but it was important I kept her in her place. Especially if she was going to be my lover.

I pinched my lips and a moan escaped from deep within. She had me hypnotized as I watched her hips bounce from side-to-side. My masculinity was heavy as it strained against my briefs.

There was only one time before Alex that a lover was as willing to let me fuck her without properly introducing ourselves first. And it just so happened that she was also an intern brought to me by the great professor, Ted Fields.

Call me a sucker for young, naïve women—but it was true. There was no denying it. I had my reasons for taking them to bed; and teaching them my ways was only half the fun.

That was what Ted was really worried about—that the same thing would happen again.

Maybe Alex was his best student. But so what? There was more to it than just that. And though he rarely brought up what happened with me and the last intern, I knew he still had some tough questions for me.

Ricky glanced over his shoulder and winked.

Alex turned to see who he was waving to, and when she saw it was me, her expression tightened.

A part of me still believed it was Ted who was most interested in laying her down in his bed. I wasn't interested in bringing Alex to bed. What I really had my sights set on was making her my Submissive.

And that would happen. All in due time.

I weaved between the crowds and made my way to the set decorators.

Putting Alex with Ricky was all part of the plan.

It was no accident. I wanted her there. Inside his trailer. To take care of him and study his moves.

But more than that, I hoped that she might learn if he knew anything about the money Wes said was never found.

It was a gamble. A risk I hoped would play out in my favor.

I get the money. I win over the girl. Game over.

The only possible flaw to my grand scheme was that Alex could fall for Ricky somewhere along the way. Hell, he was already putting his moves on, and after what I assigned her to do, she probably wouldn't mind trading me in for him.

Ricky was good enough to have her. Damn good. But not as solid as I was.

It was up to me to let her know who she really wanted. I was the boss. The one she listened to. And when she knew that she was mine, she'd do anything I asked.

84

Alex

Pain lined my eyes.

My hands cupped beneath the facet, filling them with water, before splashing it over my face.

Anger painted my complexion and nothing seemed to wash it away.

It was just awkward to be around him. I stretched my face and circled my jaw, making my ears pop. I didn't know what to expect after what we did last night. A part of me knew it would be uncomfortable at work today.

But nothing told me it would be like this.

Everything was going so well in costume. Then he had to reassign me and put me under Ricky Moran.

"Listen to me," I whispered to myself as I dabbed my face dry.

If it was anybody else, they'd be psyched to be so close to such a big Hollywood hot shot. And on any other day, and under different circumstances, perhaps I, too, would be stoked for the opportunity.

Except today wasn't just any other day. Nash did this on purpose and I couldn't place my finger on why.

Ricky was nice. He made me feel comfortable and it wasn't hard for me to warm up to him as he walked me to his trailer. That was good. Real good.

But he wasn't the one I wanted to flirt with. Nash's words from last night still plagued my thoughts. *"There will be more, and you should always be ready."*

Those were his exact words—verbatim. The same words that kept my mind speeding around the race track all night, preventing me from getting a good night's sleep. But there was a huge contradiction with what he said and how he acted today.

The words he spoke last night didn't come to mean what I thought he meant by them. Maybe I was over-thinking everything, making it into something more than it really was. I didn't know.

The toilet flushed behind me and Val, another intern, stepped out of the stall.

I smiled through the mirror's reflection.

She smiled back but paired it with a dismissive glance that I didn't know how to interpret.

I wondered what that was about. It wasn't like we were competing for a job or anything. So why the attitude? It totally caught me off guard. I brushed it off as quickly as I could, giving her the benefit of the doubt that she didn't mean anything by it. After all, I didn't know her all that well, so maybe she was just like that—bitchy.

"What team were you thrown into?" I tried to be nice and start a friendly conversation.

She scrubbed her hands and huffed. "Lighting."

"Close to the action." I smiled.

"It was fine." She looked up at me while she massaged soap into her hands. "Nash is keeping the Assistant Director spot open.

That's what I *really* want." She dropped her gaze and turned her head away.

I shuffled my feet and pushed the hair out of my face. "Huh, I hadn't heard that."

"Yeah." She glanced at me for a brief second. "And I want it." She smirked an evil grin. "And I'll do anything it takes to get it." She laughed but it came out more like a witch's screech.

My brows tightened as I thought about her words. I was positive Professor Fields would have told me about it. He told me everything. "Where did you hear that?" I asked.

"Word gets around." She turned off the water, shrugged her shoulders, and shook out her hands as she reached for a towel. "I heard your day went straight to the toilet." She glanced over her shoulder to be sure I heard.

"Literally." My eyes rolled as I sighed.

"At least it was Ricky Moran's trailer you got to clean." She turned to face me and finished wiping her hands dry. "Not everyone gets a glimpse inside that."

"I guess." I leaned against the counter and crossed one ankle over the other.

She stepped forward and said, "Nash must really hate you."

My heart skipped a beat and my breath hitched. I stared straight into her beady reptilian eyes.

"I mean, first he tears you apart on our first day." She paused and curled one side of her mouth up. Then she turned on a heel, flinging her hair into my face. "And now he makes you the cleaning lady." She laughed.

I hated how much truth there was behind what she said. But what could I do? "Tomorrow will be another day." I pushed off the counter and moved outside.

Val followed me and asked if I needed a ride home.

"Nah, I've got some errands to run," I lied, playing it cool. It couldn't have been further from the truth. In all honesty, I just didn't want to be around her any more than I already had. Taking the bus was so much better than listening to her babble on about how great she thought she was.

"I have a car." She stretched her neck forward and jingled her keys.

"Maybe next time."

"Suit yourself." She spun around and never looked back.

There was so much on my mind as I moved out to the street and headed down the sidewalk toward the nearest bus stop. Could Val be right? Was Nash purposely making an example out of me?

But what about last night? Was that some kind of example, or lesson, he wanted to teach *only* me? And what for?

None of it made any sense.

Why didn't I know about him keeping the Assistant Director position open? That was the one spot *everyone* wanted. Including me.

When the bus finally approached, I stepped toward the curb, hanging my toes over the edge, and thought how I could end this personal misery I inflicted upon myself every single day—by taking the bus everywhere—if I just had the courage to spend the money I found.

85

Nash

I watched Alex step out from the bathroom with another intern.

"Hey, Mikey." I squeezed the shoulder of Mike, the costume director. "Come across any boxes out of the ordinary?" Alex stopped to talk to the other woman and I kept her in my line of sight so she couldn't slip away.

"Shit, Nash. That's been my life for the last twenty years." He bent over and picked up a suit left out for tomorrow's scene.

I chuckled at the truth of his statement.

"What you should be asking is why things don't get put back in place so I have a fighting chance of finding them when I actually need them." He gave me a look as he moved across the floor to the wardrobe like it was my fault that nothing ever got put away. "Why you asking anyway? You know this place as well as I do." He flicked his gaze in my direction as he pulled a hanger from the closet.

"No reason." I turned my head to find Alex stuffing some papers into a folder before closing it up and filing it away in her bag. "It's just that you never know when a lost treasure will reemerge and be of real use to our current project."

Even though I was talking with Mike, I couldn't keep my eyes off her.

Alex's tits dangled free as she bent over, giving me the most amazing view of her deep cleavage; the very same gorge I wanted to drive my cock between on its way into her mouth.

"Nash."

I blinked and turned my attention back to Mike.

He gave me a skeptical look and brushed off the suit before hanging it back up. "We had this place pretty well organized before we began shooting." He straightened his spine and let his eyes drift casually across all the boxes he had spread out on the floor. "If my guys would have found anything, it would have been then." He gave me an easy nod.

"You trust your guys?"

He stepped forward and planted his hands on his hips.

I showed him my palms, not wanting to intentionally pick a fight. "All right. I got it. You would have told me if you did," I conceded.

Mike relaxed and went back to work.

I turned my head and saw Ricky walking on the far side of the room. "Let me know if you do come across anything."

"Yeah, yeah, whatever you say," Mike mumbled as I galloped across the floor to catch up with Ricky.

Ricky stopped and laughed when he saw me hurrying toward him. "Please tell me you have another intern ready to do my chores."

I forced a laugh. "Did she do a good job?"

"Trailer is clean as a whistle." He rounded his lips and whistled a single note. "Even my toilet." He nodded.

"Excellent."

"She's cute, too." He lowered his voice and came closer to my ear as if not wanting anybody else to hear him say it.

A flash of jealous anger tightened my muscles.

"Not my usual type." He broke eye contact and looked over the top of my head. "But under the right circumstances—like during a dry spell—I might find enough interest to explore more of what she has."

My fists clenched at my sides and I hated how he was talking about the woman who drove me wild. She wasn't his type. He liked long and lengthy versus short and curvy. Besides, he wouldn't know how to handle a woman like her.

He cast his gaze back to me. "Anyway, thanks for that. It really needed the polish. I'll let you know when it needs attention again."

"Don't get used to it." I winked.

He cocked his head to the side and gave me a questioning look.

"Just focus on the script." My voice was low and straight to the point. "We've got ourselves a busy schedule ahead."

He gave me a look like he wondered what he'd done to piss me off. I was in no mood to explain it to him. Not now. And lucky for me, the woman he was currently dating came up behind him and wrapped her arms around him.

"Don't you worry about me." He lifted his arm and she popped her head through. "I've got this character ingrained in my head."

"Good. Keep it that way."

"Hey Nash," his flavor of the week greeted me.

I turned my back without saying a word. I didn't know her name. Didn't care to know it either. She was a new face for Ricky, and was lucky I let her on set.

My eyes snapped shut and I rubbed my face in the palm of my hands. When I opened them again, Alex was gone. *Shit.* I'd wasted too much time hearing Ricky talk about nothing important and somehow I let her slip past my hungry gaze.

She can't be far.

I ran to my director's chair, grabbed my keys and sunglasses off the table, and booked it to my car. Once the engine roared to life, I zipped out of the parking lot, squealing the wheels as I rounded the corner, hoping that I'd find Alex before it was too late.

The engine purred as I pressed in the clutch and shifted into high gear.

I scanned the horizon, and there she was.

She wasn't hard for me to spot. Even from this far away, I could see her standing with her arms crossed, her flamingo-pink shirt glowing in the afternoon sunlight.

I dropped a gear and sped faster to catch up—needing to have her in my grasp.

A dirty cloud of exhaust expelled from the back of the city bus as it pulled into the stop where she was standing.

Alex stepped forward and I knew she was planning to get on.

I pressed the accelerator down to the floor and sped faster to her. There was no way she was going to get on that bus. Not if I had anything to do about it.

Slamming on the brakes, I honked my horn just as she was about to take the first step inside.

Fuck. Look at me, Alex. Look.

She turned to look but I knew she couldn't see me through the reflection on the windows. There was no way of knowing who was behind the wheel.

The next second, I flung the door open and stepped foot onto the street. "Alex," I yelled over the traffic.

She lifted her hand and shielded her brow from the sun. Her face showed recognition and her gaze narrowed.

"Come." I waved her over. "Get inside."

86

Alex

I had no idea what the hell was happening.

First Nash, then Val, and now this.

It was like the drama from the studio had found a way to infiltrate my real life and I couldn't decide if it was me or L.A. that was losing it.

When the stallion-white Tesla sports car sped up to the bus—like there was some kind of serious emergency unfolding before my very eyes—I didn't know what to think. And when it started honking, I flinched and hugged myself.

What the—

My hair flung over my shoulder as I looked around to judge other people's reactions. No one else seemed to see what I was seeing. Not a care in the world.

I turned back to the car and my stomach flipped, instinct telling me that somehow it was here for me. But who was it?

Time paused and my vision tunneled when nothing seemed to happen. I wondered if Val had followed me and wouldn't take no for an answer. It was possible, but not likely. She didn't seem like the kind to go out of her way for someone like me.

So who was this and why did it seem like they were trying to get my attention?

I squinted my eyes and shielded the sun with my hand. If only I could see inside, then I'd know who it was and what they wanted.

But I couldn't see anything.

The windshield had a wicked reflection shining off of it and I might as well have been staring into a mirror.

"C'mon, lady, we don't have all day." The bus driver tapped the flat of his palm on his huge steering wheel and gave me the stink eye. "I'm on a schedule."

"Sorry," I pointed back at the spotless white sports car. "But I think—"

His eyes widened as if saying, *Get on the bus or wait for the next one.*

My knee bent and I took my first step up the stairs just as I heard my name called over the loud traffic noises. I stretched my neck back to the car flashing its lights behind the bus.

My heart skipped a beat before a heat flash shocked my system stiff.

Oh. My. Lord.

And when I saw who it was, my whole body tensed.

What was *he* doing here?

After what he pulled today, I had nothing to say to him. Instinctively, I wanted to turn around and run in the opposite direction. But knew I couldn't.

Val's words echoed in my ears. *Nash must really hate you.*

Maybe she was right. He'd fucked me and then rewarded my submission by making me the cleaning lady.

My nostrils flared at the insult.

"Hey, lady. I really have to get these wheels back on the road," the bus driver barked.

I turned to Nash. He was waving me over.

My options were simple; get back on the bus or obey Nash and actually have a shot at making a name for myself in the ultra-competitive movie industry.

I hesitated.

The bus driver snarled.

Nash smiled.

My decision was much too easy to make.

Reluctantly, I stepped off the bus, unable to hold it up any longer than I already had. Not a split second later the doors closed and I stood there watching it chug to speed as it coughed a big dark plum of exhaust in my face.

Fucking great.

When the smoke cleared, Nash was still leaning against his car with the most gorgeous smile planted on his face. I hated him for being so damn sexy. But it was true. I couldn't get enough no matter how badly he treated me when others were around.

"C'mon. Get inside." He pushed off his car and walked around to the curb side.

I held my chin high as I walked in long strides to meet him. "What now? You need your house cleaned?"

He licked his lips and laughed. "Not exactly."

My tongue smoothed over the front of my top teeth. "Then what?"

He quirked a playful grin as he looked up at me from beneath his brow.

I looked around at the chaos—both cars and people—surrounding us. "Can't fuck me here."

He took his hand out of his pants pocket, leaned over and opened the door to the backseat. "Wanna bet?"

87

Nash

I wasn't going to do it. It hadn't even crossed my mind.

But when those words escaped her beautiful lips, how could I resist?

She bent over and stepped into the backseat. All I wanted to do was bury my face in her ass. God damn, she had the roundest globes of any woman I'd ever known and I wanted them so fucking badly slapping against my thighs as I fucked her hard and deep. Just the sight of them made me painfully hard.

I licked my chops and followed her inside, pushing her to the opposite side of the car where she stared at me, blinking rapidly.

My gaze dropped to her plump, full lips, as her tongue slid across the bottom one, wetting it. I wanted it pressed against my mouth as I curled my tongue over hers, tasting the sweetness that created the ache between my legs.

She twirled her long hair over her shoulder and looked down at her feet.

My gaze roamed freely, traveling down her V-neck exposing

her bronzed skin, and over her round chest before landing directly between the thighs she had pressed tightly together.

"Are you going to just stay parked here?" There was a warm glimmer in her eye.

"Is that a problem?"

She looked to the empty front seat. "At some point another bus will need the space."

"And they'll just have to figure it out." My cock twitched when I saw her nipples poking through her blouse.

"So you don't care?" Her fingers fidgeted inside the palms of her opposite hands.

I shook my head once before my eyes lifted up off her chest and met her gaze. "You're mad."

She turned her head and looked out toward the vehicles racing by on the road.

I reached out and grabbed her hand. "It's because I had you clean Ricky's trailer, isn't it?"

She flipped her head around and squinted her eyes when she met my gaze. "I'm better than that. You know it, too."

My fingers circled over her bony wrist and I yanked her across the car, laying her belly flat across the tops of my thighs.

"Nash!" She protested at the suddenness of my reaction, squirming beneath the weight of my strong hands.

My jaw clenched as I worked to pull her jeans down past her waist and over her ass.

"What the fuck!" Her legs and arms flapped.

I flattened my hand and slapped her bare ass, hard.

She yelped.

I grinned and slapped her again. "You don't know what you are."

She twisted her spine in an attempt to look at me, but her eyes were covered by her hair.

My hand came down hard on her ass in a series of quick paddles. "You'll know what you are when you've had every position on set." My hand raised high over my head. "Including cleaning," I growled, laying down the strongest spanking yet.

Her back arched and she growled in frustration before I lifted her up off my lap, tossing her back to the opposite corner where she belonged.

She fought to straighten her hair before shooting daggers at me with her eyes.

"I can't have you on set." My eyes narrowed as I watched her chest rise and fall, and I knew by the look she was giving me now, she was sopping wet—completely turned on by the punishment I just inflicted.

Her gaze cast down to my swollen bulge. "Why?"

I waited a long moment before responding. And as she looked to me for an answer, her eyes pooled with tears that threatened to spill over her cheeks.

I sighed, broke eye contact, and ran my fingers through my hair. "You're too much of a temptation."

Next thing I knew, her hand hovered over my arm. She gently began stroking light brushes over the hair on my arm with her fingernails.

My crotch ached like nothing I'd ever experienced before. And when I found the courage to look into those amazing tropical green eyes of hers, there was no stopping my hand from reaching out and cupping her face inside my palm.

She bit her bottom lip and closed her eyes as she leaned her face deeper into my hand.

"Open your eyes." My thumb stroked her flush cheek, loving the way her soft skin felt on the pads of my rough hands. She was so fucking beautiful and I knew that she was the one I wanted to make mine.

"It doesn't have to be like this," she said, opening her oval shaped eyes.

She was right.

It wouldn't be easy. "If you want to stay on set, there are some rules—specific only to you—that you're going to have abide by."

She took my hand and moved it to her mouth. "Anything." She kissed the pad of my index finger.

And no matter how gorgeous she was, there was work that needed to be done to make her perfect—to make her into the woman I needed her to be.

My fingers trailed across her jaw, over her collarbone, and in a splash, I pulled her blouse down, freeing her round breasts.

Her breath hitched as her eyes darted between mine.

I leaned over and studied her soft flesh closely. "If you want to make it in this industry, you're going to have to do something about these clothes." I pulled the pink fabric off her body so she could see what I was referring to.

"What's wrong with my clothes?" She leaned back with disgust tainting her voice.

"They're cheap." I squeezed her tit.

She bit her bottom lip and mewed.

"Imitation. Everyone knows it." She started breathing heavily as I rolled her nipple between my fingers. "Get new ones."

My mouth opened and I sucked in her peaked nipple between my teeth.

She fisted my hair and said, "I can do that."

When I pulled back, my cheeks hallowing out as I released her nipple, it puckered and snapped back into place. "Good."

She slumped down further into her seat, bringing her finger to her mouth.

My gaze cast down between her thick thighs, still exposed and vulnerable from when I pulled her pants down only a minute ago. "Get sexier panties, too. Understand?" My finger trailed over the cotton.

She nodded once as I cupped her mound.

Her eyes closed and I wedged my hand beneath the hem of her

waistline and raked my fingers through her curls. "You need to shave this, too." I pulled her hairs.

She licked her lips and nodded. "Anything."

"I need it bare."

"Okay," she whispered, a soft breath brushing my lips.

I took her nipple back into my mouth and slid my finger between her folds, finger fucking her until she came.

88

Alex

I hated how easily I gave myself over to him.

His finger curled inside me and I pulled his face against my chest harder.

Holy fuck.

The way his satin-like tongue felt as it worked over my crazed nipple was more than my body could handle right now. It was supple. Perfect. And oh so deliciously well done.

Nash had me on fire and my panties drowning in their own pool before I had time to even know what was happening to me. He was just that good.

It made me sick that he could make me feel so cold on set, only to flip one hundred and eighty degrees and have me running from the brush fire to keep my skin from burning off with the way he was looking at me now—eager and full of desire.

"Oh, fuck," I moaned and spread my knees wider.

He slipped another finger inside and twisted it as he pressed my swollen nub with his thumb.

I bit my bottom lip and struggled to breathe.

The man knew what he was doing. He had experience. That was why my mind fought my body about what was right and what I knew I should be considering wrong.

Under any other circumstances, I'd tell him to fuck off and be a gentleman. Grow up and be a professional. But remembering how he rocked me into oblivion last night in the alley made it all too easy for me to hand over access to my most precious jewels. I knew damn well he'd spin me off my axis once again, if only I opened the door to my house and invited him inside.

His tongue lapped over my nipple and his fingers sloshed between my legs.

My pulse quickened as I thought back to the way he pulled me across his lap and spanked my ass. He'd caught me by surprise. No way did I expect that. Not ever.

I'd told him what I was worth—I was more than a cleaning lady—yet he put me in my place, and for good reason; I hadn't proved my value yet. Lucky for me, I'd take that kind of punishment any day of the week.

Spank me, Nash. Then fuck me with your gigantic cock.

Fuck me. That was hot.

He was serious.

Aggressive play that had me smoldering under his fierce dominance, and I couldn't wait to experience more of what he had in store.

My back lifted off the seat as his tongue circled my nipple, causing it to tighten painfully hard. I tightened my sex around his fingers, intensifying the feeling of how his strong knuckles felt against my center walls.

"Nash, oh God," I mewed as my eyes rolled to the back of my head.

He circled and rubbed my clit more intensely, and I tightened my grip around him—clawing my nails into his thick head of hair. A moan escaped and he laughed. My chest heaved as my body heated to the likes of molten lava just before exploding through waves of pleasure.

He slowed his finger-assault and massaged my lips with my juices as I shuddered through my orgasm.

I hugged his head close to my chest and opened my eyes. "Oh shit." I started laughing uncontrollably.

Nash was still completely lost in my body as he flicked his tongue over my breasts. "You taste fucking amazing."

"Nash." I pulled him away. "Look."

He lifted his head and rotated to the window behind him. "Who gives a shit?" He turned back and dove his head between my tits.

I giggled but only because he'd just blessed me with an incredible climax.

There was something about him fucking me here; doing what he was doing with people walking by, cars roaring past, and this woman sitting at the bus stop who seemed to be able to see us inside, just staring and enjoying the show, that made his sex appeal hotter than I could have ever imagined was possible. But I still had to ask. "Can she see us?"

"So what if she can?" He pulled his fingers from my wetness, leaving me feeling empty and depressed.

The woman never looked away, and the longer she stared, the more weird I felt about the whole thing. "You get off fucking in public, don't you?"

Nash lifted his chin and smirked at the same time he pinched my nipple and leaned back.

He didn't care. It was almost like he got off on the risk of getting caught or having other people watch. That was what had my head spinning.

What made him want to do it? Because it certainly wasn't my style. No. I was always a closed door kind of girl when having sex.

"Don't worry. My windows are tinted for a reason." He winked.

My brow arched and I wondered how many other women he did this with.

I didn't want to know.

"Just in time." He looked out the rear window.

I pushed myself up and took a look myself—the bus. "Fuck." I pulled my pants back up over my hips and pulled my blouse shut.

Nash just laughed as he crawled to the driver seat. "You better hurry. I think it's your bus."

I glared at him as he stared at me in the rearview mirror. Quickly, I gathered my things and opened the door closest to the sidewalk.

"Alex." He turned to look at me.

I twisted around to find Nash's dark piercing eyes sparkling. "Remember what I said."

The bus honked its horn at Nash blocking the spot.

"New clothes. Shaved pussy. Got it," I said like it was no big deal as I hurried to make sure I didn't piss off yet another bus driver today.

He smiled. "Let me know when that happens."

I gave him a questioning glance back.

"That's when I'll fuck you with my tongue." Then he sped off, disappearing into the traffic.

89

Alex

I caved.

He made me weak.

I did what I promised I wouldn't do—*again.*

My feet left the bus floor and I hugged my knees to my chest and stared out the window, knowing that I had a long while before my stop.

What the hell did I just agree to?

A man across the aisle was talking to me, trying to get my attention, but I wasn't in the mood.

Men on the bus loved to flirt. Like, all the time. It drove me nuts. What was it about a lone female on the bus that invited such an open invitation? It never made sense. Unlucky for them, I was never interested. And no surprise, they weren't my type. None of them had what I knew I wanted.

He kept talking and gave me no choice but to turn and show him the back of my head.

Now, if they were attractive, then maybe I'd give them a chance. But that was the thing. They weren't. No, I needed a strong man with good hygiene. Someone who made me believe they could protect me. Sex me up so good I could forget anyone else existed. And the more I went on thinking about the kind of man I needed, the closer it resembled Nash.

Nash—he had *all* that.

And perhaps that was why I let him find a way to undress me, not once, but twice, without any kind of real, actual protest.

I wanted it and he knew it.

I pulled out my phone and thought about messaging Kendra. She wouldn't believe who'd been rocking my world these last couple of days. But no matter how much I wanted to tell her about Nash, the money, and how he kept finding a way to shower me in the most spine tingling, toe curling orgasms known to womankind, now wasn't the time.

The bus slowed its speed, pulled over, and stopped. The man who wanted to talk with me said, "Goodbye, sweetie," and left the bus.

I breathed a sigh of relief as the weight of his creepiness lifted off my shoulders.

When the bus pulled back into traffic, my gaze cast down to the front of my blouse.

I loved this guava colored blouse more than anything I owned. This outfit wasn't cheap. It was the most expensive thing I had. It was my best. By far. Nothing in my closet even came close to competing. And I didn't take my time getting dressed this morning because I wanted Nash to tell me it was cheap or imitation.

I grinded my teeth as my eyes closed.

God, if he'd seen the rest of my closet, I'd have no chance. But it was the best I could do. I owned the clothes and shoes I could afford, and I didn't have the money to spend getting newer, fancier, much more expensive clothes than what I had now.

At least not my own money—but I *did* have money.

Who made those kinds of requests, anyway?

New clothes. Shaved pussy. You got to be fucking kidding me.

I shaved my legs, trimmed my curls, but a bare pussy? Really? That wasn't a request. It was a *demand*. A plea only made by a control freak.

But it was also an ultimatum—do it or he'd send me on my way. "Adios, Alex. Good luck getting into Hollywood *now*."

My arms squeezed my legs, clamping my thighs tighter together.

I knew exactly what he wanted and what I needed to do—get a wax. Wax my legs, my pussy, and, of course, my asshole. And when I did, tell him so he could flick his tongue over my clit and up and between my folds.

I laughed and shook my head as I tucked a strand of hair behind my ear.

There was only one real problem I saw with all this. New clothes, shoes, waxing, and the makeup that would follow all cost real money. Money I did not have, and money that was not mine.

Who was this man I kept allowing to push me around? And why did I allow it?

It wasn't me to let men walk all over me.

Nash had somehow become the exception to my rule. A guideline I followed for the last six years.

Of course I wanted to do everything he asked of me. Because the second I did, he'd find a way to knock me off my axis with that seriously long, thick cock of his and punish me into hot orgasmic bliss.

My teeth clamped my bottom lip as I chuckled.

He'd fiercely fuck me with everything he had. No doubt about it. And that was what I really wanted to happen. To live in a fog induced perma-orgasm created by Nash Brooks, morning, day, and night.

Slow.

Fast.

Hard.

Finger.

Tongue.

Cock.

And in whatever way he needed. I'd allow him to do anything as long as I kept walking away feeling like I did now—like a woman who had the best sex of her life.

A man walking on the sidewalk caught my attention. He was carrying a duffel bag, similar to the one I found last night, and instantly my feet were pulled back down to earth.

I hadn't thought about the money very much today. There wasn't any time to do so with everything else that was going on, but I needed to seriously consider my options.

With each beat of my heart, I could hear it telling me what I *should* do—report it to the police and forget I'd even held it in my hands.

But I didn't always do what was right.

And I certainly didn't want to regret giving it away. Especially knowing that it was the kind of money that could change my life for the better.

My head told me something different. That the mess that had became my life would take me years of financial success to equal that which hid beneath my bed right now.

There was no denying I was getting kicked out of my apartment.

There was nothing I could do to change that.

Nash said I needed new clothes and to take care of some personal items if I were to stay working close to him.

I couldn't change that either.

These were cold, hard facts that defined my reality. Whether I liked it or not, it was what it was and the time to decide what future I had was now.

Using the money I found, and spending it as if it were my own, would solve both those problems. I could get a place all to myself. Finally live on my own without the bullshit that came with having a roommate. I could purchase expensive clothes that would keep Nash hard, and I could start playing the part I'd seen myself playing for so long now—superstar Hollywood filmmaker Alex Grace.

But two questions kept resurfacing over and over.

Whose money was it?

What if they found out I had it, and had spent it?

My hands shook, knowing the consequences would be dire. Perhaps even life threatening. No one just had a quarter million dollars in cash unless they were into something dangerous themselves. That was the one thing I could confidently agree with myself on.

My forehead dropped to my knees as my stomach rolled over on itself.

The only comfort I found was in smelling Nash's cologne still lingering on my clothes. A moment later I could taste him on my lips. Then he had my breasts in the palm of his hands. And soon my thoughts drifted out to sea as his cock stretched me, filling me completely. By the time I snapped out of my fantasy, a dream that was quickly getting away from me, it was my stop.

I walked straight to my apartment building, still clouded with images of Nash. Rounding the stairs up to the second level, I strode down the hall and stopped when I heard an all too familiar, and dreadful, sound.

Even from out here, I could hear my roommate fucking.

"That cunt better not be in my bed," I said to myself as I opened our front door, thinking back to Kendra's comment.

Her moans and his grunts filled the apartment, leaving me with a disgusting taste in my mouth. I rubbed my arms and couldn't help but feel like a mold was growing on me. I felt gross and it was all because of her.

It should never feel like this when coming home, I thought to myself.

I ran to my room, shut the door, and pulled the duffel bag out from under my bed.

This is it. Use it to get out of here. Make your life better. You deserve it.

Her screams got louder, like a small dog yapping.

I unzipped the bag and picked out a brick of hundred dollar bills.

My entire body shivered when I heard her tell him to fuck her harder.

The money smelled like freedom.

My brows drew tightly together as I listened to her come.

I couldn't take another day of this. Even if *she* was the one to kick me out.

My thumb flipped through the brick of cash I had in my hand and blew my bangs off my forehead.

My mind raced.

I knew what I had to do. It wasn't the choice I should be making, but it was the only choice I saw.

I had to go through with it. It was the right thing to do. A risk I was willing to take. For me, my future, and where I knew I needed to go. This dream of being a Hollywood filmmaker was just something I couldn't shake. I'd wanted it for far too long, and now it was within reach.

I didn't stumble across this money. No. It *came* to me. The universe was conspiring to give me what I wanted. And it was up to me to take what I wanted before someone else ripped it out from beneath my nose.

I stuffed the cash back into the duffel, zipped it shut, and slung it over my shoulder. Reaching for my phone, I dialed Kendra. When she answered, I said, "Girl. Let's go shopping."

Continue the story in On My Knees Box Set, NOW AVAILABLE! Click here to download it today.

ALSO BY CJ THOMAS

City by the Bay series

Ruin Me Box Set

Promise Me Box Set

Save Me

Take Me Box Set

Hollywood Dreams series

Beyond Tonight Box Set

On My Knees Box Set

Capture Me

Heat

ACKNOWLEDGMENT

I want to thank all of my readers for being supportive with each new story I write. It's because of you and your willingness to WANT to read my stories that make this all possible. Mwah!

I also want to thank my editor, LNS, for bringing my stories to life and constantly providing constructive advice on how to improve my craft. The same goes to my street team and beta readers, for without you, I'm not sure I would have the confidence to continue living inside my characters' heads day after day.

And last but not least, my family for giving me the love and inspiration to keep writing.

Never miss a release date. Sign up for my Newsletter!

www.CJThomasBooks.com

63434208R00273

Made in the USA
Lexington, KY
07 May 2017